THE BERINFELL PROPHECIES
BOOK THREE

THE
TIDE
OF
UNMAKING

Other Books by . . .

WAYNE THOMAS BATSON AND CHRISTOPHER HOPPER

The Berinfell Prophecies
Curse of the Spider King
Venom and Song

WAYNE THOMAS BATSON

The Door Within Trilogy
The Door Within
The Rise of the Wyrm Lord
The Final Storm

Pirate Adventures
Isle of Swords
Isle of Fire

The Dark Sea Annals
Sword In The Stars
The Errant King

CHRISTOPHER HOPPER

The White Lion Chronicles
Rise of the Dibor
The Lion Vrie
Athera's Dawn

THE BERINFELL PROPHECIES
BOOK THREE

THE TIDE OF UNMAKING

BY WAYNE THOMAS BATSON
AND CHRISTOPHER HOPPER

SPEAR HEAD

NEW YORK • BALTIMORE • SEATTLE

To the One who makes all things new, who grants vision to the blind, who breathes life into the dead: our pens, as well as our lives, are ever at Your disposal, Jesus.

Published by Wayne Thomas Batson and Christopher Hopper in alliance with Spearhead Books.

Exterior and interior layout and design by New Life Media | www.newlifemedia.me
Thanks to Thomas Nelson, Mandi Cofer and goodwp.com for your inspiration.

Author photos by Jennifer Hopper | www.jenniferhopperphoto.com

ISBN-13: 978-1479205783
ISBN-10: 1479205788

Printed in the United States of America.

CONTENTS

PRINCIPAL CAST

Tommy Bowman: Curly-haired leader of the Lords of Berinfell, raised in Seabrook, Maryland. Known in Allyra as Elven Lord Felheart (Fell-heart), son of Lord Velaril and Tarin Silvertree. Gifted with keen vision and marksmanship.

Kat Simonson: Raised in Los Angeles, California, known for her constantly changing hairstyles and blue-tinted skin. Known in Allyra as Elven Lord Alreenia (Al-reen-ee-yuh), daughter of Beleg and Lord Kendie Hiddenblade. Gifted with telepathy.

Autumn Briarman: Petite blonde raised outside Depauville of upstate New York. Known in Allyra as Elven Lord Miarra (Me-air-uh), daughter of Lord Galadhost and Salura Swiftstorm. Gifted with incredible speed.

Johnny Briarman: Burly blond brute raised outside Depauville in upstate New York. Known in Allyra as Elven Lord Albriand (Al-bree-and), son of Elroth and Lord Tisa Ashheart. Gifted with fire generation.

James "Jimmy" Lewis Gresham: Redhead raised in Ardfern, Scotland. Known in Allyra as Elven Lord Thorwin (Thor-win), son of Lord Xanthis and Dreia Valorbrand. Gifted with foresight.

Kiri Lee Yuen: Child prodigy cellist and violinist raised in Paris, France, whose adopted parents were killed by Wisps. Known in Allyra as Elven Lord Lothriel (Loth-ree-ell), daughter of Charad and Lord Simona Oakenflower. Gifted with the ability to walk on air.

Jett Green: *(Deceased)* Raised in Greenville, North Carolina, Jett was a star athlete. He was known in Allyra as Elven Lord Hamandar (Ham-and-ur), son of Lord Vex and Jasmira Nightwing. Killed in Vesper Crag by laying his life down for Kiri Lee. Was gifted with incredible strength and healing.

Taeva: Mysterious and exotic, Princess of the Taladrim.

Louwin: Taeva's closest attendant.

Miss Finney: Originally Jimmy's Sentinel, and a cunning warrior.

Guardmaster Eldera "Elle" Goldarrow (Galdarro): Originally Tommy's Sentinel. Known in Allyra as Goldarrow, and promoted to the preeminent military role of Guardmaster.

Guardmaster Olin Grimwarden: Commander of the military forces of the Elves and their allies.

Lord Asp: Supreme leader of the Drefids; ruthless and maniacal.

Mr. Charlie: Dreadnaught protector of Tommy Bowman. Known in Allyra as Merrick Evershield, but prefers *Charlie*. Never got over his adoption of the United States' "Deep South" culture.

Regis McAuliffe: Originally assigned as Jimmy's Dreadnaught in Ardfern, Scotland.

Mumthers: Most respected and beloved Elven chef in all of Allyra. Portly and jovial.

Bear: Giant wolf known formerly as the Keeper of the Cistern, Guardian of the Keystone, found by the Seven within Terradym Fortress.

Migmar: Barrister King of the Gnomes, known for his obsession with dragonroot.

Thorkber: Migmar's right-hand Gnome.

Overlord Bengfist: Imposing Gwar General loyal to the plight of the Elves.

Shardbearer Jastansia: Guardian Soldier of the Saer.

Kate and Allan Simonson: Adoptive Earth parents of Kat, North Hollywood, CA.

Hazel and Austin Green: Adoptive Earth parents of the late Jett, Greenville, NC.

Vault Minister Ghrell: Hot-headed leader of the Nemic race.

Priest Dhrex: Chief counsel to Ghrell; serves within the Sacred Sanctuary of Allyra.

Magistrate Forlarn: Leader of the Saer.

Sardon: General Secretary of the Conclave, and Saer kinsman of Forlarn.

General Eragor: One of Asp's chief Generals.

General Caerfasz: Lean and lanky Gwar pilot.

Skax: Northern commander of Asp's assault force.

Admiral Cuth: Commander of the Northern Elven Fleet.

Admiral Blackburn: Commander of the USS Saddle River, a DDG51 Class Destroyer en route to New York City.

The Spider King: Former mutated ruler of all Gwar, slain in the battle of Vesper Crag by the Lords of Berinfell.

The Conclave: Official gathering of leaders representing the six Allyran races: Elves, Gnomes, Gwar, Nemic, Taladrim and Saer.

Elves: One of the ancient races of Allyra.

Lyrian Elves: A very strong race of Elves, known for their dark skin and striking violet-colored eyes.

Sentinels: Very wise, very traditional Elves who are rumored to still follow the "Old Ways." Elite Sentinels are assigned to protect the Seven Lords.

Dreadnaughts: Elite warrior Elves who practice Vexbane and Nightform (also known as *Mandiera*), profoundly effective forms of combat. Elite Dreadnaughts are assigned to protect the Seven Lords.

Gnomes: Experts in maps, they wander far and wide, and have a longtime feud with the Elves.

Gwar: One of the ancient races of Allyra. Gwar are known for their brutish strength, grey-toned skin and their affinity for spiders.

Taladrim: A northern, sea-faring race.

Nemic: Winged, insect-like race of the arid regions in the south.

Saer: Serpentine-like mountain dwellers in the west.

Drefids: The Spider King's ghoulish assassins. Drefids have four deadly claws that extend from the knuckles of each hand.

Cragons: The monstrous black trees of Vesper Crag.

Wisps: Enemies of old. Vapor-beings, shape shifters. Thought extinct. Only Holy Words and a weapon together can kill one.

Warflies: Giant, mutant dragonflies used by Asp for his militaristic exploits.

Warspiders: Spiders that are so large they can be ridden like horses. Red Warspiders have lethal venom.

PRINCIPAL LOCATIONS

ALLYRA

The world where the six Allyran races live: Elves, Gnomes, Gwar, Nemic, Taladrim and Saer.

Locations on Allyra include:

Berinfell

The capital of the Elves, who once resided across the many continents of Allyra.

Nightwish Caverns

A vast network of caverns beneath the Thousand-League Forest, used as an emergency home by the Elves of Berinfell.

Vesper Crag

Former volcanic home of the Spider King and spawning grounds of Drefid covens.

Moon Hollow

The heavily forested home of the Gnomes in northern Allyra.

Tere Solium

Arid mountain-desert to the south, home of the Nemic.

Thynhold Cairn

Impregnable mountain stronghold of the Saer to the west.

Taladair

Bowl-shaped island off the coast of Allyra's northern shores, home of the Taladrim.

Kileverand

Port city on the north coast of Berinfell.

EARTH

The world where humans live.

Locations on Earth include:

Canadian Northwest
Seabrook, Maryland, USA
Greenville, North Carolina, USA
North Hollywood, California, USA
Depauville, New York, USA
Midtown Manhattan, New York City, USA
Texas Stadium, Irving, Texas, USA
London, England, Great Britain
Musée du Louvre, Paris, France
Shanhaiguan Pass, Hebei Province, China
Petropavolvsk, Avacha Bay, Russia

A Haunting Discovery

OLD ELEABOR Thrain woke, spun out of his chair, and fell to his knees on the cold cottage floor. "Huh, wha—?" His heart hammered against his ribs. He breathed in short gasps, and sent little vapor ghosts writhing into the air.

He stared bug-eyed into every shadowy corner of the room and wondered frantically what exactly he'd heard.

Being the only caretaker on duty at Innskell, the largest cemetery in Allyra, could make any Elf jumpy, but Eleabor was more steely than most. And he'd grown used to night noises that would make the younglings squirm: owls, wolves, screechers, wailing loons and such—nothing like those would startle Eleabor. This had been something different.

There'd been a strange scratching. No, more of a scraping, like slabs of coarse stone grating across each other. In his semiconscious mind, Eleabor had thought it part of a dark dream.

But then came the jarring crash.

It was as if something had shattered or been blasted apart, and the concussive sound woke Eleabor. He knew it had not been a figment of his slumbering mind at all.

"Doesn't help that it's so dratted cold tonight," Eleabor muttered as he clambered to his feet.

His candles had guttered out and, in the dark, he couldn't find any flint. So Eleabor sifted by feel through the tools hanging on the wall until he found a dremask lantern. He unscrewed its cap and blew the dust out of its well. The dremask ore within didn't feel too tarnished. *It probably ought to light.*

Eleabor pulled a small, hardened glass vial from his belt and popped it open. He tilted it carefully over the lantern and let just a single drop of ultra-cold *friosche* fall onto the dremask. The volatile metal flared to life immediately, filling the crowded room with cold, white light.

He put the cap on the lantern and swung it round. "Don't nuthin' in here make a sound like that," he muttered to himself. "Maybe the workshop."

He left the tool room and wandered nervously into a larger but just as crowded room. This was where he and the other stonecrafters sculpted, carved, and engraved the monuments.

There were hundreds of blank slabs of granite, marble, slate and verdigen. Shadows danced around them as Eleabor held up the lantern. But none of the stone looked to have fallen over or broken. He squinted and scratched at the single ribbon of gray hair that dangled from his otherwise smooth pate.

Eleabor shone the lantern into every corner of the room. Elven statuettes of pale maidens with empty eyes stared back at Eleabor, and he shivered.

"N-no, nuthin' in here," he whispered and hurried from the room.

Back in the tool room now, he thought mightily about trying to go back to sleep. But that was ridiculous really. No sleep would come. He'd heard what he'd heard. And now he was certain of two things: the sound had come from somewhere outside, and it wasn't anything natural.

Eleabor grabbed his old rychesword and left the caretaker's cottage.

Innskell was twenty acres of gravestones, tombs, mausoleums and markers in the bottom of Forn Mauer Vale, a vast hollow just outside Berinfell City. The caretaker's cottage had been built on one of the taller foothills and, but for the trees, Eleabor could see almost the entire property. On a clear night, that is. But on many nights, especially when there was a wet chill in the air, Eleabor's view would be considerably impaired.

Mist, mist, everywhere mist. Tendrils of vapor poured down the terraces, shrouded the trees, and drifted silently among the graves. Eleabor did not believe in spirits. No caretaker could and still keep his sanity. But the mists of Innskell were nearly enough to provoke Eleabor to reconsider. The shredding vapors moved with spectral grace and seemed to travel with some inscrutable purpose, at times with the wind but often against it. The mists traveled within the wrought iron gates of Innskell even when there was no wind to be felt. The moon itself, so high and glorious, could not escape the mists either. Gray tatters covered its face like grave clothes, rotting here and there for pale flesh to show through.

Eleabor looked up through the trees at the distant walls of the formidable city of Berinfell. He wished for the thousandth time that he had a squad of flet soldiers garrisoned at Innskell. Then, his nerves wouldn't be so frayed and he wouldn't dread the nightshift.

Of course, he knew he could get help if he needed it. A horn hung on the wall back in the caretaker's cottage. Winding that potent clarion would get Eleabor some attention from Berinfell. *But if there really was trouble,* he wondered, *would the troops arrive fast enough?*

With such thoughts, Eleabor trekked into the murky night. He ambled along paths he'd trod hundreds of times, but the mist and the night made them look eerie and strange. His footsteps sounded both outrageously loud and somewhat muffled, and he found himself lightening his footfalls.

The burial plots grew up all around Eleabor as he moved deeper into the yard. They were sectioned off by hedges, trees or fences of cobbled stone. Almost a hundred yards from the caretaker's cottage and, so far, there seemed nothing amiss.

That's when he heard it.

A pattering sound, very different from the blast that had awakened him. No, this sounded like a panther charging up a forest path. Eleabor's rychesword wobbled in his hand as he held the lantern high and called, "Who are ya? What ya be doin'?"

No one answered. The pattering continued. The sound grew closer. A patch of young trees wavered slightly.

"I said, who are ya—"

A blur. A shadow moving among shadows. Something large tore up a side path to Eleabor's right. Sword and lantern high, Eleabor gave chase. He soon realized he was outclassed. The thing, whatever it was, was pulling away with ease. Eleabor ducked out from under the eaves of the tress just in time to see a dark figure vault over the Innskell gate.

It had only been a momentary glimpse and just a blotch of darker darkness. But given the breadth of its shoulders, Eleabor felt sure it was a Gwar.

"Blasted hoodlum," Eleabor muttered. Sure, the Gwar had a right to visit the dead just like everyone else, but what in Allyra was this one doing in Innskell in the wee hours? "Up to no good, I'll wager."

Eleabor spun on his heels, fear replaced by fury, and trod back the way he had come. "Now to see what this joker was up to," he grumbled.

Even since the Accord, Eleabor still felt the Gwar should keep to their own. There'd always been some Gwar in Berinfell, even long before the war. But now the city was like some dang cross-cultural hub, Gwar and Elfkind mixing as freely as old allies.

Not the way of things, Eleabor thought. And surely, surely, Gwar should be buried somewhere other than the Elven cemetery. Why, Innskell was the burial places of all the former Lords! To think that Gwar could pollute the soil, well, that was maddening.

Eleabor worked himself up to a frothy lather of anger. Tombstones and monuments passed by in a blur. But some absent part of his mind still wondered about the noise that had woken him.

Eleabor swung the lantern back and forth, searching for any sign, any inkling of damage. But once, he swung the lantern to his right when he should have swung it to his left. He saw a large crypt vault, illuminated in the lantern's pale white light. Everything to Eleabor's left was blotted out in inky darkness. Eleabor didn't see the yawning pit. His next step found nothing but air. He flailed, tossed the lantern, and fell.

His rychesword jammed into earth about halfway down, knocking Eleabor backward. He landed hard on his backside in about ten inches of icy water.

He jolted to his feet, sputtering and growling. "Dang, hoodlums!" Eleabor shouted. "I could'a broke my neck!"

He was almost exactly eight feet down. He looked up at a ragged rectangular patch of sky and realized into what he had fallen. An eight-foot-deep hole in the ground in a cemetery could only be one thing.

A bit of ethereal white light glowed above. The lantern must have come to rest fairly close to the edge. Hesitantly, Eleabor looked down around his feet. He'd worked among the dead for forty years, but still had no comfort where the living did not belong.

Whatever casket or coffin had been interred here, it must have been a grand one. But there wasn't much left of it. Huge pieces of stained alder and maple floated in the chill water. *The blasted Gwar must have taken a sledgehammer to this casket*, Eleabor thought. And then, realizing that there were no skeletal remains visible in the wreckage, Eleabor had a darker thought about the Gwar's purposes here.

Visions of body-snatchers and black rituals skittering in his mind, Eleabor looked frantically for a way out. But graves didn't come equipped with ladders.

He threw his sword out and over, then jumped up at the side, feeling much like a bug trying to escape a jar. He grabbed fistfuls of wet soil and managed little more than to splatter himself dark with mud. But at last, he found a handhold. There was a deep cavity in the grave wall and a sturdy tree's root within. Eleabor was wiry and thin, so he easily grasped the root and yanked himself upward.

Oddly, he found another similar handhold just above and to the right. It was exactly where he needed it to be. In fact, there were equally spaced divots for his feet as well. It may as well have been a ladder. Eleabor clambered out in no time.

He did his best to wipe himself off, then retrieved his sword and took up the lantern once more. He held the light over the open grave and looked down. The casket shredded like that, well, Eleabor had never seen the sort.

In fact, the more Eleabor thought about it, he couldn't imagine a Gwar sneaking into the cemetery, digging up a grave just to pulverize a casket. *If that was it,* he thought, *where was the body? And if the body was the Gwar's object, why smash up the coffin?*

The lantern's white glow only revealed more disturbing details.

Eleabor had dug a lot of graves. He'd also had the unenviable task of moving dozens of graves from parts of the cemetery where sinkholes had opened up. In so doing he'd learned a great deal about the work. Older graves, for instance, were much, much harder to disinter. Any grave ten years or older, the dirt would settle and pack. It would mesh with the soil all around it. Digging it would be no easier than putting a shovel through untouched earth.

But Eleabor noticed that this grave still held its rough, rectangular shape. Couldn't be more that five, six years old. *Seven tops,* Eleabor was sure. *And where's all the dirt anyway?*

The dirt from the grave hadn't been piled up beside the ditch. Even a reckless laborer would leave some kind of bank. There should have been a ring of soil or mounds or something. Eleabor wandered about the gaping black hole, but there was no rise of any sort.

It had rained overnight: a cold, pelting downpour. That would wash a fair amount of soil away. But not all of it.

Eleabor frowned and felt as if the chill rain had begun anew. Only it hadn't. He shivered and started the walk back to his cottage. *I'll have to report this, of course.* It wasn't his fault. Thousands of graves spread all over Innskell. He couldn't be expected to watch them all, at the same time, by himself. And yet, he was the caretaker.

Maybe the Elders would see fit to assign a night detail of soldiers to make hourly sweeps. "That's what we need," Eleabor muttered as he passed a tall mausoleum. "Maybe then an Elf could get a good night's—"

Eleabor stopped as if smacked by an invisible hand. The ghostly lantern's light fell upon more destruction. Chunks and jagged shards of stone littered the ground all around the mausoleum's eastern wall. At first, Eleabor thought the wall itself or maybe some stone monument upon it had crumbled. But looming closer, Eleabor saw that the wall of the grave building was unscathed. Well, there was a fairly large crack in the wall. But nothing seemed to have broken off.

Eleabor picked up a piece of the broken rock. Turning it this way and that, he was pretty sure it was high-grade marble. He turned around and looked back the way he had walked. Not fifteen paces back was the dug up grave. Come to think of it, Eleabor had seen the frame for the grave cap. If the family had a fair amount of gold but didn't want a big mausoleum, they often had a grave cap of good stone crafted. The cap itself was usually six arm length's long and three wide. It was a full eight inches thick too.

Eleabor shook his head. Those blasted things were heavy. It usually took a team of four Elves to cap a grave. Eleabor looked down at the broken stone. The light fell upon a few engraved letters. A letter "e" and something cut off. Maybe a "t." Good engraving, fancy, deep lettering. Eleabor turned more and more of the stone. It was so obliterated that he couldn't find a single whole word. The closest thing he found was a chunk of marble with "mande" on it. *Maybe this means something in one of the old languages?* Eleabor didn't know.

He looked back at the open grave. It was as if someone had lifted off the grave cap and tossed it against the mausoleum's wall. But no single Gwar had such might.

Eleabor swallowed. He began to wonder if what he'd seen had been a Gwar after all. It might have been some creature, some backwoods creature no one had ever seen before. Something strong enough to break old Eleabor in half like a toothpick.

Eleabor turned to walk away and put his foot into a pile of fresh mud. He looked down. There was fresh, muddy soil all over the side of the mausoleum, except for a rectangular outline the size of a grave cap. Clumps of soil lay scattered all over the sod as well.

Eleabor had seen enough. The lantern shaking as he scurried away, Eleabor wondered what could have created the destruction he'd witnessed. And he wondered what "mande" meant.

He stopped cold. In fact, standing in the center of an erupting volcano wouldn't have warmed the chill that came over him. He spun on his feet, looked from grave to grave.

"Aww, no," he whispered. "Not that grave. No, no, can't be."

But the more he thought about the location of the obliterated burial plot, the more he became certain he knew just who had been buried there.

Rubbing his temples, Eleabor wondered if maybe he could find another job.

Premonitions

MRS. SIMONSON stared at the LA skyline spreading out behind her office picture window and gasped. The view from the top of the skyscraper was spectacular, vast…and empty.

No picturesque view, no posh office, no seven-figure, high-profile job could dull the ache she felt as keenly as a stab wound. More than a month had bled away since her only daughter Kat disappeared. A month full of murderous days, grinding through the jarring moments following the abduction. *The waking nightmare,* she called it. She rubbed her temples, elbows on her desk.

She wasn't sleeping well. Wasn't eating well. And therefore wasn't working well. Everyone at the office told her she needed a break. She agreed, but their beach house in Newport was the last place she wanted to go. Too many memories of Kat there. So she did what she'd always done and plunged into her work. But whatever creative energies she'd once called upon to distract her from life, they weren't working their magic now. Bidden or unbidden, the memories—and the questions— would not relent.

The North Hollywood Police Department eventually turned the case over to the FBI. International trafficking, they'd said. Most likely a cartel. Darkened SUVs, military grade weaponry, the broken stone wall surrounding the property, and the disappearance of the household's Mexican house keeper. Most likely a ransom game for the Simonson's daughter.

Only one problem: there'd been no demands.

"We're so sorry," the lead detective had said to Mrs. Simonson.

And with every frantic phone call she made to the FBI in the weeks that followed, she got the same reply: "We're doing all we can with the leads we have." But there were no more leads, and that meant the authorities weren't doing anything really.

There was the *magical paper note*, as she called it during the first few days of the aftermath. But it wasn't exactly something the FBI would believe, much less spend time and money investigating.

Still, seeing Kat's own curly-cue handwriting on the golden paper, then watching in amazement as it vanished right before her eyes, gave Mrs. Simonson some initial assurance that Kat would be fine. *It was a clue, wasn't it?* But where could it lead? And how could she follow...if the note was gone?

Before long, she wondered if the magical paper note had been real at all. By the second week, she was sure it was an aberration, and by the third, the family psychiatrist had explained it as a coping mechanism.

Speaking of coping mechanisms, she thought. The temple rubbing wasn't helping the throbbing headache...or any other aches for that matter. She turned away from the window and found the photograph of her husband staring back at her from across the desk.

He claimed he hadn't seen her for more than a few minutes a night. Maybe just a brief encounter in the kitchen at the coffee machine, or sometimes barely waking up to mumble something to her as she walked in the door at some absurd hour.

Even the company CFO, Woody Gregg, noticed the long hours she was pulling. He appeared in her office doorway and gestured for her to follow. She entered the hall and followed him to an alcove near his office.

"Kathryn, I can't imagine what you're going through," Woody said. "And I know it's not my place to talk, but I'm not so sure *On Your Mark* needs you as much as your husband needs you. This is business, and business does matter. But, we aren't exactly struggling here. Look around." Woody gestured to the audaciously stylish office floor that made up LA's top advertising firm. "Go home, Kate."

There was almost no traffic on the 101 at 2am on a Tuesday. *A good thing, too.* Kate knew she was swerving. Her vision blurred from tears and mascara. She could scarcely imagine the black streaks running down her cheeks. Not even her best waterproof makeup could withstand this sort of flooding. But what could she do? Retreat...and tears...well, that was just how she dealt with heartache.

Allan, her husband, was different. He always had been. He turned to his faith whenever things got tough. He even claimed her leap to stardom was because of God. Now, faced with the most difficult trial of their lives, Allan was going to church. "There's strength in community," he'd suggested, pointing to his small group invitation. "I don't know, I just feel God helping me there. Through people."

"I have plenty of people around me at work," Kate argued.

"You know it's not the same."

"Why? Because we have to all read the Bible and sing Kum Ba Ya in order to get God to help us?"

Allan had been visibly disappointed...again. And while Kate was dying on the inside—knowing her husband was right—she wouldn't give in.

Hands on the steering wheel, Kate imagined how frustrated Allan must be. She blinked back more tears. For several years, Kat had acted toward *her* the very same way she was now treating her husband: not really listening, retreating, even pushing away. It seemed adoption was even stronger than blood. *Of all the things to teach her, and now she's gone.*

Kate smeared more black makeup across her left cheek with the back of her hand, trying her best to stay within the yellow lines. She hadn't looked at the speedometer for a few miles. That's when the blue and red lights flashed in her rearview mirror.

"For crying out loud," Kate muttered, then snickered at the irony of her statement—the first time she'd smiled in a while. She eased the SUV to the shoulder, leaned over to pop open the glove box, and fumbled for her registration, then slipped her driver's license out of her pocket book. She could hear the police car door slam shut behind her, then saw the glow of the flashlight try and punch through her tinted windows. How was she going to try and explain her way out of this one? *I'm sorry, Officer, but my daughter has been abducted by a drug cartel. Maybe you saw it in the news? Anyways, I'm real sorry, and I won't ever speed again.*

Yeah, right.

And can I have a lollipop too? Maybe play with your radar gun?

What was the point anymore? She didn't care. She didn't care about anything. She didn't even feel like trying.

Three raps on the window with a knuckle. Kate smashed down the button on her armrest as colored lights played over her face, blaring from the rearview mirror. When the glass was low enough, she squinted up into the blinding light, unable to make out if it was a man or woman. So she went with the generic in her usual *get the first word in* approach.

"Good evening, Officer. No, I don't know why you pulled me over, and I don't know how fast I was going. But my destination is *home*, and I'm coming from *work*. Here's my license and registration."

The Officer didn't take her credentials. Kate waited.

This is strange. Some sort of interrogation maybe?

"OK, yeah. The tears are from being upset. No, I'm not drunk or high. I'm *crying*. Grown women do that from time to time. Like you haven't—"

"Mom, I'm okay."

Kate froze. The voice behind that flashlight. "Kat?"

"Don't worry."

"KAT! Dear God!" Kate reached out, trying to push the flashlight out of the way. But the figure—her daughter—stepped back. "KAT?! Is it really you?"

"I'm fine, Mom. Don't worry. But it's hard to get through...from this distance."

Kate threw the door open, tried to leap from her seat, but was held back by her seat belt. She looked down, fumbling with the button. "KAT! WAIT!" The seatbelt came free. Kate swung out of the driver's seat, her feet hitting the asphalt.

Her daughter was ten steps away now, flashlight still aimed at a blinding angle. Kate raised her hand. "KAT! COME BACK!"

The violent blast of an air horn sounded to the left. Kate didn't even have time to blink as a roaring eighteen wheeler barreled into her daughter.

And just like that, Kat was gone.

But so was the police car behind her.

Kate stood in the middle of the far right lane, hands grasping the hair on her head. "What—what—" She spun around, bewildered. *What just happened here?*

Another pair of headlights approached her from the left. The car slowed then swerved, horn blaring. Kate stumbled back toward her vehicle. "Oh, God. What's going on here? What am I *doing*?"

She slide into the driver's seat again and closed the door. "I'm delirious," she said aloud, then slumped her head onto the steering wheel. "I'm losing my mind."

Then she thought of Allan. She could see his face: the soft smile, the peaceful eyes, the confidence.

Just envisioning his face changed something in her. Suddenly the crying came from her heart, rather than her head. And that's when she knew...not what she *wanted* to do, but what she *had* to do. She had handled a lot of things in her life on her own.

"But, God," she whispered between sobs. "I just can't handle this. This is too much. I need—I need Your help."

Uninvited

"SHHHH!" KAT warned. Through a curtain of dark purple hair, her eyes flashed with urgency. "I hear his thoughts. I think he's coming."

"Aye," Jimmy said. "It's him." His confirmation came from the momentary glimpses of the future that were his gift. "Hurry! We dun'na have much time."

Using preternatural speed, her own gift, Autumn dashed around the chamber and gathered up all the planning scrolls.

Kiri Lee leaped up from her seat at the table and started climbing, walking up invisible steps of air like anyone else would a stairway made of stone. "Here!" she called, gesturing with her hands.

Autumn encircled all three tables, and then tossed the scrolls up above her head—

—Where Kiri Lee caught them and climbed higher in the air, up over the doorway's arch just as Tommy walked in.

"Crud, Autumn!" Johnny muttered, frowning at the plate in front of him. "You knocked my lunch onto the floor."

Jimmy elbowed Johnny and whispered, "Shoot oop, will ya."

"Ow," Johnny muttered, his brows beetling. He flexed his thick forearms and cracked his knuckles ominously toward Jimmy.

"Oh, joost stop. I already know yu are'na gonna hit me."

Tommy halted at the doorway. He scratched the back of his head, whirled a lock of his curly hair around a finger for a moment, and looked suspiciously at his friends.

The room was utterly silent. Even the fire, burning merrily in the room's vast fireplace, ceased to crackle for a moment.

Kat looked at Tommy, then up to Kiri Lee, just a few feet above his head. She was slowly sinking…losing altitude. Even with her gift, Kiri Lee couldn't defy gravity forever.

"*Climb!*" Kat thought urgently to her airborne friend, sending her message telepathically.

I can't, Kiri Lee thought back. *Tommy will see the movement.*

"*But you're sinking!*" Kat thought urgently.

Nothing I can do. Kiri Lee clutched the scrolls to her chest. She squinted and tried to think light thoughts. *As if that might hold me up a little longer.*

"Uh, what's going on?" Tommy asked.

"What do you mean?" Kat said, her smile luminous due to her blue skin tone.

"Noothin's goin' on," Jimmy added, reddish brushy eyebrows raised innocently. "We're actually a wee bit bored. What are yu doin'?"

Tommy's eyes narrowed. "I have forest-shooting with Goldarrow in a couple of hours. I was hoping to practice a little beforehand." He paused and scanned slowly around the room. "I was looking for Kiri Lee to help me train. Have you seen her?"

Kat glanced up. In that quick blink, she saw that Kiri Lee was now only a foot above Tommy's head and still slowly falling.

"You know Kiri Lee," Johnny said, bouncing a small fireball between his palms. "She's uh, probably just hangin' around somewhere."

"I'll go train with you," Autumn said, zooming right to Tommy's side. She took his arm and nonchalantly led him a step out of the chamber. "I can't get airborne like Kiri Lee, but no one shoots faster than I do."

"We'll see about that." Tommy turned to walk with her. He gave her the hundred-watt grin of self assurance, complete with dimples and said, "But it's a little harder when you're balanced in the crook of a tree."

"At least I'm not afraid of heights," Autumn replied.

Tommy's grin vanished. "I'm not either anymore...well, not much."

"Hey, be careful out there, Autumn!" yelled Johnny.

"Really?" Autumn called back. Johnny was protective of her to a fault, something she'd been trying—and failing—to cure him of for years. It was hard to blame him. They had lived as brother and sister on Earth for thirteen years, and Johnny had always taken the big brother role seriously. But returning to Allyra, they had discovered, among other things, that they weren't related. Even so, Johnny couldn't or wouldn't stop overprotecting her. She rolled her blue eyes at him but smiled. And then, she and Tommy were gone.

"Whew!" Kiri Lee said, floating to the ground. She landed on the left side of the door. "I thought he'd never—"

"Oh, one more thing!" Tommy said, bounding back into the chamber.

Kiri Lee slammed herself against the wall beside the doorjamb, then froze.

Tommy said, "Goldarrow was telling me there's a mandatory Lords meeting next week. You guys know anything about that?"

Kat stepped forward and to Tommy's right. "You know how tense things have been with the Conclave of Nations lately. Meetings always pop up. It might even have something to do the rumors about Grimwarden. I heard he might even show up."

"Really?" Tommy exhaled loudly. "Mannn, have I missed him. Well, cool, okay. I'll see you guys around."

Tommy turned and sprinted back down the hall.

"That was close," Kat said. "Nice reflexes, Kiri."

"I thought for sure he'd seen me," Kiri Lee said, exhaling a sigh of relief. She shook her head to get her lustrous dark locks out of her face.

Kat shut the chamber door. "Okay, now back to business," she said. "Kiri Lee, you've got the music covered. Jimmy, you good handling the games?"

"Aren't I always?" he asked with a wink.

Kat laughed. "Go light on the pranks, Jimmy," she warned. "I want this to be special for Tommy. He's been feeling down lately."

"Have'na we all," Jimmy muttered. "Seven years, it is. Still hurts."

Kat blinked rapidly and swallowed. "We still need to wrap up food," she said, glad to change the subject.

"I think I've got the menu figured out," Johnny said. "I've got a killer new recipe for pandaran wings."

"No' yur talkin'," Jimmy said. He and Johnny smacked hard high fives.

"Not just junk food," Kiri Lee said. "I want my veggies."

Jimmy laughed. "I'll bring ya some celery, then."

"No problem," Johnny said. "I've got it covered. Besides, Mumthers is going to do most of the cooking. I, still, uh…tend to burn things."

"Mumthers," Kiri Lee said. "Oh. Oh…wow. Now, I really can't wait for this party."

"Is he really comin'?" Jimmy asked. "Grimwarden? Do yu think he'll come?"

"I don't think he'd miss Tommy's birthday," Kat said. "There really is a lot of pressure on with the Conclave. They're getting curious about Grimwarden's doings. Some say he's rebuilding Whitehall, but I guess Goldarrow would have told us something."

"I think he'll come," Kiri Lee said. "Goldarrow would kill him if he didn't."

Later that evening Kiri Lee was alone in her chamber. She stood in front of a full length mirror and combed her long, silken hair. Dozens of strokes, mostly unnecessary. With very little effort, she had perfect black waves.

Still she combed on. Stroke after stroke, she'd lost track somewhere in the hundreds. It helped her think and comforted her when her thoughts turned dark.

What gives me the right to be here? she thought, meeting the convicting stare of her own eyes in the glass.

It had been seven years now in Allyra. In mind and body, she was very much a woman. *Elf maiden,* she reminded herself as one pointed ear peeked out from her hair. Wounds inflicted so long ago by the Drefid assassins upon the infant Lords were healing. Other wounds were not.

Kiri Lee wandered away from the accusing eyes in her mirror. But she kept stroking her hair. Three bluish-white dremask-braziers burned silently on her chamber walls, and she passed like a shadow in their midst. She stopped in front of one of the grand chamber windows, her reflection in the decorative glass gratefully distorted.

Deepening night lurked outside. The storm had passed, and the moon wandered the skies well east of Berinfell. Kiri Lee thought of the land that lay a great many leagues east. Vesper Crag. *It's where I died. Or should have.*

She remembered the wracking coughs, the muscle spasms, the seizing up while her heart hammered. The Wisp's poisoned blade had plunged deep. She'd lain in a pool of her own blood and felt her life draining away...

Until Jett came to her.

Jett Green, one of the Elven Lords who had lived the first thirteen years of his life on Earth in a human family, had been gifted with incredible strength. And healing.

He'd been virtually mangled in a motorcross accident, but healed completely in days. And, by the laying on of hands, he could heal others—taking on their wounds as his own until his body could beat it away altogether.

Jett had come to Kiri Lee just as her heartbeat had began its final cadence, the untimely end to a beautiful symphony cut short by a lethal poison.

Kiri Lee faded in and out of the memory, standing before the window and stroking her hair. Always stroking her long, dark hair. *Strange,* she thought, staring into the distorted glass. She could almost imagine Jett standing there, on the other side.

He should never have saved me, she thought. *He was the strong one, the brave one, the most gifted of the Seven Elven Lords.*

But the past stood like an immovable stone monument to the futility of her thoughts. Jett had come. He'd knelt beside her and found the seeping dagger wound with his hand.

The cold that had been enveloping her seemed to weaken then. Jett took her into his arms. Warmth spread from the site of the wound and radiated through her body. Jett groaned, and they both fell to the side.

"Wait, what are you doing?" she'd cried. Jett didn't answer but his rich, dark skin had gone dreadfully pale.

He'd used his full strength, every ounce of restorative power, and spent it. On her.

Kiri Lee grimaced into the glass. *Jett died in my place,* she thought. In the seven years since, she'd tried...she'd tried so hard to redeem his choice. But weighing the sum total of her efforts, she still couldn't reconcile his sacrifice. And she knew she never would.

"Huh?" she gasped sharply.

The chill that raced up the middle of her back and tingled like a frosty breath was unlike anything Kiri Lee had felt before. Her pulse quickened. She could move, but inexplicable fear kept her still. She was alone in her chamber, but convinced beyond reason and doubt of another presence.

There in the vast window stood a silhouette that was not her own. It was a dark, distorted image…a figure tall and broad and menacingly strong. And it stood behind her.

What do I do? Her thoughts crackled with terror. *I have no weapon. There is no room to climb the air. The window is far too thick.*

There was really only one choice…one chance.

Mandiera.

It was Old Elven for Nightform, the ancient martial art the Lords had been practicing for the past two years. It was considered more lethal even than *Vexbane,* and to Kiri Lee it was like a native language. She advanced in Mandiera as if it was a symphony, quickly surpassing her peers.

Still, with the intruder so close behind her, there was no guarantee.

She moved like thought itself. One moment, she was as still as the most breathless night. The next, she slid sideways like a shadow glimpsed in the corner of the eye. She began a turn, rotating at the hips even as she dropped into a half-split. Once her feet were anchored, she used the coiling torque to generate extra force. Her sharp elbow came round like a pickaxe and would have driven into the intruder's lower back, compressing vertebrae at the junction of the spine and hips.

The move would have felled a Gwar, but Kiri Lee's flowing strike slid through nothing but air. She couldn't have missed. No one except for maybe Autumn moved that fast.

Kiri Lee's momentum thew her into a spin and she almost fell. Instead, she leaped and launched a snap kick. But there was no one there.

She dropped into a crouch. Her heart pounded. She willed her breathing to calm and listened. There was no sound. But there was still the presence she had felt before.

How can this be? she wondered. The hulking figure had stood almost directly behind her. He could not have moved away so quickly without so much as making a sound.

Kiri Lee moved slowly, gliding like mist toward the window. She gazed once more into the dappled glass. She caught her breath. The figure was still there. Only, he wasn't behind her. Now she understood. He was outside, standing on the other side of the glass.

Knowing it was foolish, Kiri Lee moved closer to the window. She swallowed. Unless the glass magnified the figure, he was beyond huge.

His movement startled Kiri Lee. He lifted a vast hand and pressed it against the glass. Kiri Lee took an involuntary step backward, but then she returned.

Somehow, this shadowy being didn't feel like a threat anymore. In fact, there was something vaguely familiar about the shape and stature of this being. If only she could see his eyes, she thought, then maybe she might know.

She came closer still to the glass, and before she could think clearly and restrain herself, she put her own hand up to the glass, matching the dark figure's hand. Just inches separated them now.

She gasped. The window began to vibrate. It felt like the glass was bulging toward her. She jerked back her hand and started to step backward.

An earsplitting crack. Huge shards of thick glass crashed to the floor. A powerful hand came through and caught Kiri Lee's forearm in a vice grip.

She screamed. The mighty hand released. Kiri Lee saw just a glint of eyes through the broken glass as the figure retreated into the night.

Confusion. Terror. Shock. They struck Kiri Lee like hammer blows. She fell to the ground, an akimbo heap among the broken glass.

The world was swallowed in sudden darkness.

The darkness at last abated. Kiri Lee became aware that she was no longer lying on the floor of her chamber. She lay on something soft. There were five strange globes hovering over her.

The globes had eyes.

She caught her breath. A soft hand found her shoulder.

"Kiri Lee," said a voice. "It's me, Kat. Can you see me?"

Kiri Lee's vision cleared and she realized that the globes were her friends' faces. She blinked, and there they were: Kat, Tommy, Jimmy, Johnny, and Autumn—their expressions hovering between relief and deep concern.

"The flet soldiers heard you scream," Tommy said. "They found you on the floor. The window was shattered all around you. What happened, Kiri Lee?"

She blinked and shook her head. Tears blurred her vision. "It was Jett," she said. "He was here."

●

Grave Questions

JETT GREEN.

His name hung in the air like an uninvited specter. Each of the Elven Lords had carried differing measures of guilt for Jett's death. They hadn't been smart enough, fast enough, or powerful enough to prevent it. And whatever the years had done to dull the pain of guilt and clot the wound, Kiri Lee's claim had torn loose the scab.

When Guardmaster Goldarrow entered Kiri Lee's chamber, she found the Lords utterly still and silent. The grim mood was such a wall of gloom that she practically skidded on her booted heels.

She saw the broken glass, saw Kiri Lee sprawled on the cushions, and her heart skipped a beat. For a moment, she feared the worst.

"Lords…" Goldarrow whispered. "Kiri Lee, what…what happened here? Is she…?"

Kiri Lee leaped up from the couch and threw her arms around Goldarrow. "I saw him…he was here," she cried. "He touched my arm."

Goldarrow exhaled relief. She held Kiri Lee close and said, "Who did you see, dear? Who was here?"

Kiri Lee pulled away to arm's length. "It was Jett," she said. Her dark eyes were huge and pleading.

Goldarrow looked to the other Lords. They offered no explanation.

Goldarrow gently brushed the hair from Kiri Lee's forehead, caressed a few locks back over her delicate pointed ears. "Kiri Lee," she whispered, "while we all wish it were not so, Lord Hamandar, Jett, is dead. He was slain seven years ago."

Kiri Lee pulled away, strode on the air a few inches above the broken glass and stood in front of the shattered window. "He was here," she said. "He stood on the other side of this window. Jett broke the glass."

Tommy went to her side. "Someone broke the glass," he said gently. "But, it couldn't have been Jett."

"The glass is so thick," Autumn suggested. "And it's dark out still. You couldn't have seen too clearly. It would have been too hard—"

Kiri Lee spun and faced her. "Didn't you listen?" she demanded. "He was here. He touched my arm. Don't you think I know his touch? Don't you trust me?"

"Of course we trust you," Kat said, joining Kiri Lee and Tommy.

"We trust yu, Kiri," Jimmy said, "but we don'na understand. We saw him die. We put him in the ground. He can'na come back."

Kiri Lee wept, but shrugged off any attempts at comfort. "I know all that!" she cried. "I'm not a child. I...I don't know how he could be here, but...he was."

The room fell uncomfortably silent once more.

Autumn sat on the edge of the couch. Her foot tapped nervously, making a rapid staccato pattering sound.

Johnny bounced a chunk of broken glass in his palm. A ring of smoldering white appeared around it. The glass melted swiftly and bubbled in his hand.

Jimmy rocked on his heels and stared at the floor.

"I know how I sound," Kiri Lee whispered at last. "I know what I'd think if I were you: *she's the one Jett died for. Her guilt has frayed her sanity at last.* Maybe it has. Maybe, but I don't think so. If there's anything I remember, it is the feel of Jett's touch. He healed me, remember? He healed you, Autumn. Don't you remember what it felt like?"

Autumn looked away.

"Well, I won't ever forget his touch," Kiri Lee said. "He broke through the window to touch me again. And I felt him."

"That settles it," Tommy said.

"Settles what?" Kat asked.

"Kiri Lee's not crazy," Tommy said. "And while I don't know who or what she saw, it's clear that we need to take this visitation seriously."

"A Wisp?" Jimmy said, "yu think it might'a been a Wisp?"

Kiri Lee shivered visibly. "I...I hadn't thought of that."

"I don't know," Tommy said. "But there's one way to find out."

"Jett's grave," Goldarrow whispered. "You propose we visit his grave?"

"It's the only way to know for sure," Tommy said. "We'll go at first light."

"Now," Kiri Lee said. "I want to go now."

"But it's still a wee bit dark," Jimmy said.

Kiri Lee glared at him.

"Ah," Jimmy said, "now it is, then."

Eleabor Thrain's shoulders and back ached as if he'd just wrestled a Gwar infantry unit. Since he'd taken over the chief caretaker position, he'd never worked so hard as he had this night.

Eleabor tossed his shovel into the corner of the workshop and made his way back to his chair. His comfy chair. He patted the cushions and ran his hands lovingly over the backrest.

He glanced through the eastern window. The sun would be up in no time. Layers of mist floated among the gravestones and monuments, out in the blue-gray twilight.

Eleabor wiped the sweat from his brow and was about to plop down in the chair when dremask lights appeared out in the mists. They moved swiftly, bobbing closer like so many will o' the wisps. They were upon the cottage threshold before Eleabor could blink.

"Caretaker Thrain?" came a voice. Torchlight danced on his cottage ceiling, and seven visitors stood before Eleabor. He recognized them instantly and suddenly felt as if he stood in quicksand.

Guardmaster Goldarrow and the six Great Lords of Berinfell, he thought, swallowing deeply. *Now that's a first for me, and no mistake. And…maybe a last.*

Eleabor swallowed and bowed low. "My Lords," he muttered, "I…I'm honored by your visit. But, er, I must admit to some confusion. The hour is very early, and I had no notice of your coming. Is something amiss?"

Goldarrow stepped forward. "Good caretaker, we have an errand most urgent," she said. "Please conduct us to the resting place of Lord Hamandar Nightwing."

A chill raced up Eleabor's spine. *How could…?* There was no answer to that question in his old mind. He felt pangs of guilt like waves of filth splashing on the sewer banks. "Uh, of course, of course," he said. "Please follow me."

Eleabor grabbed the dremask lantern he'd shuttered only moments before and set off reluctantly for the monument. He took a circuitous route so that he'd have time to think.

Telling the truth was only right and proper. He'd simply have to explain that he'd fallen asleep while on duty, allowing some Gwar hoodlums to come in and wreak havoc among the dead. *Oh, and why, yes, they did rob Lord Hamandar's grave…all on my watch.*

As appealing as that admission sounded to Eleabor, there was a rather large hurdle; one that prevented him from telling the truth, that might just earn him the gallows if the Lords discovered what he'd done.

The sun was still blessedly far below the eastern horizon, allowing the tendrils of night to hold Berinfell in its grasp for yet a little longer.

As Eleabor followed the final turn past the grand resting place of the Lords of Old, his heart thudded so loudly in his chest, he thought it might burst. He stopped a dozen feet from Lord Hamandar's monument and turned his dremask lantern so that the most direct light fell elsewhere.

But Guardmaster Goldarrow and the Lords would have none of it. They jostled by Eleabor, surrounded Hamandar's grave, and held their torches and lanterns high.

Eleabor refused to breathe for several interminable moments, waiting for the questions to fly. And then the accusations.

"What do you make of this?" Goldarrow asked at last.

Lord Felheart Silvertree, called by his earthly name, Tommy, said, "I don't know what to think."

Their eyes all seemed to shift back and forth between the grave and Lord Lothriel Oakenflower...Kiri Lee.

"I can't understand it," she said, her cheeks already splashed with tears. "I saw him."

"But the glass?" Lord Thorwin Valorbrand said. "It's not yur fault. Yu could'na seen too clearly—"

"I know what I saw, Jimmy," Kiri Lee retorted, but the conviction drained from her words as she spoke. "He touched me. I can't doubt my own senses...can I? Well, can I?"

"Wisp," Goldarrow muttered. "Had to be."

"That could explain it," Tommy said. "Kiri Lee, do you think— could it have been?"

Kiri Lee knelt at the gravesite and ran her fingers over the costly marble gravecap.

Eleabor tried to swallow his heart back down to his chest. She knew. She had to know. *I'm as good as dead,* he thought.

Kiri Lee stood and exhaled deeply. "It must have been a Wisp," she said. "But to what end? And under whose direction?"

"This bears long thought and keen discernment," Guardmaster Goldarrow replied. "Come, it has been a long night. Let us return to Gladhost."

"Consult the Prophecies?" Tommy asked. Goldarrow nodded.

"My Lords?" Eleabor Thrain blurted out. "Forgive my intrusion, but I don't understand—"

Goldarrow raised a hand. "No, good caretaker," she said. "It is our intrusion. Doubtless this place and your occupation here are hard enough without our unannounced invasion during the wee hours."

"It is no trouble," Eleabor muttered, trying to maintain some kind of eye contact but failing miserably. "But...what has drawn you here? If there is some assistance I might provide—"

Goldarrow smiled and actually put a hand on Eleabor's shoulder. "No need to concern yourself," she said. "We came to Innskell hoping to find, well...I am not certain what we were hoping to find or that *hope* is even the correct term. In any case, we have found nothing amiss here."

She turned to walk away but stopped suddenly. "One question, good caretaker," she said. "You know Innskell better than anyone in Berinfell. Do you see anything amiss with this monument, the final rest of our friend?"

Eleabor couldn't squeak out a word. He shook his head vigorously.

"Have you seen anything strange this night?" Tommy asked. "Anything at all out of the ordinary?"

Eleabor felt like he'd swallowed broken glass. His stomach twisted, and something railed at him to tell the whole awful truth. But again he shook his head. *No.*

Tommy nodded. Goldarrow and the Lords turned to depart, and Eleabor followed.

Somehow, the journey back to his caretaker's cottage seemed even longer than the trip to Hamandar's tomb. Guilt weighed most heavily upon Eleabor as he watched the Guardmaster and the Lords departing Innskell, the rising sun painting their backplates and cloaks in dawn's pink and orange.

Eleabor thudded into his favorite chair, but it brought him no comfort. He couldn't believe he'd pulled it off. He'd taken one of the pricey marble tomb caps from the storage chamber and hewn it to a design like to Lord Hamandar's. He'd even engraved it from memory, and in record time, though far more sloppy than he cared to admit. And somehow, the Lords and the Guardmaster hadn't noticed.

A stark image would not leave Eleabor's mind though. He could not push it away. It was the tears streaming down from Lord Lothriel's huge dark eyes.

Eleabor's job was safe, but he felt somehow his soul was not.

Cloak and Dagger

THRUM.

ERAGOR hated the sound: the muted buzz of the daggerflies, thousands of them, recently hatched and thrumming their wings as if there were no tomorrow.

Close enough, thought Eragor as he lumbered along the central duct. Blasted daggerflies lived only a month. The Chief Practitioner hadn't found a rite to extend the lifespan beyond that. It didn't really matter much, not with the sheer numbers they'd been breeding, with five-hundred more each day. The delvers had tripled their shifts just to create enough cavern space to house the things.

And now: *Thrum.*

Six square miles of corridors, catacombs, chambers, and caverns hidden beneath Canada's mountainous Northwest Territories—all that space—and not one place a self respecting Gwar could go to get away from the sound. Eragor halted outside Lord Asp's chamber and put his hand up to the stone wall. It was faint but even here, a restricted space far from the hatcheries and hangars, he could feel—and hear—the vibration. *Thrum.*

Twin doors of black wrought-iron marked Lord Asp's quarters. Eragor lifted his fist to strike the door but froze.

"You…are bidden enter, General." Asp's resonant voice drifted out from under the doors like smoke. Few words, but somehow filling the hall…suffocating.

Eragor swallowed. *Hate when he does that.*

He adjusted the leather at his collar beneath the chestplate, shoved the doors inward, and then strode inside. Asp's chambers were far from the tiny, honeycombed living quarters used by the soldiers. Six steps in, and one found a multilevel, cylindrical library that went up a hundred feet or more, like a silo. A diffused shaft of light rained down from an ice window high above. Earagor wondered if Asp had taken every old book, scroll and manuscript from Earth and brought them here. It was dizzying to look up at them all.

"My lord?" Eragor called. There was no answer.

Eragor squinted, but Asp was nowhere to be seen. The Gwar went forward, out of the natural light in the library into the unnatural glow of green dremask in Asp's laboratory. On one long table, all manner of oddly-shaped, glass containers bubbled away over open flames. Some were clear. Some viscous. Some faintly luminous. And others as dull as dead eyes.

One of the largest containers, a gourd-sized globe filled with a sloshing, bruise-colored fluid, fed into more than a dozen rubber tubes. These emptied, one tiny drip at a time, into an army of small vials. A massive book lay open nearby. Eragor ran his fingers across the page, following the script as much as he could. He knew as much of Asp's wiry script as any Gwar might, but it was nearly impossible to decipher. Something about blood and fire and…control.

Eragor looked up suddenly and found himself staring into cold, blue wolfs eyes.

He staggered backward a few steps and ripped his war mallet from its holster. He didn't swing the bludgeon. The wolf, he saw now, was already quite dead. It lay motionless, sprawled on a four-legged grate.

The wolf had been a magnificent creature: a hundred-fifty, hundred-seventy-five pound gray with a lush pelt. Gone now.

The wolf had been split from its torn-out throat down to its abdomen. Its blood still dripped into a metallic catchment. From there it seemed to be siphoned off in several directions and—

"General."

Eragor jumped again, spun and made no aggressive movement with his weapon. No aggressive motion whatsoever. His Commander, Lord Asp Bloodthorne, stood before him. Towered over Eragor to be precise.

And at six foot six inches tall, the Gwar general was not easily dwarfed.

But Asp was Drefid-kind and...something else.

"You have come all this way." His voice cascaded down from the darkness beneath his huge hood. Not even a glimmer of eyes. The words seemed disembodied. "You bring news, then?"

Eragor stared at the Drefid's gnarled hands, the only part of Asp not hidden by the cloak. He knew well that, with a thought, Asp could summon long, razor-sharp talons from those fists. "I-I do," Eragor said. "The Practioners have succeeded at last. They've diluted the Gnomic cloaking paste without affecting its, uh...unique properties. It won't hinder the Warflies or daggerflies now."

"Of course the Practitioners have succeeded," Asp said, walking past Eragor to the long table.

"You knew?" Eragor cleared his throat. "But it was just now...how could, well, I just came to tell you."

"Relax, General," Asp said. "I am endowed with many unique skills, but not among them is the ability to see through walls."

Eragor swallowed. "How then did you know?"

There was a wet clicking sound, and Asp used his talons to turn the page of the huge tome. "Motivation, General. I was simply confident that my will would be carried out. You may have noticed that the Practitioners who succeeded were not of the same team that began the work some months ago."

Eragor blinked. Come to think of it, he hadn't recognized any of the Gwar and Drefid Practitioners who'd succeeded. The Gwar laughed nervously. "What? Did you send the first team to clean the spider pens?"

Asp skewered the dead gray wolf and flung it into a wide cask in the corner of the chamber. "No, General. They failed," Asp said, casually wiping his talons on his cloak. "I gutted them and hung their carrion for the spiders to feed upon."

Asp turned back to his thick book, read a moment, and said, "You cannot afford to have a message misunderstood, you see."

Eragor felt as if his collar had tightened three sizes. "Lord Asp," he managed to croak, "I have understood your message...completely."

Asp stood very still for a moment. His hooded head bobbed once. "You continue to impress me, General," Asp said. "Join me at the table."

Eragor approached.

Asp pointed to the text. "Could you follow...my recipe?"

Eragor shook his head and involuntarily stepped backward. "Your work," Eragor said, "is beyond my skill."

"Is it?" Asp turned and bent toward Eragor. "I believe you underestimate your potential."

Scarcely eighteen inches separated Eragor's face from his Commander's. So close that Eragor felt Asp's chilly breath, but he couldn't penetrate the shadows of Asp's hood to see his face. Not that he wanted to.

Asp turned back to the table. "Do you see what I am brewing here?" Asp asked. "I am close. So close. The wolf's blood was key, and yet I still do not understand why."

Eragor peered more closely, watched the bruise-colored liquid drip into the smaller vials. He asked. "What is it?"

"It is what changed me," Asp said. "After all, General, it's not about what you are...but what you may become."

Asp turned suddenly, and his cloak swirled around him like a dark curtain. There was a glimpse, the briefest impression of Asp's torso.

There was something very unnerving about that impression. A bend or hinge where there shouldn't be, a rigid edge or jagged point—whatever it was, Eragor didn't like it. He chastised himself to never again look inside Asp's cloak.

The master strode out of the lab, and Eragor followed at his heels.

"I have found something extraordinary," Asp said, stopping in the center of his library where the ethereal light fell upon him from above. "Among the humans, there are great works to be read. Surprising, but true. I have plundered their vaults and brought many hundreds of their books to rest here among my own. There is history, lore, even primitive religion. And one not so primitive. One moment."

Asp suddenly leaped up into the air. His cloak flapped, and he came to rest on a rail at the second level of his library. He clambered sideways a moment and then jumped out into the open air. He landed on another rail a level higher up.

Eragor watched as the Drefid leaped from side to side, from one section to the other. He went up and up until he was just a shadow flashing across the small circle of light high above. Then Asp returned, descending the same way, and landing with a dull thud right next to Eragor.

Asp held a thick black book in his hands. "This," he said, "is inspired work."

Eragor squinted at the title. *"On the Origin of—"*

"Species, yes," Asp replied. *"By Means of Natural Selection, or the Preservation of Favoured Races in the Struggle for Life.* In this book, General, are the same teachings as the Dark Arts Masters. I am convinced that this, this Darwin, was one of our own from long ago. His wisdom is

beyond mankind. Strength, General, rules all and outlasts all. Survival of the fittest. This book confirms what I have always believed...what I have always seen. Do you understand?"

Eragor stared at the book and shook his head.

"But you will," Asp said. "When I solve the last remaining problems and perfect the venom, you will understand all too well. You see, General, I am the apex creature, the strongest of all. The Dominant. The *Favoured Race*. But we must all be stronger still so that we may endure through the ages. For there is much to do. The Vulrid declares it."

Asp raced into his laboratory and returned with a vial of the purple liquid. "What of you, General?" Asp asked. "Will you evolve? Will you drink with me?"

Eragor stared at the vial and blinked. "I...I do not know. Of course, if your book—uh, the Vulrid commands it, I—"

"No?" Asp said. "Of course not. You're no fool. You would see it tested on slaves first. As would I. It is time, General."

Eragor had anticipated this much at least. "Which base?"

"Yellowknife," Asp said. "Only about 200 personnel, but plenty of what they call mechanized weaponry. Take Warspiders and daggerflies. Cloak everything and go in bright daylight."

General Eragor nodded. "Tomorrow afternoon then," he said. "And I'll take Caerfasz. He's one of our best pilots."

"Mix it up, General," Asp said. "Take a handful of raw pilots as well. Let them cut their teeth on this little test."

Eragor looked away.

"You will succeed, won't you?" Asp asked.

There came that wet clicking sound, and Eragor said, "Of course, my Lord. We will succeed."

"I have no doubt," Asp replied. "One more thing: bring me back a few humans...alive. I need to perform more tests."

Thrum.

The sound was much louder now. It brought the kind of pressure that summoned pounding headaches. Eragor thought his skull might explode but, given Asp's expectations, he managed to hold it together. The mission itself was very motivating as well. It wasn't every day he got to fly. And it wasn't every day that he got to kill. Headache aside, it was going to be a good day.

That was until Eragor stormed into the hangar and caught sight of Caerfasz reclining in a pile of leather saddles like it was his own personal easy chair.

"Caerfasz!" Eragor growled. "We fly in ten minutes!"

Caerfasz, a burly pilot with extremely long legs for a Gwar, crossed those legs and casually opened one eye. His only reply was, "So."

Eragor ripped his twin warhammers free and charged toward the seemingly lazy pilot. "So? SO!" Eragor shouted. "I don't care how well you fly, you answer me with respect! We've got to saddle up these daggerflies—"

"Done," Caerfasz said.

Eragor stuttered a moment. "Done? Well, we still need to load the arc stones in each—"

"Done."

"The other pilots need to be brought up to speed on the route through—"

"Done an hour ago."

"Spider harnesses?"

"Yup."

"What about the cloaking pumps?" Eragor asked. "They need time to build up the pressure—"

"Look, General," Caerfasz said, clambering to his feet. "The reason you asked a guy like me on this trip is because I get things done. If it's ten minutes to air, then you can know we're already ready."

"But I don't see the Warspiders...the daggerflies."

"But ya hear 'em, right?" Caerfasz asked.

"Louder than ever."

"They've already been coated," Caerfasz said. "Gnomes aren't good for much, but their cloaking paste does the trick, eh?"

Eragor scanned the hangar. The vast chamber had been blasted and carved from the root of Mount Andromeda within Canada's Columbia ice field. It was shadowy, lit only by dremask braziers, but the Gwar see vividly, even in dim light. And yet, all Eragor could see were piles and crates of supplies and a few Gwar soldiers milling about. He could, however, hear the thrum of the creatures' wings, loud and clear.

"Well, I'll be a maladon's hindquarters," Eragor said at last, breathing out a loud sigh. "You've actually managed to exceed my expectations."

Caerfasz bowed. "Lord Asp doesn't care for mediocrity."

"No, no, he does not." Eragor said, holstering his warhammers. "Yellowknife Military Base awaits us. Let's paste up and fly."

Chief Warrant Officer Cam Strauss had stayed up way too late the night before, plugging away at the combat simulator. Now it was his watch from the Yellowknife tower. Sure the air traffic controllers were there: Master Corporal Harold "Hal" Carmichael and Signalman Isabel LeSage. They did the hard work, but Cam was manning security, and he was not up to the task this afternoon, especially as the clock crept past 2:00 p.m.

Glad I'm not in charge of flight plans, he thought. *I'd nod off, hit a button with my nose, and send a troop transport into the side of a mountain.*

He had nodded off once already. He'd fallen asleep on his feet and nearly planted his face into a bank of servers. Since then, he'd swilled two cups of Tim Horton's coffee and figured that would keep him more-or-less alert until his duty ended at six.

So when Cam looked over the airfield and saw one of the base's CC-138 Twin Otter utility transport aircraft hanging in the air in front of the tower, he had to do a double take. He rubbed his crusty eyes. He blinked. Finally, he slapped himself. No, it didn't go away. And it didn't change. The aircraft was still there, hanging, almost hovering in the air… upside down.

The Twin Otter began to rise. Cam tapped on Corporal Carmichael's shoulder. "Hal. Hal, you seeing this?"

"Idiot!" Hal exclaimed. "Can't you see I'm busy?"

"Hal?" Cam repeated. "Hal, look out the window!"

Hal looked up at last, but the plane had risen out of sight. "What? I don't see anything." He leaned forward, closer to the glass, and looked up. "Blasted—get back!" Hal dove.

The aircraft plummeted from a height well above the top of the tower and slammed into the tarmac. A mushrooming fireball erupted skyward, and a jet of angry orange-burning aviation fuel spewed across a half-dozen armored vehicles.

A concussive wave shattered the windows of the tower, followed by a strange strobing flash of bluish-white.

Cam found himself face down in a pile of broken glass. The last thing he heard before the tower exploded was a deep, resonant *THRUM*.

Eragor dug his boot heels into the daggerfly's thorax, just behind the eyes, forcing the creature into a swift dive. He leveled and swung the daggerfly in low, ducking anti-aircraft fire with relative ease.

Human soldiers streamed out of every exit, trying to get to the armored vehicles, helicopters, jets—anything to defend the base.

But it's no good, Eragor thought. *You can't see us. Your machines can't see us. You are at our mercy.*

"Mercy?" Eragor laughed aloud. "We do not have any mercy today." His daggerfly was now hovering forward, mere feet above the ground. He slid his left boot down the thorax and then scraped the toe upward several times.

The daggerfly responded, curling its bladed abdomen down. Generating tremendous torque with its thick segments of abdominal muscle, the daggerfly swished the blade about, cutting through soldiers like a machete through saplings. The men ran in horror, unsure of what assailed them, but certain that if they didn't flee, they'd be next.

Eragor pulled up from the carnage and watched as sides of buildings caved in, armored vehicles were crushed or tossed, and fighter jets exploded. It was obvious that Caerfasz and his team had loosed the Warspiders.

Eragor couldn't wait to get back to the hold to make his report. As ruthless as Lord Asp could be to those who failed him, he was also known to bestow special privileges to those who succeeded.

General Eragor had led his squadron of daggerflies into the teeth of modern technological warfare...and prevailed. In a mere forty minutes, Yellowknife Base had been decimated, the human slaves captured.

He had to laugh again at the ease of it all. When the time came, Eragor knew, Asp would unleash an attack on the powers of Earth unlike any they had ever faced before.

Birthday Surprises

TOMMY STOMPED up the corridor on the way to the Great Hall. "Mandatory Lords meeting," he grumbled. "And I have to go. HAVE to. I thought the Lords actually ruled around here. I can't believe this... especially tonight."

He pounded between two long tables in one of the lower dining halls and wished his Lordly gift, ultra keen archer's eyesight, had come with nuclear vision beams. He could just imagine blasting the goblets and pitchers off the tables, rattling all the plates and utensils, and maybe melting the suits of armor that guarded each corner of the room.

Yeah, that would help.

A little.

Tommy stopped walking a moment and cringed inwardly. *Twenty-one today,* he thought, *and here I am acting like a tantrum-throwing toddler.* A tingle on the ridge of his ears and a fresh batch of goosebumps reminded him that servants of Ellos were made for better.

Tommy sighed and continued on. He ducked under the western archway and picked up speed. But then he paused at the fork in his path. Both passages led eventually to the Great Hall. He decided to go the long way through the Ailianthium. It was Tommy's favorite place in the rebuilt city of Berinfell.

A cavernous, high-ceilinged chamber with great, curving windows above, and high, sculpted archways open to the outdoors, the Ailianthium contained three acres of living trees. It had taken scores of Elves years to transport the trees, most from the Thousand League Forest. And these were no mere saplings, not in the commonly understood sense, anyway. Mature chalicewood, black hazelnut, maiden ash, and even a few silver mattisbough—the trees towered over the marble footpaths that networked at their roots. Several ambitious limbs even managed to tickle the ceiling some ninety feet above.

Tommy's pace quickened as he drew near. During the day, the sun's light danced in the Ailianthium's trees and dappled the world in every green and gold ever seen in the world of men or Elves. But night was Tommy's favorite time to visit. The dremask chandeliers turned the Ailianthium to magic. If they were all lit, and if a subtle breeze played through the archways, it was as if millions of multicolored stars danced among the trees. It reminded Tommy somehow of Christmas trees, only on a far grander scale.

Christmas trees.

Tommy sighed. It had been a long time since he'd thought about Christmas. Being at home with his parents and decorating. It was lovely… and painful. At first, Tommy couldn't bear to exile the memories, visions of his parents and his childhood. But the scent of pine, gingerbread, and pumpkin pie vanished like smoke as Tommy came to the Ailianthium's root-entwined threshold. Something was very wrong.

The Ailianthium was always beautiful, sometimes mysterious, but never dark. Not pitch black like this. Never.

Tommy glanced back over his shoulder. No flet soldiers either. *Should have noticed that sooner,* Tommy thought. He reached for his bow and silently berated himself for leaving his favored weapon back in the training yard.

"Looks like it'll be the sword, then," Tommy whispered. He

stepped into the inky darkness and drew his rychesword. From the moment it left the sheath, the weapon felt odd. The balance was off...or something. Tommy wasn't sure. He didn't spend time considering it. He had to focus everything on his vision.

Elves could see in the dark better than humans, but not usually anywhere near as well as the Gwar. But, with his gift, Tommy could nearly see as well in the darkness as a Gwar could. What he saw in the Ailianthium still left too many unknowns, too many potential dangers. The trees towered, columns of gray with boughs reaching out high overhead. Their foliage created a ragged, broken canopy of darkness. And up near the high ceiling, there were strange, bulbous shapes that Tommy couldn't identify.

Something moved.

Ahead, a shadow flitted out from one trunk and disappeared just as quickly behind another. Not quite confident enough in Nightform, Tommy dropped into a Vexbane stance known as *Jendurath*, Elven for *viper*.

He crouched low with legs flexed, right foot forward, left foot perpendicular. He rotated his torso counterclockwise, lifted his sword hand to shoulder height but turned the blade to horizontal. He was compact, coiled, ready to strike.

The tenets of Vexbane demand that combatants identify everything—anything—that might be used as a weapon or a component of a weapon. With Vexbane, an Elf was never unarmed. Tommy had his blade, but there was much more. In the shadows, he noted a bulging chalicewood root, curling up from the ground in a kind of loop. A well-timed shove could send an enemy tripping over it. Tommy imagined the movements, felt the necessary muscles tense and twitch. It would be easy enough.

There was a crook in the neighboring hazelnut tree, offering endless possibilities. Trap an enemy blade? Leap from it into a kick?

Maybe, if his foe was off balance, he could even use it to break its neck.

The shadow moved again, the motion: a wraith passing between trees, whipped Tommy into instant focus. *No,* he thought. *Not a wraith. Wraiths.* A second shadow moved in a different corner of the Ailianthium, followed by a third. And then something even further back…something *very* large…produced a low growl.

This changed everything. Tommy's mind began calculating angles. He uncoiled, slid a few yards up to a perfectly vertical ash tree, and took a deep breath. It would have to be Nightform after all.

Tommy slowed his breathing and eased back against the tree. One of the shadows drew closer, now a mere forty yards away. Tommy allowed himself to sway like the trunk of a willow in a summer breeze. A half breath later, Tommy had flowed to the other side of the ash. His blade traced the contour of the trunk. He saw the movement coming, now from behind and to his left. He heard the stealthy footfalls.

He counted: *One. Two.*

It wasn't a guess—he knew—exactly where the first assailant would be. Tommy flowed around the perimeter of the trunk, dropped low, and drove his blade up under the shadow figure's left shoulder blade. He expected to hear a wet crackle as the arm severed at the joint, but heard only a dull thud. There was no time to wonder. He spun and slammed the blade into the already caving enemy's side.

While the first intruder crumbled, Tommy listened. He heard the rapidly accelerating footfalls padding from two directions. Tommy used the fallen enemy as a ramp, leaped for the lowest limb of the nearby ash, and swung effortlessly around its trunk. He came down 280° later, right behind another shadow figure.

He swept the blade hard into the back of the enemy's knees. But Tommy didn't let him fall. He caught the intruder as he fell backward and slung him into the unseen third assailant. There came a heavy *whump*, like dropping a sack of grain on a hard floor.

Tommy almost smiled, the satisfaction welling up, but that was when the booted heel slammed into his back. Tommy flew bodily and smacked hard onto the tiled floor. Pain radiated across his shoulders and down his back. There were tingles and numbness in his right arm. But Tommy rolled twice and surged up to his feet.

That was when the lights began to flash.

Dremask lanterns of many colors blazed to life and then vanished while others kindled. Flashes blinked on and off from every direction. It was like being in a multicolored strobe light.

Tommy heard the footfalls, including those of the giant beast that had waited in the woods, but he was too disoriented to act. It was all he could do to flex his abs before the booted heel struck him in the gut. He groaned, folding inward to absorb the blow even as he stumbled backward.

The figure came on again, but this time because of the blinking lights, Tommy saw him. One-on-one, Tommy shifted back to Vexbane. The enemy lifted a peculiar oblong blade and seemed to be aiming for Tommy's head. Tommy waited and then uncoiled. His blade met the enemy's with a sharp crack—not the ring of metal. An intruding thought almost threw off Tommy's timing. But Tommy bounced his blade off the parry, spun, and feinted a strike at the enemy's legs. Instead, Tommy put a side kick into the assailant's lower back. He flew forward and hooked his foot in the looping tree root. The enemy went down in a jumbled heap.

Tommy raced from the clearing and found a tile path leading north. He took it and sprinted for the other side of the Ailianthium. He charged with all his might, his heart pounding, but with the odd blinking lantern flashes, it felt like he was running in slow motion. He glanced left and then right...and growled. There were enemies fifty yards away on both sides, matching his pace, and surging from tree to tree. A giant shadow stalked him as well, a massive monster he knew he couldn't outrun.

One of the assailants moved with supernatural speed. Maybe it was the light, but this warrior left the others behind and raced ahead into a thicket. Tommy adjusted course and took a leftward angle. A plume of white flame flared up on Tommy's left. He felt the blast of heat and swerved back to the right. Something darted by him, grabbed the crook of his right elbow, and flung him around.

Tommy found himself surrounded by five figures clad all in black, and the monster looming behind them. The strobing lanterns revealed that each enemy bore a sword, mace, or club, and they were closing in, tightening the noose.

Uh, oh.

Tommy thought of the fluidity of water coursing through a boulder-strewn riverbed. It was the perfect Nightform image. Tommy allowed his body to relax. He rolled his neck loosely, flexed each major muscle group in turn and let them loosen. The enemies came closer, just out of reach.

Tommy knew that, if he let them close off the circle, he'd have no chance. But the flashing light had triggered a pulsing headache. His muscles involuntarily began to tense. The pain was excruciating. He tried to focus on the steps, the angles, the counters, and defenses, but it was too hard. He had no choice now. He'd have to launch into the first couple of moves and improvise the rest.

Tommy turned in place, waited for the shortest enemy to lunge, and then leaped. He planted his foot on the enemy's knee and used it to propel himself up. Flying at shoulder height and feeling for the moment very much like Kiri Lee, Tommy kicked one of the combatants in the chin. Still in the air, Tommy used the momentum of the blow and swung his blade at the head of the next warrior.

But the head wasn't where it was supposed to be. The enemy was up in the air, right in front of Tommy. Flabbergasted, Tommy began to fall. Something stuck him hard in in the shoulder.

A flurry of blows pounded Tommy to his knees. He waited for the slash that would take his head, but none came. Suddenly, a booted foot slammed his rear end so hard that Tommy flew forward.

His sword cartwheeled ahead, and Tommy fell into an exhausted pile. When Tommy looked up, silvery blue light illuminated the figure towering over him. Tree trunk legs, a barrel chest, broad shoulders—made all the more massive by dark armor—this mighty warrior seemed descended from a race of giants. He reached over his shoulder and loosed a terrible, twin-bladed battle axe.

And then…he began to laugh.

Huge shadows descended slowly from the ceiling, falling in bulbous clumps all around Tommy. Blinking stupidly, he rose to one knee just as the huge warrior took off his helm.

What? Tommy could scarcely reconcile what he was seeing. *Balloons?*

"Happy Birthday, Tommy!" Grimwarden bellowed.

All at once, the dremask lanterns stopped flashing and became steady. A thunderous cheer went up from the hundreds of Elves who filled the wide stair to the Great Hall. A huge tongue covered him in hot drool, that of their beloved, giant wolf, Bear. Now drenched in steak-flavored saliva, Tommy shoved the pooch away. "Well, you got me," Tommy confessed, wiping his face. "You got me good."

"You really didn't figure it out?" Kat asked. She rubbed a knuckle on her right hand so intently that the flesh there turned slightly purple rather than the usual blue. "Really?"

Tommy laughed, rubbing his shoulder. "You ought to know, Kat," Tommy said. "Not like I can hide anything from you."

"You certainly could," Kat said. "A promise is a promise. I won't read your thoughts unless you give me permission."

Tommy rolled his eyes playfully. "Rest assured, Kat. If I woke up tomorrow with pink and purple Gwar ballerinas pirouetting around my bed, I wouldn't be as surprised as I am now. You guys just about beat the snot out of me."

Laughter crackled around the long table on the Lords' Dais, echoing and filling the far end of the Great Hall with more mirth than it had seen in many years' time. No laugh was deeper or louder than Grimwarden's.

"Hwah, whu, ha! Tommy, you should have seen...Hoo, hwah... should have seen the look on your face when you saw me!"

"I thought I was coming to a council meeting!" Tommy grumbled. He took a long sip of splendine punch from his goblet. "Is that how you treat all Elves on their twenty-first birthday?"

"Twenty-one is an important age for all Elves," Goldarrow replied. "It is the Threshold Day, and we all celebrate it in one fashion...or another."

"But for practitioners of Vexbane, Nightform, and other martial arts," Grimwarden explained, "it is customary to run the Gauntlet upon their Threshold Day. It is a chance for a young warrior to prove his mettle—which, Tommy, I'd say you did and then some. It's not often that a warrior must be outnumbered and face the combined powers of the Lords, all while being blasted by dremask flashes. You did well, Tommy."

"I bet you all had fun knocking me around," Tommy said, still wiping some of Bear's saliva off his face.

They all denied it...at first.

"Okay," said Jimmy, "so maybe we had a wee bit of fun at yur expense."

"Sorry about hitting you from behind," Autumn mumbled with a chuckle.

"I guess my wall of fire gave you a bit of a scare!" Johnny said.

Tommy laughed loudly. "I did NOT see that coming," he said. "But nothing scared me more than Grimwarden. I thought you were going to behead me!" Tommy huffed out the words and pointed at Grimwarden's side. "New axe?"

"Yes, yes," Grimwarden replied, patting the twin-bladed weapon. "The first of its kind from the Nightwish Forge. Strentium edge and wicked sharp."

"It's got to be better than this thing!" Tommy tossed his sword to the middle of the table. It slid to a stop between the muffle cakes platter and a bowl of nockels. Only, it wasn't Tommy's sword or even a real rychesword at all. It was a practice blade fashioned from the hard wood of a maiden ash tree. "How did you guys manage to switch this with my real sword?"

"That was easy," Kiri Lee said. "I switched them while we were forest-shooting. You'd gone to collect arrows."

"Did you hide my bow too?" Tommy asked.

"Yup," Kiri Lee said. She crouched beneath the table for a moment. When she stood up, she had Tommy's rychesword and bow. She slid them to Tommy. "You should be more careful with these, you know."

"With sneaky friends like you anyway," Tommy replied.

Just then, a beautiful flourish of music trilled.

"Ah, that's my cue!" Kiri Lee said. She nimbly leaped up from her chair and trotted across the air into the massive gathering of Elves assembled in the hall.

"Where's she going?" Jimmy asked.

"Do you not know?" Goldarrow said. "The Berinfell Symphony plays tonight. It is time for dance!"

A few heartbeats later, the soft voice of a harp ascended to the Lords. Other stringed instruments followed, reeds and woodwinds too, and the delightful bouncing harpsichord. The cavernous Great Hall came alive with an inviting symphonic melody. Elves left their seats and tables behind and began to whirl and sway to the music.

"Ya don'na have t' tell me twice!" Jimmy yelled. He was up and at Regis' side in a flash. "M'lady, would honor me with—"

He needn't finish the sentence, for Regis took his hand and hauled him down the stairs to the dance floor.

"What? Wait!" Grimwarden thundered. "What are you doing, you cantankerous woman!"

Goldarrow had Grimwarden by the arm. "Cantankerous?" she exclaimed. "Now if that isn't the pot calling the kettle black! Now, get up, you great lummox, and treat me to a dance!"

Grimwarden's bushy white eyebrows danced, but in a variety of frowns. "You know quite well that I...DO...NOT...DANCE!"

But Goldarrow would have none of it. She mussed the old war-general's hair and finally pulled him the rest of the way to his feet. "Don't believe a word he said," Goldarrow told those who remained at the table. "Olin Grimwarden used to be the most graceful dancer among Elves in Berinfell. And as I recall, once told the Lords that *real Elf men dance!*"

"What?" Grimwarden groaned. "You make me sound like a butterfly or some such! I blunder and stomp! *Graceful?*—rubbish!"

"Oh, do stop this whining," Goldarrow said. "Remember, I'm now your superior officer, and I'm ordering you to dance. And you too, Lords, though you outrank me by far. This is a night to be jovial, to celebrate. Go, join the dance."

With that, the Guardmaster and former Guardmaster left the Lords' Dais. Tommy, Kat, Johnny, and Autumn were left at the table, staring at each other.

"Well," Johnny said, "this is awkward."

The laughter diffused the situation somewhat. Autumn said, "I wonder what amazingly handsome flet soldiers are still available down there." Autumn left her seat and whooshed down the stairs.

"They better mind their manners!" Johnny called after her. A lick of flame kindled in his palm as he tromped away down the stairs.

That left Tommy and Kat.

He looked up at her, saw the dremask torches flickering in her huge, expectant eyes, and then stared at his goblet of punch.

"Oh, I'll make this easy on you!" Kat said, taking Tommy's arm. "But only because it's your birthday!"

Before Tommy could say a word, Kat whisked him down the stairs and into the mix of swirling Elves.

Tommy's right hand was planted on Kat's narrow waist. He held her other hand straight out to his left. Both hands began sweating instantly. His heart pounded louder than the symphony's percussion section. It was all he could do to remember the simple steps to the Elven waltz.

They danced, gliding easily across the hall, whirling on the sides and sliding back. But all the while Tommy couldn't think straight. Breathing didn't work so well either. He had to inhale through his mouth or he'd smell Kat's perfume. And every time they turned, he had to jerk his head super quick to avoid eye contact.

"Why are you so nervous?" Kat asked.

Tommy swallowed. *Why am I so nervous?* he wondered. *This is my best friend in the world.*

"Well?" Kat demanded. Her hands were on her hips now.

"I uh—"

Shouts from the corridor on the east side of the Great Hall stopped the music.

Tommy whispered a silent prayer of thanksgiving. He'd been granted a reprieve, precious time to think of an answer to Kat's question. But when the guards on either side of the entrance drew their rycheswords, Tommy reconsidered his good fortune. Bear, who'd been enjoying the party with a roasted cow femur beside the main door, turned his head and raised his hackles in a deep growl.

"Lords!" Tommy cried out. "Arm yourselves and meet me eastside!" Tommy left Kat and darted up the stairs. He was back down in a flash, armed with his blade and bow. The shouting grew louder now.

"...do not care what the occasion is!" someone yelled, a strange accent on each syllable. "*Varnest kul sh'i uyudiffex!* Let us through!"

"With all due respect, your highness," said another voice, "this is a matter for council tomorrow. The High Lords will see you then."

"Tomorrow is too late!" the voice cried out. "Untold thousands are dead! Do you hear? And thousands more may yet perish, *skans vir allan zhik!*"

The other Lords, Grimwarden, Goldarrow, and a host of flet soldiers fanned out behind Tommy. They all stared at the opening to the eastern corridor.

"Who would intrude on a night like this?" Kiri Lee asked.

"I don't know," Tommy said. "The voice...it's strange, sounds almost Russian or Eastern European, maybe."

"Someone...someone from Earth?" Johnny asked.

No one answered. No one dared.

More angry shouts came from the corridor. Torchlight lit the curving walls. Flanked by a detachment of flet soldiers, three hooded figures burst into the room. The lead figure called out in a feminine voice, "Lords of Berinfell, we seek audience and are in most dire need!"

"The Lords of Berinfell answer your call!" Tommy called down to her. "Advance to us and make no sudden move. Speak plainly: who are you and what is your need?"

The three hooded figures approached. They bowed in the general direction of the Lords and then lowered their hoods.

"I am Taeva, Princess of the Taladrim," said the leader, an exotic looking young woman with blazing eyes. "My homeland, Taladair, is in ruins!"

"Ruins?" Grimwarden echoed. "But your people are steadfast...

fierce in battle. What befell you?"

Taeva nodded. "I thank you for your words, graybeard," she said. "The Taladrim are tested and proud, but we were overmatched... slaughtered. An army of untold power converged upon Taladair. They had weapons...*shia gin su fallac!* Weapons of fire and cunning the likes of which we have not seen before."

"An army?" Tommy said. "Whose army?"

Taeva glanced over her shoulder at her two attendants. They nodded in return. "It was the Spider King's army," Taeva said. "And they burst forth...right out of the sky."

The Coming Storm

"YOU MUST be mistaken," Goldarrow said. "The Spider King is long dead."

Grimwarden was quick to step between Goldarrow and the furious Taladrim visitor. "With all due respect, Princess," he said, "this conversation is not meant for all ears."

Grimwarden signaled for two flet soldiers at a nearby gate. He whispered something to them and then announced to the crowd that had gathered for the party, "Carry on, one and all! The Lords must depart for a...diplomatic matter. They will return before the night's end. So carry on. Make merry! Enjoy the hospitality of Berinfell!"

The orchestra began again, minus Kiri Lee, and the Elves did indeed return to making merry. Then, Grimwarden discreetly led the Lords and their new guests out of the chamber. They traveled a seldom used corridor, and the former Guardmaster moved with such speed and surety that no one would have guessed he'd been away from Berinfell city for several years. After numerous twists and sudden turns, Grimwarden paused at a narrow cleft in the right hand wall. He turned and his eyes were huge and glassy in the torchlight. "This is Treblewood," he said. "It is a chamber of council and will offer us every necessity the Hall of Lords might…with one distinct advantage. In this secret place, we will not be disturbed."

A fire blazed in the hearth, wood popping and spitting as the smoky scent of cherry oak filled the stone chamber. A few candles scattered throughout the space helped cast off the thick darkness that seeped in from the corners and crevices of stone, but it was the fire's radiant glow that kept the chill of the rain at bay. Flame-orange hues splashed the underside of the stone mantle and illuminated the faces of the Six, all seated in low, leather chairs. Grimwarden and Goldarrow stood on either side of the fireplace. Mr. Charlie and Regis, both Dreadnaught warriors, stood guard by the only exit on the far wall. Fletmarshall Finney, hand on the hilt of her rychesword, paced the back of the room.

The firelight warmed the chamber, but it also made the visitors from Taladrim more mysterious…alluring even. Especially Taeva, Princess of the Taladrim.

The hooded cloak she wore was knit together of shady greens, grays, blues, and browns. It would camouflage her against almost any setting but was of a design that would also render it attractive in any but the most formal environments. The hood hid her hair from view, but a few very dark strands spilled down her forehead and crisscrossed above her arched brow. Her flesh was a peculiar gray color. Not the bleak gray of winter clouds, but more like gray marble, rich with tones of purple, pink, and even blue.

Tommy watched intently as Taeva pulled her feet up into her chair and sat back. Her dark, emerald-green eyes flickered like a stormy sky above the rim of the steaming mug she cupped between her hands. Tommy looked away.

Johnny watched Taeva as she inhaled deeply of the dark, amber cider. She sipped slowly, lowered the mug to the table, and dragged the long nail of her thumb across her lips to wipe a dribble of cider. Though her face was taut with fury, a hint of a smile—one part relief, two parts satisfaction—appeared at the corner of her mouth.

Jimmy watched the Princess arch her back. She pushed off her hood and freed her hair. Long, gently spiraling locks poured down over her broad cheekbones and ended near her pointed chin. But locks of this length were layered in with much longer ribbons of hair. These fell all around her unusual ears. They were somewhat pointed like the Elves' ears, but shorter and swept back, the shape more like a raptor's wings. She wore three plain gold rings, spread equally from lobe to tip in each ear. Taeva reached up suddenly and pulled her hair up into a loose braid. Jimmy looked away.

An attendant finished filling their mugs of spiced cider, indicated the large cauldron and ladle hanging from an iron arm beside the hearth, and then bowed, leaving the group alone in the small chamber.

"This is savory and heartening," Taeva said, taking another sip. "Apples, you say?"

"The best of Berinfell's orchards," Tommy confirmed. "I can show you how to make it later...if you, I mean, depending on...well, after."

The girls looked over at Tommy and then to Taeva. Kat resisted the urge to roll her eyes. She looked at Taeva and groaned inwardly. Exotic, fierce...gorgeous. And that hair? It was the color of dark chocolate and deep raspberry, and fell in luxurious waves. Kat had experimented with every colored dye known in Allyra but had never been able to manage that lustrous hue.

"Tommy could definitely assist us," Johnny piped up. "But I probably have a little more experience with making cider than him. Apple-farming." He sat up a little straighter. "Family heritage, you know."

"I see," said Taeva, placing her lips on the rim of the mug and taking a long sip. Even as she did so, her chin trembled slightly, and a single tear slid down her cheek. Tommy, Johnny and Jimmy were transfixed.

Grimwarden cleared his throat. "I am sure distractions are welcome, Princess," he said, casting a momentary glare at each of the Lords. "But I am certain that you did not travel these many leagues to discuss cider recipes."

"No," Taeva said. "No, I did not." And, as if someone suddenly flipped a switch, Taeva choked on her cider and lurched forward, hand to her mouth. She regained her composure for the most part, but her next words were spoken as if half-caught in her throat.

"Slowly," Goldarrow said. "Let the words come."

"It was horrible...and maddening," Taeva said, smoothing out the gravel in her deep voice. "For ages, Taladrim thrives, powerful, protected and—we deemed—impregnable. The city gone...so many dead. And there was nothing I could do." She coughed.

"Easy," Tommy said. He leaned forward in his chair so that his hands were inches from Taeva's. "Whatever we can do to help your people...we'll do it."

"But he'll be coming here, too," said the Princess. "No one is safe. No one."

Jimmy leaned forward, trying to catch her eye. "Princess Taeva, yur safe here. With oos." He extended his hand.

"Thank you for your reassurance," she said, gently patting Jimmy's hand, the last pat more of a push away. "But I really don't think you know who you're dealing with."

"Well who is it then?" Kat interjected. Tommy shot her an exasperated look, but Kat ignored it. "Taeva? We conquered the Spider King, so we can't help but be somewhat skeptical."

The Princess wiped away tears with the back of her sleeve. "You faced the Spider King, you say?" She sniffed. "Then you know the root of this enemy's power."

"The root?" Kiri Lee spoke up. "Whatever do you mean?"

"The Spider King, the ruler you defeated, performed one last freakish act in the mire below Vesper Crag. The myth is that the Spider King bit a Drefid in the leg, transferring all of his power to that host."

"A Drefid?" Autumn winced.

"His name is Asp, a former general, powerful in the Dark Arts… cunning and utterly ruthless. If the Spider King was a foul demon, Asp is his Overlord."

Tommy leaned forward, his eyes narrowing. "How would you… how could you know this?" he asked.

Taeva's head turned so fast that her earrings jingled. "What? Do you think it impossible that the Taladrim would know something that the Elves do not?"

Tommy blinked. "No, that's not what I meant," he said. "Honestly, I don't know enough about your people or your military to assess your scouting ability. But even if the Spider King did manage to stave off death in the wreckage of Vesper Crag long enough to bite some wandering Drefid, how could anyone have been there to see it?"

Taeva voice fell to a menacing whisper. "Asp was there to see it. That Drefid miscreant explained in great detail as he threatened my family. And if you had seen Asp, as I have, then you would not doubt his word."

Tommy's mouth snapped shut audibly. Jimmy slid slowly back into his chair. The fire hissed before them, flickering light dancing on the features of their sullen faces.

"Perhaps, you should start over, Princess," Grimwarden said. "Tell your story…" He sent withering glares at Tommy and Kat. "And we will not interrupt again."

The Princess of the Taladrim began, her voice taking on the ethereal quality of the old ones, elves too advanced in years to contribute with labor, so they told stories. Only, unlike the babes that sat around the elder's feet consumed with childish wonder, the Lords listened to Taeva's foreboding words as one might await the news of a close friend who had suddenly passed away.

They stared into the hearth, watching the flames devour the logs, the white-hot, throbbing pulse of wood turning to embers. It spread up each log like a disease, chewing into the core and splitting the wood in a slow ache, until there was nothing left but ash—a scene not far off from how they imaged the land of Taladrim looked by the time Taeva's haunting tale was through.

Far north of Berinfell, just off the coast of Allyra's Northern Shores and the famed Coral Bridge, lay the remote realm of the Taladrim, a geographical oddity as beautiful as it was dangerous. The massive island of Taladair was a perplexing feat of creation. Made of solid black granite, it appeared from the air as a great overturned shield forged of stone and resting low in the sea.

No history records when or how the Taladrim came to dwell there, but they inhabited a near unassailable fortress ready-made for generations of defense. From above, the surrounding seas might seem a threat to cascade over the rim of the shield, swallowing the inner island completely. But no tempest-driven sea could ever dream of scaling those hundred-foot rims. Instead, the surrounding waters remained tame, becoming little more than a vast moat, and yet another layer of protection.

Over the centuries, the Taladrim had delved a massive sea gate from the granite. It was the only point of egress at the waterline, and the entrance to Gahl Harbor and Taladair's fleet of long-hulled ships.

Jaco-Mirthel, Captain of the East Wall Sentry, stood watch at his high post and was the first to notice the peculiar storm building. He'd been on guard since just before midnight, and now that the sun was rising, he was eager for the comfort of his bed. Yet the sky seemed to take a long time in warming. Too long.

"See that there?" he nudged his counterpart, a young cadet named Lynthnel, who'd lost his battle to sleep an hour ago.

"What? Who?" Lynthnel sputtered to life.

"The horizon, there." From their lookout, Jaco pointed to the edge of the world where water met the heavens. Only the heavens were a tumult of flashing light harbored in billowing clouds, thick enough to blot out the sun.

"What is it?" Lynthnel rubbed his eyes, thinking he might still be asleep.

"A storm out of season," Jaco replied, now squinting. "And unlike any I have seen before."

A flash. In a flickering moment, long spindly fingers of lightning shot down to the ocean and danced along the surface like an electric hand. It almost seemed to seek purchase, to grasp and pull itself forward before disappearing back into the roiling clouds.

"It's moving," Jaco noted. "Toward us." He fidgeted with his trident, fingering one of the points.

"Should we call it in?" Lynthnel asked, unable to take his eyes off the apparition.

The clouds took up more and more of the sky, rolling westward. They cast a dark purple hue to the water below, lighting up a sickly yellow wherever the bolts of lightning flashed.

"Jaco?"

"What?"

"Sorry, sir. Shall I call it in?"

"Aye, call it in," Jaco said. He knew the entire signaling manual by heart. "Attention, warning, eastern front, prepare for storm."

Lynthnel strode to the far side of their lookout and pulled the signal horn from its cradle in the roof. He removed the leather sleeve from over the conch's mouth piece and placed the shell to his lips.

The first long blast cut into the morning air like a blade. The note sailed from the rim, down over the most steeply situated houses just beneath the lookout, and then out across the flattening bowl until it reached the spire-mount in the very middle.

The palace mirrored the odd tension between the elegance of the sea and the harshness of the black granite. Long, smooth lines of stone swept skyward to form the towers and outer walls, only to be adorned with hard, angular summits that comprised the turrets, peaks, and dwellings of the royal family. At its highest point, the palace was far above sea level without, and below the rim within.

The second cry from the horn—the double blast for warning— sent the gulls rising from their roosts, beating the air in an effort to rise above the city. The Taladrim stirred, and Jaco knew the King and Queen would be awake any second. If not already. As Lynthnel gave the third verse of the signal, Jaco looked back to the east. The storm had halved the distance from the horizon now.

"What in heaven's name can move that fast?" Jaco muttered to himself.

Having dispensed the warning's fourth verse, Lynthnel replaced the horn and turned back to see the storm. "So fast..." he said in wonder. "It will be upon us in—"

"Retrieve the horn once more," Jaco ordered, not turning from the sky.

"Sir?"

"I'm changing the order," Jaco insisted. "Retrieve the horn."

"I don't understand. It's a fierce storm to be sure, a fast-moving weather front—"

'Stand aside!" Jaco pushed his way past Lynthnel and reached up for the horn.

"But, sir," Lynthnel made to question again, but then he saw it, too. There, in the middle of the storm. "What—what is that?"

Jaco took a deep breath and blew with all his might.

"Your lordship," came a muffled voice behind the door.

The King sat upright in bed, checking to make sure his wife was covered. "Enter."

A face poked in, eyes averted. It was his chamberlain as expected. "A signal from the wall, your lordship."

"I hear it," said the King. "What does it say?"

"The guards are closing the Sea Gate. A storm comes from the east."

"The east?"

"Aye, and quite bad at that."

"It has been many a fortnight since I've seen one from the east," the King replied, rubbing one eye. He climbed from bed and made for the windows. The chamberlain beat him there, undid the latch, and opened the floor-to-ceiling glass-latticework panes. The gulls were flying to the west and the heavy winds brought the salt scent into the city afresh. The King examined the sky.

"Your orders, sire?" asked the chamberlain.

But the King did not respond at first. Merely puzzled. He sniffed the air again.

"Sire?"

Suddenly a fifth trilled horn blast came from the rim. The King did not need his chamberlain to interpret for him this time. "That is the call for Defenses."

"What would you have me do, your lordship?"

"Ready the men to their stations. Take my wife and Taeva to the loft. We're under attack."

"Attack, sire? From what?"

"I don't know," the King replied. "But I trust my guards. That call is serious. An enemy lurks to our east…somehow cloaked by the storm front. There is something else. I smell it upon the wind. A reek of decay as if death comes in the clouds. Go now!"

While children helped their mothers batten down every window and door that swung free, all the Taladrim men of fighting age poured through the garrison and donned the armor of their people: lightweight green plates of woven sea fibers able to stop a spearhead from penetrating the skin. Their streamlined helmets, fashioned from the same material, covered everything but the eyes, nose, and mouth, and permitted them to swim without becoming water logged. Archers were provided their bows and three quivers of arrows, while the spearmen were handed the symbol of Taladrim—the golden trident.

The armed warriors of the city spread out to their stations, some bounding up to the ramparts along the rim, others filling the alcoves along the waterline where the ships were nestled in to harbor. Platoons readied massive harpoons mounted along the rim, while others manned large winches that strained against tawny ropes. The soldiers ground away as enormous green-plated panels of calcified sea coral ascended from inside the rim. The panels rose as one around the entire circumference of the city, gently arching inward as they climbed skyward. Eventually they met in the middle, forming a dome whose apex closed shut hundreds of feet above the spire-mount.

Taeva bit her nails as the final rays of sun were shut out far above her.

"There, my beauty," said her mother, stroking Taeva's hair from within the confines of the loft, a fortified sanctuary near the summit of the spire-mount. "Do as I say. Our safety is the utmost concern here."

"Mother, the city?" Taeva complained, leaning toward the exit.

"The city has survived every storm and every attack for hundreds and hundreds of years," she said. "We must keep you safe."

"I sicken of safety."

"Nonsense, Taeva. Enough." She snapped her fingers.

Three attendants appeared in the shadows behind their royalty, sworn to meet every need unto death. Since all of the Taladrim's would-be assailants arrived by sea, and the greatest natural threat was a flooding, keeping the Queen and the Princess as high as possible was paramount. "All will be well. It will pass soon. We're untouchable."

Taeva did not respond. As much as she wanted her mother's hand to work its magic on her soul, just as it'd done on countless sleepless nights in her past, all she felt were cold fingertips caressing strands of hair behind her ear.

"Honestly, mother," Taeva said. "I am far too old to have my hair stroked like this."

"You are never too old," the Queen replied.

Taeva sighed. But it was more than the hair. Doubt lay heavily upon her. No matter how soothing the words, Taeva simply did not believe her mother this time. Something was very wrong about this particular morning. Her mother's pride was clouding her judgement. Perhaps for the last time.

The two of them sat on a deeply cushioned bench and stared out through a large picture window. The darkness within the city was combatted by fire light. Torches and braziers sputtered to life throughout the cavernous space until the whole thing looked like a massive candlelit funeral procession.

"Perhaps it's prophetic," Taeva whispered to herself.

"What's that, my love?" the Queen asked.

"Nothing, mother. Just mumbling."

And then the winds came. They howled, beating against the bowl, and sent shuddering spasms up through the domed plates. The spire-mount groaned. Taeva and her mother grasped the sides of the furniture as their turret swayed.

"Great Ellos!" the Queen exclaimed as a crack of thunder reverberated through the city. The attendants fell to the floor behind them, one of them crying out as her head hit the granite floor.

Taeva spun around. "Are you all right?"

"It's Louwin," said one of the elder ladies. "She'll be fine."

Then all at once the wind ceased.

The Queen sat clutching Taeva, perhaps more for her own good than Taeva's. The attendants sprawled on the floor, Louwin whimpering. Nothing else stirred.

"A wind tempest?" Taeva asked her mother.

"Must be. We're in the eye now. Although…" The Queen stared out the picture window.

"What is it mother?" asked Taeva.

"I don't ever remember an eye being so still. Listen." She paused, exiting the room through a heavy door set beside the picture window. "Not even the sound of distant wind." She and Taeva stood on the balcony.

Suddenly a small shaft of morning light burst through a small opening near the top of the dome directly above them. Taeva and her mother shielded their eyes. "Can you see what it is?" Taeva asked her mother.

"No," replied the Queen, squinting painfully.

Something whirred up high, like leather speeding cross rope.

"I see something," the Queen said. "Someone."

"They're sliding down a line," added Taeva. "And they're descending onto the palace!"

"Quick, back inside," the Queen ushered her daughter through the door, slamming, then locking it shut.

"An attack?" Taeva dared suggest. The attendants gasped.

"The intruder is but one," the Queen pointed out. "Possibly of our own, caught outside of the enclosure during the storm." The attendants came closer, now all five women watching the single dark figure descend behind the palace walls. But the Queen noticed something peculiar about the stranger. She put a hand to her stomach.

"He's in the courtyard," Taeva said. "We've got to see who it is."

"Taeva, wait!" But before her mother could stop her, Taeva was out the chamber door and bounding down the spiral stairs through the palace. "Taeva!" her mother yelled again, taking to the same stairs with the three attendants in tow.

But the Princess did not pause or answer. She fled as fast as her legs would carry her.

The Siege of Taladair

WHEN TAEVA burst out the doors of the palace entrance, she was surprised to see so many centurions gathered in the courtyard. Each was poised in atack form. They brandished their tridents, surrounding a lone figure who stood in the middle of the chamber.

"Father!" she cried out, seeing the King on the edge of the group.

King Silnoc turned at her voice. So did the stranger. Heedless of the hedge of weapons and the guards' efforts to hold her back, Taeva pushed her way through to her father.

"Taeva, stand down," he ordered her, his eyes weary, bloodshot, and sad. "You should not have come. It is not safe—"

"Safe? But it is merely—" The Princess cut off her own words. She looked first at her feet, at the dark blood spreading in a pool. The blood of her people, soldiers, the elite Chamber Guard even. So many of them lay, dead.

Then she looked up at the stranger. He seemed frozen in motion and somehow larger than life, like a bronze statue. But there was nothing heroic about this being. He was garbed all in black, and a dark, oil skinned coat hung on his skeletal form like a loose grave cloth eaten through by moths. It draped over his left arm that he held forward like a barricade, and fell from his aloft right arm like a serpent's wing. Long, razor sharp blades of bone extended from his fists.

A Drefid, Taeva realized. *But different. Worse.*

He wore some kind of peculiar jutting armor. There were spikes and bulges, clefts and ridges—especially at his shoulders and back. And he wore a dark, conical helm with a curving horn protruding at each jawline like pincers. A narrow gap began at his chin, thinned to a black line at his nose, and then spread into scowling mask eyelets. Orbs of cold, white fire burned within and glared out, daring anyone to move against him.

The ominous stranger retracted one set of claws, pointed a boney finger directly at Taeva, and said, "And her."

"No!" the King protested. He took a step forward and drew his sword.

"Ah, ah, ah," the intruder waved that same finger. "Remember what I said, Silnoc. Consider it a favor knowing your precious daughter will live long after you."

"Father?" Taeva said in surprise. "What...what is this thing saying?" She couldn't bring herself to say *man*. But her father could not take his eyes off the stranger.

"Dear Princess," said the intruder, his voice deep, rough hewn, and yet still resonant. "I have come seeking the help of your father's kingdom."

"Not another word, Asp," commanded the King. "Your business is with Taladair, and I am its ruler."

"Help for what?" Taeva asked.

"Taeva!" her father turned back toward her. "You speak out of turn. Go, find your mother!"

"She will remain," the being called Asp replied coldly. "She asks an appropriate question. Why have we come? The answer is simple: *survival.* I seek Taladair's aid in defending my people."

"Father?"

"Committing mass murder is more like it," the Silnoc corrected.

"War," Asp said, clearly directing his words to Taeva. "Your nation is no stranger to war, to taking the initiative rather than waiting for an antagonistic foe to force the fight. And yet your father continues to refuse me."

"You ride the dark wings of a storm," said the King. "You murder my guards. Of course, I refuse you. Be gone from here, accursed." Silnoc leveled his sword at Asp's chest.

If Asp noticed the blade, he did not show it. "We are wasting precious time," he said.

"And what's this about me?" Taeva asked.

"A small matter," Asp said.

"I am never a small matter," she quipped, lifting her hands. Her fingers began move, as if she played an invisible harp.

Asp's pale eyes blinked once.

"Daughter, you have no place here," said her father. "This is not some noble request for aid. Asp demands our assistance and threatens all of Taladair."

"A threat?" Taeva echoed, her fingers increasing their speed.

"I cannot afford mistakes at this critical point," Asp said, restraining his tone. "If Taladair will not side with me, then I must conclude that it stands against me. Add your blades to mine, or I will destroy this realm. And...take you." His eyes seared into hers until she looked away.

After a moment, Taeva realized she wasn't breathing. Her fingers stopped moving, but not of her own will. She looked down at her feet. Her legs seemed disconnected from her body.

"Father, I—"

"Not a word," he replied. He spun back to Asp and said, "Taladair is its own. We are sovereign. We will never align ourselves with your bloodlust."

But the statement was barely off his tongue when Taeva asked,

"Would you vow to leave my people in peace if I come with you?"

"TAEVA!" her father practically gagged. "That is enough! This fool has the audacity to rappel into our sanctuary, demand our allegiance, and make outlandish claims that he can destroy our city with the swipe of his hand. Do not entertain him with vain pleas."

Asp spoke softly, saying, "I accept your offer."

"There is no offer!" the King blurted out. He thrust his sword forward, but Asp's blades extended in a blink. He caught the King's sword between two of his bony extensions, and in the flick of the wrist, he snapped off a foot of the King's sword.

"Begging your pardon, your lordship, but I was speaking to your daughter." Asp's head moved ever so slightly in her direction. "If you come with me, I would consider sparing your people."

"This is absurd!" the King took another step forward, but stopped, glancing down at his neutered sword.

Suddenly Asp's eyes flared. "As we have spoken," he growled, his words laced with fire, "a legion of my warriors placed arc stone charges along the base of your precious walled city."

"Arc stones?" the King said. "These walls have endured arc stones before and with ease."

"Not like these," Asp said. His smile was half hidden by the helm, but ghoulish nonetheless. "I have journeyed far...far beyond horizons that you could imagine. And I have learned how to intensify the impact of a simple arc stone one-thousand fold. Your walls will crumble."

"A thousand fold?" the King echoed. "That's impossible."

"Impossible for small minds like yours to imagine, King Silnoc," Asp said, spittle flying from his mouth. "But seeing is believing, is it not? My soldiers are watching me from above. Should you and your guards somehow manage to fell me, they will set off the arc stone charges. If I return without your word, or your daughter, we will likewise set off the explosives. In either case, Taladair will come to an end."

The King blinked at Asp, but his free hand drifted to his leg and the lethal dart sling holstered there.

"Do not test me," Asp seethed. "Decide."

No one moved.

"Decide," said Asp.

Still the King could not speak.

Taeva trembled, hoping no one saw her. She stared at the frightening intruder. How could a bluffing stranger appear so confident? Unless…unless he could actually do as he claimed.

"DECIDE!"

Taeva stepped quickly in front of her father, blocking any clean shot. "I'll go with you," she said.

Before anyone could act, Asp grabbed her hand and pulled her to his chest.

"NO!" the King cried out, lifting his dart sling. His draw was fast. Against any other foe, he would have sent the dart shaft deep into his target's eye, extending well into the brain.

But Asp was unlike any Silnoc had faced before. Asp swung his razor claws and severed the King's hand at the wrist.

A beat later, a hundred tridents leveled against Asp, but he gave a single tug on the line running up from his harness. A second later and the pair shot skyward, flying up through the shaft of light like an arrow.

"AFTER THEM!" the King cried. "Archers! But don't hit the Princess!"

Centurions launched a salvo of precisely aimed darts. But they bounced harmlessly away from Asp's cloak or missed entirely.

In the blink of an eye, the King of Taladair had lost everything.

"LET ME GO!" Taeva demanded as she thrashed. "I never even

said goodbye to my mother!"

"Not the most appropriate command, Princess," Asp said, nodding downward.

Taeva gasped at the sudden height, and yet still struggled. But Asp's grip was like slow-forged iron. Taeva realized coldly that escape— even to death—was impossible.

The wind sailed through her hair until they neared the dome's ceiling. Their ascent stopped short of the hole that had been ripped through the top of the dome. A beefy hand reached down. Asp took it and he and Taeva were pulled topside, standing suddenly in the open air beneath a turbulent sky.

"Take her," Asp said, shoving Taeva to a Gwar warrior clothed in battle gear. His one hand nearly covered her torso. There was only one other Drefid on the dome, presumably Asp's right hand. Where was his army? Where were his explosives?

"So this is it then?" Taeva asked Asp as he turned away.

"What's it?" he sneered over his shoulder.

"You were bluffing."

Asp released a crackling, humorless laugh. "My dear Princess," he said, staring her down with his fiery eyes, "know that my threats are never idle. Pity that history will not remember the once-proud Taladrim in this, the greatest conquest of all. But others will take their place. Others less proud, perhaps."

Taeva's heart flash-froze in her chest. "You mean you—"

Asp turned to the other Drefid. "Open the portal. Once we're through, bring it down." He looked back at Taeva. "Bring it all down."

"NOOOO!!!" Taeva screamed, trying in vain to tear herself from the Gwar's grasp.

Asp's Drefid assistant produced a small chest. He flipped open the lid and pinched a few grains of a powder. These he sprinkled into the air. Sparks kindled immediately. The Drefid spoke words in a language

Taeva had never heard. A circle of mist appeared, and a small cloud formation grew with astonishing speed. An aura of blue electricity flashed from within the growing circle of darkness, then stretched into a thin sheet of blue as the cloud formation grew in diameter.

"You should be grateful, Princess," Asp said, without meeting her gaze. "I spared your life. And this is but my latest gift to you."

"I want nothing from you apart from my people's safety!"

"Disappointing," Asp said. "Are you certain, Princess? Is there not something you would do with ultimate power?"

Taeva blinked back at the madman, her thoughts spinning into a long-hidden corner of her mind. She hesitated just a moment. A black instant.

"There is something…isn't there?" Asp asked.

Taeva shook her head violently. "NO!" she screamed, her venom surprising all around. "Nothing from you! Keep whatever power you think you have!"

"You betray your heritage," Asp said. "Your miscreant mother's hopes will die with you." He looked up at the Gwar guard. "Send her back."

Stunned, Taeva cried out, "What?"

The Gwar carried her toward the hole in the dome.

"Wait," Taeva said. She knew the rope was gone. Only a bone-shattering fall remained. "You can't do this!"

"Your sense of authority is misguided," Asp replied. "Titles mean nothing in this world. There is only power and blood. You have chosen neither."

Asp looked to the other Drefid and nodded. The growing, miniature storm drew closer, as if he was pulling it in on a tether. The high winds felt as though they'd pull everyone off the dome. Thunder shook the air.

Taeva was three steps from being cast away. The sizzling blue screen of light hovered just a few feet overhead.

The Gwar stood ready to throw her in, then escape through what Taeva could only guess was a portal. But she was not going to die this way, thrown like a fish carcass into the middle of her own courtyard. No, she would at least put up a fight. And having been trained by the Taladrim Master of Arms himself, she could more than hold her own.

But this Gwar was her largest opponent yet. She could not best him with brute strength. She had only agility, surprise, and…a dagger.

In the split second it took for the Gwar to peel her away from his body and force her forward, she felt his grip loosen. Not enough to get free, but enough to shift her body. Which she did, twisting herself to the inside and faced him.

She slid the dagger from her boot and dragged the blade up the Gwar's torso. The Gwar yelped and yowled, but Taeva wasn't finished.

With blazing speed, she ran her feet up his legs, chest, and locked her knees behind his head. She went limp, her deadweight pulling the Gwar forward.

The warrior groaned, trying to jerk backward. But Taeva's surprise had forced him to take a step. Then another. And before either of them realized what was happening, the Gwar's third step was into the Taladrim world under the dome.

Swallowed by blackness speckled with torch fires that looked like thousands of stars, the pair tumbled through space, hurtling toward the courtyard floor. Now free of the Gwar's oppressive grip, Taeva hammer-punched her foe in the soft part of the neck under the chin. With a two-fisted plunge, she slammed the dagger into the Gwar's chest. The warrior flailed for the weapon, but Taeva held it firm.

Seconds from impact. And no ideas came to mind. At least she wouldn't be a slave to Asp. The Gwar batted at her, trying wildly to tear her form his head. Taeva suffered a deafening blow to the right ear, but managed to stay clear of the menace's clutches. Until she realized that was the opposite of what she needed to do.

Taeva quickly withdrew the dagger and tossed it away. Then she took the Gwar's burly, armored chest face-on in a great bear hug. The warrior must have been surprised by the sudden posture change; he threw his arms around her and squeezed her against his torso as if he might break her back.

And that was the last thought the Gwar ever had. His massive back took the full force of the landing. Bones crushed, and a last violent blast of air shot from the Gwar's mouth. The impact left a crater in the granite and shot bits of rock into the surrounding gathering of guards.

Taeva opened her eyes. The warrior's arms lay across her, but tight only from their own weight. She could see dust in the air, and guards with torches walking toward her. They were saying something but her ears were ringing. She blinked. Their mouths were moving. Hands reaching. Then finally the ringing stopped in her left ear.

"Princess!" she heard them yell. She reached a hand out toward them. Someone peeled back the Gwar's arms. "SLOWLY! SLOWLY!"

Taeva blinked again. Hands slid underneath her. That's when she felt the searing pain in her ribs. She thought she screamed, but she didn't hear it. Only more yelling from the men.

"CAREFUL! EASY!"

The next face she saw hovering over her was the King's. Her father's. She felt his finger tips move some hair out of her face. Her head throbbed. And the pain in her ribcage mounted.

"INSIDE!" his face contorted as he yelled at his men. "NOW!"

"There - there, Princess," Louwin said, easing a glass of water to Taeva's lips. "Drink easy."

Taeva tried to sit up, but the burning around her upper chest became too unbearable. She winced, spat the water out, and eased back down onto her bed. She didn't remember being carried to her room. Just falling. Falling. Descending into blackness with a sea of fire to swallow her below. "What...what is—"

"The doctors say you've broken ribs," Louwin interjected. "You have massive bruising and need to stay put. But they don't believe you've ruptured any vital parts. It's a miracle really." Louwin offered her a drink once more, but this time she kept a hand pressed against Taeva's shoulder to keep her from sitting up. Louwin was young, but a studious learner, and took easily to her job as royal attendant.

"Where is Father?"

"I believe he sent the men to inspect the dome, as well as the exterior of the city."

Taeva coughed, throwing herself into a convulsion.

"Princess?!" The glass of water fell to the floor as Louwin tried to steady Taeva. But still the Princess hacked, crying through the staggering pain, trying to catch her breath.

"EXPLOSIONS!" Taeva finally got out between coughs. The strong taste of iron filled her mouth.

"Princess, you're bleeding!" Louwin withdrew a white handkerchief and cupped the Princess' chin. But Taeva batted it away. She swung her legs over the edge of the bed. "No, Princess! You mustn't move!"

"THE CITY! THEY'RE GOING TO COLLAPSE THE—"

The world seemed to rock sideways. Taeva and Louwin were both flung to the ground. Taeva cried out in agony, her ribs smacking into the granite floor of her bedroom, while Louwin screamed in terror. But the tumult was so loud neither girl heard the other, only the thunderous cacophony of explosion after explosion shaking the foundation of their city. Every glass window in her room shattered, furniture toppled, and belongings dashed to the floor.

Taeva was sure the tower would come crashing down with them inside. If she was going to face death twice in one day, she at least wanted to see what assailed her. She rolled over onto her stomach in anguish, then used her elbows to crawl through the glass shards to the picture window. She propped herself up on the ledge, now slippery with her blood, and caught her breath.

The walls that had shielded Taladair against rogue waves, storm surges and violent tempests...were disintegrating. Cracks like streaks of lightning, illuminated by daylight from without, splintered across the surface. And wherever the cracks intersected, huge sections of the wall began to fold in on themselves, plummeting downward.

Taeva watched on in horror, deaf and mute from the destruction unfolding before her.

Worse still was watching thousands of torch lights snuffed out, starting with those on the outside of the city's circle. The lights were swallowed by a black carpet that spread quickly over the entire city. Every home, every fortification, every storefront.

The unthinkable had happened. The very thing that kept their city safe below sea level had become their worst nightmare.

Taladair was flooding.

Without the walls, the city would be swallowed whole. And there was nothing the Princess could do but look down in horror.

That's when the sound of the wall shattering and the waves rushing in were met with something else, something even more terrifying.

A deep and arduous groan rumbled clear above her head. Taeva looked up to see the plates of the dome sliding against each other. They screeched and shuddered like metal armor binding around a soldier's body in battle.

And then it all came down.

Taeva covered her ears, mouth agape and eyes weeping, as the walls and ceiling of her beloved city came crashing down onto her people. She screamed, but the deadly din around her was too suffocating for her to hear.

The sudden appearance of daylight blinded her. She tried to maintain her witness to the atrocities unfolding before her, but the light was too great. Taeva buried her eyes in the corner of her arms, blood dripping down her torso. The violent sounds reverberated throughout her room, and she waited for her tower to be struck down. It swayed precariously, battered by the ocean waters now teaming at its base. Surely the dome would pummel it into the rubble and burry her and Louwin in the watery grave of her people.

Taeva was thrown back from the window and landed on her back. She felt more glass bite into her flesh and winced.

The groaning again. This time, punctuated by sharp cracks. Her room seemed to spin. Bits of rock showered her body. Larger, crushing chunks crashed beside her.

More explosions echoed outside of her room. The smashing of stone, the grinding of metal, the roar of the ocean. And somewhere in it all she swore she heard the cries of people. Of children. Of mothers screaming after their babes. Of husbands calling after their wives. Or was she just imagining it?

It wasn't until she heard Louwin whimpering somewhere behind her that Taeva realized the sounds were subsiding.

"Louwin? Are you still here?" Taeva asked. "Are—we still here?" The Princess slowly pulled her arms away from her face, now bloodied and drenched with sweat and tears. Even with her eyes closed the light was overwhelming. She gave her eyes a minute to adjust. Louwin was still crying somewhere in the room.

Taeva blinked. The roof above her head was half there; beyond the scraggly remains floated the whimsical puffy white clouds she so loved, gently slipping underneath a deep blue sky.

"Louwin?" Taeva coughed out. She looked around what used

to be her room, now resembling a rock quarry more than it did a state room. Louwin was hiding under the Princess' writing desk against one of the only completely intact walls. She looked all right. Whether she'd *be* all right was another question. Taeva crawled to her and tried to get her attention. But Louwin was shaking, eyes wide open, muttering something to herself.

"Louwin?" Taeva asked.

"…Take care, take care, yes, yes…that's my assignment 'mum…no, I'll fetch more water…"

"Louwin, it's me, Taeva."

"…Yes, Taeva is in her room 'mum…"

"Louwin," Taeva said her name again, then grabbed the girl's wrist. The touch sent a shock wave through the girl and she started screaming.

"DON'T TOUCH ME! DON'T TOUCH ME!" She flailed Taeva's hand away and sunk deeper into the shadow of the writing desk.

"Louwin! You're alive! It's me, Taeva!" The Princess then reached up with whatever energy she could summon and grabbed Louwin's face with two hands, forcing the girl to look at her. Louwin's eyes went wild, darting around every which way.

"LOUWIN!" Taeva yelled, "LOOK AT ME!"

The girl shuddered.

"LOOK AT ME!"

Louwin winced at the sound of Taeva's voice.

"Look at me, Louwin. I'm right here."

Louwin blinked a few times, then focused on Taeva's face. A deep breath. Then full recognition. "Princess!" Louwin cried, then fell into Taeva's crippled form on the ground and sobbed into her shoulder.

Taeva tried to get into a sitting position but the pain was too great. She let Louwin have her way until she composed herself. "I need you to help me up," Taeva finally said. Her servant complied, and Taeva's body convulsed with the waves of pain.

Taeva's eyes rose over the jagged rock wall and gazed upon utter atrocity spreading beneath her. She cupped her mouth. Louwin sobbed, trying her best to steady Taeva.

Their tower stood in the churning waves of the ocean, a lone spire looming in the late morning sky. The walls were gone, collapsed to pieces along with the dome, now a swill of debris and flesh. And beneath it all lay their city, a watery grave for untold thousands of their people.

Huge air pockets underneath the city still bellowed, sending an unending stream of bubbles to the surface. Within another few hours the sea would swallow the remnants and nothing would remain, as if a few millennia-old civilization had never even existed.

Louwin half coughed, half spoke. "Look, my lady!" Clinging to a piece of wreckage almost directly beneath them were at least five souls, maybe two or three more hanging on along the sides.

"We've—we've got to help them," Taeva said, breathless. She forced herself to stand.

"No, Princess, you—"

"If I'm going to die of my injuries, my last bit of energy can certainly be used in salvaging those that remain of my—" she coughed, forcing her to her knees. She cupped a splatter of blood in her hand. "—my people."

Louwin made to protest but Taeva would have none of it. She regained her feet and made the arduous journey down the tower. Whole sections of the wall were missing, giving way to more views of desolation as they descended. More than once, Louwin helped Taeva leap over gaps in the staircase. Finally the pair came through the grand doors of the annex which was now mostly submerged in water. Across the room were the palace doors, and beyond that, the courtyard.

The courtyard. *Father.*

It was the first time Taeva had thought of her parents. Had they survived? It wasn't until she thought about swimming over to the palace doors that she noticed bodies floating in the room. First one. Then two.

Then too many to count.

Guards mostly. But then she saw her.

"Oh, Princess," Louwin said, both hands now covering her mouth and fresh tears streaming down her cheeks. "It isn't—no. It can't possibly—"

But the Queen's extravagant dress was unmistakable. Taeva's mother looked serene in her watery bed, eyes fixed on something in the distance, staring at the annex ceiling. Her face was calm. All terror gone. She seemed weighted to one side. That's when the Princess noticed her submerged hand clinging to something...

...another arm. Her father's, his body held down by his armor.

Taeva was too numb to feel. Couldn't feel. She just stared.

She probably could have stood frozen there on the balcony all day if it weren't for the screams. The voices on the wreckage just outside the building. Someone sounded hurt. They were calling for help. Clarity was starting to take shape in her mind. Action.

"Here," Taeva said to Louwin as she gave her hand. "Hold me while I reach for that board." It was the remnant of some furniture gifted to the High Court by the Elves of Berinfell somewhere in their nation's past. Now this gesture of goodwill would be used as a water craft to rescue her countrymen. *Ailianthum wood*, her father had always told her whenever they passed it...something about how it was most precious to the Elves. And that's when Taeva knew what she must do.

When whoever was left to be rescued was accounted for, she'd take them all south. The Elves would take them in. She was in charge now. Her parents gone, her kingdom destroyed. She had to get her people south. Or die trying.

And if she did survive? What did the Taladrim Code require?

Revenge.

Revisitation

KATE SIMONSON couldn't say that she'd found Jesus anymore than an orphan could claim to have found a family.

I'm like Forest Gump, she thought, remembering a scene from the famous movie. When Sergeant Dan had asked if Forest had found Jesus, he replied, "I didn't know I was supposed to be looking for Him." *I didn't know either. But something happened to me. Something supernatural.*

Was it a real connection? She couldn't be sure. But it felt somehow wholesome...nourishing even. And that was good enough.

So far, she hadn't had another incident like the police-car-pull-over episode three weeks ago. But since then, she'd started going to church again. She felt a connection there, a connection to God, sure. But also a kind of kinship to her husband...and even somehow...to her missing daughter. Something about the atmosphere at Hope Community Church. The freedom people had when they worshipped. The encouraging message the pastor gave.

She still didn't get it completely. Couldn't lift her hands. Couldn't sing. But it was having an effect on her. *He* was having an effect on her. She felt lighter when she walked back to her SUV. She felt lighter when she was around Allan.

Allan. How she loved him. He'd been so faithful, especially through the constant depression, the nightmares, the unexplained walk-outs during dinner. He just kept loving her. "I'm not going anywhere," he'd say when it got really bad; she thought he'd be crazy not to walk out the door. But he didn't.

"You can't change the choice I've made to love you, no matter what, Kate," he'd said. "I don't care how nuts this gets. I'm staying."

And that's when it clicked. His words. They sounded so much like *HIS* words. *I'll never leave you or forsake you.*

But it still didn't rest well with what she knew in her head. God had abandoned them, hadn't he? How could He let Kat get abducted like that? If God was so good, like the pastor always said, how could He let bad things happen to innocent people, like Kat?

While her head constantly tormented her—wrestling with scripture and making up arguments to throw at the pastoral staff—it was Allan who was living the faith right in front of her. She didn't get Jesus so much, but she could see Allan. Flesh and blood. Walking this out in front of her.

Kate found Allan chopping cilantro for enchiladas in the kitchen. "Thank you," she said.

"For what, babe?" He didn't even look up.

"For..." How was she supposed to say it? "For...you know."

He chuckled. "Uh, I do?"

Kate went back to stirring the beans for their side dish.

"Yes, you do."

Allan smiled. "You're welcome."

Kate sat on a bench overlooking the shore. A few people surfed. Fewer sunbathed. It was colder than usual, and she wished she'd brought a sweatshirt.

Wait. Why am I here? she wondered. She couldn't recall getting into the car. She didn't remember the drive. Come to think of it, she didn't remember planning a trip to the beach at all.

I'm waiting for someone. Allan maybe? No, not him.

A few gulls fought over a scrap of flotsam drifting in the waves. Most people thought the birds were so pretty...pure white harbingers of the ocean. Not Kate.

Obnoxious, she thought. *Rats with wings.*

"Thought you might be cold," came a familiar voice.

Kate turned.

Before her stood a young lady...late teens, perhaps, early twenties. Kate thought she looked older than she should be. More mature. Her hair was dark purple with hints of indigo wherever stray sun rays lingered. Her large, sepia brown eyes gleamed, sparkling with happiness. They were knowing eyes, full of wisdom and experiences beyond Kate's imagination.

She was still blue, of course, her skin smooth like porcelain but deep blue with a blush, here and there, of violet. Still beautiful.

"Here Mom, put it on," Kat said, handing her a gray UCLA sweatshirt. Her favorite. "You're going to catch a cold like you always do."

"Thanks, beautiful," Kate said, taking the sweatshirt. Kat sat down beside her and scooted up close. Kate could feel the warmth of her daughter's body.

How odd. Why are both of us being so nonchalant? Kate wanted to scream. To smother her daughter with hugs. To jump up and down and call Allan, call the family, the police, the media. Everyone! Her daughter was here, right here, in the flesh. But something kept her from crossing that line. Something elusive. Did Kat feel it too? Surely she was just as happy. Wasn't she?

"I miss surfing," said Kat.

"I miss watching you surf," said Kate. There was a long pause. Somehow Kate knew they were both thinking the same thing. And then they said the same thing at the same time.

"The beach house." They laughed a little. Smiling. Thinking.

"I miss it," said Kat.

Kate took a deep breath. "I do too. Haven't been back since..."

"Since I left."

"Yeah. Since you left. Wish I knew where you went."

Kat looked up. "But you do."

"I do?"

"The letter that Anna left for you and Dad."

Kate's emotions were stirring. "I don't remember..."

"Sure you do Mom."

"No...no..." All those irrational thoughts—the ones that got her in trouble...got her in a counselor's office—those thoughts came flooding back again. "It wasn't real."

"Yes, Mom, it was re—"

"Please stop, Kat," Kate said. "I can't...I can't handle..."

"You have to handle it, Mom."

"No Kat...I can't..."

Kat grabbed her mom by the shoulders. "Listen to me."

"There's something wrong with me. It's post traumatic stress, that's all."

"It's me, Mom. Not some disorder. It's Kat." She shook her head and smiled. "I'm far away now, but I'm safe. I have friends too, good friends. People I can count on. You and Dad would be happy. There was so much I would tell you, but it's difficult to concentrate hard enough for so long. I'm using my gifts, Mom, my Elven gifts. I can project this far for just a short—"

"No! This isn't possible."

"Yes, it is, Mom."

"I can't," Kate whispered, squeezing her eyes shut. "I can't."

"You have to, Mom. I can't keep this up much longer. Listen, Mom."

"No, Kat!"

"LISTEN TO ME."

"Kat, I can't!"

"WAKE UP!"

"I…I can't…"

"WAKE UP, KATE!"

"But I—"

"YOU'RE DREAMING."

"Dreaming? But Kat—"

"Babe, you're dreaming. It's me, Allan."

Kate opened her eyes. And all at once she was back at the beginning. Losing her grip on reality.

A Game of Words

"HAVEN'T WE heard enough?" Tommy asked.

No one replied immediately. The fire crackled and hissed. Taeva and her attendants formed a taut triangle of eye contact.

"The Spider King's lieutenant lives to carry on his master's ambitions," Tommy went on. "He has become some kind of ultra-Drefid thing, and he's already murdered thousands. Other lives still hang in the balance."

"What do you propose?" Goldarrow asked.

"We launch a full rescue mission," Tommy declared. "If there's a chance Asp and his armies are still in Taladair, we must empty Berinfell. Overwhelm our enemy, rescue our friends, and search. New portals could mean the way is open to Earth once more."

"Meet force with force," Taeva said. "You are most wise, my lord."

"Too wise for his own good," Grimwarden muttered. "You cannot leave Berinfell undermanned. With all due respect, your highness, we know nothing but what Princess Taeva has told us. Maybe Asp is wreaking havoc in Taladair, and maybe he wants Berinfell's armies out on a wild skeemu chase so that he can wreck our city."

"Grimwarden!" Tommy objected.

"We come to you for aid," Taeva said, "and you accuse us!"

"The Bloody Fall of 3927, Princess!" Grimwarden thundered. "Or do you not know? I would think Taladair's finest historical archives would be open to you. Even so, leave this hall. Go and dig in the courtyard to the south. It would not take you very long to find soil that has mixed with Elven blood, blood spilled by Taladrim weapons. Your people invaded our city once before. Why should we trust you now?"

"Outrageous!" Attendant Louwin exclaimed.

"I told you they would not listen," Attendant Celandria said. "The Elves have nev—"

Taeva held up a hand. "Wait, wait!" she said, tightly controlling her voice. "You have every right to question us, graybeard. You've spent the better part of seven years bringing Berinfell up from the ashes of the last invasion. And, of old, the Taladrim have seldom been anyone's ally. I assure you, if we could have driven off this foe, we would not be here. This Lord Asp, as he calls himself, is the Spider King reborn, that same who sought to exterminate Elves from Allyra. He is as much your enemy as he is ours. Send scouts. Do what you must, but please hurry. What remains of my country withers with each passing day."

"Is that what you think we should do, Guardmas—Grimwarden?" Tommy asked. "Do we send scouts to verify?"

"If you wish my counsel, Lord," Grimwarden replied, "you shall have it. But you, the six of you, must take whatever action you deem wise. By your leave, I would send scouts upon Scarlet Raptors to verify Taladair's fate and assess their need. But I would also summon the Conclave of Nations, and that immediately. If what the Princess tells us is confirmed by our scouts, and we have not convened the Conclave, I fear the delay would mean the blood of innocents on our hands."

Tommy blinked. He turned to the other Lords and received slow nods from them all. "Send the Scouts," he said. "And summon the Conclave. We will meet in three days time. Pray that our scouts return by then."

�֍

"You cannot attend," Goldarrow said, her hand pressed firmly into Grimwarden's chestplate. "You are retired, after all, remember?"

"Yes, yes, I know," Grimwarden replied, his scowl hardening. He leaned against a pillar in a hall outside Berinfell's military barracks. "But I should be there. Ambassadors, diplomats, politicians—for all their words, they say little of value. They seek favor and advantage for themselves but let their people founder. I would give them much to think on."

"Yes. Yes, you would," Goldarrow said. "And that is why they forced our hand...forced you from your rightful command as Guardmaster of Berinfell. Still, it was a blessing in disguise. You have made Berinfell stronger than ever before."

"Perhaps," Grimwarden replied. "But all this sneaking about... wears on a man. I am no criminal. I should have nothing to hide."

"*Should*...have nothing to hide," she said. "But if Berinfell and the Elven race is to be protected properly, then hide you must."

"It's no easy thing," Grimwarden muttered, "hiding thousands of warriors."

Goldarrow grabbed up her long, silken locks and tied it up in an elegant golden tail. She smiled warmly. "Nor was it easy hiding the remnants of Berinfell from the Spider King, and yet you managed it."

Grimwarden scratched at his beard. "Mmhm, how did you get so wise?"

"By keeping company with the wisest Elf I've ever known," she replied. "Now, get yourself away to the barracks. The flet soldiers stuck here could use the encouragement. Go on now, before some stodgy politician spies you and wonders what you're up to."

"Let them wonder," Grimwarden said wryly. "Maybe I'll give

them a wee something to satisfy their curiosity."

"*That*," Goldarrow said, "would *NOT* be wise."

"It's been too long, Migmar," Tommy said, stooping to shake hands with a diminutive Gnome fellow.

"In reckoning of my own, passed have four years," Migmar replied. His acorn-shaped green eyes twinkled beneath wickedly curled brows. Elf and Gnome, they stood in Conclave Chamber, a remarkable domed piece of architecture in the center of Berinfell City.

Migmar stroked his long sideburns and said, "Visit us you more often, Elf-boy."

"I'd like nothing more," Tommy said. "So long as you don't throw us in chains again."

"Trespass you not our land anymore," Migmar said. "Welcome you as friends now." With one hand, the Gnome scratched an unruly shock of hay-colored hair. With the other, he took a bite of a twisted piece of root.

Tommy frowned. "Migmar, that's not dragonroot—"

"Chew now, I do, only when nervous," Migmar replied. "Worry you not. Sitting Migmar with Strubthak, Thorkber and Sarabell over there."

Tommy shook his head. "I feel for them." The discussion volume in the room dropped suddenly. "Ah, looks like we're getting started."

Migmar bowed. Tommy returned the gesture. As they parted, Tommy thought he heard a strange sound, but he refused to investigate.

He continued to his seat and was somewhat relieved that Migmar sat on the opposite side of the massive meeting table. The other Gnomes, Strubthak, Thorkber and Sarabell, wore somewhat queasy expressions, complained audibly, and seemed to be trying to scoot their chairs away from Migmar.

"Order, sssth!" General Secretary Sardon commanded, the snake-like appendages flicking from his muscular jowls, one of many peculiarities that marked the Saer race. "Sss-come to order."

"Did yu hear, that?" Jimmy whispered to Tommy. "Sounded like he said 'Scum to order.'"

"Should I be offended?" Tommy whispered back.

"Present company excepted," Kat spoke into both their minds.

Goldarrow's green-eyed glare fell upon the Lords like fiery searchlights.

Still snickering, Tommy looked away. His eyes traveled clockwise past the other lords. The Conclave of Nations had met four times since its inception in 1413, and not always with all six Highborn races in attendance, as they were this day. But Tommy still found it hard to keep from staring. It was like being in the cantina scene of Star Wars. The beings of Allyra were that diverse.

Seated between two pairs of his red-clad Nemic Priests, Vault Minister Ghrell leaned to the side and thoughtfully rested his chin on the bony hinge of his folded wing. The Nemic were fliers, lean and strong, and absolutely cunning. In a game of chess against a Nemic child, Tommy found his game lost after one errant move, his third move overall. The Nemic were fiercely independent, however, and it was something of a miracle to have Ghrell agree to join the Conclave at all.

Migmar and the Gnomes sat beside the Gwar representatives, followed by the Saer Magistrate, Forlarn, and his kinsman at the podium, Sardon.

The General Secretary rapped all six bony knuckles of his gnarled hand across the edge of the podium. The staccato sound silenced the room. Many watchful eyes gleamed around the massive, black granite table.

"This emergency Conclave gathering isssth hereby commenced,"

Sardon announced. Two lips of his triangular mouth parted vertically like curtains, with a horizontal third lip undulating below. Most Saer speech, though clear, came with an odd drawl. And Sardon's inflection was more pronounced than most.

"Thisssth meeting," he said, "there had better be good reason, ah, for it." His enormous red eyes were deeply hooded by a thick overhang of brow that arched down sharply above his nose. Even so, his goat-like, rectangular pupils were quite visible and, for the moment, locked onto the Lords of Berinfell.

On Sardon's left, the Gwar Overlord Bengfist laughed, a slow grumbling sound like a roll of distant thunder. The slabs of muscle on his upper body—neck, shoulders, arms—shook like quaking boulders.

"Goldarrow, Guardmaster of Berinfell to be recognized," Goldarrow said as she stood.

Sardon waved a hand dismissively. "The Conclave recognizssth Goldarrow, of coursssth."

"Thank you, General Secretary," Goldarrow said. Her voice, at first polite, became stern. "I think you all know the Elves of Berinfell well enough to be certain we would not have called you here for any reason beyond beckoning tragedy. For those who have not had history with the Taladrim, allow me to introduce Princess Taeva, as well as the kingdom's two surviving royal Prefexes, Louwin Siir and Celandria Ryeot."

"Surviving?" Bengfist, the Gwar representative, blurted out. "An unfortunate word. What has befallen Taladair?"

Goldarrow nodded solemnly. "Princess Taeva will tell you of her plight."

"The Conclave recognizssth Taeva, Princesssth of the Taladrim." Sardon bowed his head once.

Taeva stood, took a deep breath, and told her story.

Tommy listened to, or rather, watched Taeva's delivery. She was much more dramatic with her story this time. Her body rocked and swayed. Her hair fell out from its braided captivity and swung free. And the way she moved her arms as she spoke…it was as if she were weaving images out of thin air.

Tommy felt a touch dizzy as he listened. The small hairs on the back of his neck stood on end. And his mind wandered once more among the scenes conjured by Taeva's words.

When Taeva finished speaking at last, some sudden sound startled Tommy. He looked away from the Princess and briefly made eye contact with Kat. He looked quickly away feeling somewhat guilty, though he could not discern why.

The sound had been the Gwar leader, Bengfist. He banged his ham-sized fist once more on the table. "Outrage! Outrage!" he growled. "Why do we sit here like dotards, sleepy and content, waiting as desperate minutes pass? To war, I say! To war!"

"Overlord!" Sardon shrilled his voice to be heard over the swirling murmurs. "Overlord Bengfist, pleasssth! This is the second time you've addresssth the Conclave without, ah, formal recognition."

"But if a new Spider King has risen," the Gwar rejoined, "we must not waste time with parliamentary procedure. We must swing our hammers and dash his brain—"

"Whether there is truly a new Spider King, issth for the Conclave to consider," Sardon replied. "But thissth Conclave exists to champion wisdom over rash decisionssth."

"Lord Felheart Silvertree, to be recognized," Tommy said, using his formal name.

"Ssspeak on, Berinfell Lord," Sardon said, his knuckles clacking on the podium.

Tommy nodded. "As you all know, we fought the Spider King at Vesper Crag, but what you may not know is how he came to be what he was. He was bitten."

The murmurs arose again.

"Yes, he was bitten," Tommy said. "I don't understand it all, but by some enchantment, alchemy, or chemistry, he had turned his wife—his own wife—into some kind deformed creature. He used her to begin his race of Warspiders. When her chance finally came, she bit him...drove her venom into him. She meant to kill him, I think, but instead, her venom transformed him, made him ten times more powerful than before. If the Spider King somehow bit the Drefid Asp, I can only dread the might he could now wield."

"But the Ssspider King was ssslain," Sardon replied. "Bengfist can confirm thissth."

"My people pulled his half-rotted corpse out of the rubble of Vesper Crag," Bengfist said. He clenched his massive fist so hard the knuckles crackled. "Still, he was a practitioner of the Dark Arts. That is the alchemy to which Lord Felheart spoke. The Spider King learned the Dark Arts from his dealings with the Drefid clans. Logic and history could dictate the truth of Princess Taeva's tale."

"Are you suggesssting, then," Sardon said, his red eyes narrowed to slits, "that the Spider King managed to raise himssself from the dead and then, ah, bit the Drefid Asp?" He crossed his long, gangly arms and sneered. Even the serpentine appendages crossed over his chin.

Bengfist shrugged.

One of the Nemic Priests became animated and leaned in toward Vault Minister Ghrell. "You see," the Priest whispered. "The Drefids are the ones meddling with the Dark Arts."

Ghrell's deep breath nearly doubled the size of his chest, but he said nothing. He turned and assaulted the Priest with such a glare that would raze a forest to the ground.

Tommy looked to Goldarrow, but had no answer for Sardon's question.

"Are you all forgetting?" Taeva said. "I was there! I saw Asp, standing arrogantly in my father's own courtyard. I saw what he could do! Have I come all this way to lie? If so, to what end? My people are dying…we need your help!"

"Perhaps," Sardon said. "Perhaps we must all, ah, come to your aid. But, there seemsssth something quite fantastical in your ssstory. How can we, in good conscience, release Conclave forces without confirmation?"

All at once, the room exploded.

"Would you see the Taladrim wiped from the face of Allyra?" Taeva shrieked.

Bengfist was on his feet now. "My race was enslaved!" he bellowed, "because we failed…to…act! March, I say! March for blood!"

Even Migmar's voice, high and light as it was, managed to mix into the chaos. "March us not into war!" he cried. "Unless wills it does the Conclave or attack does the Spider King to the Moonchildren!"

"People of the Conclave!" Goldarrow shouted. "This solves nothing! Take your seats!"

"Order!" Sardon shrilled. "Order thisssth minute!"

"This is getting bad," Kat spoke into Tommy's mind. *"Should I have Johnny flare up?"*

Tommy was about to answer, when a voice louder than any, clear and resonant like a hammered bell, called out, "ENOUGH!"

Vault Minister Ghrell of the Nemic flapped his wings once, a sound like a cracking whip. In a flash, he tossed a handful of metallic marbles out onto the table. They rolled loudly a few feet and came to a stop in a circular pattern at the exact center of the table.

Then, with his other hand, Ghrell tossed dozens of shimmering fingers of sharp metal high into the air above the table.

BLADES! The thought registered in Tommy's mind too slowly. He barely had his hand on the hilt of his rychesword, when the Nemic's blade weapons dove down out of the air. They fell fast, as if some army of archers clung to the domed ceiling and shot them down from their bows. With loud *thwacks* and cracks, the blades pelted the table, sinking deep into the hard wood.

Though the table had been scored with enough blades to kill everyone in the room, not a single one of them had come dangerously close to any of the Conclave members. It had been a demonstration only. A demonstration that left the room utterly silent.

"There," Vault Minister Ghrell said, "now that you have all come back to your senses, I motion that we stop arguing and vote."

"Second!" Migmar yelped.

General Secretary Sardon snorted. "Thank you, Minister Ghrell, for your timely sssuggestion. But, in the future, would you find some other way, ah, than a *fussilade barrage*, perhaps?"

Ghrell folded his wings and took his seat. His expression was grim as always, but he seemed satisfied somehow.

Sardon held both hands spread open, and they looked like twin tree canopies in winter, gnarled and barren. "Very well," he said, scowling. "We will vote. Let all—"

Just then, an Elven flet soldier entered the chamber. She made no effort to hide her presence from the group but rounded the table straight to Goldarrow. She whispered in the Guardmaster's ears for several long moments and then came to Tommy.

Tommy could scarcely believe what he was hearing. "Are you certain?" he asked.

"One cannot mistake something of this magnitude," the flet soldier replied.

"What isssth the nature of thissth interruption?" Sardon demanded.

"I apologize, General Secretary," Tommy said. "But our scouts have returned from Taladair at last."

The room erupted in conversation, but Ghrell cleared his throat and all noise vanished.

"What word, ah, from Taladair?" Sardon asked.

Tommy glanced at Taeva and took a deep breath. "Taladair is in ruins," Tommy said. "It is as the Princess described: untold thousands dead, but—"

The crowd drowned Tommy out.

"But listen!" Tommy called out, summoning a deeper tone that he rarely used. "Listen to me! Our scouts report all that Princess Taeva told us; in fact Asp has somehow caused the Dollniant Sea to overflow the walls. The city is flooded out. Three legions of enemy soldiers remain there, picking at the flotsam like sea birds."

"We are too late!" Taeva cried.

"No," Bengfist said. "There is still time to avenge!"

"Vote," Sardon said. "If you call the Conclave Legions to Taladair to assault this new threat and rescue the survivors, if any exist, then place your weapon upon the table, blade facing the table center. If you refuse this call, place your weapon upon the table with the haft toward the center."

Tommy looked to Goldarrow. She nodded, so Tommy drew his rychesword and put it on the table. He turned it until the curved blade pointed toward center.

Taeva did the same with one of her daggers. Bengfist put his waraxe facing center as well.

The younger Nemic Priest again tried to speak to his people's ruler. "There, Vault Minister, all the evidence you could want that it was the Drefids, not the El—"

"Silence, Dhrex!" the Vault Minister commanded. "You are an upstart, barely past Allyran Rites. Things are not always as they appear."

Ghrell's flexed his wings and drew a wide-bladed broadsword. He placed it haft to center. Saer Magistrate Forlarn placed his mace the same way. And, to Tommy's exasperation, Migmar placed his thwack hammer, haft to center.

"The vote is tied," Sardon said. "The Conclave has ssspoken its

will. As duly commissioned General Secretary, I cast the deciding vote."
He place a long, gnarled stave on the table.

"Which end is which?" Kat whispered into Tommy's mind.

No clue, Tommy thought back. It was maddening.

"My vote settles the dispute," Sardon said. "Conclave forces will
not go to war. We are adjourned."

There were cheers from some parts of the room, angry complaints
from others.

Tommy gathered the Elves, Taeva, and her attendants. "Cowards,"
he whispered.

"Did you expect any different?" Goldarrow asked.

"From Migmar," Tommy said. "Yes. Yes, I did."

"But he lost a lot of his people in Vesper Crag," Autumn said.
"Maybe half their population."

Tommy shook his head. "I know, I know, but still."

"Is that it?" Taeva asked, her voice trembling. "With a simple
raising of hands, my people are doomed?"

"No, that's not it," Goldarrow said. "We have another option, but
we can't talk here."

Sport of Champions

DECORATED WARFLY pilot Caerfasz soared unseen, high above the Texas stadium where the humans watched their precious professional football team play.

No ground or air radar would report the Warfly's presence. There would be no military response, at least not until it was far too late. The Gnomes' invisibility paste had seen to that.

It's all up to the Drefids, Caerfasz thought. *Asp better be right about this.* As a high ranking Gwar soldier, Caerfasz was more than a little distrustful of the mysterious Drefids and their Dark Arts. Bewildering and powerful, the Drefids—Asp especially—could do things beyond the reach of the former Spider King. But their power was volatile, mercurial even. What worked once might not work again or in the same way. One error in the formula, one slip of the tongue, could mean the difference between immobilizing an enemy or simply making him itchy.

No, Caerfasz liked things he could count on each and every time. Like the heavy warhammer slung on his back. It was guaranteed to break the spine of his foe. Or the *narcan powder* held in massive pouches on each of the Warfly's legs. *Now, that's the stuff,* Caerfasz thought. *Guaranteed to send any creature into a deep, helpless sleep.*

Caerfasz banked his Warfly in a wide arc and gazed down at all the humans gathered in the stadium for their game. They looked like ants. Ninety-thousand ants, content in their trap and completely unaware of the doom that was coming.

But the Drefids needed to come through. These humans had advanced communication technology. Not only were ninety-thousand spectators watching the game in person, but untold millions could watch on light boxes all over the world. The Drefids were tasked with knocking out this communications system. Each and every one of them. No one outside of the stadium could witness what was about to happen. All it would take was one missed communication stream to get to the outside world.

And then, the military would be alerted. Their response would be swift and severe. Caerfasz doubted that Lord Asp would appreciate a problem of this magnitude at this stage of his plan. *That would mean my head,* he thought ruefully.

A red flash down below. *The signal!* Caerfasz exulted. He watched as there were five more flashes in sequence.

"It is done!" Caerfasz cried aloud. He put his warhorn to his lips and winded a mighty blast. His squadron of Warflies would respond by spreading out into their oft-practiced attack formation.

They couldn't see each other, but they knew where they would each be at any given time in the maneuver. Caerfasz had seen to that. He'd had to kill eighteen good pilots for mistakes they'd made while training. But it was worth it. There would be no mistakes today.

Caerfasz took his Warfly into a shallow dive. He heard the crowd roar below. Apparently something exciting had happened in the humans' mundane little sport. *Nothing compared to what I am about to do.*

Caerfasz and his other pilots leveled out twenty feet above the playing field. Just before they raced over the players' heads, each pilot reached beneath their Warfly's neck armor and stroked the creature's flesh. Each Warfly then scratched two of its limbs together, breaking apart the narcan powder deposits. It released a fine white mist that fell more gossamer than snow.

One of the football players had apparently done something heroic, Caerfasz thought, for this player...he was leaping, spinning, shaking his hips and rear end in some strange ceremonial dance.

But then, the player went as limp as a boned fish and fell to the ground in a heap of pads and muscle. Other players began to collapse as well, some in mid-step. The coaches and players on the sidelines looked on in horror. They rushed onto the field to help their fallen comrades, only to stagger and drop themselves.

A dark hush fell on the thousands and thousands in the stands. The stadium announcer broke the silence. "Ladies and gentlemen, please remain in your seats. Medical personnel are—" A deafening blast of feedback cut him off.

Screams and panic broke out. People clambered over their seats, trying desperately to find a clear path to the aisle stairs. The pushing and shoving reached lethal intensity. A man was knocked backward over a rail and fell into the causeway, dead. In the most crowded places, people fell; others trampled them.

"Narfak!" Caerfasz cursed. Letting the merchandise destroy itself was not part of the plan.

The Gwar Commander took decisive action. He loosed two short blasts on his warhorn, so that his team would move immediately to the second phase. He and his squadron of Warflies took their potent narcan payload and spiraled up over the stadium seats.

Row after row of spectators fell dormant until, at last, the entire stadium was ghostly silent. Then, the Warflies descended upon the roof and high fixtures of the stadium and perched like invisible gargoyles.

Caerfasz made a final sweep of the stadium's perimeter. Little movement: a few cars coming or going. But no law enforcement. No flashing lights. No military.

I'll be a Warspider's egg, Caerfasz thought. *The Drefids actually pulled it off. Maybe the Dark Arts aren't as unreliable as I suspected.*

Caerfasz gave three long blasts on his warhorn. It was answered by a strange, muffled tone that seemed to come from beneath the football field.

On a section of the field, empty of fallen players and coaches, the turf exploded upward. Clumps of earth the size of trucks careened into the air, and gigantic, gray segmented worms burst out of the ground. Each one had eight small black eyes and a gaping, leech-like maw.

Behind these serpentine beasts, thousands of Gwar warriors began to emerge. Many rode Warspiders and dragged massive, walled carts behind them. They positioned themselves, ten-deep, at the bottom of every stadium section.

Caerfasz signaled once more to his squadron, and the ferrying began. The Warflies used their many appendages to gently grab up fifteen to twenty people at a time. They descended rapidly to the carts and carefully dropped off their loads. Waiting Gwar and Drefids positioned the unconscious humans so that they could not smother themselves.

The fully-loaded Warspiders clambered back into the holes from which they'd come, took one of several subterranean passages, and dropped off their prisoners at Asp's brilliant brainchild: the subterranean railway. Asp had reasoned that the humans could keep their random, naturally formed aquifers. He'd simply *build* transportation wherever he wanted it.

Ground and sky forces worked together with breathtaking efficiency and speed. Caerfasz knew that the entire operation needed to be complete in fifteen Earth minutes or less. Moving ninety-thousand humans in fifteen minutes was no small feat, but Gwar and Drefids had practiced for so long that they made it happen.

The stadium now empty—even the food stands and bathrooms had been scoured—Caerfasz prepared to leave. He couldn't help but smile, looking at the vacant seats. "There," he muttered, as he nudged his Warfly to enter one of the holes. "That ought to be enough slaves for Asp to set his plan in motion."

Minutes later, deep beneath the surface, Caerfasz triggered the arc stone charges that had been strategically placed beneath the field and throughout the stadium.

There was a blinding blue-white flash. Steel and concrete twisted, crumbled, and vaporized. The Texas stadium, built over six years at a cost of over a billion dollars, was reduced to rubble and dust in a matter of seconds. No one would find the imploded tunnels or any evidence of the Gwar and Drefids' presence there.

For the humans who investigated the scene, they would find only that ninety-thousand people...had vanished.

Unfolding Secrets

"I DON'T like her," Autumn said.

Kat and Kiri Lee raised their eyebrows, but they could hardly disagree. There was definitely something about Taeva that didn't sit right. The three lords sat in a small anteroom following the conclusion of the Conclave meeting, nursing their loss by changing the subject; and Taeva was as good as any distraction at the moment. The guys wouldn't join them for a little while longer, choosing instead to see some of the so-called "leaders" safely on their way.

"Plus do you see the way the guys are smitten with her?" added Autumn. She tried to impersonate her brother: *"Apple-farming family heritage.* Really?"

"They do seem distracted," agreed Kat, thinking of Tommy's pandering. She felt annoyed. Annoyed that the guys weren't giving the girls as much attention...and annoyed that she cared so much about attention from the guys in the first place. Especially from Tommy.

There was more. A hint of fear maybe? There was something about the guys' instant infatuation that seemed unnatural. Kat couldn't put her finger on it. It wasn't tangible or visible, like a spot of yellow mold on an orange. Whatever it was, Kat found that she didn't like—didn't trust Taeva.

"We'll have to watch her," said Kiri Lee. "Carefully."

"All the same, I think we should keep this between us," added Autumn. The other two nodded.

There came a knock at the door.

"Come," said Kat.

"M'ladies," said a female attendant pushing open the door, then stepped aside.

"Grimwarden," the three lords said in unison. They rose immediately to meet him.

"If only such smiles greeted me behind every chamber door, I'd be a better Elf," he said. "I thought I'd find you in here."

The three girls hugged him and dismissed the attendant.

"We left the parting pleasantries to the guys," said Autumn.

"I don't blame you," Grimwarden murmured. "Given the display you just witnessed. When Goldarrow told me all about it, it was all I could do not to—"

"Not to lop their heads off with your rychesword?" Kat suggested.

Grimwarden chuckled. "Not exactly as tactful as I was thinking, but no less appropriate."

"So what are we going to do?" asked Kiri Lee.

"That is why I have come." He gestured to the overstuffed furniture in the corner of the room. The four made themselves comfortable, and Grimwarden lowered his voice. "I have a plan."

"I knew you would!" said Autumn. "I knew he would," she echoed, turning to Kat and Kiri Lee. They smirked. "What? I did."

Grimwarden smiled warmly. "Mark of a career warrior, I suppose," he said. "Anticipate the enemy's moves, and prepare. It just so happens that I have been preparing Berinfell for just such a time as this. After that meeting, after the scout's report, one thing is certain: we cannot leave Taladrim to rot."

Just then, there came a thud at the door. Grimwarden hit his feet in a heartbeat and, sword in-hand, bounded over the furniture. He flung the door open and a stout shadow fell inside.

"Overlord Bengfist?" exclaimed Kat, now on her feet with the others.

"I'm very sorry to bother you, Lady Lords," he said, wringing his massive hands. He looked to Grimwarden. "I was just walking by and tripped, and the the next thing I knew—"

"Overlord Bengfist," Grimwarden interrupted, "had you truly tripped and fallen, then, my old friend, I doubt this frail door would still be on its hinges."

Taking their cue from Grimwarden's tone, the girls relaxed and looked at each other. But why had Bengfist been listening in on their conversation?

"Ah, well yes, Grimwarden," Bengfist murmured, the gray skin flushing pink on his broad cheekbones. "You've always had a way with words."

"Perhaps in friendly conversation," Grimwarden said. "But I doubt if my words would have done much to change the minds of those short-sighted fools at the Conclave."

"And thus why I'm here," Bengfist said, his expression hardening. "Oh?"

"Tell me, Guardmaster, since when have you ever been one to take *no* for an answer, especially from the likes of politicians?"

"I no longer possess the rank, my friend," Grimwarden admitted, raising his chin.

"Humph," Bengfist grumbled. "Maybe not in title. But no man can shed his real identity, especially a chunk of granite like you. Hmph, humph, the allegiances of the faithful run with those loyal to preserving all of Allyra. And not just for now as some would argue, but forever." Bengfist looked conspiratorially over his shoulder, then lowered his voice. "And I can't imagine for a second that you're disappearing back into the Thousand League Forest with your ears bent and your blade broken."

Grimwarden looked into the hallway beyond, and seeing it was clear, ushered Bengfist further into the anteroom and closed the door.

Once they were all comfortable—Bengfist taking the largest sofa-like chair all to himself—Grimwarden resumed his previous train of thought. "I have assembled a small force of Elves loyal to Allyra's defense."

"I KNEW IT!" shouted Autumn, who was immediately met with shushing fingers and at least one hand trying to cover her mouth.

"If this is to remain a secret," Grimwarden warned, "then it must be kept in the strictest confidence." He looked around to each of them. "No mistakes. No leaks."

"So what are you proposing we do?" Bengfist asked.

"Well, first we need to make it back to Nightwish."

"Nightwish?" asked Kat. "They're assembled in Nightwish?"

"It was the perfect place," said Grimwarden. "We knew it well for obvious reasons, and it's the last place any snooping Elf would ever want to look." The Elves' long plight underground made the term Nightwish tantamount to an expletive following their return to Berinfell.

"Grimwarden, please don't take my inquiry the wrong way," said Kat, "but how long have you been keeping this from us? This is quite the matter to be hiding from the Lords of Berinfell, wouldn't you say?"

"Your lordships," Grimwarden bowed his head. "It has been more than five years that I've been training the Elves in Mandiera. I fully admit my actions of developing a secret army without your knowledge are reprehensible—if not treasonous—deserving severe punishment. However, I might contest—"

"Oh Grimwarden, we get it," said Kat. "And none of us," she looked at Autumn and Kiri Lee, "would ever question you, let alone punish you."

"I am most grateful for your trust," replied Grimwarden. "But still, if I may, I'd like to explain myself, as I'm not the only one who knows."

"Really?" The girls leaned in.

"Goldarrow, Mr. Charlie and Regis are also thoroughly aware. We had long feared there would be an uprising, either from the rogue Gwar survivors, or perhaps from the Drefids. So when the Conclave waxed complacent, ensconced in Berinfell's newfound luxury, we decided to take matters into our own hands. Our reason for not alerting you, however, was an issue of service."

"I don't understand," said Kiri Lee.

"In short?" asked Grimwarden. "Plausible deniability. Should the Six have known of our efforts, there would be no way for you to remain true to your word when negotiating these many long years with the Conclave. Our secrecy secured your integrity."

While Kat and the others found the new information a bit startling, though not entirely surprising, they could not fault the Guardmaster nor their esteemed Sentinels for having the Six's best interests in mind. Over the last several years, the Six had grown up; they'd become diplomats when tensions grew high, and tenacious when politicking grew tenuous. Grimwarden's secret had in fact forced the Six to mature within the affairs of the Conclave, all the while safeguarding Allyra from future attacks. And they were all better for it.

"If anything," Kat finally spoke up, "we honor you for your harrowing act of faith. And when we can, all of Allyra shall know of the secret weight you have carried these many years, especially in the face of outlandish accusations of cowardice."

"Hear, hear!" cried Bengfist, slapping the flat of his hand with a fist.

Grimwardem bowed his head again. "Defeating this Asp will be honor enough," he replied. "Let us do what needs doing, and then, I don't care who you tell."

"So how do we get to Nightwish?" asked Autumn. "It's a rather long way, right? And how can we just leave? Our corporate departure will be noticed."

"We will depart the city at dusk," Grimwarden said, "take alternate routes, and converge north of the city. From that point, the Scarlet Raptors I've eyried there will bear us to Nightwish. We will assemble our forces there, and then travel north to Kileverand where we'll commandeer the city's fleet and set sail. Admiral Cuth is an old friend."

"But what will explain our disappearance from the city?" Kiri Lee asked.

Grimwarden winked. "This was Goldarrow's idea," he explained. "Even the Lords of Berinfell need to brush up on their training, now and then. The Six shall depart for a combat retreat, to learn and test a whole host of new moves and weapons."

"Well," Autumn said, "that's true enough, except that we'll be fighting for real."

"It seems you've thought this through," said Kat. "You really are quite sneaky, you know that?"

"Elle, er...Goldarrow, I mean, tells me that all the time."

Bengfist pounded a fist into his hand and asked, "When do we leave?"

"Ah, well, there is one minor problem," Grimwarden said. "Bengfist, I wasn't expecting your aid on this mission. You'll likely wish a few of your trusty lads to join us, but I'm afraid I don't have enough transport for more than yourself. Spare Scarlet Raptors are hard to come by in Berinfell these days. If I begin asking around, others will get curious. We cannot afford any mistakes."

"I understand," Bengfist said, nodding. "My Commanders will stand-by here with our troops. They shall ever be at your disposal, Guardmaster."

Grimwarden winced at the term again but realized there would be no dissuading the Overlord from using it. Bengfist was a loyalist to the core, and Grimwarden loved that about him.

"We will rout the lingering remnant of Asp's forces!" Bengfist growled. "I suspect that Asp will not be among them. Pity."

"There is a need for more than fighting," Grimwarden said.

"The survivors?" Kat asked. "The scout said there couldn't be many."

"True," Grimwarden said, crossing his arms. "But few Elves know of the catacombs. I doubt our scouts did."

"Catacombs?" asked Kiri Lee. "As in underground tunnels and chambers?"

"The same," said Grimwarden. "Used for storage, and in the event of an assault, the safety of their women and children. Much the same as your parents prepared the escape route and Nightwish Caverns."

"So why didn't Taeva mention it to us?" asked Kat.

"Given the destruction she experienced," said Grimwarden, "I suspect she feared to hope. She teeters on the edge, even now. The edge of depression, desperation, or something worse. I am not sure which. You can only imagine the turmoil she's enduring."

"I guess," Kat replied flatly, surprised that Grimwarden already seemed to trust Taeva when she was clearly up to her neck in guile.

"Taeva may fear all is lost," the senior Elf went on. "But I believe the catacombs could very much be intact. They were first carved by the ocean out of solid granite, and then fortified by Taladrim engineers. It would take more than a flood to collapse them. The wrenching question that remains is whether any Taladair citizens made it down there before Asp blew the walls off the city. If some did, they are trapped now, and it's our job to get them out."

"Not that I disagree with you, Guardmaster," interjected Bengfist, "but a search and rescue mission is not really what I had in mind."

"Nor I, Overlord Bengfist, but we have a call to protect all of

Allyra's citizens, not just our own—wouldn't you agree?"

Bengfist nodded.

"And if there are survivors," Grimwarden went on, "they may hold clues as to where Asp was heading next. We can't afford to let that information disappear on the sea floor."

"I admit your reasoning is sound. Perhaps I simply wish to confront Asp with my warhammer sooner rather than later," Bengfist said as his knobby fingers absently stroked the giant mallet on his hip.

"And it will come, Bengfist. It will come. But Asp is a cunning foe, and one misstep on our part could be disastrous. I sense that whatever respect we held for the Spider King, it should be multiplied for Asp. Careful preparation and strategic, deliberate action must guide our every move."

Bengfist finally pulled his hand away from his warhammer and leaned toward Grimwarden. "So when do we fly?"

When all the visiting dignitaries had finally been escorted to the edges of Berinfell, Tommy, Johnny and Jimmy found the girls in the Lords' training chambers, a long vestibule just outside the throne room. Their surprise at seeing Kat, Autumn and Kiri Lee dressed in travel attire was only bested by discovering that Grimwarden and Bengfist were also there—donning their own gear: heavy boots and floor length, oil skinned cloaks.

Tommy, Jimmy and Johnny exchanged perplexed glances.

"We must have missed the memo," Tommy said, checking his back and closing the door. "So...uh, where are we going?"

The band of travelers looked at each other before Kat spoke up. "Nightwish."

"Excuse me?" Tommy mumbled.

Johnny and Jimmy engaged in a contest of whose jaw could hit the floor quickest.

"I'm not certain I understand," Bengfist said, scratching his chin. "What's there to excuse? Did you burp or far—"

"It's an expression of surprise from Earth," Grimwarden explained quickly, angling the back of his hand against the corner of his mouth.

"Oh. How strange," Bengfist replied, thinking the Gwar response of *roaring* was far more direct.

Grimwarden stepped forward and explained what he'd shared with the girls about his secretive band of elite Elven warriors hiding in The Underground, as well as the logic of sailing north for Taladair. He included his apology and explanation of deniability, then bowed low.

"Grimwarden," Tommy said, "you really overstepped your authority here."

Kat's hand flew to her mouth. The others hung on Tommy's words. Grimwarden's eyes widened.

"No," Tommy went on, "there's really no excuse. You took thousands of elite soldiers away from Berinfell's defense."

"Well, but I..." Grimwarden stammered. "I mean to say, they weren't elite when they left Berinfell. It was the train—"

"To think that we have trusted you all this time," Tommy said, stepping forward.

"Tommy!" Kat exclaimed. "He was only trying to protect—"

Tommy held up a swift hand. "No, no, Kat. There must be consequences here."

"I understand," Grimwarden said, tucking his chin into his chest plate.

"I really don't think you do," Tommy said. "This amounts to a kind of treason. But since you've already exiled yourself, I can think of only one other punishment."

"Young Lord," Bengfist implored, "don't do this! I assure you,

Grimwarden has been nothing but honorable in this."

"As leader of the Lords of Berinfell," Tommy proclaimed, "I pronounce your fate. For creating a secret army without the knowledge or approval of Berinfell's Six Lords, I hereby sentence you to…ten jumping jacks, ten push ups, and ten up-downs. Oh, and Mumthers has to pack us lunches for the trip!"

After a moment of stunned silence, everyone in the room fell into fits of side-splitting laughter. It went on for some time, until rib and abdominal pain forced a retreat to sobriety.

"Hoo!" Grimwarden gasped. "You, you really had me going, Tommy. Shame on you! I might have died there!"

"That's for my birthday surprise," Tommy replied.

Grimwarden grinned. "Well met."

"Now, then," Tommy said, "so when do we leave?"

"Immediately," Grimwarden said.

"I'll go get Taeva," Johnny said, stepping hastily backward.

"No, yu always take forever to get packed," Jimmy said. "I best be gettin' the Princess."

"No, guys," Tommy said. "Leave this burden to me."

"Uh," Kat said, raising a finger. "Does everyone think that's the best idea?" She looked to Grimwarden, then to the girls.

"No," replied Johnny. "You're the leader, Tommy. You should let us handle—"

"Let me handle it, yu mean," Jimmy said.

"Seriously?" said Autumn. "You guys are kidding, right? You're acting like a bunch of—"

"What Autumn's trying to say," interrupted Kat, "is that perhaps revisiting her homeland so quickly after the attack might be too traumatizing for Princess Taeva. Perhaps she should remain here until we return."

"That makes no tactical sense whatsoever," Grimwarden said,

eyeing Kat suspiciously. "We need her despite whatever discomfort she may endure. No one among us knows Taladair better than the Princess. Lives of her people are at stake."

"Grimwarden's right," Tommy said, turning. "The decision is made: I'll go get her."

Kiri Lee made to protest, but Kat put a hand on her shoulder. Kiri Lee frowned and mouthed *Why?* Kat didn't answer, but Grimwarden glared at them both.

"Go quickly, Tommy," Grimwarden said. "We'll meet beyond the Northern Gate in half-an-hour. Goldarrow, Mr. Charlie and Regis are already on their way. Move independently. We can't afford to be followed as a group. And Tommy, make sure Taeva's equipped for flying."

Tommy nodded and was out the door, followed by Jimmy, Johnny and then Bengfist. "Ladies," said Grimwarden, "May I have a word?"

Kiri Lee rolled her eyes.

"I heard that," said Grimwarden.

Kiri Lee blew the hair out of her face. "Grimwarden, how could you possibly hear—"

"Maybe you missed my class on that technique back at Whitehall."

"Funny."

Grimwarden eyed the three lords. "So, do you three want to tell me what's going on?"

"Nothing, sir," said Autumn.

"Nothing," he repeated slowly. "Right. And Warspiders give birth to strawberries. Come now, I may not yet have had the privilege of wedding a fair maiden, but I've spent more than enough time around women to know when a grudge is afoot. What do you have against Taeva? I hear it now or you stay behind."

"Stay behind?" Autumn objected. "But you can't command the lords—"

"My dear Lord Autumn, how difficult do you think it would be for me to persuade the male lords that you three should stay behind?"

Autumn swallowed. "Not too hard," she grumbled.

"There, now enough playing coy," Grimwarden demanded. "Berinfell cannot afford to have our plans undermined, least of all from within. So let's have it."

The three girls swayed uneasily, each looking to the floor or the ceiling—anything but to Grimwarden.

"As you wish." He strode past them and reached for the door.

"Wait," said Kat at last. "You're right."

"I almost always am, my dear," answered Grimwarden.

"See, it's just that—"

"We don't trust her," interjected Autumn. Kiri Lee nodded.

"Have you reason for this judgment?" Grimwarden asked.

"Well, she..." Autumn fumbled. "It's just that..."

Grimwarden waited a moment, then nodded with his lower lip furrowed up into an arc. "I see." He clasped his hands behind his back. "Lady Lords of Berinfell, it may well be that Princess Taeva comes to us with hidden motives. She has not told us all, that much is plain. Time will tell. But, be that as it may, might I suggest that you rise above the trivial trappings of lesser Elves and lay your jealousies aside? We have no use for them once we embark. Nor can any of us afford for our mission—or the fate of our world—to be commandeered by the insecurities of unbridled emotions. Yours most especially. Do I make myself clear?"

"You almost always do," replied Kat.

Grimwarden grinned. "I'll see you in twenty-five minutes."

After each individual had successfully slipped into the forest without drawing undue attention, the group gathered and made their way north of the city on foot, diverting off the main road and heading deeper into the wood. Grimwarden and the Sentinels led the way, covering a great deal of ground with their forest craft. Bengfist found it difficult, both to keep up and to employ anything close to the stealth of the others.

Twenty minutes later they found three Elves standing guard in a small clearing. A palisade pen had been erected in the shade of a great maple off to the side. Tommy noted that, within the pens, little more than a dozen Scarlet Raptors wandered about, as far as the birds' lead lines allowed them anyway.

"All is well?" Grimwarden asked the foremost guard who saluted him.

"Neither hare nor howl, Guardmaster," said the Elf.

Tommy winked at the Five beside him; apparently Grimwarden wasn't as opposed to his old title as he'd indicated previously.

"Good to hear," replied Grimwarden. He turned to the team. "Mount up. We leave immediately."

Tommy, Johnny and Jimmy helped the girls up onto their birds. The girls could not help but notice the extra care the lads rendered to Taeva. Grimwarden noticed too.

Kat was about to comment, but as soon as she felt Grimwarden's eyes on her, changed her mind. "Ready, Guardmaster!" she intoned.

Grimwarden nodded with the passing hint of a smirk, then turned his raptor aside and pressed his heels into the feathers. The grass rippled in waves as Grimwarden's flying steed climbed into the air, talons pawing at empty space until they cleared the treetops.

"After you, ladies," said Tommy.

"Indeed," Kat replied.

The fourteen other Scarlet Raptors soared skyward, filing out of the Thousand League Forest like a thin, red line of butterflies sailing across a green carpet.

On and on they flew, staying close to the treetops, and keeping their conversations to a minimum. Tommy watched the sun start its measured descent toward the horizon in the east, remembering back to the first time he'd entered Nightwish almost eight years prior. They had run through the Lightning Fields in Vesper Crag, fleeing into a tunnel, where the Seven eventually discovered the headwaters of an underwater river.

"Will you ever forget that first boat ride?" Tommy yelled over to Jimmy.

Jimmy was clearly thinking along the same lines; he smiled and shook his head a little. "I'll not forget. Nor Grimwarden, I imagine. Most painful for him, I'll wager."

Tommy grimaced. He'd shot an arrow directly through Grimwarden's outstretched hand in order to keep the Guardmaster and Jimmy from disappearing into a whirlpool. It felt so long ago. They had just become teenagers; now they were each entering their twenties. Time felt like it was flying as swiftly as the Scarlet Raptors beneath their seats.

Tommy's thoughts wandered, as did the others', wondering what it'd be like to be back underground. They wondered how much it'd changed, how strong Grimwarden's warband really was, and just what awaited them in Taladair—and beyond. While their memories had grown dimmer in recent years, muted by the constant beauty and excitement of abiding in Allyra, the Six remembered Earth, imagining what it must look like today, so many years later.

Fourteen shadows passed up above the trees, silhouetted by pale moonlight beyond. But below the forest air was filled with the sounds of birds roosting in their nests and all manner of woodland insects conducting their evening symphony.

Then, as if someone had given instructions to the concert master to silence the orchestra, the entire medley of sounds dissipated, until nothing so much as moved beneath the leafy canopy above.

A moment later and a sharp crackle sizzled through the air like the pop of a firework. A brilliant blue light flashed and illuminated the forest floor as if in midday. Then the strange aberration expanded, rippling out through the forest in all directions, wrapping around trees with the surface tension of a pool of water, yet without any mass above or below the plane. It shimmered, having the appearance of a liquid mirror. But instead of reflecting what it saw, it seemed to hold the imagery of an alternate space within. An alternate world. An alternate time.

Once the phenomena seemed to reach full strength, the trees that intersected it suddenly fell in on themselves, their upper portions pulled by gravity into the blue plane, trunk and limbs and leaves. Whatever passed into the horizon above did not exit below; tree trunks appeared as if they'd been cut by a laser in a wide, circular field.

Before any onlooker could ascertain what was below—or above—the surface, the aberration snapped shut with a whipcrack and disappeared, leaving the forest floor in darkness.

Silence consumed the woods again, and the new meadow that'd been created, along with a strange smell. The creatures within never did regain their night song, as most of them were long gone.

"We'll land right there," Grimwarden said after more than an hour, then gave the signal to descend to a small dark patch in the midst of a thick grove of tall trees, illuminated only by the full moon above them. Tommy thought the space looked oddly familiar.

The birds touched down, clearing the space of dead leaves and sticks, before tucking their tired wings and settling down for a well-deserved sleep. The Six knew better than to remain atop a sleeping raptor; they occasionally suffered from very fitful rest, and snapped at imaginary prey in their sleep. Rider beware.

All the riders, including Bengfist and Taeva, slipped from their mounts and followed Grimwarden into the darkening forest. The cicadas were well into their serenade, and the warm air sat heavy and still in the musty smell of the deep wood.

"I never thought I'd say this," said Kat, "but it feels good to be back."

"Aye," said Jimmy. "I know just what yu mean. Those were hard days," he thought aloud, "but good ones all the same."

They marched single file further down a deer run until they came to large stone the size of a two-door car. Tommy knew this rock. Grimwarden placed one hand under a small opening at the base, but before he could do anything, Tommy stepped forward.

"May I?" Tommy asked.

"You remember, then?" asked Grimwarden.

"I do," replied Tommy. He slipped his hand where Grimwarden's had been and pulled up. Miraculously, the stone pulled up and away like a giant hatch, revealing a sizable hole that disappeared into a sloping tunnel.

"Fake stone," Tommy smiled. "To guard the sun bathing tunnels."

"You remember well, Lord Felheart," said Grimwarden. "After you," he gestured with his hand.

Tommy led the way into the tunnel and was soon completely enclosed in darkness. The cave smelled of wet soil and mildew, and the sound of his feet hitting the floor was absorbed into the walls like a sponge.

"Perhaps this will help," came the voice of the only Raptor Guard allowed to proceed with the group. Tommy heard the sound of water pouring from one vessel into another, and then the cave burst to life in a dazzling blue light.

"Dremask Vein," Tommy said, looking at the small cluster of stones inside a handheld glass container. The guard had poured some cold water on the rocks to start them blazing. "Quite the new canister you have for it."

"Aye," said the guard. "Makes it easy to carry around, for times like this."

"Indeed," Tommy replied, smiling at the constant ingenuity of his people. It seemed many wonderful inventions came out of their hardships in Nightwish, and in fact had never stopped coming. The proof was being handed to him. "Thanks."

"My honor, your Lordship."

Tommy continued down the passageway with the others following directly behind him. "Think you can remember the way from here?" asked Grimwarden.

"I think so," said Tommy. As he led the way he felt someone come alongside him. He knew her smell before he could see who it was: Kat. While he'd never said much to her in the way of his feelings—choosing to learn the art of lord-craft to better serve Berinfell's people over a relationship with her—he could not deny the feelings he had for her, well, since pretty much the first time he'd laid eyes on her. Tommy hoped Berinfell's season of peace would permit time for such pursuits, but if anything, it diminished them. Still, here in this cave, it was like they were young teenagers again and the feelings remained strong.

Toward the back a second flash of light appeared. "Here you go," Johnny said to Kiri Lee, holding his hands aloft behind her so she could see ahead.

"Thanks, Johnny," she replied. Tommy looked back and thought he noticed the faintest smile on her face.

Oddly enough, Jimmy had picked up step beside Regis—the girl who had once been so much older—but with Allyra's time difference, had become relatively compatible. Regis appeared indifferent, but Jimmy had clearly put off his early infatuation with Kiri Lee to pursue the Elf maiden who had once masqueraded as a pubkeeper from Ardfern.

Tommy ran his fingers through his hair. The only person who seemed out of step was Autumn. Her affinity for anyone had died with Jett. And while she never confessed any such longings, it was apparent that Jett's care of her when she was ill had provoked a powerful case of the hero effect that so many patients and doctors experienced throughout time.

And then there were Goldarrow and Grimwarden, a likely pair, but never acknowledged by Grimwarden. No one could fluster the legendary warrior like she could. And yet there were no military rules preventing them from a relationship at this point. While Tommy suspected it was their stoic sense of duty that prevented an advance in their intentions—and scolding the notion that love was reserved only for the young—he more often thought marriage may be the only thing Grimwarden was truly afraid of.

Before long, Tommy's mind moved from the romantic involvements of his pack to a deep rushing sound steadily growing from the distance.

Daladge Falls.

The tunnel meandered through a dozen switchback turns, descending deeper and deeper before finally leveling out and opening up. The sound of rushing water had turned into a roar, and soon the cave filled with mist.

"Look!" said Kat. She pointed past Tommy, then raced ahead, bathed in the dremask lantern light. The group moved forward and Tommy raised the lantern.

Towering high above them were the falls they had first come crashing down, emptying into the basin that formed the apron of Nightwish. With the falls to their right and the glow of the city around the corner to their left, the scene was spellbinding. Massive dremask chandeliers hung from the vaulted ceiling further down, while countless wall sconces flooded the periphery with pale blue light.

"It's so romantic," said Taeva, her first words of the entire trip.

"Romantic?" asked Kat in disgust. "You do know that thousands of Gwar and Elves lost their lives here, right?"

"Um, no," said Taeva slightly taken aback. "I am sorry. My words were poorly chosen."

Kat knew she had failed miserably in heeding Grimwarden's warning, and was sure his eyes were drilling the back of her head. "Uh, but I agree, it's still magnificent, Taeva. Thanks for, for the compliment."

Tommy thought he saw Taeva roll her eyes. "Right then," Tommy said. "Grimwarden?"

"To the city," said Grimwarden. "They're waiting."

The small team marched along the upper bank of the river as the lights grew stronger and more frequent. The roar of the falls behind them was replaced by another, less monotonous, more deliberate one. There was a rhythm to it.

The group turned the final corner and came upon Nightwish proper.

There before them was a throng of warrior Elves, pumping their rycheswords in the air, all chanting a line in the Elvish tongue of old.

"What are they saying?" Taeva asked.

It was a moment before anyone replied, each listening to the sing-song cadence of the defiant chant.

"It's a line from the Rainsong," said Tommy. "An ancient prophecy of our people."

"How does it translate?" Taeva asked again.

Tommy took a few steps forward, lost in the dangerous beauty of the phrasing. His mind suddenly elsewhere, his mouth translated the lyrics for Taeva. "By the hand of the justice bane, we dispatch the ruthless, wicked and foul. Let injustice suffer our wrath. The Lords of Berinfell take up their thrones, the Mighty of Allyra."

They all stood listening, captivated by the scene stretching out before them.

"Uh, Grimwarden?" asked Kat.

"Yes, Lord Alreenia?" Grimwarden replied.

"I thought you said you had assembled a small force of Elves."

Mind Games

IT WAS oddly nostalgic for the Six to be bunking in their old Nightwish staterooms again. Things were exactly as they'd left them so many years ago on the day the tribes made their exodus back to Berinfell: the same furniture, the same dremask braziers, the same wardrobe of underground work clothes and royal garb. There was very little they'd wanted to bring with them, choosing to embrace their victory and a renewed life above ground rather than cling to the darkness of this place.

Still, Nightwish had a certain romance to it as Taeva had accurately—if not hastily—pointed out.

The feelings, however, would be short-lived, as Grimwarden wanted to depart for Taladair just after midnight, hours after they'd entered Nightwish. For those submerged in Taeva's homeland, time, and likely breathable air, were running out. Every minute counted. Grimwarden set everything in motion so that the Nightstalkers could depart within hours of the lords' arrival. There was just enough time for the travelers to grab a quick, but much-needed nap.

"Where are you going?" Kat whispered, trying not to wake Autumn or Taeva.

Kiri Lee froze, surprised she'd been caught. "Out. Can't sleep."

"Me neither. Want some company?"

"Sure," she said, though inwardly she wanted to be alone.

"My, how easily we forget one another's strengths," Kat smiled. She tapped the side of her temple.

"Oh. Right." Kiri Lee frowned. "But you promised not to listen in unless we gave you permission."

"I did promise," Kat replied. "And you did give me permission. You said, 'I have no secrets from you.' Remember?"

Kiri Lee squinted and then smiled. "Oh, yeah...right. Listen, I'm sorry about what I thought. It's just—"

"Don't worry about it, Kiri. I get it. Go get some air."

"OK. Thanks, Kat. Just need some alone time."

"You don't need to explain yourself, girl. I told you, I get it."

Kiri Lee thanked Kat, appreciating her humility, and scolding herself for not being truthful with her mind-reading friend. Then she slipped out of the room and made every effort to ease the latch into place.

Kiri Lee kept to side corridors so as not to be seen by any Nightstalker patrols. She obviously had nothing to fear, but she'd rather move undisturbed and even unnoticed. Eventually she arrived at one of the underground hubs—a large domed room with over twenty tunnels burrowing to various locations on the surface. The engineers had carefully created hubs like these, along with an intricate schedule to ensure each Elf in Nightwish had their allotted amount of time in the sun, while likewise keeping them out of harm's way to any Gwar sorties.

She chose a random tunnel marked Hibiscumi 4-b in First Voice script, indicating the type of shrubbery topside—essential for camouflaging any sunbathers—while also identifying the quadrant and sub-lot. The tunnel led her on for ten minutes before Kiri Lee came to a latticework hatch covered by the roots of a flowering bush. She waited for a minute, listening. An old habit. But of course now, enemy Gwar scouts weren't hunting in the Thousand League Forest. She chuckled to herself and pushed the thatched cover aside. She emerged into a wooded glade drenched in moonlight and cloaked in a sea full of stars.

The scene was just what she needed. A place to recharge, to think. To recenter on Ellos and prepare for the days ahead. It had been many years since she'd seen battle—real battle, not just simulations—and she wondered if she was ready for it again.

Peace was a balm that all too soon blurred the memory of trifling with the affairs of the wicked. But it could also dull instincts. A warrior could lose her edge. Surely the passion to protect was still there, but could she do it still?

Could she kill if she had to?

Kiri Lee found a small boulder to sit atop. Holding her knees close to her chest, she shuddered, the cool night air prickling her skin. The fingers of her right hand absently played across her stomach until they touched the scar, the imperfect flesh left behind from the wound that had nearly ended her life. The wound that had indirectly taken Jett's life instead.

She missed Jett. Not in a romantic way, of course, though he certainly was handsome. And heroic. No, Autumn had always liked him, and she wouldn't dare violate Autumn's memories, even with unspoken curiosities hidden deep inside her own heart. Friends didn't do that to one another. Ever.

But what did it matter anyway? Jett was gone.

But what if he wasn't?

The image of the intruder outside her window. Wisp? Phantom? Or could Jett somehow…someway be alive?

Gooseflesh continued to erupt all over her arms and neck. *What if Jett's alive?* She allowed herself to muse for the moment. *What would I tell him?*

Thank you, Jett.

Too insincere. Too common. Anyone could say thank you.

I owe you my life.

Melodramatic. What did it mean anyways? Lifelong indentured service?

You saved me from—from...

A shadow passed through Kiri Lee's peripheral vision. She spun right, and her heart leaped into her throat. Feeling exposed, she stood up and took to the air, ascending five or six steps toward the leafy canopy.

There it was again, this time slipping between the trunks in a copse of trees. She couldn't make it out, but it seemed big. A large wolf possibly. Or even a bear. Whatever it was, it was moving silently. It didn't want to be seen or heard. It was hunting. A true predator.

Kiri Lee instinctively reached for her dagger, but she was in her sleeping gown. She would have to avoid fighting tonight, if she could. *Flee and hide,* she thought. *That is the plan.*

From twenty feet above the ground, she turned slowly, looking for the thatched tunnel cover hidden on the forest floor. She saw something up ahead, a dark spot in the shrubs. It was in the correct general area. She'd have to chance it. If enemy or beast, she'd have one shot to escape. If Elven Nightstalker patrol, she'd have one shot to avoid having to offer a lengthy and embarrassing explanation.

She took a deep breath, then set off sprinting through the air like an Olympic runner, only she careened down an invisible race track.

Within the span of her first lunging steps, she could scarcely hear, what with her pulse blasting like a drum in her ears. She was roughly twenty-five feet away, her eyes narrowing on the tunnel entrance.

But her gut told her the creature was making its move too. She could feel its presence, a shadow closing in just as she dashed for the tunnel.

Get there, Kiri! Come on!

Her muscles burned though she pressed against only air.

The last five feet she dove. Her hands reached for the hatch.

She struggled to throw the cover back, the lower corner snagged on something. It wouldn't budge. She wrestled with it, expecting an attack at any moment.

But the hatch would not move. She spun and rolled and came to a breathless crouch, scanning the darkening forest. The air was still. Nothing moved.

She bent down, fingers shaking, as she searched to release the trellis cover from whatever hindered it.

Foolish girl! She saw now and remembered. The root.

All of the sunbathing hatches had camouflaged triggers or latches on the outside. Shaking her head at her own fear, Kiri Lee knelt at the knobby root of an immense, old oak. She twisted the center segment of the root forward until she heard a dull click. Then, still feeling silly, she pried the door open.

All was well.

Until the shadow passed behind her again.

This time she spun around and yelped, seeing a lone figure standing beside the boulder she had sat atop.

Kiri Lee froze, suspended by fear.

By shock.

Blending with the dark shadow-play all around was a face. Distorted. Confused. But one she would never forget. The face of the boy who'd saved her life and forfeited his own.

"What's this about?" asked Tommy, rubbing his eyes. "Couldn't this wait another hour?"

"For real. I was having a dream about pizza," said Johnny. Then seeing Tommy's rueful expression. "Seriously, it's been so long."

Kiri Lee had pounded on the boys' door until they'd answered, then demanded they meet in two minutes in a secluded chamber further down their bedroom corridor. Then she roused Autumn and Kat, leaving Taeva alone, and led them on a sleepy walk to the meeting place.

"I know, I know," apologized Kiri Lee, "but you need to hear this."

"Go on," said Tommy. "We're here, aren't we?"

"I could not sleep, so I went above for some air. You know, clear my head, that kind of thing. I was thinking about everything we've been through, and preparing myself mentally for battle again. It's been a while for all of us, right?"

"Are we here to discuss your self-reflections on war, Kiri Lee?" asked Tommy.

"Man, I can'na believe this," said Jimmy. "I'm going back to me room."

"Me too," huffed Autumn.

"I saw Jett."

The Five looked at her.

"Not this again," said Jimmy. "It was a dream, Kiri Lee. Johnny dreams of pizza. You dream of Jett."

"Hey!" Autumn objected.

"In the forest this time," Kiri Lee explained. "He walked right up behind me."

Tommy ran his fingers through his curly hair. "Kiri Lee, don't you think you may have been dreaming? We already went over this."

"I'm telling you, Tommy. It was him. Nearly scared me to death. I saw a shadow, and made a mad dash for the tunnel entrance, thinking it was a wolf or a bear or something. And when I turned around, it was Jett. And it wasn't through a thick window this time."

"Are you absolutely sure?" Tommy asked. "I mean, we checked his grave, we asked the caretaker—"

"Do you think it's that easy for me to forget the face of the person who saved my life?" Kiri Lee looked at each of her friends in the eyes, willing them to believe. "Never. This time I'm telling you, it was him.

THE TIDE OF UNMAKING

He looked different. Confused. Not fully himself. In fact, I don't think he even recognized me. Before I could even think what to say, he was gone. But it was him."

Tommy looked around the room. Whatever sleepiness there was before, it was gone. His friends were all awake and sober-minded.

"You sure it wasn't a Wisp?" Kat asked. A few of the others nodded, as that was their conclusion from the alleged sighting in Berinfell.

"How would a Wisp have known exactly where to find me in the Thousand League Forest?" Kiri Lee replied. "Berinfell, sure. But up here? No way."

"But you said he didn't recognize you," said Kat. "Surely if it was Jett, he wouldn't have any trouble there. As you said, no one's going to forget an exchange like that."

"Unless he's brainwashed," said Johnny. The others looked at him. "You know? Or brain dead. Maybe, he never died at all, but he's so messed up that he doesn't really know anything, like amnesia."

"But...but we saw him die," Autumn whispered.

"That still doesn't explain the grave site," Kat said. "But it does explain why Caretaker Thrain was acting so funny. His thoughts were so scattered not even I could read them. I thought he was just in shock at having the Lords of Berinfell show up in the middle of the night; not exactly a routine visit."

"Do you think he was hiding something?" asked Autumn. "Maybe he knew Jett's grave was empty. Maybe he was trying to keep it from us."

"Why hide something like that?" asked Johnny.

"Because," Tommy said, trying to put all the pieces together, "who would ever trust him as a caretaker again? Having a Lord of Berinfell get exhumed on your watch isn't exactly the best thing for your resume."

The Six stood there, each pondering the rationality of it all. It felt more like a conspiracy theory than a viable plot, but Kiri Lee was family. And she was desperate. There was no way they were going to crush her hopes.

"As far as I'm concerned," Tommy said, "Jett's alive." He looked squarely at Kiri Lee. "But I'm sorry, Kiri Lee. We have our marching orders for Taladair, so we can't conduct a search ourselves."

As her head fell, her face disappeared behind a curtain of dark hair. "But..."

"However," Tommy went on, "we will make sure that a team of Nighstalkers stays behind to search the area."

"But what if they find 'im?" Jimmy asked. "What if Jett's not himself, and they fight?"

"They wouldn't stand a chance against Jett," Autumn said.

Tommy blinked. "There's no easy solution here. We just have to believe that Jett, even if he's not himself, would never turn violent against his own people."

"Yu'd better be right, Tommy," Jimmy said. "Yu'd better be right."

March of the Nightstalkers

GRIMWARDEN FEARED what they might find in the submerged wreckage of Taladair. *Watery graves, most likely,* he thought.

The intelligence, however, far outweighed whatever horrors waited beneath the surface. They needed a lead, a loose end that would give the Nightstalker army a tactical advantage in their pursuit of Asp. Yes, it was first and foremost a rescue mission, but the reconnaissance was vital.

And what to make of the supposed sightings of Jett? Goldarrow had relayed the story of Kiri Lee's first encounter in Berinfell. To have another such experience here in Nightwish was a little hard to dismiss as chance. Had it been a Wisp? Surely that was it. But if so, why had the creature come now after seven years? Up to no good, that much was assured.

But if not a Wisp, what then? Grimwarden didn't believe in ghosts, and the alternative was beyond his mind's boundaries to accept.

"I hope you slept well, my Lords," said Grimwarden stepping over the threshold to the lords' barracks. Goldarrow followed just behind.

"Aye, Guardmaster," Tommy said. "I slept well enough. To be honest, the coming mission made it hard. One moment I'm imagining our approach to Taladair, the first sighting of the enemy, and how we'll respond. The next, I'm running through Vexbane and Mandiera forms in my head. I don't feel tired, though."

"The lack of sleep is no small thing, Lord," Grimwarden said. But within, he thought it a good sign. *Mark of a true warrior, a leader,* he thought. "Perhaps you can rest after the first march."

Tommy grinned. "Nah, there'll be plenty of time to rest when we're dead."

"Hey!" Jimmy objected. "That's my line."

"And a morbid line at that," Goldarrow chided. "There's no cause for such talk, especially among Berinfell's Lords."

Tommy and Jimmy immediately began studying their boots. Each lad mumbled, "Sorry."

"What about you, Kiri Lee?" Goldarrow asked. "Did you sleep?"

She nodded. "I think after the shock of seeing…well, after the encounter, I think my adrenaline wore off. I crashed. Slept like a stone."

"Good," Goldarrow replied. "Be comforted. When we return from our mission, we will get to the bottom of this. Perhaps the Nightstalkers we've tasked with the search will turn up something."

Tommy looked up abruptly.

"Fear not, Tommy," Goldarrow said. "If it is Jett, the Nightstalkers will not engage him. They will tranquilize him."

Tommy sighed heavily. "I hope that works."

"Good to see that you have all dressed," Grimwarden said, purposefully changing the subject. "However, the attire you wore from Berinfell will not be suitable any longer. You need Nightstalker gear."

"Nightstalker gear?" Kiri Lee echoed.

"Indeed," Goldarrow replied. "Better by far than any armor you've ever worn."

"The Guardmaster says that only because she helped design it," Grimwarden explained. This earned him a slap on the shoulder from Goldarrow. "What I meant to say is that the Nightstalker gear is the finest in all of Allyra."

"Much better." Goldarrow crossed her arms.

"Yes, but is it fashionable?" Kiri Lee asked.

"I think you lived in Paris too long," Autumn said.

"In any case," Grimwarden grumbled, "you'll get your new gear after we eat."

"We seemed to have lost Princess Taeva, however," Kat said. The lady lords had dropped off to sleep one-by-one. But when they awoke early in the morning, Taeva was gone.

"Not to worry, Lord Alreenia," said Goldarrow. "She was summoned by Regis to go with Mr. Charlie and get outfitted for our expedition. Your sizes, for obvious reasons, are all well known to our seamstresses, even here in Nightwish. But Taeva arrived with only the clothes on her back. Our battle dress may be foreign to her, but even a sturdy pair of boots and a tightly woven cloak are universal assets to even the most foreign among us."

"Ah, we thought she'd run off," said Kat.

"Really?" inquired Grimwarden with the slightest sarcasm in his tone. "And where might she have *run off* to?"

"Well, not like that," Kat stammered. "We just wanted to make sure she was okay."

"Very good then," said Goldarrow. "Mumthers has—"

"Mumthers is here?" the Six exclaimed, each adding their own endearing comments to the news.

"As I was saying, Mumthers has prepared a small meal for us. Then you will receive your new gear."

Grimwarden said, "Eat well, and don't be shy about taking more than your fill. After this meal...we march to Taladair. And we will march hard."

"Small meal?" Tommy exclaimed, staring at the spread on the mess hall tables.

"Me and Autumn are no strangers to family cooking," Johnny said. "But not even Aunt Paula could put out a feast like this!"

"Not even close," Autumn confirmed.

"Oh, it's nothing much," Mumthers said. She was as portly an Elf as one might find in Allyra, but she was still a cyclone in the kitchen. She beamed at the Six, her warm, coffee eyes sparkling. She smiled with such infectious kindness that even Drefids might use proper table manners with Mumthers around.

"It is a banquet!" Kiri Lee said, her eyes locking onto the desserts.

"Now, aren't you kind, dearie," Mumthers said. "But you shouldn't go on so. This is just a few things really: roasted gessette haunches, herb-rubbed boar off the spits, racks of kurgan stag ribs, sweet Amberwood corn on the cob, rushes of red potato shingles deep fried in goose fat, crushed gickers in scallion and garlic gravy—rosco sauce too—sage bread with chive butter, steamed spiral beans, spreadatch fresh from the garden with ripe bloomatoes, oh…and muffle cakes, mallow-brownies, cinnamon-nutmeg twisty loafs, chocolate-chip, scarlet berry cookies, ketelo fruit, and splendine punch. Like I said, nothing to go on about."

The Six practically tackled Mumthers, showering her with love, appreciation and gratitude. Then, they dove for the tables.

Johnny had a steaming spiral bean half way to his mouth, but when Mumthers shouted, "WAIT THIS MINUTE!" it threw off his bean accuracy. The curling, green legume went an inch up his nose.

"Don't even think about eating," Mumthers commanded, "lest you give Ellos thanks first."

With his cheeks burning, Tommy led the assembly in a prayer of thanks for all the provisions. At the end of the thanksgiving, the Six tore into the food, each of them only too happy to heed Grimwarden's advice. They knew it might be their last good meal for some time, and they'd learned long ago to savor food and company when presented.

After saying their goodbyes to Mumthers, the Six descended into the arsenal where their battledress awaited. Each of them were fitted with new, black, hardened-leather helmets and articulated breastplates, each piece reflecting Goldarrow's design. They donned thick war cloaks of a purple so deep it was nearly black, and laced up soft leather boots with metal nose caps. Wide belts wrapped their waists and held protective plating over their upper thighs.

The armor and fabrics were surprising light and unrestrictive, yet unquestionably resilient, something Grimwarden insisted the new designs have in order to pair well with the Mandiera fighting style. When clothed, each of the Six felt like an armored, black shadow, able to step in and out of view, and amply protected from even the heaviest of blows.

"Very nice," said Johnny, flexing his larger biceps and admiring the craftsmanship. "But will it burn?" He looked to Grimwarden, then Goldarrow.

"Try it," Grimwarden suggested.

Johnny summoned a small flame in his right hand and picked up the corner of his cloak in his left. Like spouting napalm from a blowtorch, Johnny poured a sticky blast onto the garment fully expecting to see it consumed. To his disbelief the fire not only didn't take, but was completely extinguished.

He looked back to Grimwarden. "I don't understand. I mean, I've never—"

"A recent discovery," Grimwarden said, cocking an eyebrow. "On the western edge of the Thousand League Forest, there was a substantial fire. The Elves there managed to quench it. But in the charred ruin, I found a peculiar moss growing on the verdigen stone there. It hadn't been so much as singed by the blaze. Goldarrow ground up the moss and made a resin from it. We treated all of your gear with the stuff. Thought you'd like it."

"LOVE it," replied Johnny. "Just so long as my enemies don't figure it out."

"Oh, they won't. This one lives and dies with us Elves. Your whole battledress acts the same way, as do all of yours," Grimwarden indicated the others with his hand. "Just in case there are any *accidents*." Johnny was about to protest. "Not that Johnny would accidentally roast anyone." Grimwarden raised his hands in mock defense.

From there, the team moved into the armory. Tommy was handed a brilliant new bow of black yew, and three quivers of ironwood arrows. "Tipped with dremask," said Grimwarden. "Just to make sure whatever you shoot down *stays* down."

Each member was given a sleeker version of the rychesword; lighter, faster, and sharper. It reminded the Six of a Samurai blade. Only this sword was completely black, without the faintest hint of metallic reflection. "So it won't give away your location if shown in the light," Grimwarden said as he angled a blade beside a dremask brazier.

Their belts were fitted with a small medical kit - something they never had to worry about when Jett was around - as well as a black dagger that looked like a miniature version of their Mandieran rycheswords.

Lastly they were each given a backpack to fit underneath their cloaks. The packs were stuffed with food rations, water, bedding and a waterproof, tear-proof map of the known lands of Allyra.

"What's this?" asked Kat. She held up a second map and unfolded it.

"Ah," said Goldarrow, "I think you'll recognize it."

Kat's eyes went wide as the familiar lines of North America unfolded before her. The Six each unfolded their own maps with equal awe. It had been so long since they'd seen a map of Earth. Kat's memories of public school came rushing back: the smells of the locker room, the sounds of the cafeteria and the dry, grating voice of her Earth Science teacher as he droned on about sedimentary rock and tectonic plates.

"I don't understand," said Kat.

"To be honest, we're not sure where this adventure will take us," said Grimwarden. "Nor how long we'll be gone. So we've tried to prepare for the unexpected, even if that means returning to Earth."

Even hearing Grimwarden mention such a possibility was startling.

Go back to Earth? Tommy could scarcely consider the thought. After all, he'd spent the better part of seven years convincing himself that he'd never be able to go back.

The Six had each toyed with the idea in their own way, but with the portals closed, and their memories slowly fading, it had turned more into fleeting fiction than pending probability.

Grimwarden and Goldarrow led the Six back up to city's center, and stood on the same dais nearest the river that they had arrived on so many years ago. The entire city spread out around them, and then grew up along the walls. Taeva and Overlord Bengfist waited there on the open terrace with Mr. Charlie and Regis.

Taeva's dark complexion, mingled with the shadowy effects of the Mandieran battledress made her even more striking...even more mysterious.

"Looking good!" Johnny said.

"Why, thank you, Lord Albriand," Taeva said, running her hands down her leather plate armor, "though it feels a bit cumbersome on me."

"Not a bit," said Jimmy. "Looks smart on yu. On both of you," he glanced over to Regis. She seemed a bit surprised, and Jimmy had to look away, then forgot about Mr. Charlie. "Beggin' yur pardon, Mr. Charlie; I should have included yu too. You look—"

"Here now!" interrupted Mr. Charlie. "A man knows when he's surrounded by beauty: he's always the last to get complimented. And I'm right fine with that, son; don't ya' dare go there."

Everyone chuckled.

"Right yu are," said Jimmy. "Not a word more on that."

"And no compliments for me?" Bengfist feigned grumbling.

"Why, your Overlordship," said Autumn with her best Gone-With-The-Wind, southern drawl, "I do declare, the armor makes you look like you have muscles on top of muscles."

Bengfist, half bemused, laughed and blushed—and even took a brief bow. Everyone laughed even harder now as Bengfist admitted he'd rather stay in his own battledress than adopt some "Elven tree garb."

Finally Grimwarden stepped forward. "It's time," he said. "Goldarrow?"

"Right away sir," she said, then signaled to a set of guards to the far side of the open terrace where they stood.

A moment later, blasts sounded from the battle horns high above. The Six waited, listening, until they heard the sounds of marching. Footfalls echoed from deep within the Caverns, rising up like the chorus of a thousand drums beating in quarter-note rhythm. Soon the passage started filling with soldiers, Elves dressed from head to foot in the same Mandieran uniforms that the Six wore. They flowed into the city center, and then spilled out into the tunnels and byways.

Tommy and the others expected the procession to end any second. But it didn't. The Elves kept coming and coming and coming. There seemed to be even more than those present at their arrival the night before.

"So many," Kat whispered aloud.

"Aye," said Jimmy, shaking his head.

"Just shy of five-thousand to be precise," said Grimwarden.

"A legion?" asked Tommy.

"Indeed," Grimwarden smiled.

The footfalls stopped, and soon there was the pregnant pause of a legion of Elven warriors waiting with anticipation for instructions from their leader. From their Guardmaster.

Grimwarden felt keenly that this would be the last time they would ever see Nightwish. Abandoning the underground was evidence of success; that was not what concerned him. Rather, he feared that there were many Elves standing before him who—when this was all over—would never see Berinfell or even Allyra again.

"They are yours to address," Grimwarden said to Tommy with a bow.

"On the contrary," Tommy smiled, "I believe it's you they need to hear from. I insist, Grimwarden." Tommy glanced at the other Five who all nodded. "We all insist."

"Very well," said Grimwarden, pulling himself upright. He turned to the waiting throng and swallowed. As everyone knew, public speaking wasn't his specialty—public *yelling*, perhaps—but not public speaking.

"So here we are," Grimwarden began, his commanding voice echoing throughout the main cavern. "Each of you trained, each of you tested. Berinfell's elite. I say without hesitation, Allyra's elite. And I of all people am the most honored, knowing I have the privilege of beholding your greatness. Your bravery. Your fortitude.

"For these last seven years you have paid a dear price. Stolen away from your families with no other reason than your country had need of you. Your world had need of you. No promise of ever returning. You've lived in secret, and given yourselves to the ways of Ellos. You've invested in Mandiera as if your lives depended on it. For indeed they do; but more so, the lives of those we will never live to meet. The generations beyond.

"And so I say again: here we are. Committed to pursuing the plague of evil to the furthest realms, and even into realms beyond if we must. We will pursue the darkness, we will pursue the night until it has nowhere to hide. Nowhere to run. We are the Nightstalkers!"

The army raised their Mandieran rycheswords and shouted as one. Their deafening cheer seemed to shake the walls of Nightwish like a seismic ground tremor. Then, without provocation, and in perfect unison, they dropped their sword arms such that they crossed wrists over their chests. And together they shouted, "ENDURANCE AND VICTORY!"

Tommy felt as if an electrical current raced through the cavern, touching each with power beyond measure. He looked to Grimwarden, saw him blinking in astonished pride. The Guardmaster looked to Tommy and shook his head.

Tommy said, "I know."

Johnny leaned over and whispered something to Tommy. When they parted, Johnny said, "Well, can I?"

Tommy felt like a massive bubble ready to burst. There was a thrill racing through him that he could not explain...something far beyond chills and goosebumps...something supernatural.

"May Ellos guide your hands, Johnny," Tommy said. "Give them all something to remember."

Johnny stepped forward. He held up his hands, and the caverns fell silent. Johnny glanced back at the Lords and the others. "You might want to step back a bit," he said.

They did. Only Taeva remained where she was, but Autumn grabbed her arm and yanked her back.

Just then, Johnny made fists and slammed his elbows down hard to his sides. With a primal yell, he threw his hands up in the air once more. When he opened his fingers, there came a white-orange flash that left everyone blinking. Heat washed over the balcony, and the air around Johnny's hand shimmered like a heat mirage.

Ten inches from his outstretched fingers, a pulsing golden flame surged toward the cavern ceiling. Johnny grunted and clenched his teeth with the effort. Soon, waves of fire seemed to be gushing upward, and the darkness of Nightwish Caverns fled into the farthest corners and crevices. An undulating sea of golden flame coursed on the ceiling, and every being who witnessed it gasped in awe. It swirled around the base of every stalactite and even consumed each point.

"FOR ELLOS!" Johnny bellowed, and he cut off the flow of fire.

The roaring ocean of flame ebbed, receded, and disappeared in moments. The Elves gasped once more, perhaps even more deeply, for the flames had found the veins of a dozen different metals hidden in the ceiling's stone. The metal ore glowed white hot or blue or green or even a florescent purple—and it streaked across the cavern ceiling like multicolored lightning.

"To Taladair!" Tommy yelled, drawing his rychesword. "May our enemies tremble at the coming of Ellos' army! To Taladair!"

The Nightstalkers answered, and the march began.

The Elven army made good time, traveling by foot through the upper reaches of the Thousand League Forest. They surged east of the Spine, and arrived by nightfall of the third day at the northern coast of Berinfell. Even Bengfist managed to keep pace with the fleet-footed Elves. They slept for only three hours in the port city of Kileverand before conscripting the city's entire fleet of war ships and setting off in the middle of the night.

"Due north," Tommy told the Admiral of the Elven fleet.

"As you wish, my lord," replied Admiral Cuth, never one to argue with the Lords of Berinfell...or any paying customers for that matter, though he did give them a deal on account of seeing Grimwarden once again. "The skies are calling for fair winds by morning, holding steady for the week. The fleet should arrive in two days."

"Thank you, Admiral. Your services are greatly appreciated," said Tommy.

"As is your presence among us, Lord Felheart."

The Six and Princess Taeva made themselves comfortable in the bow of the lead ship, admiring the endless views of the ocean and the dolphins that accompanied their advance in the heat of day. The afternoon winds were strong and steady, allowing them a broad reach due north toward Taladair.

For her part, Taeva was pleased to have found a number of Taladrim sailors in Kileverand who'd been at sea when Asp struck. Having no port to come home to, and being too late to find anything worth rescuing, they took their leave in Admiral Cuth's service, their own ships all but destroyed from Asp's far-reaching storm. Thus, upon seeing the Princess and her company arrive at the port city, they were only too happy to pledge themselves to her service and join the rescue mission.

The first night aboard was rough, as the winds from the afternoon heat had stirred up the seas to an unsettling height. More than one forest Elf spent the evening heaving into the salt water and wishing that the planks they slept upon were those of a tree-ensconced house. And it soon became a running joke that Overlord Bengfist said and repeated, "Even if the alternative is to burn, I will never step aboard another ship for as long as I live."

Jimmy, in fact, developed a rather convincing impersonation of Bengfist. Stomping unsteadily around the deck, Jimmy crowed nervously, "When can I get off this sea-going demon?"

Even Bengfist himself had a laugh at that.

Precious few Nightstalkers, only those who had grown up near the coast, seemed to enjoy the night hours, rocked to sleep by the methodical shifting of the waves.

Even through the midnight hours, the fleet edged further north under light winds. By morning, their pace improved considerably, and the ships were carving their course more swiftly than even Admiral Cuth had anticipated.

"At this rate we should make Taladair by evening next," he said to the group gathered at the bow. "Clear skies and the sun on our faces, now you see why we live for these conditions."

"Aye," said Jimmy, thinking back to his fond days sailing in Ardfern. "As soon as we're doon with this Asp fellow, I'll be back for a wee sail if that's all right with yu, Admiral Cuth."

"My ship is ever at your disposal, Lord Thorwin," the Admiral said with a slight bow. To the group he said, "If you'll excuse me," and then left the foredeck and made his way aft.

"They'll be no diving on Taladair tonight," said Goldarrow.

"She's right," said Taeva. "We'll need as much light as we can. Wait until morning tomorrow."

But Grimwarden was shaking his head. "We can't afford to wait that long."

"Guardmaster," said Tommy, "you know I'm not one to question your wisdom, but do you think pushing the army this hard is prudent? Diving at night?"

"I don't think we have much of a choice, Tommy. Every minute that we delay, a civilian below may meet death in the catacombs. And every minute that we delay, Asp is advancing his plans, perhaps swallowing other cities in his misplaced wrath. While these facts might not move the Conclave, they certainly move me. We have a foe more dangerous than the Spider King, and unlike him, Asp does not seem tied to any one location. There seems no Vesper Crag upon which to focus our might. He's on the move and leaving a swath of decimated, innocent lives in his wake."

"How exactly do you propose we dive in the dark then, Guardmaster Grimwarden?" asked Taeva.

"With this," he said, producing a small chunk of dremask. "We Elves have been using it for generations, mined from deep within the Nightwish Caverns."

"A bit of rock?"

"You'll see," said Johnny. "It's pretty cool stuff. But not quite as cool as the light I make, and my flames always works underwater too."

He opened his palm, revealing a rotating ball of fire.

"Impressive," said Taeva with an odd, knowing grin. It seemed almost as if she and Johnny shared a secret.

A few minutes later, Tommy took Johnny aside and asked, "What's that about? All the grins?"

Johnny blushed and shrugged. "Not sure," he said. "Must be she likes me."

Just as the sun began its evening decent, Taeva rose suddenly from her late afternoon nap and stared intently at the horizon.

Tommy and the others had seen her jump up.

"What is it?" Regis asked. "What do you see?"

Taeva looked to the heavens, then back down to the South. And finally out to the East to confirm her suspicions.

"We've come to Taladair," she said. "My homeland."

"What?" The others leaped to their feet.

"I can feel it," Taeva said, her voice strained and cracking. "We've arrived."

"Already?" said Mr. Charlie, stretching. His eyes were puffy and half open. "Dang gum it, I was about on to my third nap of the day."

A young Nightstalker laughed nearby. He and Charlie both had missed the grim reality in Taeva's words.

Grimwarden made her look at him. "You're sure?" he demanded.

"Without question," Taeva said, suddenly holding her hands to her heart. Her eyes were looking somewhere off.

"She really does feel it," Kat whispered to Grimwarden.

"Oh, no," Kiri Lee whispered through her fingers. She gazed at the open water. "Does this mean? The city...an entire city cannot just vanish beneath the waters...can it?"

"Admiral!" Grimwarden shouted. The Admiral looked to him from the helm. Grimwarden made a circular motion with his fist. Before the Admiral could even give an order, the Elves had already read the Guardmaster's communication, and the ship became a bustle of activity.

Admiral Cuth shouted routine orders down the ranks of his commanding officers. All but two of the main sails were doused and stowed, unused lines were secured, and the anchor and anchor lines were readied.

"Princess Taeva, we'll need you at the helm to guide us in," said Grimwarden.

"Yes," she replied, her eyes coming back to here and now on the boat. "I can manage. We'll have to sail through the reef. Once we're through, we'll be in shallower waters and within range of the—" she cleared her throat, "—the bottom of the city inside the old walls."

Grimwarden escorted her aft while the Six, Goldarrow, Regis, and Mr. Charlie followed. Arriving at the helm, Taeva asked the Admiral, "Do you mind?"

Glancing from her to the wheel and back to her, he looked surprised. "Uh, no, Princess, not at all." To his First Mate, he announced, "Princess Taeva has the ship."

"THE Princess HAS THE SHIP," repeated the First Mate, followed by a third echo of the announcement further down the vessel.

Taeva grasped the wheel with two hands and planted her feet on the deck. "Signal the boats to follow me in single file. Do exactly as I do. The channel through the reef is quite narrow."

"Understood," said the Admiral, then relayed a message up the mast to the lookout.

Taeva narrowed her eyes, then sent the ship hard to starboard. At once the men trimmed the sails to match and waited for Taeva's next move. One by one the fleet slowed and then came in line with the lead ship, following Taeva's eager course. Meanwhile Taeva watched the waters of the port bow with keen interest.

"You see there," she pointed.

"Where?" Kiri Lee asked. "I see only waves."

"No, she's right," said Jimmy. "About a hundred yards out, there's a slight change in the water. Almost…almost like it's shallow."

"I see it," said the Admiral.

"That's because *it is* shallow," said Taeva. "It's the reef."

Confirming her assessment from on high came the voice of the lookout: "REEF OFF THE PORT BOW, FIFTY FATHOM LENGTHS."

"Well, I'll be," said Mr. Charlie. "And here we would have—"

"Been dashed to pieces," said Admiral Cuth. "Fine sailing Princess. Fine sailing, indeed."

"We're not through yet," said the Princess. "Taldrim ships aren't this big." She glanced down. Weren't *is the proper tense now. All those beautiful ships, gone,* she thought. *All those beautiful people…*

"It's all right," said Kat as she placed a hand on Taeva's back. "You can do this."

Taeva was about as surprised as the others. But Kat had seen what she'd missed before. Her jealousy had shielded it from view. Taeva cared about her people, just as Kat cared about the Elves. It was no different.

"It's the depth I'm worried about," said the Princess. "When we pass through the channel up ahead, it's narrow, but these ships should manage. It's how much they *draw* that should concern us all."

"Any chance we could anchor here outside the reef?" asked Jimmy.

"I'm afraid not. These waters are too deep, and we'd risk being smashed up against the reef even if we did have enough line. Plus I wouldn't recommend swimming over the reef unless you like summoning sharks with the scent of your blood."

"Inside the reef," Jimmy said. "Inside the reef works."

Taeva slowly brought the ship northward back into a broad reach. Then she gave the command.

"READY ABOUT!"

The crew sprang to action, holding lines and preparing for the second call to bring the ship about to port.

"HARD TO WIND!"

The ship lurched to port as Taeva spun the wheel to starboard. The crew shouted, and the sails billowed. Elves raced across the deck from starboard to port, scampering like mice in a room full of cats. The bow moved across the horizon until the sails filled with wind again, snapping their booms tight against the main sheets. They were heading straight for the reef.

The Six could feel the acceleration of the ship as it sped off toward the southwest. They marveled at Taeva's sailing skills, as did the Admiral who was clearly pleased that his vessel was not so large and ungainly for the Princess in spite of her initial claims.

"Ensure they follow my course exactly," Taeva reminded the Admiral. He had the First Mate holler up to the lookout once more.

Taeva read the water like a scribe reads parchment scrolls. Her eyes scanned the waves incessantly, and then moved from the horizon to her sails. She made constant adjustments to the wheel: three pegs to starboard, two to port, two more to port, six to starboard, and so on.

"She's bringing us in by feel," said Admiral Cuth to the group gathered behind him, never taking his eyes off the Princess. "Incredible. Never seen anything like it."

"Hold on," Taeva finally said.

"What? Why?" said Grimwarden.

"I said hold on. This might be a little rough. We need more sail!"

"MORE SAIL!" said the Admiral.

"MORE SAIL!" said the First Mate. "RAISE THE FORESTAYSAIL!"

The crew set to work, lines flying and fabric billowing. The sail flew up in mere seconds. Taeva hoped the burst of speed would be enough. She glanced behind their ship.

"Make sure they do the same!" She pointed to the vessels behind them. "AND TELL THAT ONE TO GET IN OUR LINE!"

A beat later, the Admiral's ship lost enough momentum that everyone stumbled forward. A sickening sound ground across the keel from stem to stern. "Come on!" Taeva shouted to the ship. "Keep going!"

More grinding emanated from under the hull. Tommy and the others were beyond worry. They looked to the Admiral, but instead of concern the Admiral was smiling.

"Admiral?" Tommy inquired.

But the man waved him off and continued to glance between the sails and Taeva. To himself he muttered, "Fascinating."

Finally the last scrape traveled the length of the ship, and a moment later the boat was free of the reef and moving through clean water.

Shouting went up from behind them. Everyone on the bridge looked aft. The third vessel back had foundered, striking the reef on the port side and listing to leeward.

"Admiral," said Taeva, offering the helm back to him and with a wave of her hand. "She's all yours."

"I have the helm."

"ADMIRAL HAS THE SHIP," called the First Mate.

"The good news is we made it through," said Taeva.

"A formidable sailer you are," said the Admiral. "And the bad news?"

"We'll be the only ship through until that boat is burned," she pointed backward.

"It can't be salvaged?" asked Grimwarden.

"Sir, I've grown up in these waters; no ship has ever made it off the reef."

"Then burning it will have to be handled by you, Admiral," said Grimwarden. "We don't have time. We'll take a small team down and find what we can. You burn any ship that can't be salvaged. Tell the rest of the fleet to steer clear of the reef. There's no telling what or who we'll find, so getting a clear and quick route out of here will be essential."

"Understood, Guardmaster," said the Admiral. "We'll be ready."

Diving on the Dead

THE RUINED realm of Taladair waited beneath the waters. On the surface, the sea was peaceful and calm, undisturbed, as if a great city had never been there at all. But just a glance into the depths would tell a far different story. Each of the Elves geared up for the dive, preparing the mind was another matter entirely.

It was decided that Tommy, Jimmy, Johnny, Kat, Grimwarden and Goldarrow would follow Taeva through the wreckage of Taladair and to the entrance of the catacombs. From there, the team would attempt to gain entry into an airlock that Taeva described as the entrance of the catacombs, and then see what hope there was to discover. If there were in fact survivors, as Grimwarden had projected, a second team would then come down to relieve the first and rotate through the night until all were rescued.

Admiral Cuth produced a chest of flippers and crude underwater breathing devices that fit over the head. Taeva looked at the strange apparatus. The bulbous, bronze helmet had a glass face and a protruding filter over the mouth.

"It's filled with terrock moss," the Admiral said. "Produces something similar to the air we breathe when it gets wet. Probably not as efficient as what you're used to, Princess, but it will do the job."

Taeva hefted the helmet over her head and secured the collar snuggly around her neck; it seemed counterintuitive, like being strangled, but she understood it'd keep the water out.

"You'll get about twenty minutes out of the stuff before we need to pack it with new moss," said the Admiral. "Remember, *twenty minutes*." Taeva nodded. To the rest of the team, he continued: "And if you find anything worth saving down there, we'll have plenty of these," the Admiral produced a resilient material that the Six thought resembled a black garbage bag. "Open one up underwater and the moss inside will fill the bag with enough air for three adults to breathe and ascend to the surface. Like sticking your head inside a balloon and holding onto the sides."

Once the team was outfitted, they jumped overboard and gathered for the dive. The water was warmer than the team expected, except for Taeva, of course. Upon contact with the water, each diver's dremask torch sputtered to life. They plunged beneath the surface and breathed in the mossy air of their helmets.

The team descended slowly upon the remains of the island city, their torches casting a pale blue aura around each diver, like lightning bugs flying through a dark summer night.

When Taeva began to see the first signs of ruins, she could feel her heart quicken, the sights threatening to strangle her. To others, it might just seem like a random spread of rubble, but for Taeva, it was all that was left of her home. She realized she knew the street she was hovering above. She even knew the cottage. It belonged to Laurice's, a dear childhood friend. Where had Laurice been when the walls came down?

Next door was the Thruvions' home, a childless couple who always opened their doors—and larders—to the neighborhood children. And across the street was Taeva's favorite bakery. And three doors down was the tannery, then the lower barracks, and...and...

Taeva coughed, bubbles engulfing her. She suddenly felt trapped, like the ocean was caving in on her. The surface was too far away. She couldn't make it. She tried to fight the emotions rising in her chest, but they were too strong. Bile filled her mouth, and she forced herself to swallow it, thinking she might drown on her own spittle if she didn't.

Suddenly a hand touched her. She wanted to shout, to kick and scream. But the hand seemed gentle. Authentic. Taeva turned to see Kat's face covered in glass and the glow of blue light casting deep shadows over her features.

"It's okay, Taeva," Kat spoke to Taeva's heart. *"I'm right here with you. Just breathe in and out. Slowly. Breathe…in and out. You cool?"*

Taeva didn't understand the last part.

"Ah, forgive me," said Kat's voice, now light…almost merry. *"It's an Earth expression. It means, are you all right?"*

Taeva didn't know if she could speak so clearly without using words like Kat could, so she nodded. Then tried one word: *Thanks.*

Kat nodded. *"You're welcome."*

The two turned and continued on, gliding over the city.

Homes had been decimated, buildings collapsed, and debris strewn in every possible locale. It wasn't until the bodies started to appear that the rest of the team felt the same terror that Taeva had just experienced.

Any of the deceased from the initial explosions and resulting flooding were washed away to sea. But far more of the Taladrim were trapped beneath the wreckage. It was these unfortunate souls that the team saw now: arms protruding from underneath large stone fragments that had crushed their torsos; bloated fingers grasping for rescue that came too late; faces staring off into eternity with mouths gaping wide in horror. The sites were so disturbing that even Grimwarden, who had seen more death than any of the Elves, had to avert his eyes.

"Keep going," Kat said to Taeva, even her thought-voice tremulous. *"I'm right behind you. We're all right behind you."*

Taeva swam on, now heading for the center of the island, descending to the lower-most portion of the upside-down shield that was her beloved homeland.

A tall spire rose in front of her...the remains of her tower. Where it had poked above the water when she left, it was half its size and fully submerged, presumably suffering more damage from the tireless onslaught of the ocean in just a few short days.

Taeva motioned the team onward, indicating the remains of a building on the backside of what appeared to be the palace. Swimming around the building, Taeva drew close to what had been the main entrance. But it was blocked by fragments of the spire, never to be moved by Taladrim hands again. She pointed down, indicating where they needed to go.

It was Grimwarden who began working at what he thought was a side window, or at least a hole that might be big enough for everyone to get through if he could just pry lose the column that lay against it. Tommy and Jimmy swam over and lent their backs to pushing away the pillar. Dust clouded their vision, but the column finally gave and fell away. Once the sediment cleared, Grimwarden held a torch up to a two-foot by two-foot hole just big enough to swim through. Bravely, Taeva swam over and entered first.

Once inside, the team found a very different scene. They hovered through a dimly-lit palatial vestibule, left almost entirely intact. A brilliantly colored rug rested on the marble floor while a golden chandelier swung above, still half-filled with candles. Though askew, large portraits hung on the walls, faces of the deceased. Taladrim flags draped over railings and curtain-rods fluttered, as if an eerie breeze still stirred their fated threads.

Taeva summoned everyone forward with a wave, urging them deeper into the building and through at least three sets of twin doors. Soon, however, the path became less obvious as she took turns away from what appeared to be the main corridors. They grimaced as they swam under more than a few bloated bodies, corpses still filled with air pockets that pressed them to the ceiling like macabre balloons.

Grimwarden busied his thoughts with practical matters. He touched the filter of moss in front of his mouth; he guessed it had another twelve. Probably less. They'd have to keep moving quickly.

Now Taeva was swimming down staircases, switching back and forth, plunging deeper and deeper into Taladrim's core. Eventually, they spilled out into an ample sized room designated by two guards that lay against the ceiling, spears still in hand. Taeva seemed focused on them until Kat summoned her thoughts back.

"Is that the vault door?" Kat asked her.

Taeva looked over to Kat. *Yes, that's it.*

Kat motioned to Tommy and the others. *"Down there,"* she told all of them. *"It's the entryway."*

The team approached the solid metal door and Grimwarden examined the large hand-wheel that sealed the cover shut. He was about to try it when he noticed a dial in the center of the wheel.

This is a most unfortunate development, he thought.

"What is it?" Kat swam up.

They locked the door. Grimwarden pointed to the deceased guards above.

There was a third body floating beside the guards…a much smaller corpse. Tommy eyed it carefully, trying to see past the fog clinging to the inside of his mask. He squinted. It was a child, holding a toy, face frozen in a blank stare. His back tingled as if an icicle dripped down his spine.

Kat saw also. *"Focus!"* she demanded of them all. *"Focus, or we'll be no good to anyone."*

Kat immediately called to Taeva, *"There's a dial lock. It needs a combination. Any ideas?"*

Taeva looked as surprised and frustrated as Grimwarden. *A*

combination of numbers? I...I...have no idea!

Tommy edged closer and put his hands up in a questioning gesture as if to ask what was the matter. Kat explained the appearance of the combination lock to him, then Jimmy and Goldarrow.

"*Whatever we do, we better do it quick,*" Kat said to everyone. "*We're nearing the threshold where we won't have enough air to get us back topside.*"

"*Taeva?*" asked Kat.

I'm sorry, I really have no—

"*You need to try, Taeva. You're the only one. And if there really are survivors behind this door, you have to try for them, for the remnant of your people.*"

Lord Alreenia, I don't even know who set the combination in the first place let alone what it might be. Maybe it's on those guards.

"*You know as well as I do the guards would never keep it on them. Try, Taeva. And you can call me Kat. Just Kat.*"

All right. But—

"*Try.*"

The team pushed away as Taeva grabbed the wheel and looked at the dial. She didn't move for at least a minute.

Kat could hear the team's nervous thoughts...they feared they might be added to the number of this underwater tomb if they didn't end this first dive soon. She was just about to reach for Taeva when the Princess started turning the dial.

The clicks were loud and clear underwater. She spun the dial slowly. The team watched each number pass the large arrow at the top of the collar. Suddenly Taeva stopped and started the other way, the clicks continuing their steady delineation. Back the original direction, Taeva continued halfway around the dial before finally ending on "72."

With both hands firmly on the wheel, she tried turning it.

It didn't budge.

"*We have to go back,*" Kat said. "*You can taste the air getting stale, thin.*"

Wait, thought Grimwarden. He placed his hands beside Taeva's and joined with her. Suddenly the wheel broke free and started to move.

"You did it!" cried Kat, shaking Taeva's shoulder from behind. Taeva lost her grip and slid sideways in the water. Both girls faced each other and smiled. *"Well done, Taeva."*

Grimwarden finished turning the wheel and then pulled the steel door toward them. It groaned loudly, the sound shooting back up the stairways and down the corridors. The Guardmaster held his torch out in front of him to reveal a long chamber a little wider and taller than the dimensions of the door.

It's an air lock, Kat heard Grimwarden say in his mind. *Tell everyone to get inside quick.* And then a thought reserved only for himself and the God he served: *Ellos, help us. If this doesn't work, we are all dead.*

Kat relayed the instructions (minus Grimwarden's concern) and everyone swam in. Jimmy pulled the door shut and worked the inner wheel back the other direction. Meanwhile Grimwarden searched for the lock mechanism: a switch, a lever, another wheel—anything.

Just as Kat sensed he was about to start panicking himself—something she'd never seen him do—a roaring, mechanical *kuh-thunk-thunk-thunk* began grinding beneath them.

Moments later, Taeva pointed to the ceiling. The water level was lowering. Soon they found themselves head and shoulders above water.

"Let me try the air first," Grimwarden said from behind his round, glass mask. "Just to make sure it's breathable." The team nodded and Grimwarden removed his helmet. He took a deep breath, exhaled, then inhaled again. He waited a moment longer, testing his balance and vision. Satisfied he gave the go-ahead.

The team removed their helmets and congratulated each other. "This is incredible!" said Jimmy.

"I've never been in anything like this," said Kat. "Just amazing." The small corridor had a brushed metal ceiling and walls, while the floor was grated with iron slats.

"So what was the combination, Taeva?" asked Goldarrow. "I'm curious."

"Bet it was her birthday," said Jimmy.

"My birthday?" asked Taeva. "Why would—"

"Never mind," Jimmy waved, forgetting many of the Allyrian races didn't mark their birthdays with dated numbers.

"So what was it?" Tommy asked.

"Random numbers really," she said. "I could just hear the mechanics more clearly underwater, that's all."

"Very clever of you," said Goldarrow. "Clever, clever girl."

"Now, that's brilliant," said Jimmy.

Grimwarden spoke up. "Lords, we need to find out who's behind this door."

"Right you are," said Jimmy. "Let's do this."

Grimwarden offered the wheel to Taeva but she declined. "It should be you, Grimwarden. I'm not sure I can handle any more—"

The Guardmaster raised a hand. "No more needs to be said, Taeva. I understand." Grimwarden began spinning the wheel. He thought that perhaps people would be gathered on the other side, hoping he would hear their gasps of surprise at the wheel moving on their side.

But nothing sounded. Just the groan of a poorly oiled spindle releasing pressure on the hatch.

When the door was released, Grimwarden eased it back, standing aside. He purposefully left his dagger behind, figuring even the sight of a visual threat might provoke any survivors to paranoia; plus his hands were weapons enough for anything he'd encounter down here.

"After you," whispered Tommy.

Grimwarden moved over the threshold and into what appeared to be and smelled like a damp cave. The immediate good news was that the cave wasn't flooded and that the air quality was still good. Grimwarden's dremask torch cast long shadows down the rocky floor of unfinished stone. The team followed behind him, each trying to keep their breathing quiet...listening...hoping.

Kat could hear each of the team members reasoning as they walked.

No signs of life, but someone had to be down here.

If not, why were there two guards stationed in the entryway?

Why was the door locked?

Johnny held a fiery fist aloft, casting more light into the tunnel from the far rear.

Eventually the team emerged into to a large chamber, the ceiling of which was almost out of reach of their lights.

"HELLO..." announced Grimwarden, his voice bouncing off the walls and disappearing down an infinite combination of sub-tunnels.

Nothing stirred.

"Johnny," Tommy nudged him, indicating the ceiling. Johnny aimed a blast of his liquid fire at the center. The napalm-like stream stuck, casting a warm, organic glow throughout the hall.

"Look there," Jimmy pointed. Casks and seaweed bags were strewn about the room on a sandy floor.

"Rations," said Taeva.

Grimwarden knelt beside them. "Someone's been here recently," he said. "Fresh footprints."

"So it seems some of your people did survive after all," said Kat. Taeva's chest drew in a deep breath as she reached for Kat's hand. Kat froze, unsure of how to respond to the Princess's sudden display of affection.

"Let's not get ahead of ourselves," said Tommy, fingering through a barrel of moldy grain. "I'm guessing these rations weren't as fresh as their providers might have intended."

From a few paces ahead, Grimwarden held his dremask torch close to the sand. "Seems the majority of the tracks head down this tunnel here." He indicated a branch where the ceiling was just about shoulder-height.

"Keep your ears and eyes peeled," said Tommy. "Let's move."

The group started down the offshoot from the main chamber, their footfalls absorbed by the soft floor. The only sounds were the occasional bronze helmet bouncing off the narrowing granite walls or someone clearing a throat. The path itself was random, long straightaways followed by sudden switchbacks, and odd climbs over, under or around giant rock outcroppings. At last the passage seemed to be opening up again.

Grimwarden was just about to ask for Johnny's flames when a knife shot out from beside him, jabbing him in the soft part of the shoulder beneath his leather armor.

He clamped the blade in the muscle, then twisted his torso, wresting the blade from his assailant. His rychesword was drawn and crossed with his dremask torch, both sweeping around to illuminate a pale-skinned woman with cat-like eyes. She made no move to defend herself further. She stood their, erect and solemn, eyes unmoved as Grimwarden's blade rested a hair's width from her neck's smooth skin.

"If you have come to kill us, please be swift," she said.

"Lena?" came Taeva's strained exclamation.

The woman did not even try to contain her shock. She turned sideways, her eyes flashing in Johnny's firelight. "Princess Taeva?"

Taeva pushed through and embraced the woman, the two holding each other as the Princess began weeping. "I'm…so glad…I can't believe… it's…"

"I'm so glad to see you too," the woman replied. Slipping away from Taeva's clasp in order to see her eyes, she asked, "But tell me: Why so long to come? We feared the worst had happened. We were preparing to fall asleep down here and wake in the hands of Ellos."

Taeva opened her mouth, but no words came out. Kat heard

her. *She has no idea.*

Finally Taeva managed three words. "It's all gone."

"What?" Lena stared, stunned. "What do you mean? What is *gone*?"

"The city. Taladair. It's all gone, Lena."

"Gone?"

Tommy had withdrawn the blade from Grimwarden's shoulder and was nursing it with a strip of wet fabric. "Your world has been attacked by a being known as Asp," Tommy said. Lena looked at him suspiciously.

"He's Felheart, a Lord of Berinfell," Taeva said. "I've solicited the Elves' aid, and they have generously answered. This is Grimwarden, Goldarrow, that's Alreenia, and Thorwin. And the one with the flames is Albriand."

Tommy continued. "Asp blackmailed your King in exchange for the service of your army, but your King refused. As a result Asp unleashed a destructive force upon Taladair the likes of which no one in Allyra has ever seen before."

Lena was clearly stunned. "But how could our entire city, our entire island be decimated? It's not possible."

"Asp made it possible," said Kat, stepping forward. To Lena's mind she added, *"Please don't try and understand it all now. We're here to help you and get those who've survived to safety."*

"A thought reader," said Lena.

"She is," said Taeva, tears still streaming down her cheeks. "And someone you can trust."

Kat glanced over to Taeva.

"How many of you are there?" Grimwarden asked Lena.

"We are two-hundred and twenty-nine," said Lena. She thought again. "We *were* two-hundred and twenty-nine. Lost three last night. Forgive me."

"I'm so sorry to hear that," said Goldarrow.

"As am I," said Lena. "But it will be made right when I exact payment for their lives on this Asp," her voice suddenly defiant.

"A little vengeance complex, anyone?" Johnny whispered to Jimmy.

"Yu think?" Jimmy replied.

"It's all right everyone," Lena spoke over her shoulder. "The Princess is here. You may come out."

Grimwarden asked Johnny for more light. All across a chamber about half the size of the previous one emerged a sea of tiny, pale faces. Children mostly. A few mothers had also made it to safety, but those caring for infants; it seemed this was a refuge for children only—no doubt by the instance of their mothers and fathers who'd perished above.

At seeing the Princess, the children moved toward her, suddenly unaware of their hunger. They swarmed her with hugs and kisses as she knelt to take each of them in an embrace.

Griwmarden moved around them to Lena. "I'm sorry about the shoulder," she said.

"I'm not," said Grimwarden. "Now I know who to keep beside me in battle." Lena smiled. Pulling her aside from the bustle of the children he asked, "Tell me, did you hear or see anything just before you came down here?"

"Sir?"

"Other than the destruction?"

She shook her head. "I'm sorry, Grimwarden. All I was told was to escort the children as deep into the catacombs as I could, and to not come out for any reason until we were summoned."

"You are brave."

"I am alive. My people are dead. Who's brave?"

Grimwarden was impressed with her selflessness, if not slightly troubled by the Taladrim's fatalistic mentality. "So other than Lord Felheart telling you about Asp just now, you have no idea about the attack or where he might be heading?"

"No, I'm sorry," said Lena. "I truly wish I could help you."

Grimwarden thanked her and left her to the children. He stood aside watching them. Frustrated. They'd rescued these children. But he had been hoping for more. Anything more. These children were alive today, but with Asp on the loose, it didn't assure they'd be alive tomorrow.

"Excuse me, soldier Elf?"

Grimwarden looked down. A small Taladrim child no more than three feet tall pulled on the leather plate over his thigh. "Yes, child." Grimwarden crouched low.

"Is the bad man still outside?" The child's eyes were wide, full of glistening fear.

"The bad man?"

"Yeah. The one that hurt all those people. The claw-man."

Grimwarden's heart began to quicken. "Tell me little one, did you see the bad man?" The child shrank back, looking left then right. "It's all right," said Grimwarden as comforting as he could manage. "Did you see the *claw-man* up there before you came down?"

The child nodded.

"Where were you?"

"In the palace. I snucked outside to play. Don't tell my Mi a' ma."

Her mother. Grimwarden's heart nearly cleaved in two. "I won't," he choked on his words. "I promise."

"The bad man said he was leaving. To hurt more peoples."

"Leaving? Do you remember where?"

"My Di a' da's best friend, Grumsken Vertic, he's a Saer. Mi a' ma said Di a' da left for there a few weeks ago."

"Your daddy's best friend?" Grimwarden asked, trying to track with the child. "I don't understand."

"Do you think the bad man will hurt my Di a' da there?"

"Your Daddy's—" That's it. She must have overheard Asp talking to the King; it would be just like a power-crazed lunatic to reveal too much of his hand…only to be thwarted by a mere babe. "Thank you, my child," Grimwarden kissed the little one on the top of the head. "Your Daddy will be safe if we can get there in time." Grimwarden stood up. "Tommy! We need to get topside!"

"What's up?"

"We need to get the Admiral to oversee their evacuation with those moss bags."

"Why, where are we headed?"

"To save the Saer. If it's not to late."

Principal Negotiations

"MAGISTRATE FORLARN will not be a problem, then?" Asp inquired, his words measured and precarious, like a knife teetering on a table's edge. The darkness of the narrow mountain corridor didn't seem to bother him, and he kept up with his Saer guide step-for-step.

"Sssth, no. He will not oppose you," Sardon replied. "Hisssth vote confirms that much. But he may not be convinced that your, ah, venture isssth worth the risk. Many are loyal to him."

"Can he be bought?"

"Have you crystal?" Sardon asked. "Have you archives of wisdom?"

"An entire world full of both."

"Then, yesssth, Forlarn can be bought. Ah, hsssth, wait." Sardon stopped in mid stride. He slapped his huge hand into a black crevice between bulging rocks. "Yessth, I thought so," he said.

He worked his multi-joint fingers inward, making an odd scraping sound. At last, his hand emerged. Clasped between his two long forefingers was a moon-colored, segmented worm. Sardon held the wiggling creature up for his companion to see. "A delicassthy," he said. "Slagmite worms are rarely found here…anymore."

One of Sardon's jaw appendages whipped around the worm and,

in a blink, curled it into his mouth. There were several wet popping sounds, and the Saer swallowed. "I am sorry," Sardon said. "I ssshould have shared."

"That," Asp said, "was disgusting."

"Sssth. Do not reproach a gift from Thynhold Cairn. The Saer capital city is not known for its hospitality."

"You can keep your worms. We have our own." Asp was more than a foot taller than Sardon. When he lifted his robed arm and pointed, he nearly knocked the Saer down. "Shall we continue?"

"There may, ah, be one complication," Sardon said. "Dregory. He issth the chief underminer. More, he is a former soldier, ah, a hero to the Saer commoners. He could limit our success."

"I know the type all too well. I will show him something that will change his mind."

Seated on a throne of brilliant white crystal, Saer Magistrate Forlarn rapped his knuckles across the armrest and said, "Lord Asp, you arrive suddenly at Thynhold Cairn, with many thousandssth of fighting troops. Have you really come seeking aid? Or are you here to threaten?"

A dozen Saer soldiers, the Shardbearers, showed their disdain for the visitor by striking the ends of their staves to the floor. The Saer dignitaries in attendance filled the room with their hissing disapproval.

Asp stood alone in the hollow surrounded by the Saer Crystal Thrones and the magistrates seated upon them. The myriad glimmers of light from all the luminous shards seemed to dim wherever Asp strode. As he drifted closer to Forlarn, Asp's hooded robe became indistinct… less now a garment and more a shroud of living mist.

Asp stood perfectly still and said, "I have come for neither. I don't need your help. And my army is present, not to coerce, but simply because we are in haste. No, Magistrate, I've come to offer opportunity. My campaign on Earth will prove to be lucrative, but it cannot wait."

"But at the cost of Saer blood?" Forlarn asked.

The other Magistrates squirmed on their crystal seats and hissed.

"There issth risk with all such ventures," Sardon said.

Magistrate Forlarn said, "There were those at the Conclave of Nations who believe you are a tyrant, Asp, a destroyer of cities. And still, I cast my vote—the Saer vote—to refuse action against you. But to volunteer the bulk of the Shardbearers into your service...in a world that is unknown to us is foolhardy."

"Well said, Magistrate." The voice came from a much older Saer sitting in the front row of the vast audience that encircled the crystal thrones. His forehead and brow were creased from a combination of age and frequent glowering. But in spite of his years, he was more bulky with muscle than most Saer. His arms and shoulders bulged from the leather vest that he wore. "This issth not our fight," he said.

"You're right, of course," Asp said, nodding toward the older Saer. "Dregory, correct? I've heard much about you, a resolute warrior by all accounts—and wise. This fight does not belong to the Saer. This is mercenary work. I want decisive victory—and swift. And for that, I will pay generously."

"What kind of pay?" Magistrate Forlarn asked, sneering. "The Saer care nothing for gold, silver, or vanadium."

Asp spread his arms wide. "We're talking about the spoils of an entire world."

This time, Sardon himself hissed. "Shall we shy away when sssuch treasures await?"

Forlarn leaned forward, and his jaw appendages whipped wildly. "Treasures? You don't mean—"

Asp nodded. "Crystal deposits ten times the size of those in Allyra, and—"

Forlarn's mouth smacked wetly. "T-ten times the size..."

"Yes," said Asp. "At least. And the libraries, this world has the most advanced archiving system I have ever seen. Not tens of thousands but rather millions of volumes of knowledge available at your fingertips."

Forlarn's misshapen mouth curled into a rapturous grin. "You would deliver all this over to ussth?" he asked. "All of it?"

Asp nodded. "We will take other riches, of course," Asp said. "These humans have many things of value. But crystal is of no use to me. And their compiled wisdom doesn't interest my people, Drefid nor Gwar. Earth would be yours to pillage."

Red glimmered out from Forlarn's narrowed eyes. He turned and whispered something to a magistrate on his left, and then the same to his right. The message appeared to travel the circle of magistrates. The Saer leadership exchanged knowing glances. Then they drummed their fingertips upon the crystal, filling the chamber with a melodic tinkling that sounded like windchimes.

Magistrate Forlarn stood. "It is decided, then," he said. "We will join your crusade, Lord Asp. We will commit seventy percent of our general forcesssth to your cause in exchange for mining and archival rights to this Earth you speak of. Done and done."

"A wise choice," Asp said. "You will need such numbers to carry your plunder."

"SEVENTY!" Dregory thundered. He leaped up from his seat in the audience and stormed up to Magistrate Forlarn's throne. "That would leave usssth defenseless here. Have you all gone mad?"

The magistrates hissed. "Magistrates, esssteemed guests," Forlarn intoned gently, "this is an unprecedented offer and may prove to be the greatest cultural advancement in Saer history."

Sardon spoke up. "Dregory, your caution is well respected," he said. "But perhapssth, missplaced? What enemy has Thynhold Cairn to fear? The Elves? Ha, no! Our mountain would be safe even with, ah, ten percent of our Shardbearersssth."

"You, you all speak with poisoned tonguesssth!" Dregory growled. "And eyessth too wide with greed. What if our enemy standssth before you? Taladair is no more, thanks to *his* doing!"

"Again, Dregory, you prove your reputation is well-earned," Asp said, each word clipped. "My forces are formidable. We did put down the Taladrim, but understand, it was they who provoked us. I brought the offer of riches to them. Their answer was to sneer and demean my people. You all know the contempt between the Taladrim and Drefid races. It was unfortunate."

Whispers slithered through the chamber.

Dregory scratched at his chin. "That feud is well-known," he said. "And yet, we have only Lord Asp's word as proof. And what of this phantom world he speakssth of? Have any of you seen it?"

"Would you like to?" Asp asked. The room fell silent.

"I would," Dregory said.

"Then, allow me a moment," Asp said. "Saer Magistrates and citizens, I ask patience of you. What I am about to do will not be easy for you to comprehend. And, what we do not comprehend, we fear. I am about to create a portal for Dregory to pass through, but it will stretch your perspective to see it."

Asp took a small bottle of liquid from his robe pocket. He spoke in whispers for several seconds. Then, he held the bottle aloft and smashed it to the stone floor. A gleaming line of liquid spattered across the floor. A bluish spark kindled at one end of the line and danced its way to the other end. Others like it followed. Asp bent down, speaking more whispers, and then reached to either end of the spilled liquid. Then, he pulled upon it, and the liquid rose from the ground like some kind of curtain or blind. Asp lifted it higher and higher, until he stood erect, and before him shimmered a door-sized sheet of...something.

The magistrates and spectators gasped and spoke in fearful

whispers. They could see through the strange door, and the chamber on the other side was still clearly visible. But the bluish electricity raced in frenzied patterns across it.

"Dregory," Asp said. "Ready to see the new world?"

The older Saer hesitated a moment, but then descended the curling stair. He approached Asp and nodded. Then, he said, "You go first."

"Very wise," Asp said. "As you wish." Then Asp strode through the portal and was gone.

The Saer muttered and exclaimed. A few called for Dregory not to go. But the majority urged him on. And so, Dregory stepped through the portal.

The noise in the chamber escalated to a roar until, moments later, Asp and Dregory returned.

"Tell them, Dregory," Asp said. "What did you see?"

Dregory blinked. "There isssth another world," he said. "Its sky was deep blue. The land issth vast and green...and beautiful. There was a shining city on the horizon, though I do not know its name. I have no doubt there are riches in both crystal and wisdom to be had."

"You see?" Sardon exclaimed. "It issth ripe for the picking. Alert the Shardbearers! We will—"

"But," Dregory said. "I do not believe we should do thisssth thing."

Hisses filled the room but none larger than Asp's. "You do not know what you are saying," the Drefid replied, his voice low and blunt like a hammer.

Forlarn grumbled. "You are of a different generation, Dregory, afraid to change. Afraid to try new things. Your ambition has left you."

"Maybe," Dregory said. "But I am alssso wiser. That world out there...it seemsssth a quiet place. Quiet but full of life. What have they done to us? What right have we to plunder their world? What right have we to kill them all? Nay, we should not do this thing, Saer. I have seen this world, and to me it issth innocent."

"Perhaps you should look again," Asp said.

His movements were almost too swift to follow. He turned and his robe whirled with him. Something came out of his hand, making it appear as a grotesque claw. He grabbed Dregory and, with one arm, shoved him halfway into the portal. Then, Asp whispered something. The portal glowed. Electricity crisscrossed its surface. And then the portal snapped closed with the sound of a whip.

Asp tossed the lower half of Dregory's body to the ground and asked, "Is there anyone else here who doubts my word?"

The Vanishing Army

"DREGORY WASSSTH too inflexible," Sardon said as he clambered onto his lance cat. He seated his feet in the stirrups and wrapped one of the leather reins around his long forearm. "Inflexible and loud, yesssth. But did you, ah, have to cut him in half to make your point?"

"Object lessons are invaluable tools," Asp said. "They will not forget what they have seen."

"No, no, they will not forget," Sardon replied. "But you have alienated the working classessth. Some of our generals and their Shardbearer units will remain in Thynhold Cairn. I fear we have less than seventy percent to offer you."

Asp squeezed his toes into the upper abdomen of his Warspider, and the creature began to crawl. "It is enough," Asp said. "Our numbers are sound."

"What about the Nemic?" Sardon asked. "They are alwayssth good for a fight, and they thirst for many thingsssth this Earth may offer."

"The Nemic are already in the fold," Asp replied. "But they will not be needed on Earth."

"Did you see that, Jast?" Shardbearer Rhystalec asked. He peered through a slightly misshapen spyglass that was wedged neatly into the crennel of his lookout position. His partner didn't answer right away. She was nestled into her own nook, a pocket of stonework built into the mountains of Thynhold Cairn.

Jastansia changed the focus on her own spyglass. "The treesssth are moving," she replied. "So?"

Rhystalec muttered a curse and then asked, "Do you feel any wind?"

"A bit of a breeze," she said, "here and there." Then Jast sat up very straight. She reached swiftly over her shoulder and pulled free her shard stave. "But a breeze would not move the trees like that."

Rhystalec looked again. The cliffside forest was more turbulent than he had seen it, even in a gale storm. The massive canopies writhed and shook. Branches tore, and untold numbers of leaves scattered. It wasn't just one place either. Rifts opened in the foliage all over, bending and twisting boughs.

"What do you make of it, Rhyssth?" Jastansia asked. "Should I get to the summoning bell?"

"Might be wise," Rhystalec said, tearing himself from the spyglass momentarily. "I've never seen such a thing, have you?"

"No," she replied. "Not aside of that vortex that dropped down from the storm back in 212."

"That was a bad one," said Rhystalec. "But then, we had the black sky, and a doomfinger we could see. This...I don't know." The sound of crumbling stone pulled him back to the spyglass. He watched the edge of the forest. Trees still swayed and shook, but now, rocks and gravel tumbled down the cliffside in dozens of places. A shrill screech sent a cold thrill through his body.

"What was that?" Jastansia asked, panic choking her words.

"Nothing good," Rhystalec said, rising to his feet. "That is certain. Go now, get to the summoning—urkk!"

Right before Jastansia's eyes, Rhystalec's chest burst. A bloody mess opened on the right side of his chestplate, and the Shardbearer was lifted bodily into the air. His limbs wheeled uselessly. He struggled like a beetle on a pin, crying out a gurgling scream.

Jastansia ran to help her friend, but something that felt like log of timber slammed into her forearm. Her shard stave cartwheeled into the air and clattered over the edge. She screamed and clutched her forearm but only for a moment. She looked at her dying friend and took a step forward.

But Rhystalec's eyes bulged. He held up a spasming hand and cried out, "No!" Then he was tossed backward over the wall. He plummeted out of sight, into the chasm below.

Jast spun on her heels. "Ellos, save us all!" she cried out as she loped toward the stair ridge that curled around the cliffside. She stumbled and just as she went to one knee, something incredibly hard smashed into the stone at the level her head would have been. She was showered with dust and flecks of stone, but didn't wait until she could see clearly. She kept low and raced to the stairs.

Something brushed her leg and she teetered a moment. She glanced for a split second over the edge at the yawning abyss but threw her gangly hands at the rock face. Her Saer fingers found crevices and she kept from falling. She was steady for just a few seconds before something stabbed into her thigh.

Pain lanced up her spine. Blood soaked into the leather plate armor and dribbled down her leg. Instinctively, she reached down to the wound. By touch, she found an arrow shaft protruding from her leg, but she could not see it. "What madness isssth this? How can—"

SCREET!

The shrill cry was close enough and loud enough to make her ears ring. Jast grabbed the unseen arrow shaft and snapped it off a few inches from her flesh. Then she ran. Ducking down behind fences of stone whenever she could, she stumbled along the narrow footpath. A mad chorus of cries and screams followed her as she hit the first step of the spiral stairs that led up and around the outside of Thynhold Cairn's bell tower.

Every time she pushed off with her right leg, pain erupted. She could feel the arrowhead grinding against bone and shredding muscle. She knew she was losing a lot of blood, maybe dying, but fear drove her on. Fear that something had come to her city—her lifetime home—something that no Saer had ever experienced before. Perhaps, something beyond their ability to defend against.

The bell tower loomed above, and she climbed. A strange, cold wind swirled. CRACK! Something struck the base of the tower beneath her. Blue fire flared below, and gray smoke plumed upward. Jast screamed, but kept running.

Just three turns remained before she could reach the platform and sound the alarm. He right leg felt numb, and she slipped once on the second turn. That's when she heard the clicking, clattering sound. She looked behind her and down, just for a moment. And there, in the billowing smoke, a terrifying shape formed.

It seemed a monstrous spider made of shadow, and it was clambering up the tower only twenty feet below. A gust of wind chased the smoke away, and the creature was gone from view. But Jast knew better. It was still there. Still climbing.

Jast groaned in agony, slamming her feet down upon the stone, grabbing the clefts of rock with her long fingers and wrenching herself up. She dove onto the platform, rolled onto her side, and snatched the heavy hammer from its cleft under the tower rail. She rose to her knees and wheeled the hammer over her head. The massive mallet head struck the body of the huge bell. A deep chime pealed out from the tower.

An angry screech answered, and something heavy stepped up onto the tower's platform.

The bell swung ponderously back and forth, sounding once, twice, a third time. But, before it could sound once more, it jerked to a stop in midair, colliding with something unseen.

SCREET!

Jast clutched the bell hammer and slammed herself backward against the rail. Her red eyes scanned the platform furiously. Her jaw appendages whipped to and fro, as she tried desperately to sense something, anything that would give away the creature's position. *How can I fight what I cannot see, cannot sense?*

The summoning bell swayed a little to the left. Then Jast knew. She leaped forward and swept the hammer, low-to-high, into the seemingly open air right of the bell. It collided with a nauseating crunch. There was an angry screech, and a gout of black blood spurted. More blood trickled and ran along an uneven contour hanging in the air.

"I see you now!" Jast yelled. She swung for the blood and missed. Something slammed into her shoulder, but a glancing blow. She recoiled and slid a few yards left, trying to keep the summoning bell between her and the beast.

The strategy paid off. The bell moved, and so did Jast. This time, she swung the hammer like an ax. It hit home.

Crack. Screech. Blood.

Jast pivoted right and watched spots of blood spatter the platform in front of her. The summoning bell suddenly flew forward with such force that it tore free from its housing. The thing was charging her. There was no place to go but over the edge of the bell tower.

Jast gasped out what she thought might be her last breath and tried the only thing she could think of. Pain screamed from her wounded thigh as Jast dropped into a split. She held the hammer's head out in front of her. The second the beast barreled into it, Jast planted the haft on the floor and used the weapon to lever the creature up and over her head. The hammer splintered in her hand. Something struck Jast a blow on the jaw. As darkness swarmed in on her mind, she heard the percussive snaps of evergreen limbs.

When Jast awoke, she felt like she'd been trampled by a herd of maladons. Her head pounded, her shoulder and forearm throbbed, and her thigh burned. But all the pain meant she wasn't dead.

"Thank Ellos," she whispered hoarsely. Clenching her teeth and groaning, Jast clambered to her feet.

Her head swam. She was dizzy and swayed. After steadying herself on the rail, Jast became aware of the clamor all around her. Crashes, cracks, screams, commands, wails, thuds, explosions and the steady rumble of many armored feet.

The sounds of war.

Jast leaned on the rail and gasped. Thynhold Cairn burned in a hundred places. Saer defenders lay dead or dying all around. All the avalanche traps had been sprung, and many enemy beasts—spiders, flying creatures, and massive wormlike monsters—lay crushed, half-visible by their own blood and gore. Several towers had been thrown down. The western ramparts were wrecked. And the living, Saer and invader, still fought on amidst it all.

Jast instinctively reached over her shoulder for her shard stave, and then threw her head back and moaned. It was gone. It was all gone. Everything.

She felt a chill tremor. Maybe it wasn't all gone.

The Saer Heart, she thought, the chill becoming a hard freeze. *The Deep Archives.*

Jast was already moving, careening down the tower stairs. Crystal and wisdom, valued by the Saer above all other things, and Jast knew of no more precious stores of each than the Saer Heart and the Deep Archives. As she thundered across the only plank bridge she could find, she desperately fought the decision that was coming.

Both the Heart and the Archives should be guarded. Saer troops should have fallen back to defend these last bastions of their racial identity. But the attack had been so sudden, the enemy invisible. Maybe there had been no time to mount a defense or seal the chambers. Jast would have to choose which one, a literal fork in the road.

The Shardbearer skidded to a halt below a low cliff overhang, and snarled. The bridge gate was in ruins. There was only one other way in on this side of the mountain. Jast turned from the path and leaped into the waiting arms of a tall pine. Half-falling, half-climbing, she slipped down to the needle-covered rock. Then, she sprinted back eastward until she came to a spiny hedge that curled some ten yards around a jut of stone.

Jast cut herself a dozen times, plunging through the foliage, but she found the hidden east entrance. The heavy iron cap hadn't been accosted. She wrenched her back turning the thing, but she managed. Then, she dropped down the ladder to a shadowy tunnel.

Jast plunged forward knowing that, in a few hundred feet of tunnel, she would be forced to make the choice. She knew of a cache of weapons on the way, but that would do no good against this enemy. No matter what she chose, there was only one hope: to trigger the chamber seal. But which one?

SCREET!

The monstrous screech seemed to come from behind her and in front. *Dear Ellos!* she thought. *Perhaps the choice has been made for me.*

The Home Front

KATE AND Allan didn't share their secret with anyone. And it was probably better that way. Who would believe that they were having telepathic communication—albeit one way—with their daughter? There was no way to prove it, no evidence to show that they both weren't stark raving mad. To share their theory with anyone meant alienating any clear-thinking person, including all of their friends and family.

And if someone did believe them, that could potentially be far worse. Images of men in dark suits and sunglasses, storming their home and taking them to some underground research facility—threatening images like those were hard to avoid. After all, the government would be very interested to know that there was another world out there. Another world that could perhaps be exploited. If Kate and Allan were the only keys to that world, they might never see the light of day again.

Keeping this knowledge to themselves would not be easy. To resist searching for someone to confide in, someone who might help would be harder still. But if it meant Kate and Allan at least had a chance at finding their daughter, then that secret, they knew, was worth guarding with their lives.

Kate stopped seeing her therapist, and both of them started going to church with renewed purpose. They trusted each other, and they trusted God. Eventually, somehow, someway, they'd find her.

Kat was out there, somewhere.

None of the Elven Lords' adoptive parents were without distress in the weeks following the Lords' disappearances.

Jimmy Gresham's mum and dad in Ardfern, however, were least affected. They quickly accepted the unknown fate of their adopted *problem child*, and gave themselves fully to their natural offspring. Yet even they wondered what became of Jimmy, secretly regretting they had never spent more time with him.

Mr. and Mrs. Bowman had worked hand-in-hand with the police on a statewide manhunt that eventually encompassed most of the mid-Atlantic states, resulting in a stymied attempt to locate Tommy. "Have You Seen Me?" posters of their precious, curly-haired son plastered the cork boards of every local business. But Tommy Bowman had vanished, seemingly without a trace.

The Briarman's followed a similar path seeking Autumn and Johnny, making more than a few appearances on national television programs pleading for the return of their twins. The few call-in tips that came led law enforcement to a string of dead ends. Mr. and Mrs. Briarman became reclusive, turning inward to grieve their losses.

But none seemed as troubled as Austin and Hazel Green.

No one seemed to put the multi-family teenage disappearances together; after all, there were thousands of child abductions every day around the world. But the former tailback for the Carolina Panther's got the most national, and even international press from the disappearance of his son, Jett. His former Panther teammates rallied behind him and Hazel, and the team's owner made a very generous donation to the Missing Child Benevolence Foundation. But like most important things in the media, the story lost momentum, and people moved on.

Then one day, something happened. Hazel had been worried sick about Jett. She wasn't sure why exactly; that sunny afternoon was no different than any other. But something brought Jett to mind in a fierce way—so fierce, it sent her to her knees. She began praying for him. *Interceding* was what Bishop Arlington called it. She rocked back and forth on her knees in the kitchen, weeping. Her prayers turned from intelligible English to deep groans. Then in the midst of her deepest heart cries, a wave of absolute anguish washed over her. It was as if a forest full of the sounds of crickets and cooing birds went absolutely silent, as if every standing tree had been brutally and suddenly felled. Only barren wasteland remained in her soul. She curled up on the floor and sobbed until she had no more tears to cry.

Austin found her there after he came home from a round of golf cut short by the onset of his own depressive episode. Hazel wouldn't respond to him, and seeing her there broke his heart. So he did the only thing he could think of to do: lie down and curl up behind her. Husband and wife, father and mother, the two of them lay there until dawn, spent from long hours of crying, and having no concrete reason why it was so intense this time.

But it was. Very intense.

Gut wrenching, nerve fraying, body writhing pain. No report from the FBI, no local sheriff knocking on their door. Just an indistinct impression that something had happened to Jett, and there was absolutely nothing they could do about it.

Days later, things improved for Austin and Hazel, at least as much as things could for a couple that had lost their most prized possession. Life moved on, church moved on, investments moved on. Numbness replaced agony. Grim courage replaced numbness. Mission replaced grim courage.

And rightly so. Nothing and no one could ever replace Jett. But they had committed his destiny to Jesus long ago. "After all," Austin had reminded his bride on numerous occasions, "we were merely stewarding him. He was God's first, and God's last."

Austin and Hazel praised the Lord for the few beautiful years they had Jett in their care. The sense of guilt they carried would probably never fully relinquish its hold, Austin surmised. But at least life would go on, and they'd discover other *divine orders* they would need to be faithful to. Financially, they'd helped more than one family in need, and that felt good. Hazel volunteered at a local food kitchen, and both she and Austin served selflessly within the church.

Eventually something shifted even further. Austin and Hazel were growing closer through the turmoil of Jett's loss. Instead of feeling married but distant, they felt married and in love. *Whole* even. In fact, there were moments during the day where their family felt complete again...like Jett was upstairs working on homework, or in the backyard working at his agility drills.

Pastor Duke said that the grieving process had come to an end, and that fond memories would take its place. It certainly felt like that was happening. But there was something more. Something they couldn't explain to anyone but themselves. They'd share a look, and both Austin and Hazel knew Jett was with them. He was alive in their hearts again. His memory would never leave them, and that was enough.

Hazel was folding laundry while Austin was in the den, watching Sports Center to catch up on the game he'd missed in place of a benefit concert they'd attended earlier in the evening. The music was good, but wasn't either of their styles. Hazel was humming to herself in the laundry room when she heard something upstairs.

"Dear?" she poked her head out into the hallway and peered down to the den. She could see the changing lights from the TV flashing within the room. "Austin?" she was a bit more direct.

"Yeah?" she heard her husband respond with his usual lower timber.

"You hear something?"

A beat passed, and then Austin appeared in the hallway. "What's that, dear?"

"Did you hear something? Upstairs?"

Austin cocked his head, listening, then absently aimed the remote at the TV and pressed the mute button. He listened more closely.

"No, dear. Probably just—"

There it was again: a heavy *thud*. Hazel froze. Something, or *someone* was definitely upstairs. Austin's face went cold, the same expression he used to wear on game day.

"I'll check," Austin said. "Stay there." He nodded at the laundry room, then told her to lock the door.

Austin moved to his study and fetched a key from his top desk drawer. Across the room stood his gun cabinet. He unlocked it and retrieved a .45-caliber Colt revolver. He slid open the cylinder and made sure it was loaded. He'd never had to use his gun collection on anyone, and hoped he never would; but with his notoriety came many threats, both public and anonymous. So arming himself in order to defend his family became a priority...something that plagued him to this day... something that he was not able to do for Jett.

He walked out of his office and crept up the master stairwell, moving lightly for a man of his size. Another thump from somewhere above, far end of the hall.

An undulating creak of the floor, another dull thud. Austin felt his pulse quicken. Someone was definitely in the house. *Broke in through a window*, he thought.

Austin held the revolver low in a doubled-handed grip like he'd

THE TIDE OF UNMAKING

been taught by one of his FBI buddies. His heart pounded in his chest, but he slowed his breathing, willing himself to a calmer state. *The calm before the storm*—that's what he called it back in his playing days. He needed it now more than ever.

I've lost my son, he thought bitterly. *I won't let no one touch my Hazel.*

The next thud threatened to take a door clear off its hinges. *Jett's door.*

Austin crept down the hallway and saw a dim light shining underneath the door to Jett's room—a room neither he nor Hazel had touched since Jett disappeared.

Austin's blood boiled. To think someone was in there, that someone had the audacity to tamper with their deceased son's possessions…it angered him enough to shoot first and ask questions later. He paused just beside the door and listened. Scuffling. But no talking.

Austin took a deep breath, then reached for the door handle. He twisted it ever so slightly to see if it was unlocked. It was. *One, two, three…*

He threw the door open and raised his .45.

Then dropped the gun.

Thynhold Cairn

"GRIMWARDEN," TOMMY said, glancing backward to be certain that Taeva was out of range, "what Asp did to Taladair…it was like a force of nature."

"That, my young Lord, is exactly what it was," Grimwarden replied. "But no nature that Ellos ever intended. Long have the Taladrim relied upon their walls and domes. Rightfully so, at least, until Asp managed to let in the sea. It is more than a miracle that any of the Princess' people survived at all."

His mount whickered. Tommy's steed answered with a snort. Having seen the devastation of Taladair, Admiral Cuth called in every favor he had to supply the Nightstalkers with mounts. Horses, lance cats, mountain rovers—even a few maladons—anything that could save the Elves wear and tear and speed them on their journey.

"What of the Saer?" Tommy asked, absently rubbing the horse's neck. "Do they have an army, anything that could withstand Asp's forces?"

Grimwarden nodded slowly. "The Saer are well fortified," he said. "Asp will not be able to trigger a cataclysm such as in Taladair. I suspect he will have to claw for every inch of rock and stone in Thynhold Cairn. It is like a hornet's nest made of the bones of a mountain. The Saer should be able to defend their realm much longer, unless..."

"Unless what?" Tommy asked.

"Nevermind," Grimwarden said. "It was something Goldarrow told me, something about the Conclave. But I am not certain it has any bearing here." Grimwarden spurred his mount and rode ahead to catch up to Goldarrow.

Tommy wondered. Grimwarden's suspicions had the uncanny habit of being dead right. But the old Guardmaster was as resolute as they came when he didn't want to share information, so there was no point in pursuing it. Maybe the Saer would fare better against Asp. Maybe they wouldn't. The Taladrim probably thought they were well prepared too.

Tommy shuddered. There it was again, like a cold finger tracing the spine, a sense of creeping dread. Ever since Taladair. Ever since he saw that poor child still clutching the toy he'd been playing with...before the flood waters came. And now, they were both forever locked in an underwater tomb.

"What's wrong?" Kat asked. She rode up on Tommy's left.

Tommy shrugged. "Death," he said.

Kat nodded and when she spoke, her words were half-choked. "I know, so many bodies, all those innocent—"

"Not that," Tommy said. "I mean it is, but it isn't."

"I don't follow."

"Seeing so many dead is sickening," Tommy said. "Horrible, but we've seen it before. The carnage at Berinfell, then Vesper Crag. Hurricanes, floods, tornados, earthquakes...thousands dead. Thousands and thousands. But it's more than the numbers. It's death itself. One minute, you're there, walking and talking...living. The next minute, motionless and cold. Nothing. Sightless eyes and a still heart. I mean, where do they go?"

"Who?"

"The dead," Tommy said, his words sharpening with frustration.

"I don't know how to say it! When they die…the soul or spirit…the thing that makes someone be someone—where do they go?"

Kat frowned. "It depends on their faith," she said. "You know what the Word of Ellos says on this matter."

"Of course I know it," Tommy snipped back.

"Well, it's true," Kat said. "Believe it."

"I do believe it, Kat. Most of the time. But when someone dies, they're just *gone*. We can't know them anymore, not here. There's like a hollow left in the world, a gaping shadow of what used to be. It…it just feels like an emptiness that won't ever be whole again. And worse, the emptiness has a kind of gravity, like a black hole. It almost feels like it's pulling at me."

"I know precisely what you mean," Taeva said, riding up on Tommy's right side.

Kat and Tommy turned. "I'm sorry," Tommy said. "I…I didn't know you could hear. I didn't mean to…"

"My Lord," Taeva said. "Do not apologize for speaking your heart. There is no joy in this speech, but there is *something*. When kindred spirits recognize one another, there can be comfort. For I have felt this grasping vacuum you speak of. I've felt it ever since I learned of…well ever since I was very young. I feel it keenly now at the loss of my family, my people, my city."

"But how do you fight it?" Tommy asked.

"Fight it?" Taeva asked. "You do not fight it. You embrace it. Death calls to us all. The Taladrim cannot escape it. Neither can the Elves. Let death's call be a reminder of how to live. Of how fleeting and precious life is. Live, Tommy. Soak in every moment…and live."

Taeva's words were magnetic. How fine it would be to turn death and dread upside down. Tommy watched Taeva ride away. He turned to say something to Kat, but she was moving on to join Taeva.

Taeva heard the clip-clop of Kat's horse coming up behind her. She bristled, waiting for a sarcastic remark or a rolling of the eyes. It was clear Kat didn't like her; and why should she, or any of the other female lords for that matter? She knew the females of any race were territorial and treacherous, though cunning enough to keep their intentions well hidden…until it was too late.

But Taeva could not dismiss the hope that perhaps Kat's behavior while diving on the ruins of her homeland was genuine…that perhaps she'd made a friend.

"How are you doing?" Kat said, now riding beside her.

Taeva looked sideways, trying to gauge Kat's tone. The question seemed genuine enough. "I bode well, all things considered," she replied.

Kat nodded, but refrained from speaking for a few moments.

Was that it? Taeva thought. *No taunt? No snide remark?*

Finally, Kat said, "I'm sorry. About your people."

Taeva looked straight ahead. *Digging at fresh wounds, she is.* "It is a loss I must carry alone," replied Taeva, "and cannot expect another to know."

"That's true," said Kat. "I cannot know exactly how it feels. But you don't need to carry it alone."

Taeva looked up.

"That's what friends are for," added Kat.

Taeva didn't know if she should reply; rather, she didn't know *how* to reply. *Friends?*

"Just saying," Kat finished, and slowed her mount to rejoin the others behind them.

Suddenly Taeva turned around. "Hey, Kat," she said. "Thank you." She paused…*how to say it*… "You know. For *down there.*" Referring to the dive.

"It was nothing," said Kat with a smile. *A genuine smile*, Taeva thought.

✳

"Beyond those trees!" Grimwarden called out. "Thynhold Cairn, the mountain city of the Saer."

Tommy gazed at the line of sky-scraping pines, but the foliage was far too thick to see through. However, as their caravan rounded a bend and followed the path down a curving slope, he caught sight of the mountain. At first, he thought it was partially enveloped in cloud. But these plumes were soot-colored, and boiling into the sky.

It was smoke.

"Don't just sit there gawking, Tommy," Grimwarden shouted. "Give the order!"

Tommy blinked. "Sorry, sorry!" He sat up tall in his saddle and called out, "Spearhead formation! Lords, take point! Guardmasters, left and right barb! Bengfist, take your *blade* down the tree line, cover our flank on the east slope!"

"Yes, hmm, hmm, finally some action!" Bengfist rumbled. He hefted his hammer high in the air and was about to signal his seven-hundred troops.

"Overlord!" Goldarrow called. "Overlord Bengfist, we are doubly blessed to count you as an ally. But please remember who the enemy is. Kill only Asp's forces."

"What? Oh, right!" Bengfist replied. "Yes, of course. Though, to be honest, I wouldn't mind putting a lump or two in that General Secretary's noggin. Sardon, hmph!"

Tommy watched Bengfist ride off, shouting orders, organizing the Flet Groups into a full blade of near seven-hundred soldiers.

"Probably the first time a Gwar Overlord has led a blade of Elves into

208

battle," Kat's voice spoke into Tommy's mind.

I like him, Tommy thought back. *He's like a scrunchy, less patient Grimwarden...with a hammer.*

"Only you would joke like that just before we charge into battle. Glad you're thinking of better things."

Thanks. Tommy spurred his mount. He sucked in the chill air and bellowed: "Endurance and Victory!"

Taeva spurred her mount and caught up to Grimwarden. "What about me?" she asked.

"What do you mean?" Grimwarden asked.

"Lord Tommy—Felheart—whatever you call him, he gave orders to all your forces, but mine."

"Princess Taeva," Grimwarden said, "you are the last of your royal bloodline. You lead the remnant of Taladair. You should remain in safety."

"Safety?" Taeva said as if the mere mention of the word was detestable. "Safety is for cowards."

Grimwarden nodded. "I see," he said. "Forgive me, Princess, but I never considered that after...well, after what happened that—"

"That I would be in any condition to fight?" Taeva asked. "Do you not know the customs of my people, Guardmaster? It is better that our race perish utterly than to diminish our honor by not fighting our sworn enemy."

"But the women...and children?"

"...Can look after themselves." Taeva took a deep breath. "Now, Guardmaster, I would not normally hesitate to join the battle, but your lord has initiated a detailed plan of attack. I want the Taladrim to compliment it rather than to hinder it. Where do you think we would be best utilized?"

Grimwarden looked over the Taladrim remnant. *Seventeen fighters altogether,* he thought. "You might best serve with Bengfist on the flank. He will—"

"Come now, Guardmaster," Taeva said. "You do not really suggest that the Taladrim ride support to the team guarding the mountain's backside. We wish…" Her voice cracked a little. "We *need* to make our mark. We *need* to fight."

Grimwarden suddenly understood. "Follow the Lords, at the front," he said. "They will be in the thickest fighting and can no doubt use doughty warriors such as the Taladrim."

Princess Taeva bowed low. "Thank you, Guardmaster," she said. "I will not forget this gesture. And do not worry. We Taladrim are fierce beyond our numbers, and I have a few tricks up my sleeve. We will earn your respect and return to jest about it later."

Tommy led the Lords and two blades of flet soldiers in a hard charge to the foot of Thynhold Cairn. Ahead, smoke swirled and billowed, driven by the cold wind. Tommy wanted to loose his bow, but couldn't see well enough, couldn't find a single target beyond all the murk.

Doesn't help that the sun's nearly spent, he thought, drawing his rychesword. *Better be ready for close combat.*

Just before disappearing into the murk, Tommy glanced over both shoulders. Grimwarden and Goldarrow each led a blade, flaring out on either side, ready to flank any enemy force. That was more than a little comfort, Tommy thought.

The grade of the terrain climbed steadily. Sudden clumps of short trees and piles of boulders forced the Elves to make one swift maneuver after the other. Tommy trusted in his mount and kept his eyes peeled for enemies. He expected Warspiders, enemy Gwar, Drefids, maybe Cragons—but saw nothing, not even their corpses.

The smoke clouds tattered and broke here and there, and Tommy began to find the dead, but they were all Saer as far as he could tell. Not a good sign.

"Where are they?" Kat's thoughts demanded in Tommy's mind.

We might be too late, Tommy said. *Again.*

The wind picked up, and the smoke began to shred and clear. Tommy and his troops came upon a scene they could not at first comprehend.

In the distance, arc stones by the dozen sailed into the sky, but there were seemingly no enemy soldiers to fire them. They just appeared and raced into the dusky thick air. There were pockets of Saer soldiers, *Shardbearers* Grimwarden had called them. And they were fighting like mad, wheeling their shardstaves, axes, and blades—but at what? They seemed to be grappling with ghosts. *They've gone mad,* Tommy thought. He halted his mount. "What's going on?"

Jimmy rode up. "We've seen this before have'na we?" he asked.

Gooseflesh spread up and down Tommy's arms. "The Gnomes."

"It moost be," Jimmy said. "I don'na know how Asp got his blasted hands on the stooff. Best yu tell Kat."

"Right." Tommy focused his thoughts. *Kat, broadcast to all: Asp's forces have the Gnomic invisibility paste.*

The words were barely conceived in Tommy's mind when Kat showed once more just how powerful her gift had become. Her thought-voice sounded a clarion call, ringing out the warning to the entire legion of Elven Nightstalkers and their allies.

"Be on your guard," Kat told them all. *"The enemy is cloaked by Gnomic invisibility paste. Look for shadows, spatters of blood, dirt and soot. More visible in dust clouds and smoke. Watch especially for Saer already engaging the enemy. The enemy is invisible, not invincible. Take them out."*

Good work, Kat! Tommy cried out mentally. Then he spurred his mount.

"Me first!" Autumn's voice came out of nowhere.

Tommy saw a blur of Nightstalker ebony and the brief flicker of Autumn's long fighting knives as she whooshed past his galloping mount as if it were standing still.

"Autumn!" Johnny yelled. "Wait for your backup!"

There was a burst of flame off to Tommy's right, and Johnny's terrified mount dashed by with Johnny bouncing in the saddle and summoning up fireballs in each hand.

Autumn's blur careened up the mountainside where a pair of Saer Shardbearers were running out of room to back up. They were seemingly overwhelmed by something unseen. Autumn raced by three times in the span of a heartbeat. There were several shrieks and a spurt of black blood. Johnny arrived a moment later and launched a stream of molten power into the bloody spot that Autumn had just struck. As the inferno kindled, there appeared the ghostly, burning forms of two Warspiders and a Drefid assassin.

Now that they could see their foes, the Saer finished them off. They raised their shard-staves in salute.

But suddenly, a deep womanly voice cried out, "One side, Elf!" There was the thunder of hoofbeats as Taeva and her Taladrim soldiers crashed by Tommy. There were only seventeen of them, but Tommy found himself fascinated watching the coordination of the Taladrim attack.

They rode virtually side-by-side at first, but as they neared the fighting, Taeva's mount slowed. The other sixteen riders split around her, plunging forward in two wings of eight. With perfect timing, the soldiers fanned out, creating lanes of attack ten-men-wide between them. While mounted, the Taladrim soldiers used their vicious tridents, which proved to be just as formidable on land as they surely were in the water.

The Taladrim wielded their weapons with vicious accuracy.

Tommy clamped his eyes shut, but a moment too late. He saw a Taladrim soldier lean from his steed, windmill his trident swiftly, and slice it into something unseen. There was a tremendous spray of blood, almost an explosion, and the now semi-invisible enemy soldier collapsed at the feet of the Saer he'd originally been fighting.

When Tommy opened his eyes, he saw the two wings of eight Taladrim soldiers collapse inward and then spread wide once more. Each time they came together, there were all manner of shrieks and cries, and Tommy found himself wishing they had seventeen-hundred Taladrim soldiers, not seventeen. At about that moment, Taeva caught Tommy's eye. She hadn't rushed forward into the battle as her comrades had. She sat stationary on her mount, well back of the fighting.

Tommy rode forward a little. What was she doing?

She had no visible weapon, but moved her hands about in front of her chest as if she was playing an invisible harp. *No,* Tommy thought. The way her fingers and hands moved so intricately, it was more like she was weaving something. Suddenly a bright green electrical arc kindled between her two hands. The ghostly electricity began to dance among her fingertips. Then, she lifted her hands high.

Tommy jumped. The thunderclap was so loud and sharp, it seemed the entire battlefield froze for that moment. A searing bolt of green lightning leaped from Taeva's hands and obliterated a stand of trees just up the hill. Chunks of burning tree trunk and debris wheeled into the air, as well as burning pieces of Warspider.

"Ellos save me!" Tommy cried aloud. "Taeva has a gift! And WHAT a gift!"

Taeva rode forward, her head scanning back and forth even as her hands continued that weaving motion. It seemed to take some time for Taeva to generate enough of a charge to launch a new bolt of lightning. But every fifteen to twenty seconds, she unleashed a flash of sheer destruction. And unlike the wild streaks that strike down from the sky,

Taeva's strokes were well-aimed. She only struck in areas clear of Saer Shardbearers. Tommy wondered how she was guessing so accurately the location of the enemy.

Still, can't afford to spectate any longer, he thought. *Gotta do my part.* He turned his mount to find the highest ground.

There was what looked like a bell tower, but it was more than a hundred feet up. Definitely a great spot for shooting, but the mountain didn't offer the easiest path of ascent. There were so many switchbacks it was dizzying, almost like a pencil-and-paper maze with too many tightly fitted lines.

Gotta try, Tommy thought. *I could do a lot of good from up there.*

"DUCK!" Jimmy yelled from somewhere behind.

Tommy flattened himself to his mount's neck just in time. He felt the rush of air as something heavy swept over him. No way to know what it was, but it sheared off the top of a nearby pine. Tommy spurred his mount forward.

"Die, yu wee beastie!" Jimmy shouted. He rode to the spot Tommy had occupied a moment before. There, he unleashed his newly forged claymore sword. He combined his mount's strength and his own and plunged the long blade forward. Three feet of the blade disappeared into something. There was an explosion of bluish gore, and whatever creature it was let out a piteous, gurgling wail. But Jimmy wasn't finished. He yanked out his blade and began a furious windmill of hacking that ended only when he leaped off his mount and drove his sword down as if he was sinking a post into soft earth.

"Great Scott, Jimmy!" Tommy called back. "I think it's dead already!"

"Can'na be too sure!" Jimmy called back, wiping off his face and neck. "It was gon'na take yer head, it was. Could'na let it do tha!"

"No, that would have ruined my whole day," Tommy said. "How did you see it?"

"I did'na," Jimmy replied. "I joost saw what it did to yu...before it happened, and figured I might put a stop to it."

For the ten-thousandth time, Tommy felt desperate gratitude for Jimmy's gift. Those brief, but timely visions of foresight had saved them all many times.

"Now, off with yu," Jimmy called. "The right hand trail will get yu there."

Tommy waved and tore up the foothills to the base of stone where the switchbacks began. A dozen twists and turns later, the trail narrowed to the point where Tommy needed to dismount. He unfastened his two spare quivers from the saddle, patted his mount on the neck, and raced up the path. Soon it became too narrow to run, and he had to sidle along more slowly. And that was galling because he needed light to shoot. If it took too long to get to the bell tower, it would be all for nothing.

Bits of stone broke away with each step. Tommy grit his teeth and tried not to look down. A blue-white flash forced the issue. Tommy watched as a small glimmer grew closer and flared to life as it came. *ARC STONE!*

Tommy was exposed on the rock face. The explosive arc stone sped closer. There was nothing he could do...but pray.

It was no long, eloquent prayer of flowery devotion and praise. Tommy's prayer was just, "Help!"

Then he closed his eyes.

Lost and Found

BLASTS OF incandescent blue and white flashed though Tommy's eyelids. The arc stone struck the mountainside. There was a tremendous *Kerraack!* Then *Whoosh!* Heat washed over Tommy and fragments of stone pelted him. He opened his eyes just in time to see a massive hump of stone break free from the face above him.

Dark gray and oblong, the huge boulder slid down in an avalanche of smaller stones. Tommy pivoted on one foot, the other dangling precariously over open air, and went face-first into the mountainside. The falling monolith careened by him, blasting the thin lip of stone Tommy had been using as a path.

There would be no going back, at least not that way, but Tommy had survived. "Thank you, Ellos," he whispered. But another flash from somewhere at the mountain's base spurred Tommy on. He clambered as fast as he could, clinging to the mountainside each time an arc stone struck. At last, the path widened. Tommy ducked under some pine boughs and raced up to the bell tower. Next was the winding staircase that wrapped around the outside of the structure. His legs and lungs burned, but he had to get to the top.

Bounding up the stairs, more arc stones tried to purge him from the tower, blowing up the stone steps beneath his feet moments after his boots had graced the surface. Finally he reached the top and threw himself over the rail, then commando-crawled to the far side. He put his hand in something wet. It looked like blood, but strangely dark purple rather than red. Hard to tell in the twilight.

Tommy pulled himself up to the rail and unslung his black yew bow. The vantage from the tower was far better than he'd hoped. A spectacularly wide vista opened up before him. He could see close to 180 degrees, combatants on every square foot of the battleground.

He saw Grimwarden and Goldarrow's blade groups breaking off from their barb points, cutting off escape for the enemy. He saw Johnny's fire flare up as he burned his way through foes. The other Lords were just as busy. But they could use eyes from above and a little bit of cover fire. With the piles of arrows he had stuffed into his three quivers, Tommy knew he could fell or wound more than a hundred enemies.

But there were two problems: invisibility and the sinking sun.

I've got maybe ten minutes of effective light, he thought. *Best use it.* He nocked a shaft, found a Saer warrior struggling at the base of a tree, struggling against something unseen. Tommy estimated where to shoot and fired. Time stopped. His pulse quickened. His eyes went with the arrow, guiding it by will to the exact spot he wanted. The shaft sunk halfway in. The invisible enemy grunted and fell into the arms of a pine tree far below.

Tommy didn't have time to exult, watching the stupefied Saer slash the air for an enemy no longer there. Tommy found his next target... and his next. Other than the few enemy soldiers already bloodied or soot covered, Tommy couldn't make them out. But he could see the evidence of their presence. He gazed from Shardbearer to Shardbearer, seeking after signs of grappling or any manner of engagement. When Tommy found it, he fired. And when he fired, enemies went down.

Like so many times on the practice range, Tommy found a rhythm: loosing one arrow, the release propelling his hand to the quiver, the arrow rotating over his shoulder, landing on his bow hand, balancing and aiming even as he put the nock to the string, and firing again. Over and over again, arrows sailed into the dusk.

Tommy heard a screech. *That was a Warspider,* he thought. He heard a deep, bellowing grunt. *That was a Gwar.* He heard a shrieking curse. *Drefid. Definitely a Drefid.* Once, he heard a disgusting, raspy, coughing sound. *No idea what that was.*

Tommy's deadly rhythm continued, foe after foe. But a flash in the sky caused a bad miss. Tommy ducked and covered his head with his hands and arms. The flash had seemed like a gigantic arc stone kindling right in his peripheral vision. A few non-explosive moments later, Tommy looked up again.

No arc stones to be seen. But above the treetops a patch of light blemished the darkling sky. Tommy blinked and squinted, but the vision refused to focus totally. It seemed as if the sky itself had been punctured, and a ragged, luminous wound remained. It shimmered and pulsed, and suddenly, something broke through. A quivering, wavering strand of pure white light poked out of the glowing patch and seemed to take hold of the sky around it. Then, another came. And another. It was almost as if a spider of light was trying to clamber out of its hidden den.

There came the sound of a whip crack, and the patch in the sky imploded and was gone.

What in Allyra was that? Tommy wondered. But he didn't have time to think, for two things occurred: a throng of flaming arrows pelted the bell tower above his head. And the sun slipped below the distant forest line.

"Time to go!" Tommy shouted. He turned, ducked down, and crab-walked to the other edge. The staircase was all but blown to smithereens. *No going back down that way.* The only alternate route—besides a straight plunge to his death—was leaping off the tower to the steep mountainside about fifteen feet to the rear. He took a deep breath and sped off the only way he could: through the pines and downhill.

Tommy busted through half a dozen tree limbs before he stopped, his torso lodged between a sheer rock face and a tree trunk. He'd have bruises for weeks, but he was alive, and nothing was broken as far as he could tell.

Get up! Get moving!

Tommy strained against the pain in the legs and arms, wiggling out of the cradle that caught him, and slipped quickly down the face behind the bell tower. Finally he passed by the base of the Bell Tower and moved along the side of the mountain. His thighs and calves burning from the twisting, downward path, Tommy stopped to catch his breath. *Kat,* he called in his thoughts. *Kat, are you there?*

"*Here,*" she said. "*Just a second.*" Her voice returned a few moments later. "*Sorry, I had a Drefid trying to cut off my head.*"

You too, huh? A Warspider tried for mine. Jimmy saved me.

"*He's pretty good at that,*" Kat said. "*Thanks for the arrow cover. You gave us the room to advance. I think we've scattered Asp's forces.*"

That's what I wanted to know, Tommy said. *But you sound nervous. We've got Asp's forces on the run. That's good news, right?*

"*I caught up to Grimwarden,*" she said. "*He doesn't think this is Asp's full army.*"

What? Why?

"*Signs of trampling in the forest. Grimwarden says there was a much larger force here and too few here now. This may only be a fraction of our enemy.*"

Great, Tommy replied, continuing his descent. *See if anyone's connected with the Saer. They should be able to tell us for certain.*

"*On it,*" she said.

Oh, and Kat, Tommy said. *I wanted to say I'm sor—*

Tommy slid to a halt.

"*What?*" asked Kat.

I heard something, he said. *I've gotta go.*

Tommy shoved himself between the competing arms of two pines and found a deeply shadowed cleft of stone. He'd heard something from this direction. It had sounded so desperate, so sorrowful...a sonorous wail for help.

"Noooo!" came the cry once more. "You cannot enter here! Get back!"

Now Tommy heard the clash of steel, shrieks, and growls. Then once more came the cry for help. It was all muffled, nearly suffocated by the mountain, but Tommy knew it couldn't be far within or he wouldn't have heard it at all.

He emerged from the pines and explored the rocky cleft. He found it went far deeper than he'd first thought. It was narrow, so he had to turn sideways to get all the way in. He found an iron door torn from its hinges and an excavated opening into the mountain. The cries and clashing sounds came from inside, so Tommy drew his rychesword, peeked around the corner, and stepped into mountain.

His surroundings changed immediately. Greenish-white dremask lanterns made a glowing connect-the-dot path that curled far out of sight. The rock on the inside was dark and smooth, and sparkled in places from small deposits of crystal. Thick, custom-forged girders of iron ribbed the corridor, making Tommy feel like he was in a tunnel. Sword out in front, he crept forward.

The scream he heard this time was so loud that it froze Tommy in his tracks for several frantic seconds. Whatever was happening could not wait for caution. Tommy sprinted up the corridor. His heart slammed against his ribs more out of fear that he might arrive too late than from the exertion. Flashes lit the tunnel ahead. There was much more yelling, the clash of steel and then...

Silence.

"No!" Tommy growled. But the cold sensation now traveling the base of his neck warned him that he was indeed too late.

The path seemed to elongate before him and the final fifty yards felt like three-hundred. But, at last, he came around the bend. The sight that awaited Tommy was both spectacular and heart-wrenching.

The corridor opened into a vast chasm, its darkness thwarted by dremask, illuminated crystal deposits of blue, purple, and green, scattered all around the arched stone walls. There in the center of the cavern was what appeared to be a subterranean country cottage.

Built of cunningly cobbled stones, bordered with stained timber, and roofed with thatch, the small building looked like any homestead one might find in the midst of a pasture or in the back woods. But this cottage sat on a stone island in the midst of the chasm. Just a few feet from any of the lodge's walls, lurked a seemingly endless fall into darkness.

A narrow stone bridge led from the front porch of the cottage and across the gulf to a peninsula where several fires burned. On the near side of the bridge a barricade of stone had been raised, and there appeared to be several dead Saer warriors sprawled across it. The lone Saer survivor, a female Shardbearer, stood. She was covered in blood but still held her ground, defiantly brandishing a warhammer.

Across the barricade, dead enemies lay, and still more enemies advanced. No longer invisible, but now soot-stained shadow-shapes, three Warspiders—two of them the most venomous red Warspiders— several Gwar soldiers, and a Drefid Commander stepped boldly onto the bridge.

The Saer called out, "Be gone! This Archive is hallowed ground!" Her voice quavered and her limbs shook.

Her courage riveted Tommy. This one Saer war maiden had survived an onslaught and now, wounded and alone, faced overwhelming opposition. And yet, she would not give in. Tommy clenched his fists so hard that his knuckles popped audibly.

No way those monsters will get her! Tommy thought. *No way.*

But how to stop them? From high ground, he could pick them off, one after the other. But they were almost on her. No time to search or even climb. Even if he fired his fastest, there was no guarantee he could pick them all off before one of them got to her. An eye-shot on a Drefid in motion was no easy feat, and the red Warspiders would take several arrows each to put down.

All such thoughts careened in Tommy's mind but, with few grains of sand left in the hourglass, he had to act.

"You heard her!" Tommy shouted. "Vermin, puppets of Asp, you will not advance!"

The enemy party stopped. The Gwar and Drefid turned toward Tommy and gazed across the shadows.

"An Elf?" the Drefid hissed. "We will have our way with her and you, Elven cur. Thynhold Cairn belongs to Lord Asp. You have come to your tomb."

Tommy laughed haughtily. "You might want to run that by the legion of Elves who are, at this moment, wiping out your futile attempt at invasion."

"Tommy?" Kat's voice intervened suddenly. *"Tommy, you there?"*

Tommy didn't answer. He had other things on his mind.

"Legion of Elves?" the Dredid echoed. The enemies growled and hissed and traded uncertain glances.

"Don't believe me?" Tommy chided. "Go see for yourself."

The Drefid held up its arms. There came a shrill, scraping sound, and long, razor-sharp, bony claws knifed out from its knuckles. The Drefid's gaze bounced from the Saer maiden back to Tommy. "You cannot deceive a master of deception. Let the world burn outside for all we care. Our prize is here."

"Your invisibility paste is wearing off," Tommy called out, edging his voice with as much arrogance and aggression as he could muster. "You're no match for us now. Behold, I am Felheart Silvertree, one of the Lords of Berinfell. Leave the maiden and assault me if you dare!" *Boy, laid that on thick,* Tommy thought. *I hope they take the bait—*

With surprising speed, the Warspiders skittered across the cavern floor toward Tommy. The two Gwar lumbered after the spiders, and the Drefid brandished its long claws and leaped high into the air.

Tommy couldn't see the Drefid up in the shadows of the cavern roof, but knew the creature would plummet right on top of him.

Okay, Tommy thought. *They took the bait. Now what?*

Kiri Lee stepped down out of the sky and landed lightly beside Grimwarden and Goldarrow.

"Well?" Grimwarden demanded.

"Bengfist was victorious," she said. "Decisively. His blade of soldiers holds the northern gate and all the wooded access points."

"The others?" asked Goldarrow.

Kiri Lee pointed west. "Between Johnny's fire and Taeva's lightning, they have the last organized bunch of Asp's troops on the run. Taeva's lightning…what does it mean?"

Grimwarden's brow lowered and pinched above the bridge of his nose. "It is potent…a mighty gift. I confess I don't dare guess what it means."

Kiri Lee nodded. "We've fought valiantly," she said. "And we've all but won today, but…"

Grimwarden inclined his head. "But what?"

"We arrived too late," she said. "Jimmy and Autumn found the Saer Heart…shattered."

Goldarrow sighed. "That is world-changing misfortune for the Saer," she said. "Those who survived, that is."

"And Tommy?" Grimwarden said. "Where is he?"

"I've been up over every inch of these peaks," Kiri Lee said. "The moonlight's bright enough, but I've seen no sign of him. He must be somewhere inside."

"What about Kat?" Goldarrow asked. "Has she tried—"

"I saw Kat on the eastern ledge." Kiri Lee shook her head. "She says Tommy doesn't answer."

Grimwarden uttered a throat-clearing grumble. "He'll be alright," he said. "I'm sure of it. Well-trained lad. The only way he'd get himself killed is if he ignored his brain and did something impulsive."

Not like Tommy would ever do that, thought Kiri Lee. She stared up at the moonlit peaks of Thyhold Cairn and shuddered.

I hope I'm right! Tommy thought desperately. He loosed two arrows, one for each of the Gwar. Just crude legs shots. *No time to follow with arrow heads into their knees.* He slung his bow, grabbed his rychesword in both hands, and thrust it hard above his head. He braced every joint and stabilized every muscle, using Nightform technique to mold his body into a tree-like, powerful base, completely supporting the rychesword.

The semi-visible Drefid fell out of the darkness and shrieked as it impaled itself.

But Tommy screamed as well. He'd succeeded in skewering the Drefid, but the creature's claws raked his forearm and barely missed his face. Tommy couldn't help but release the rychesword. He stumble-ran a few feet away, unslung his bow, and turned to the Drefid.

The thing looked down at Tommy's sword. The blade had gone into the flesh at its hip and sunk to the hilt. The Drefid grabbed the sword by the grip and yanked it free, producing a gush of black. "Fool, you cannot kill a Drefid in this way."

"I wasn't trying to kill you with the sword," Tommy said, nocking an arrow. "I only needed you to hold still."

Tommy released. The shaft crossed the ten feet between them before the Drefid could turn its head so much as an inch. The arrow plunged into the Drefid's ghastly eye socket, the force of the strike knocking the creature backward. The Drefid's body crashed without grace to the ground and sprawled like a rag doll at the feet of the oncoming Gwar.

One of the Gwar tripped over the body. His face abruptly met the floor. The other stepped on the Drefid's head and kept coming. He almost cornered Tommy and swung a heavy maul at the Elf's midsection. Tommy jagged to his left, and the maul shattered a stalagmite that had been ten inches thick.

So long as Tommy could move his feet, he could dodge those slow, heavy blows all day. He loaded up an arrow and fired into the meat of the Gwar's thick shoulder. It howled in agony. And Tommy sidestepped a few feet to fire again. But, the moment he put his left foot down, he knew something was very wrong.

The ground felt soft, like he'd stepped into clay or dense mud. And when he tried to lift a foot for the next step, it wouldn't budge. Both feet were stuck fast. Tommy yelped and stared down at the still-glistening glob of webbing clinging to his boots and spreading in an irregular shape three feet in all directions.

"Warspiders!" Tommy castigated himself for being so clumsy. The huge arachnids could hurl different kinds of webs over great distances. The Elves had learned that the hard way in the assault on Berinfell.

The Gwar who had tripped over the Drefid clambered back to his feet. The other Gwar tore the arrow out of his shoulder. They both turned toward Tommy.

The Warspiders, however, had turned toward the Saer war maiden.

Tommy fired off two quick arrows at the spiders. "Over here!" Tommy yelled. "Stupid bugs, come get me!"

"Happy to," came a low Gwar voice.

Tommy looked up in time to see a massive hunk of tree trunk, a

Gwarspike, hurtling towards his head. Too big, too heavy, coming too fast—there was no chance to duck it. Except for suddenly, it wasn't there anymore. One moment: *head-smashing chunk of timber.* The next: *gone.*

There was the clang of something metal and heavy, followed by a guttural scream.

"Yu'll not be havin' this Elf today!" Jimmy shouted. He yanked his enormous claymore from the belly of the first Gwar, ducked the second Gwar's overreaching swipe, and then drove the blade into the enemy's lower back.

"Jimmy, thank Ellos!" Tommy exulted. "Cut me free. We've got to help that Saer!"

"Autumn's on it," Jimmy said.

"But there are three Warspiders!"

"Nay, joost two. Autumn's got them."

Jimmy dragged a dagger around Tommy's boots. The web sprang away from every place the blade touched.

Tommy heard a great tumult of shrieks and screeches, and when he looked up at the stone bridge, the Warspiders were gone. *Well, except for a few semi-transparent limbs,* Tommy noted.

Dodging globs of webbing, Tommy and Jimmy raced over the bridge to where Autumn was already helping the Saer war maiden. Autumn had leaned her up against the barricade and was spreading salve on her wounded shoulder and side.

"Thank you, Elf maid," the Saer said. "You...you have come in time."

Tommy exchanged glances with Autumn and Jimmy. They both shrugged. "I am Tommy. This is Autumn and Jimmy. We are three of the Lords of Berinfell."

"Lordsssth?" the Saer replied, her red eyes widening. "Then, you were not posturing jussst to draw them off. Ah, I am sorry. You should not have risked your lives for Jastansia."

"Jastansia," Tommy said. "That's your name? We're glad to help you. You are quite valiant to stand up to—"

"Wait!" she said. "You've come to claim it, haven't you? It is yours by rightsssth and would be a worthy reward for what you have done here today."

"What is she talkin' aboot?" Jimmy asked.

Tommy replied. "No idea."

Jastansia groaned as she gained her feet. "Please, I must enter the Archive. I—"

"What are you doing?" Autumn asked. "You need to lay still, let the salve work."

"No, please," she said. "I owe you everything. Please grant me the favor of returning at least…unh…a small token."

On long legs and sure feet, Jastansia glided the rest of the way across the bridge and vanished into the strange cottage. Moments later, she returned carrying a luminous, blue crystal tube.

"On behalf of my failed countrymen," Jastansia said, handing the crystal to Tommy, "accept this with ages of regret."

Tommy stared down. "I don't understand," Tommy said. "You are returning…this? I don't know anything about crystal in Berinfell. I—"

"Open it," Jastansia said. She reached out to help him twist one end of the tube.

The crystal slid away and a heavy parchment fell into Tommy's hands. Something about it felt momentous, as if it was charged with electricity. He began to unroll the scroll.

Autumn gasped. "Is that—?"

"Tha' looks like…" Jimmy's words drifted off.

"A Prophecy of Berinfell," Tommy whispered. "One we've never seen before."

21

The Tide of Unmaking

GRIMWARDEN'S FACE was as red as an overripe tomato.

Tommy had never seen him so angry. Even Goldarrow kept her distance.

"If that skinch Sardon were here right now," Grimwarden thundered, "I would throttle him myself!"

Ordinarily no one would have dared utter such threats in the Saer's Chamber of Crystal Thrones, not even Grimwaden. But of the eight Saer Magistrates who ordinarily occupied those grand seats, only one remained: an elder named Phein. And Phein had no intent to oppose one such as Grimwarden. He slouched down in his crystal chair and absently fingered the sparse gray hair that crowned his oblong head. He sweated profusely, and his damp robe hung loose on his lanky frame. He looked like he was melting.

I would be too, thought Tommy. *If I had Grimwarden glaring at me like that.*

"What do you have to say for yourself, Phein?" Grimwarden demanded.

Phein swallowed deeply. His triangular lip flaps barely moved as he muttered, "Well...yesssth, you are right, of coursssth. But understand it was our ancestors who took the scroll."

Grimwarden slammed his fist down so hard on the armrest that a sliver of crystal shot across the chamber and tinkled on the floor. The Saer, spectating from the stands that encircled the thrones, hissed their disapproval. A withering glance from Grimwarden stopped that instantly.

"Ancestors?" Grimwarden bellowed. "Not that old dodge. Phein, my patience has worn to its breaking point. Your people have knowingly had this Prophecy of Berinfell for two-thousand years!"

"Actually," Phein said, clearing his throat, "it is closer to three-thousand yearsssth. Balsooth the Bold obtained it while we Saer helped you repair Berinfell City." He coughed. "After the failed Nemic invasion. Remember, the Saer helped you?"

"You helped yourself to our property, didn't you!" Grimwarden fired back. "Do you have any idea how significant this could be to the Elves of Berinfell?"

Phein seemed to grow just a little bolder. He said, "Balsooth found the scrollsssth in a caved-in reliquary far from your Great Hall and its archivesssth. It was among many commonplace parchments, family rolls, architectural diagrams, and such. If it is so hallowed by your people, how is it that it came to be so...discarded? How is it that the Elves have not searched for it ever since?"

If Grimwarden had looked like an overripe tomato before, he now looked as if the tomato was boiling within its own skin and might burst. "This rare and precious document was NEVER discarded!" he shouted. "And...just who says we have not been searching for it?"

"Well, have you?" Phein asked.

Grimwarden tilted his head and cracked his neck. "No," he said much more quietly. "Not to my knowledge."

"Why not?" Tommy asked. "Why didn't we search for it?"

Grimwarden glanced at Goldarrow. "I...I do not know," he replied at last. "I suspect someone thought it was an old copy, rather than the original. There are segments of this we have all read before. But there is also much that is new to us. How it could have disappeared...I cannot say."

"Perhaps," Goldarrow said, "perhaps it was one of the oldest manuscripts. Perhaps it had only ever been seen by a few and became... forgotten."

"It's like Whitehall," Kat said.

Goldarrow looked up. "What?"

"The bricked-up tower in Whitehall, remember?" Kat said. "The Scarlet Raptor showed us the Book of Prophecies. It was original and included things other Elves tried to cover up."

"Yes, Kat," Grimwarden said. "We all remember that quite well. But this set of scrolls is very different."

"How so?" Phein asked, the hunger for wisdom lighting a fire in his eyes.

Tommy and the other Lords, even the Saer spectators, leaned forward waiting on Grimwarden.

"This prophecy," Grimwarden began, "well, I have studied much under the wisest Old Ones in Allyra, and yet, I have not learned...have never even heard, mind you, of some of the elements within these scrolls."

"Like what?" Kiri Lee asked.

"Lords, you are blood rulers of Berinfell, indeed of all Allyra's Elf kind," Grimwarden explained. "You will need to read—nay—study these precious words for yourselves. We will wait for your interpretation before we take action."

"But what about Asp and his forces?" Tommy asked. "This was not his true army...we don't know where he's gone."

Goldarrow and Grimwarden exchanged glances once more but, this time, Magistrate Phein was also involved.

Tommy asked again, "Do we?"

Grimwarden sighed. "I am afraid we do, Lord Felheart," he said.

"The troops Asp left here were nothing more than a clean up crew, assigned to destroy those who would not join him in his new crusade. His full army, or at least a gigantic portion of it, was here."

"That isssth correct," Phein said. "It wasssth a vast army."

"Kat told me," Tommy said. "You found signs of troop movements. Massive areas of foliage trampled. Tens of thousands of enemy soldiers."

"More," Goldarrow said. "But what you do not know is that, when we felt Thynhold Cairn was securely in our hands, we sent scouts to follow the enemy's trail. If he was headed for the Nemic next, we thought, perhaps we could send raptors…get there first to warn them."

"Our scouts followed Asp's trail east," Grimwarden continued. "But less than a league from here, the trail ended."

"What do you mean?" Tommy asked.

"I mean the trail stopped completely," Grimwarden said. "Thousands of soldiers, Warspiders, and worse things…all marched recklessly through the foothills into the forest, and then vanished."

"More of that Gnomic invisibility paste?" Johnny asked. "That what you're saying?"

Grimwarden shook his head. "If only it were that simple. The enemy didn't just vanish from sight. The enemy vanished from Allyra."

"A portal," Tommy said. "Asp took his armies through a portal."

"There was a vast section of forest flash-burned," Grimwarden explained. "The tracks of the enemy end there. Beyond that point, the forest is undisturbed."

"Dear Ellos!" Tommy exclaimed. "Does that mean…?"

Grimwarden nodded gravely. "Phein?"

Magistrate Phein stepped down from his throne. "Asp wanted my people to come with him, to conquer, and to pillage a place we Saer had never heard of before. He claimed it wasssth ripe for the taking. He called thisssth place…Earthsss."

Tommy and the Lords sat alone in the Saer archive deep within Thynhold Cairn. Tommy held the scrolls in his lap. "I know we all want to read these," he said. "We all *need* to read these. How do you want to work it?"

"I can'na wait to get into them," Jimmy said. "But yur the leader. Yu should go first."

"A couple of us could go at a time," Autumn said.

"I could read them aloud," Kiri Lee suggested.

"I have an idea," Kat said. "What if I read it and broadcast it to you?"

Tommy looked to the other Lords, collected their nods, and said, "Okay."

Kat took the scrolls and began to read with her inner voice, and the other Lords heard her in their minds. Verse after verse, the Word of Ellos spoke to them. They had read much of the text before, studied it even. But they came to several new passages that fed their souls like cool water to parched earth.

Time passed unnoticed. Kat read on. Nearing the last page, however, they came to an unnerving series of prophecies. It was no forgery—undoubtably truth, indisputably the Word of Ellos. But that served only to make it more terrifying to read.

From all time to all time, the children who rise under the sun will bleed wickedness. Drop by wretched drop, it will flow from all who dwell in Ellos' kingdoms. Not of Ellos' hand, for what has light to do with darkness? Nay, it is the transgression of all, flowing unseen into a Black River within the firmament.

And it shall come to pass that the deceived, those of shriveled soul and diseased mind, will find their thirst for more to be far more than they can bear. They will dip their cups into that dismal torrent and become the destroyers of worlds. The river will o'erflow its banks. Malice will bleed into the soil, into the stone, into flesh, and into the very air.

By dark chants, the deceived will tear open the sky, and even the faithful of Ellos will travel into lands they were never meant to tread. With each new soul who traverses, the ocean of darkness will swell and consume. By Dark Arts, the lawbreakers will shepherd their legions across thresholds of disaster.

And, "Behold!" says Ellos. "I will not suffer their misdeeds forever. I will not hold back the Tide." And all the venom of eternity will rise up in a Tide of Unmaking. All that was, all that is, and all that might be, will be swept away, consumed utterly. Unless the Tide is turned, those living who wander return, and the Seven be Seven again.

Tommy and the Lords marched into the Saer Crystal Throne room, now emptied of its previous Saer hosts. He held up the scrolls. "This is bad," he said. "Really, really bad."

"Lord Felheart, you have many gifts," Grimwarden said. "But eloquence is not among them. Nonetheless, we agree with your assessment. Tell me your interpretation. Begin with the Black River, what do you make of that?"

"Sounded like evil," Johnny said.

"More like sin," Kiri Lee said.

"Same thing," said Johnny.

Kiri Lee shrugged.

"I don't understand the river image," Tommy said. "Is it a metaphor or some other kind of symbol?"

"I do not believe so," Goldarrow said.

"So...what?" Jimmy asked. "Don'na tell me there's a great lot of sin floatin' around in the sky."

"Ten years ago, Jimmy, would you have believed in Elves?" Grimwarden asked.

"Good point, that," Jimmy replied.

"There are other places in the Prophecies that talk about the evil of Allyra flowing into a well," Kat said. "There's a real cost to each and every sin."

"Yes," Kiri Lee said. "I recall that as well. And there is another place, in the passages just before the Rainsong, that speaks of the dark water of sin, seeping into the world. It is very powerful, catastrophic even."

"Well done, Kat, Kiri Lee," Grimwarden said. "When one point in the Prophecies is unclear, we must always interpret it by other Prophecies that are clear."

"Okay," Tommy said. "So, the Deceived...those are the Drefids. They're the ones who practice the Dark Arts. And they're the ones who first opened the portals between Allyra and Earth."

"Yes," Grimwarden replied. "Thresholds that never should have been crossed. When the original Spider King began extracting human slaves, he unwittingly began the process that would end all life in Allyra."

"And Earth," Autumn said. "The Prophecy says all will be swept away—*things that were, things that are, and things that might be.* That means Earth too."

"I am afraid you're right," Grimwarden said.

"Don't miss the most important word in that part," Tommy said.

Johnny frowned. "Tide?"

"Dark Arts?" Jimmy asked.

"Those are two words, Scotland Yard," Kiri Lee said. "It's 'unmaking,' right?"

"No, none of those," Tommy said. "The word is UNLESS. That tells us there's a chance we can reverse all this."

"Unless the Tide is turned," Kat said absently.

"Yes, but how do you propose to do that?" Grimwarden asked.

"We go back to Earth," Tommy said. "And bring each and every enemy back to Allyra. That's what started the *Tide* flowing, then that's what will undo it."

"Yes, let's do it!" Jimmy shouted. "The Nightstalkers go to Earth."

"Not so fast," Goldarrow said. "You are forgetting something."

"Something rather important," Grimwarden said.

Tommy crushed his eyes closed. "We can't," he said.

"We have to," Autumn said.

Tommy opened his eyes. "The Prophecies," he said. "They say that every new soul who traverses...every being who crosses into a world where they don't belong will just make the problem worse. Asp already has many thousands over there."

Grimwarden nodded. "That is why we have seen so many unstable portals opening and closing all over Allyra."

"I still don't understand," Kat said. "We've got to get the enemy out of Earth. We have to go."

"But if we take a legion of Nightstalkers over," Tommy said. "We could push it too far. We could trigger the end of the world."

Jimmy drove both hands through his hair. "How...can'na we do this, then?"

The Saer Throne Room became as quiet as a tomb.

"This is getting out of control," Goldarrow said.

"Long ago," Grimwarden said. "It went out of control many years ago. And these past seven years, I thought we were, well…not quite safe but at least ready. I knew the Drefids were still out there, tampering with black evils, but I thought with our secret army of Nightstalkers, we could handle the worst they could throw at us. But we had no idea what the worst could actually mean! And now, when time is critical, we find ourselves in desperate need of information that will take time to get. Just what have those Drefid monsters tapped into? How unstable are the portals already? What exactly is the Tide of Unmaking? Has it begun?" The old Elf massaged his temples and grimaced.

"The Tide of Unmaking," Autumn said plaintively. "You don't think it would really end the world? Do you?"

"Earth?" Jimmy asked. "Allyra? Humans, Elves—"

"Everything." Grimwarden spoke the word in a whisper, but it fell like a hammer nonetheless.

That was when Mr. Charlie entered the chamber. He looked around expectantly, but no one greeted him. He frowned and asked, "Why ya'll actin' like you was dunked in vinegar and lost your last friend?"

"We are in a conundrum," Goldarrow replied.

"Several conundrums, actually," Grimwarden said.

"Shoot, ain't never seen nuthin' mighty Ellos can't handle." Mr. Charlie made a rueful face. "Think ya'll would know that already, bein' Lords and all."

"Well, uhm…" Tommy stammered. "It's not that we don't have faith, but—"

Charlie put his hands on his hips. "Uh, huh."

"Ellos is good," Kiri Lee said. "It's not that we doubt Him. It's just—"

"Uh, huh."

"C'mon, Charlie," Jimmy said. "Yur not bein' fair. Is there anything Ellos can'na do? Of course not. It's just—"

Mr. Charlie narrowed his eyes. "Seems t'me ya'll just need to take a little trip back into Ellos' Word."

"That's just it, Charlie," Goldarrow said. "It is Ellos' *words* that are most troubling to us."

"I'm listening," Charlie said. "What's the trouble?"

Punctuated by additions from Grimwarden and Goldarrow, the Lords told the story. They even read the new Prophecy to Charlie. When they'd finished the whole tale, including all their fears and questions, they all turned to Mr. Charlie.

"Aww shucks," Mr. Charlie said, a twinkle in his violet eyes. "That ain't nothin' but a thing."

"Really?" Goldarrow said, fighting off a smile. "And just how do you propose we stop the end of the world, Charlie?"

"Don't got to," Charlie said.

"Huh?" Johnny said. He thought for a moment and repeated, "Huh?"

"Mr. Charlie, there's no one who respects you more than I do," Tommy said. "But, you lost me here."

Charlie laughed. "It's not some grand scheme," he said. "I don't do grand schemes."

"Then what do you mean, old friend?" Grimwarden asked.

"Look," Charlie said. "This Tide of Unmaking, whatever it is, you Lords think you can just muscle up against it? It's Ellos' will. You can toss fireballs and shoot arrows at it all day long…ain't gonna make a dent. You just gotta play by the rules."

"What rules?" Tommy asked.

"Ellos' rules, Son," Charlie said. "The Drefids broke 'em. Shoot, we broke 'em too, all us tap dancin' across those portals like they was our personal secret passages. All you gotta do is keep everyone in the right world."

"But, Charlie," Goldarrow said, "Asp has tens-of-thousands of Allyran soldiers on Earth."

"Don't make no difference," Charlie said. "They all gotta come back or they gonna die. Asp might be just as big a maniac as the old Spider King, but he don't want to get himself all wiped out. Tell him. Show him. Whatever you need to do to make him see."

Goldarrow's eyebrows beetled, then relaxed. "Charlie, that's so simple it's brilliant."

"I can do simple," Charlie said with a wink.

"We'll need proof," Grimwarden said. "Proof beyond our Prophecies, that is."

"He's got to have seen the rogue portals opening and collapsing all over," Autumn said.

"Let us hope so," Goldarrow said.

"What if we give him proof?" Tommy asked. "What if we make it as clear as we can, and he still won't order his forces to leave?"

"Then," Mr. Charlie said, "you kill him."

"And the others?" Grimwarden asked. "The other thousands?"

"I bet a bunch of 'em will hightail it outta there," Mr. Charlie said. "The ones that won't, well, you know I don't relish the killin' of any livin' thing. But if they won't leave, you won't have much choice. Ellos' Word said the *livin'* who wander."

"The dead can stay," Kat said quietly.

Grimwarden nodded solemnly. "The dead can stay."

Tommy turned his back on the group and marched past the crystal thrones into the empty spectator seats. He returned a few moments later. "Okay," he said. "There's a lot to do and a very short time to do it. Here's what I propose. We need proof for Asp. I say we send scouts out on raptors. Scatter to the four corners of Allyra and look for any signs of this Tide of Unmaking. Chart every portal, even if it collapses in a few seconds. He's got to know how widespread this is. And we need to know which portals, if any go to Earth."

"That is precisely what I was thinking," Grimwarden said. "What of the Dark Arts, the Drefids? We have allowed Asp and his kind to fester and toil in the Dark Arts too long unchecked. We have to know what we're up against."

"We go find out," Tommy said. "Maybe take a few Drefids captive? Interrogate them?"

"That might work," Charlie said. "But maybe…maybe somethin' else would be more direct."

"A Coven?" Goldarrow said. "If you could even find one, Charlie, that would be incredibly dangerous."

"I'll go," Charlie said. "Ain't no Drefid never scared me."

Grimwarden laughed nervously. "Maybe so, Charlie. But this is a nest of Drefids."

"I won't go alone," Charlie said. "I'll take a few of the Fletmarshalls with me, to watch my back."

"You are to gather information, Charlie," Goldarrow said. "Not engage the enemy. It is not wise to strike the nest while you are still inside."

"Yes, ma'am," Charlie said.

"That leaves Asp," Kiri Lee said. "Oh, and tens of thousands of enemies."

Tommy pinched the bridge of his nose. "I guess we'd better be the ones to take care of Asp. The Drefids stole us from Allyra and dumped us on Earth. It's time we return the favor."

"There's a certain poetry to it," Charlie said. "Don't ya think?"

"Something else," Tommy said. "Before we go back to Earth, we need to visit the Gnomes."

"The Gnomes?" Grimwarden said. "Whatever for?"

"Asp somehow has their invisibility paste," Tommy said. "We need some too."

"That's right smart, that is," Jimmy said. "Fight fire with fire."

"I like the sound of that," Johnny said.

"Perhaps, Mr. Charlie and his team should visit the Gnomes as well," Goldarrow suggested. "A little invisibility might be of use to your team in a Drefid Coven."

"It might at that," Mr. Charlie said.

"But," Kiri Lee said, "what about the *Seven becoming Seven again*?"

Johnny piped up, "Maybe Taeva? She has gifts, right?"

"I wondered the same thing," Tommy said. "Did you see that lightning she tossed around?"

"Aye," Jimmy said. "Where is Taeva anyway?"

"With Bengfist and the remaining Saer," Goldarrow replied. "Securing the enemy prisoners."

"What do you think, Grimwarden?" Kat asked. "Could Taeva be our new Seventh Lord?"

"But Jett," Kiri Lee said. "We still don't know about Jett, not for certain."

Grimwarden did not reply.

"I don't think ya'll need to worry about ole number Seven," Charlie said. "You just let Ellos sort that out."

"Agreed," Grimwarden said. "But that is far from our only supernatural need. We must hasten back to Berinfell. Every aspect of our mission could change, depending upon what the scouts discover. The sooner we set them to the skies, the better."

"But, Olin," Goldarrow said, "The Nightstalkers? All of Berinfell will know, and the Conclave…"

Grimwarden snorted. "I care not for the Conclave's misgivings," he said. "And, though I may be sorely mistaken, I hope that the Elves of Berinfell will not begrudge the outstanding legion of warriors we bring for her defense. Once they learn of Asp and the threat he poses, I suspect all will be forgiven."

"Lords," Tommy said. "Spread the word. Feed and water the mounts, take such food as you can, and make ready for a long ride home. And…instruct each Elf to lift our needs to Ellos. Without His aid, we are doomed."

Silvertree

"I THINK we've gone far enough west, Khali!" Flet soldier Scout Irethor yelled across the open air to his flying partner. The Scarlet Raptor screeched as he banked her a little closer to the other.

"Just a bit more!" Khali called back. "Look at that up ahead. It's a beautiful sun shower."

"We're not here to sightsee, Khali!" Irethor growled. "Come on! We've plotted dozens of portals, and Grimwarden told us not to go past the western Gray Mountains. We've got to turn 'round!"

Khali ignored him. *As usual,* thought Irethor. He gave his raptor the knee signals that would send her into a speedy, shallow dive. He did have to admit that the sun shower up ahead was rather breathtaking. The crimson sun was setting on a low mantle of gray clouds, but its rays had blasted into a storm front at just the right angle. The nearly horizontal cloud bank became almost purple in the sun. And the rain curtain beneath it sparkled like diamond prisms, yielding light of every color. Irethor was actually glad to get a little closer. He had fond memories of sun showers, of dancing with his mother on the cobbled stone streets of Berinfell. It was a warm time, a—

Irethor got a sudden chill. There was an odd burning smell in the air. The storm front was only a few hundred yards distant. And Khali was pulling away.

"Khali!" Irethor shouted. "Khali, come back!" He drove his raptor forward as fast as it would fly and banked her hard to try to cut down on the distance to Khali. It wasn't until the bird tilted that Irethor saw.

His mind could not at first comprehend what he was seeing. Down on the peak of the foothills where the rain curtain drew a stark line across the ground...things were burning.

Trees, earth, streams, even rock—it was being consumed in blue fire wherever the rain band touched.

"Khali, NO!" Irethor screamed.

But it was too late. Khali drove her Scarlet Raptor right into the rain. There was a bluish flash, a sickly crackling sound, and she was gone.

"We have a decision to make before departing to the Gnomes," Grimwarden said, gazing up into the cavernous Ailianthium ceiling. "Or perhaps, I should say, you and the other Lords have a decision to make."

"Taeva?" Tommy asked.

Grimwarden nodded. He reached up and snapped a dark green apple, one of many dangling just above their heads. He took a monstrous bite that left his beard glistening. The Ailianthium's apples had become legendary and were sought by all who called Berinfell home. "She is quite...gifted."

"But she's not Elfkind," Tommy said.

"Don't be too certain of that," Grimwarden said.

Tommy grabbed an apple. "I thought she was Taladrim...she's their Princess, right?"

"She is their Princess, but if there's one thing she is not, it's Taladrim. You saw the Taladrim survivors. Did you not note the differences?"

"Skin color, for one," Tommy said. "Taeva's frame...she seems more sturdy somehow, quite a bit more athletic."

"Yes," Grimwarden replied. "There is much to wonder about Princess Taeva. If my eyes are not deceived, I believe there is more than one race in her blood. Perhaps…several."

"She might be part Elf?" Tommy said, his voice becoming higher and more enthusiastic than he'd meant it to.

After a bite that nearly split the core in half, Grimwarden said, "I think it's a possibility."

"Then you think we should invite Taeva to become a Lord of Berinfell?"

"Lord Felheart," Grimwarden replied. "I gave you no such counsel. There may be many reasons why she should not become a Lord, but her race may not be one of them."

Tommy rubbed his tired eyes. "I'm too exhausted to think about this kind of stuff," Tommy said. "The marathon journey back from Thynhold Cairn just about ruined us. I don't think I ought to be making important decisions right now."

"I did not advise you to make the decision," Grimwarden said. "At least not without inviting a greater intellect than your own. Take the matter before Ellos. Advise the other Lords to do likewise. Then, summon a council. And do it quickly. The minutes that slip by already feel to me like opportunities lost."

An hour before the council, and Kat stood in her chamber staring at herself in the glass. Mirrors had once been her mortal enemy. They told a hard truth and, for many years, Kat could not bear the sight of her own reflection. On Earth, the bluish coloring of her skin had made her different, a monstrous curiosity. People never looked beyond the flesh to know the person she was. They just couldn't get past the surface.

With a wave of her fingers, Kat brushed a lock of hair behind her ear. Then, everything had changed. Someone told her she was an Elf. An Elf! Every once in a while, she still giggled at images of Keebler or Santa's workshop. She wasn't just an Elf. She was a Lord of Berinfell, called by Ellos, by...

God.

Those years on Earth, she'd thought she had a disease. All that time, she'd thought she was nothing. Worse than nothing. But Ellos had awakened her. He'd shown her that she was beautiful just as she was. He'd adopted her into His family and given her a mission. And now, another had come.

Taeva.

She'd arrived in Berinfell a refugee. Everything she'd ever known had been destroyed. She had become...different. Her exotic looks, while entrancing to the guys, were peculiar...otherworldly. Kat wasn't sure, but Taeva didn't look Taladrim. She didn't look wholly anything. Taeva was an outcast standing outside the door looking in...wanting in. Kat thought she knew exactly how Taeva felt. Not that Taeva would ever admit it. No. Taeva would not knock. She needed an invitation.

Kat looked away from the mirror. She whispered, "An invitation I don't think I can give."

There was something about Taeva that didn't sit right with Kat. And she had almost convinced herself that it wasn't just petty jealousy. Taeva wasn't part of the Lordly bloodline. Never in Berinfell's six-thousand year history had the bloodline been broken. That alone would disqualify her, wouldn't it?

But she has a gift. Kat couldn't dispute that. Lightning bolts were pretty hard to ignore. And no one was supposed to have Lordly gifts unless born to the Lordly bloodline. So, if Taeva wasn't part Elven, of the Lordly line, how did she get a gift? And the way her gift manifested itself...that thing she did with her arms, hands, and fingers. There was something creepy about it, like two spiders constructing an intricate web. Even now, it made Kat shudder.

And then there was the impact Taeva had on they guys. Sure, Johnny fell in love once a week, but Jimmy? And...Tommy? They just about tripped over themselves trying to gain Taeva's notice and approval. Kat laughed quietly. *Jimmy better get his head on straight,* she thought. *Or he might wake up one day with arms and legs tied to two different pack beasts, and Regis holding the whip.* No, Regis would not abide Jimmy's wandering eye. And...

Tommy! Kat growled as she stomped across her chamber and threw herself onto the balcony couch. Looking up at the descending moon, she whispered, "You and your stupid curly hair and those big puppy dog eyes. I thought you...I thought we, ah! Never mind."

She stood straight up. "What am I doing?" she asked the Berinfell night. "The world is coming to an end, and I'm a Lord of Berinfell. I don't have time for this high school...prom Princess...nonsense." She wiped the tear from her cheek as if it was a drop of acid and stormed from the room.

She took the back stairs, a spiral that meandered down a wide castle turret and eventually led out to the Berinfell marketplace. Kat left the stairs and cut across Oak Narrows, a beautiful, tree lined gallery of paintings, carvings and sculptures. It also led past Taeva's quarters.

Kat didn't know how to ask what she was going to ask. But it seemed the only way to know about Taeva for sure.

The artwork called out to Kat, especially the seascapes. Kat thought of her mother back on Earth about the trips to the shore. Kat wanted to stop and look at the paintings, but need drove her on.

She found the row of small cottages along the east wall. Taeva's was the fourth one in. The door was shut. Kat knocked. Taeva didn't come. Kat knocked once more. Still nothing. Kat shrugged and started away.

A glimmer and a flash.

Kat turned and found herself staring through a high round window in Taeva's quarters. Taeva was there, sitting on the end of a table. She had her legs crossed Indian style. Her eyes were closed. And she was doing that weaving thing with her hands. Arcs of electricity—some white, some dark red, some a ghostly green—danced between her fingers, stretching, leaping, intertwining with others.

What is she doing? Kat wondered. The only time Kat had ever seen Taeva perform those movements, it was directly before she cast a lightning bolt. Kat backed away from the window.

Kat knew she could do it, knew she could read Taeva's thoughts. Maybe she should. It might give some answers. *No,* she thought. *Taeva is a guest in Berinfell. I won't do it without her permission.*

Kat moved on. As she walked, she couldn't help thinking about Taeva's hands.

"And, 'Behold!' says Ellos. 'I will not suffer their deeds forever. I will not hold back the Tide.' And all the venom of eternity will rise up in a Tide of Unmaking. All that was, all that is, and all that might be—will be swept away...consumed utterly. Unless the Tide is turned, those living who wander return, and the Seven be Seven again."

Tommy lowered the book and gazed from face to face, his fellow Lords seated on the thrones and then down to the cabinet seats where Grimwarden, Goldarrow and the Fletmarshalls were seated. No matter how hard he tried, Tommy found he could not keep his eyes from the empty throne seat between Kat and Jimmy. He took a deep breath and said, "The word of Ellos makes it clear that the Tide of Reckoning cannot be turned back...unless Berinfell's Lords are restored to Seven. Are we agreed on this point?"

He waited, watched until he had affirmation from each Elf present. The Lords sat in hand-carved, wooden seats that had been stained to preserve the natural grain of the wood while enhancing it with a pearlescent shimmer. Before each Lord, stood a very old candle stand. A pristine white candle sat in the center of a tree canopy cunningly wrought of very pure silver. As it melted, the wax of the candle ran across the branches, here and there, following the curving boughs and glistening on the faux leaves. Some of the Lords stared curiously at these candle stands, but eventually all nodded agreement.

"So then, we are left with few options and little time. What do we make of Princess Taeva of the Taladrim?"

Johnny spoke first. "I don't know about the rest of you," he said, "But I say she's it. She's the Seventh. Have you seen her draw lightning between her hands and throw down bolts like that Roman myth god, what's his name? Sleuth?"

Autumn said, "Zeus…and he was a *Greek* god."

"Right," Johnny said, frowning. "Right. Anyway, Taeva's gift is as powerful as any of ours."

"Powerful, yes," Kiri Lee said. "But we have seen other powers at work in Allyra. The Spider King alone harnessed powers that almost defeated all of us…together. Almost."

"Are you saying that Taeva's powers are from the Dark Arts?" Tommy asked.

"No," Kiri Lee replied. "Only that it is possible to have unique powers outside of what Ellos intended."

"Guardmasters?" Tommy asked. "You've dealt with Drefids and Dark Arts since long before we returned to Berinfell. What do you say on this matter?"

Goldarrow leaned forward. "I have seen Dark Arts enchantments, and they often seem to rival the Gifts of the Lords. But there is always a difference…often felt in the heart rather than seen. The energy seems to drain rather than empower. It inspires fear, not awe. And generally speaking, the Dark Arts are not used for good."

"That settles it, then," Johnny said. "Taeva used her lightning for good at Thynhold Cairn."

"That she did," Jimmy said. "Saved me bacon, more 'an once, she did."

"We have, however, seen the Dark Arts used to masquerade as good," Grimwarden said. "Meaning no disrespect to you, Goldarrow, and know that I agree with you wholeheartedly. But Wisps are a creation of the Dark Arts. We have all been fooled by the Dark Arts before."

"Is she even an Elf?" Regis asked. "The Line of Lords demands that Elven blood flow in her veins."

"I asked the same thing," Tommy said. "But we don't know. She's not Taladrim, not pure Taladrim anyway."

"Joost look at her," Jimmy said. "Looks like she's got a bit o' everything in her. Broad-limbed like the Gwar, a little bit of their colorin' too. But there are touches o' Elves there. See her ears. They're pointed like our—er, well, like ours would be if the blasted Drefids hadn't gotten all scissor happy. Sure they slant back a wee bit more, but she's got Elven blood, no doubt in my mind."

"At least our ears are growing back," Autumn said, fingering the arched projection of her right ear. "Not growing very fast, but still."

"Have any of you asked her?" Goldarrow inquired.

"What?" several Lords asked at once.

Goldarrow tilted her head and frowned. "Have any of you actually *asked Taeva* if she's part Elven?"

Silence filled the Throne Hall of Berinfell.

"What about you, Kat?" Grimwarden asked. "Have you used your gift on Taeva?"

Kat stiffened in her seat. "We are not at war with Taeva," Kat said. "She is an ally. I will not read her thoughts without Taeva's permission."

She swallowed. "I meant no offense, Guardmaster," she said. "But I do not want to abuse the gift Ellos gave me."

"I understand," Grimwarden replied. "But it may be that we must know...depending on how you rule here today."

"And that is what we must do," Tommy said. "We must rule. Either Taeva joins us or she does not. If you have anything else to say on the matter, now is the time for it."

"Her abilities compliment ours well," Johnny said. "Especially mine. With the two of us on Scarlet Raptors, we could provide cover from the air twice as good as we've ever had before."

"But she has not trained with us," Autumn said. "She doesn't know Vexbane or Nightform."

"She fights well enough," Jimmy said.

"But will she be content in Berinfell?" Charlie asked. "She may not have much Taladrim blood in her veins, but she loves her people. Wouldn't she want to rebuild Taladair?"

"I don't know," Tommy said. "I guess we'll have to ask that too."

"She's hot tempered," Kiri Lee said. "She reacts rather than responds."

"Haven't we all at times?" Tommy asked.

"Look," Jimmy said. "Joost look at the timing of all this. We've been without Jett for seven years now. And yet, joost when the Tide of Unmaking is unleashed, joost when the new prophecy is discovered and we need a Seventh, Taeva shows oop. Isn't that joost like Ellos?"

"Ellos' timing is perfect," Grimwarden said. "Have you all prayed?"

"I have," Tommy said. "A lot."

The rest nodded.

"Well?" Grimwarden asked. "What did you learn?"

"Learn?" Kat asked.

"From Ellos," Grimwarden replied. "Did you learn His will in this?"

Kat shook her head. "No definite answer," she said. "I had a hard time focusing my mind. This seems so important, but my prayers felt like they were bouncing off the ceiling."

"Mine too," Tommy said. "A lot of my prayers have felt that way lately."

"As have mine," Grimwarden said reluctantly.

"Just because we ask," Goldarrow said, "does not obligate Ellos to speak to us. Much that we need to know, we can discover in His written word. Much we cannot tell until the right time has come."

Grimwarden nodded with gusto. "That is wisdom if I have ever heard it," he said.

"I call a vote," Tommy said. "But we do it the old way, the way my great grandsire did it in Berinfell's first age thousands of years ago. You have all worn your medallions, I see. We will douse all candles. In the darkness, pray and think and ultimately decide. If you wish Taeva to join our ranks, to become a Lord of Berinfell, then place your medallion on the silver tree on the candle stand in front of you. If you do not believe she should become one of us, then keep your medallion around your neck."

"I am impressed, Tommy," Grimwarden said. "That is an old tradition. Very old."

"I did some reading," he said. "The wisdom of our past. I thought it might help."

"It might indeed."

"Now," Tommy said. "Blow out your candles."

They did, and the throne hall was plunged into darkness.

"Once you've cast your vote," Tommy explained, "Say your own name. Attendants, when you've heard each of the Six Lords, ignite the dremask braziers."

The hall plunged into a silence as impenetrable as the darkness.

There were no murmurs, no whispers, no creaks of chairs or squeak of boots on the floor. This was a solemn time.

"Felheart Silvertree," Tommy said, his voice echoing faintly.

And, after broad spans of silence, punctuated by Lordly names, the final name was spoken.

"Alreenia Hiddenblade," Kat said.

And the Throne Hall attendants restored the light.

Misguided Vengeance

"MY LIEGE, if I may be so bold," bowed Priest Dhrex.

"You were bold once already," Vault Minister Ghrell spat. "And that is one too many times, I fear."

"I was only asking that you consider—"

"And in front of the Conclave, too," Ghrell continued. "I tell you, Priest, if you were not under the protection of the Sacred Sanctuary, I'd have your wings torn off and your body piked atop the Central Spire."

Dhrex swallowed. The image of his wingless body run through with a Nemic polearm forced bile up his throat.

The pair talked on the third balcony of the Vault Minister's palatial home high atop one of thousands of red-rock spires in the Nemic mountain-desert of Tere Solium. The sedimentary towers were perfect protection from ground invaders. Meanwhile the arid climate forced any assailing army to double their food rations, making any prolonged siege nearly impossible.

The easterly setting sun flared red against the spires and sent long tendrils of shadow across the barren, undulating ground hundreds of feet below.

"Recognizing your restraint," Dhrex continued, feeling only slightly more bold at the Vault Minister's adherence to the Spirit Laws, "and trusting in your continued veneration of the Sacred Priests, I must insist that your judgement may be misplaced in this matter, and it's my job to present you unbiased wisdom."

Ghrell's eyes burned with fury, and every thorny plate on his abdomen bristled. "Unbiased wisdom..." the Vault Minister repeated, turning his eyes away from the impertinent fool before him. "Wisdom is such a temperamental thing."

The Priest followed the Vault Minister's gaze to the horizon. "Temperamental, my liege?"

"Wisdom says this, wisdom says that. And then it changes based on the mind of the speaker. It shifts with the wind, shifts with the passing of ages."

"I can see your point, but I—"

"Yet the wisdom of our ancestors is of inestimable worth." Ghrell turned to Dhrex and drilled him with a glare. "Such wisdom is far beyond what we can manage in this day. Wouldn't you agree, Priest?" he spat out the word *Priest*.

Dhrex rustled his wings awkwardly. "Well, yes, the wisdom of those who've gone before us is certainly one of the pinnacles of our—"

"So I wonder. I wonder what wisdom motivated our ancestors to defend themselves against the woodland parasites."

"Woodland parasites?" Dhrex frowned. "I...I don't follow. If you could..."

"And when our people rose up to fight, were they not cast down from the sky and dashed upon the forest floor of the infidels? Tell me, Priest." Ghrell's eyes had an eerie light behind them. "I said, tell me. Is it not the Sacred Texts themselves which designate *us* as the First Born of Allyra? Are we not those who were called to reign and rule upon the holy grounds without and within?"

"Vault Minister Ghrell, perhaps you are misinterpreting—"

Ghrell's hand shot up and encased the Priest's throat, choking his airway.

"Perhaps it is *you*, young Priest, who needs reminding of precisely what the Elves have done to our people."

Ghrell lifted the pitiful Servant of Allyra off the floor by his neck. Dhrex's eyes bulged as he struggled to squirm free, but Ghrell held him close and spat as he spoke, "Study the ancient words, imp! Then you would see what the heretical Elves are hiding from the faithful Nemic... from all of Allyra. And—"

A blinding white light exploded in the city somewhere below, the intensity so strong that Ghrell shrank back and dropped Dhrex to the floor.

Suddenly the light changed to blue followed by the ear-shattering sound of splitting stone. Dhrex crawled to the balcony's edge while Ghrell took flight, both of them with mouths and eyes gaping wide. Spreading out over the ground was a massive, azure blanket of shimmering water. But rather than fill in the barren wasteland, it hovered in a horizontal plane, suspended in mid air.

Then, the Vault Minister and the Priest heard the screams.

Stone at the bases of no less than fifty spires cracked and splintered, and slowly the towers began to fall. But they did not shift and topple. They dropped straight down into the shimmering, surreal plane. Some sort of sucking gravity drew them down at increasing speed such that few Nemic citizens had time to fly out from their dwellings. Spires, homes of thousands, slid away into nothingness.

Dhrex suddenly realized just which spires these were. "Mother Allyra, save us," he whispered. "The hatcheries."

"NO!" Ghrell yelled, his voice instantly hoarse. He clambered toward the balcony's edge, leaped, and shot down toward the aberration.

The sound hit him like the ringing of hammers. Stone cracking, concussive waves like thunder, but something more as well. There was a kind of thin, high wail that seared through armor and flesh to rattle his skeleton. It was grief and agony on a scale Ghrell never thought possible. It was the sound of hundreds of Nemic children and their attendants shrieking in horror.

Ghrell beat his wings with the pull of gravity, diving toward the descending spires with complete disregard for his own life. But there was nothing he could do. Not even halfway to the cataclysmic event, the towers disappeared completely, the cries of the children vanishing as one.

Ghrell roared, diving faster and faster. From Dhrex's angle he was sure the Vault Minister would follow them into the mystical blue sea. But before Ghrell could reach it the plane snapped shut with a thunderous *boom* that knocked the Vault Minister out of the air.

Dhrex had forgotten about the searing pain around his neck and flew down toward the Vault Minister. The whole thing had happened so fast; the Priest was still trying to make sense of it all. As he flew, Dhrex noticed Nemic taking to the evening sky, surely searching for the cause of so much chaos.

"Vault Minister!" Dhrex called. "Vault Minister!"

Ghrell lay on his back amongst some large red stones. Dhrex descended upon him. "Can you hear me, my liege?"

The Vault Minister moaned, struggling to open his eyes.

"It's me, Dhrex!"

Ghrell hissed at the sound of the Priest's name, then coughed up blood. "Are they gone, fool?"

The Priest looked up at the circular vacancy, appearing like a field full of freshly hewn tree stumps. Dhrex nodded. "Yes, sire. All gone."

The Vault Minister swore in Nemic, struggling to prop himself up on his elbows. "Don't touch me," he said when Dhrex tried to assist. Ghrell wanted to see it for himself. He squinted, forcing his eyes to focus on the absence of so many spires in his beloved city.

The sight was more painful than anything he could imagine.

Absolute grief. He could barely think, fighting back the insignificance of the injuries that threatened to take his life in favor of the pain of losing so many innocent lives. It was incredulous too; beyond the depth of his imagination to comprehend. *How could this happen? How could such a thing be possible?* Nothing on Allyra's shining face had such destructive power.

Ghrell coughed again, using his wing to wipe blood out of the corner of his mouth. It was then, from the very corner of his eye, he spotted something in the sky. A distant blur at first, even with his exceptional Nemic farsight, but then gradually coming into focus. When it did, his heart nearly stopped.

"LOOK!" the Vault Minister cried.

Dhrex turned to follow Ghrell's outstretched finger. "I don't see, my liege. Your people have taken flight. They've come to—"

"LOOK, YOU FOOL! IN THE DISTANCE!"

Dhrex looked again, past the crimson spires, past the swarming Nemic and further back over the northern mountain range. A tiny speck hovered above the border of their lands. Dhrex blinked through three sets of corneas, magnifying the speck to 25 times its size.

It was an Elven Scout on a Scarlet Raptor.

"No," Dhrex thought. "It cannot be."

"YET, IT IS!" Ghrell snarled, climbing to his feet and shoving the Priest aside. "As I have told you!" He flapped his wings, struggling to take flight. Sand sprayed Dhrex as the Vault Minister ambled up to join his onlooking masses above. "LOOK UPON OUR FOES, MY PEOPLE!" he pointed to the horizon. "SEE HOW THE ELVES BESET US FROM AFAR AND MURDER OUR CHILDREN! COWARDICE!"

The host of Nemic fliers turned to discover exactly what their leader pointed at. Thousands of sets of eyes cycled through their lenses and focused in on the Elven Scout far in the distance.

Ghrell sat at his empty dining hall table gnawing off the heads of rock beetles. Normally he enjoyed the bowl of his favorite delicacy. But today he was absent from the pleasure of it. His thoughts were elsewhere.

"Vault Minister Ghrell?" came an attendant at the far end of the room.

Ghrell didn't even register the summons, his articulated jaw grinding away on a recently deceased beetle. He was preparing for war. But something bothered him, something he cared not to admit. And if he was going to lead his people to annihilate the Elven race, he couldn't afford to be bothered by doubts.

Still, the thought scratched the back of his skull like a disgruntled sand flea. The strange blue apparition that stole so many innocent lives... *was it really the Elves' doing? Was Dhrex correct in his caution?*

Ghrell swallowed. Perhaps he'd been too hasty to accuse the Elves of this bloodshed. Perhaps Dhrex's ideas needed hearing out.

"No," Ghrell spat the remains of a rock beetle carcass onto the floor. "No, he isn't right." He still came to the same conclusion he'd all but voiced down below: *war* would be the only response.

The attendant tried a little louder. "Vault Minister Ghrell?"

"WHAT?!" Ghrell roared.

"S-s-sir, your scouts bring word."

"Send them in." Ghrell reached for another rock beetle trying to escape from the bowl.

Two Nemic scouts covered in dust and bleached from long hours in the sun strode into the dining hall and saluted their Vault Minister.

"What news do you bring?" Ghrell said, his eyes focused on the the beetle he was slowly squeezing to death.

"Vault Minister, we bring word of..." the lead scout hesitated, then looked to the other. They'd rehearsed this before they landed, but now the words were hard to find. "...Word of—"

"SPIT IT OUT," roared Ghrell. "Or get out of my hall before I bite your heads off too."

"Well, your Vaultship, it's just that..."

"We honestly don't know what to call what we've seen," said the second scout.

Ghrell mocked them. "You *honestly don't know what to call*—what in Allyra are you babbling about? OUT! GET OUT!" Then Ghrell stuffed the beetle in his mouth.

The attendant started to usher them out when the first scout yelled over his shoulder, "It's a *Curtain of Doom*."

For the first time since they entered, Ghrell looked toward the scouts who were now almost out the door. He let the chewed-up flesh of the beetle slide out of his mouth and pile onto the table. "You said *what*?"

The attendant and the two scouts stopped, then turned back around.

"In the East, Mother Allyra bends from a plague of unmentionable description," said the second scout.

"Well, *try*," answered Ghrell.

The first scout stepped forward. "It's a wall of light," he said. "Like a rippling curtain stretching from horizon to horizon. It moves ever so slowly. Quite impressive, glimmering, colorful. But wherever the wall meets the ground, the terrain is utterly consumed."

"*Consumed*," Ghrell repeated.

"It is simply no more," said the second scout. "We fired bolts into the apparition to see what would happen."

"And?" asked Ghrell, growing weary of coaxing information from his scouts.

"Well, sir, it vanished," said the second scout. "Consumed in a flash. No more."

"*No more...*" Ghrell reached for another beetle and tore off the head with his teeth. Whatever doubts he'd suffered a moment ago, they were put to flight. Dhrex was just as pitiful with his assumptions as Ghrell suspected. *Wait until the Priest hears this,* Ghrell thought. *Then he'll see.* Ghrell cursed himself for wanting the Priest's approval so much. *If only he weren't the*—he stopped the thought from going any further.

"It's the Elves," Ghrell finally said. "Bent on wiping us from the face of Allyra." The Vault Minister stood up and pushed his chair aside. Blood was filling his face, his hands balling up into tight fists. "I want to purge Allyra of these misbegotten, pointed-eared usurpers! WAR, I SAY!" roared Ghrell. *"LET US AVENGE MURDER WITH WAR!!"*

Dhrex paced the balcony of his quarters, situated alongside the temple. "This is not good," he muttered to himself. "Not good at all."

Wringing his hands, Dhrex took a few deep breaths trying to calm himself down, trying to get clear on the situation.

"Think, think, think," Dhrex ordered himself.

He knew Ghrell was about to explode. *If he hadn't ordered war against the Elves yet,* he thought, *he's about to.* As much as he respected Ghrell, even honored him, he did not agree with him...*couldn't agree with him,* was more like it. *There was too much proof to the contrary...wasn't there?*

But the more Dhrex thought about it, the more he realized he couldn't prove the strange, blue blaze of destruction *wasn't* from the Elves. "Using the power of the Lords, it's possible," he said to the air. "But not plausible. Why would they?"

His pace along the balcony quickened. He had to think fast. Ghrell was beyond reasoning, but *he* wasn't. "I will make up my own mind," Dhrex said. "I will do what logic demands. What justice demands."

He looked to the northern horizon to a point caught between the setting sun and the encroaching darkness. "I have served you faithfully, Mother Allyra." He swallowed against what he was about to say next. "But

I sense their is a call greater than your preservation. The preservation of *life*. Of the souls created by Ellos Himself. For too long I have bowed to inferior truths, though merit they may have. There are superior pursuits, and of such, I chose."

But how could he betray his people? How could he willingly inform the Elves of Ghrell's plot knowing he'd doom his own race?

That's when Dhrex realized he had no reason to *not* suspect the Elves were bent on annihilating his people. But he had no reason to suspect them either. For all his reasonings as a Priest, he was finally making a decision based on *faith*.

And it was the best decision he knew to make.

24

Coronation

FOUR MEDALLIONS hung from the silver tree candle stand. Tommy, Jimmy, Johnny and...Kat had all voted for Taeva to become a Lord of Berinfell.

"Kat!" Kiri Lee said, "How? You...you changed your mind?"

"No," Grimwarden said. "Each Lord's reason is his own or her own. The vote stands...unless Taeva is not of Elven blood or unless she does not wish this for herself. As Lords of Berinfell, you must speak with one voice. Go to Taeva. Go now."

Taeva opened the door to her quarters. "Well...hello," she said, the words welcoming but wary. "What brings...uh, *everyone* here at this time of night?"

Tommy stepped forward and said, "We're sorry about the hour, but there is a matter we should discuss before we depart for Appleheart Village in the morning. Will you come?"

"I feel like I am back at the academy," Taeva replied, "and I've been sent to the headmaster's office. Am I in some kind of trouble?"

"Far from it," Tommy said.

"You WHAT?" Taeva asked, stepping backward and resting an arm on the throne. "Is this some kind of jest?"

"Elves do have a rather warped sense of humor," Tommy said, "but, Princess Taeva, we couldn't be more serious. So much has happened in the past few months. Our minds are all spinning. But as we looked at the most recent events, we began to see threads coming together."

"Yu showin' oop here was a big one," Jimmy said.

"The way we worked together in battle was another," Johnny said.

"The fact that you have a gift that ordinary Allyrans don't have," Tommy said.

"My power is no different than yours," Taeva said.

"That's just it," Tommy said. "We believe that Ellos has given you this gift to become a new Lord of Berinfell."

"The new prophecy means we need to be Seven again," Johnny said.

Taeva's expression softened from shock to confusion. "And you think I'm your new Seventh Lord? But I am Taladrim."

"With all due respect," Tommy said gently, "Taladair is—"

Kat broke in. "What Lord Felheart means to say is that we respect your kingdom and your position within it. If we can turn back the Tide, and you should want to rebuild your city, of course, you would be free to do so and with all the might of the Elves behind you."

Taeva blinked and her eyes met Tommy's for a moment. Then, she looked away and walked slowly behind the ornate seat that might be hers. Taeva had known royalty her entire life. She had grown up with the expectation that, one day, she would rule the Taladrim nation and wield the power of that position. But now, the hallowed Lords of Berinfell had come to offer her a place high above the throne of Taladair. This was an offer of nearly matchless power, prestige and dominion. She recalled a similar offer from another but shook the memory away. *This* was different.

In all her plotting, in all her designs, Taeva never once dreamed that she could be put in such an advantageous position. But was that all it was…an advantage? Tommy, Jimmy, Johnny and Kat—especially Kat—had welcomed Taeva as a friend, something she had never genuinely had before.

"There is one…issue," Tommy said. "You must be at least part Elven by birth."

Taeva attempted a thoughtful expression but inwardly she felt a spreading, icy cold. How much could she tell them? She had to answer them now. A delay would be seen as dishonesty.

"I am half Elven," Taeva said. "My mother was full Elven from the tribes of the far east."

"I knew it," Jimmy said.

"Cool," Johnny added.

"Grimwarden was right," Tommy said. "Will you join us then, Taeva? Fight by our side, defend Berinfell and all of Allyra?"

Tell them everything, Taeva's conscience demanded. *Tell them right now, or don't accept this invitation.* But there was another voice, a voice of fear that warned her of what her newfound friends might think…and no longer count themselves her friends. Should they know the truth.

Taeva raised her eyes, then replied, "I would be honored."

After sprinting throughout Berinfell, Tommy finally found Grimwarden in the Sun Chamber near the Aviary where the raptors were kept and cared for. The Guardmaster sat on a low mantle of stone near one of the Aviary's many fountains. He was with a flet soldier Tommy hadn't seen before.

"Guardmaster!" Tommy called. "I have grand tidings. Princess Taeva is indeed part Elven and she has agreed to become the Seventh Lord of Berinfell. The Seven will be Seven again! We must alert the herald and sound a clarion call for all Berinfell to know. And…" Tommy's words trailed off to nothing as he drew near enough to Grimwarden to see his pained expression.

"The heralds will have to wait, I'm afraid," Grimwarden said. "Tommy, this is Irethor."

Irethor stood and bowed low. Tommy returned the gesture with a nod.

"He is one of the scouts we sent out," Grimwarden explained, "to map the portals and search for any sign or evidence that the Tide of Unmaking has begun. You'll need to gather the Lords and the Fletmarshalls here. Irethor has grave news."

In the grand Berinfell Sun Chamber near the Aviary, the Lords and their military leaders sat for several moments in stunned silence. Irethor, the lone Elven scout, stood in the center of the chamber. Green, yellow and golden sunlight in all manner of leaf shapes dappled the cobblestone at his feet. But in a chamber designed with happier times in mind, even the dancing sunlight couldn't lift the Elves' spirits.

Goldarrow was the first to conquer the fear-induced paralysis the scout's news had brought. "You are certain of this?" she asked. "It could not have been some natural phenomenon? Especially powerful stormfronts have been known to cast sheet lightning. It can be devasta—"

"I am afraid not, Guardmaster," Irethor replied. "I watched Khali fly into it. In an instant…she was gone, incinerated…annihilated, ah! I don't know how to describe it."

"She was unmade." Goldarrow stared at the floor.

"Yes," Irethor said. "That is what it did to her. There is more to tell. After Khali perished, I flew down to the surface as close to the... unmaking as I dared. I was not fifteen paces from where it struck the ground. It consumed everything it touched. And it was moving. Not swiftly, thank Ellos. Just creeping along, an inch at a time. But my Lords, please believe me when I say that I am not exaggerating. I looked left and right. It stretched from one horizon to the next. It is consuming our world."

Silence gagged those in the chamber once more.

Princess Taeva began to whisper, and many heads turned toward her. "...many tragedies should come in my lifetime. Can this be real?" She blinked, ignored the attention from others, and asked, "What is the nearest village to...to this Tide of Unmaking?"

"Windy Gap," Irethor replied.

"You warned them?" she asked.

"Of course," Irethor said. "With an admonition to flee east, to warn all civilization in its path."

"That is admirable," Grimwarden said. "But it will not be enough. The Tide moves slowly, you say, but it cannot be so slow that we could reach everyone in Allyra from horizon to horizon. Still...we must do what we can. We will need to push our aviaries past their limit and start a chain reaction across this world."

"Where will we tell them to go?" Goldarrow asked. "Berinfell could hold many, but..."

Grimwarden's gaze was as weary as Tommy had ever seen. The old Guardmaster looked especially old when he said, "But...if the Tide of Unmaking is not itself unmade, then even Berinfell and its newly reinforced walls will offer no protection to any who flee here."

�֍

"Forgive us the austere nature of this ceremony," Goldarrow said. "You should have gained this medallion in a spectacular event on the Feithrill Way, the great thoroughfare of this city in front of fifty-thousand cheering Elves."

"Boot instead, yu get stook with oos," Jimmy said. "In a mostly empty throne room, that is."

"Thank you, Guardmaster," Taeva said. "If it were under different circumstances, I would be glad of the small ceremony. I do not much care for grand spectacles. And given the recent news, something small and swift is warranted."

Gathered in Berinfell's Throne Hall were the Lords, several Fletmarshalls, Goldarrow and Grimwarden. A cool breeze drifted through the floor-to-ceiling arched windows, lifting the silken drapes into slow waves. White and blue petals from the rosewoods and feint apples drifted down like snow.

"Endurance and Victory!" Goldarrow shouted.

All the attendees answered in like manner.

"Today," Goldarrow said, "we welcome a gift from Ellos Almighty, in the time of our need. We welcome a new Lord to the rolls of Berinfell."

The Lords sat upon their thrones. Taeva stood a few paces away from her chair, and Goldarrow stood before her. "The crystal face of this medallion is blank now," she said, holding up the necklace. "But with your oath, you will begin a new Tribe. The Tribe of…forgive me. I do not know your surname. What is your family name, Taeva, on the Elven side…your mother's side?"

Taeva hesitated. She wanted desperately to make up a name, but she found she couldn't. She would not betray the memory of her mother in that way. She chose to trust that the Elves of Berinfell had long forgotten the name she was about to utter.

"Her name…her name was Ravenpath."

Goldarrow's eyes narrowed. "Taeva Ravenpath," she said. "It is a beautiful name...beautiful and sad somehow. Like a memory too sweet to forget but fading nonetheless as age takes its toll."

Grimwarden raised an eyebrow. He was always moved when Goldarrow waxed poetic.

"You are Taeva of the tribe Ravenpath. You were born a stranger, but are welcomed in Berinfell as friend...as family. But you must also choose to fulfill those duties by a pure heart. Your position requires stout leadership, but also . . . relentless service. Will you, before Ellos and all these you see assembled here, assume your position as a Lord of Elves? Will you honor our creeds? And will you serve your people?"

"I will," said Taeva.

Goldarrow lifted the medallion. "Then, by virtue of blood and word"—she lifted the cord over Taeva's head—"I deem you a Lord of Berinfell. And I give you the amulet of the tribe Ravenpath. You must wear it at all times, covering your heart, signifying your everlasting Covenant to lead and protect your people, even at risk of your own life.

"Notice that the amulet itself is crafted from the most precious metals and stones, but the necklace is but a plain black cord. Remember, you—like the people you serve—are a blessed mixture of all that is precious and all that is common, and you must never stray from the right path. Now, sit, Lord of Elves. Sit upon the throne of your Tribe."

Taeva sat to the applause of all. Goldarrow's words, the oath itself had touched her at a level she hadn't thought possible. She felt something she didn't understand. *Love, perhaps?* But before she could begin to accept that as reality, two other words from the oath clambered back into focus. And no matter what Taeva tried to do to banish them, the words *mixture* and *stranger* would not relent their assault.

A series of sharp knocks on the door shattered the silence of the wee hours.

Grimwarden pried open one eyelid. "This had better be important!" he growled. "I've beheaded for less!"

Silence from the door.

"WELL?" Grimwarden thundered.

"There is a messenger in the Aviary," came the timid voice. "He brings urgent news."

Grimwarden grunted, sat up and rubbed his eyes. "Tell him to feed and water his raptor. I'll be there shortly."

"He has no raptor."

"What?" Grimwarden asked. "I don't have time for riddles."

"He flew here himself. He is one of the Nemic."

The Nemic? In the middle of the night? Grimwarden leaped out of bed. "Take him to an empty chamber in Aviary Tower," he commanded. "I will meet him there immediately! And...and summon the Lords!"

"I remember you," Tommy said. He stood in front of the other Lords and stared at their unexpected visitor. "You were at the Conclave."

"Yes," the Nemic replied still breathing heavily. "I am Dhrex, Priest of Mother Allyra, and attendant to Vault Minister Ghrell." He leaned on a fist and rested his wing upon the table.

Tommy thought the Nemic looked sickly or distressed...or both. Beneath the filed-down thorny plates, the Nemic's lean chest pulsed rapidly. The fliers heart beat twice as fast as any other race in Allyra and even faster still from the fierce exertion.

"Clearly you have driven yourself to the brink," Grimwarden said. "What brings you with such haste?"

"War," Dhrex said.

Chill wind whistled through the high Aviary Tower. Somewhere outside, a Scarlet Raptor cried.

"War," Grimwarden uttered a whispery echo. He suddenly thought he knew. "So Asp and his forces came to Tere Solium. I am sorry. We should have—"

"No," Dhrex said. "No Drefid has come to our desert. I speak of my nation waging war upon yours."

"Against Berinfell?" Goldarrow said, her words clipped with panic. "Against the Elves. Why?"

"And why would yu tell us?" Jimmy asked.

"Vault Minister Ghrell has nursed a very personal grudge against the Elves for a long, long time," Dhrex said. "5807, the memory of war between our nations, lives on vividly among us...some of us, that is. Many feel that you are at fault for all the war and strife, scouring our beloved Mother Allyra."

"Preposterous!" Grimwarden grumbled. "We fight because we must. And in so doing, we have saved this world from far worse devastation."

"You do not need to convince me," Dhrex said. "That is why I come now, betraying my people. I know that the Elves are not to blame. And I have avidly followed how lovingly you dwell among Allyra's forests. But I am one. Ghrell has most stirred up for war. And the tragedy in our kingdom will set them in motion."

"What tragedy?" Kat asked.

Dhrex told the story: the hatcheries falling into the magic abyss, thousands of innocent Nemic vanishing in seconds, and then the Elven scout spotted in Nemic skies.

"One of our scouts," Grimwarden said. "That was an unfortunate coincidence."

"A coincidence that pushed Ghrell over the edge. As for the destruction we suffered, do you know what it was?" Dhrex asked. "What it was that swallowed our spires, our people?"

"Portals," Tommy said. "Asp and the Drefids have tampered too often in the Dark Arts, traveling from our world to another, making everything unstable. Those are tears or rips in the world. And there is worse. The Tide of Unmaking has begun. That is why our scouts have flown so far from Berinfell: we were trying to find it."

"Tide?" Dhrex asked. "You mean the curtain of doom, far to the west? Our fliers have seen it also. Ghrell blames it on the Elves. He claims that to destroy Berinfell to the very last Elf is the only way to stop the curtain...the *Tide*, as you name it. Ghrell calls you *woodland parasites* and seeks your destruction."

"This is madness," Grimwarden said. "How long, Dhrex?"

"I am a Priest of Mother Allyra," Dhrex replied, his eyes darting relentlessly. "I know little of military action."

"Best estimate, then," Goldarrow said. "Please."

"The Vault Minister spoke some things," Dhrex said. "Let me think. Let me think! Ah, wait, yes...he said something about the city, after the tragedy. Nine days, he said, to verify that the other spires are undamaged and stable."

"Nine days and they march for Berinfell?" Tommy asked.

"We are Nemic," Dhrex said. "We do not march."

"What about war preparations?" Grimwarden asked. "That will take some time."

Dhrex nodded. "Yes, yes, it will. But how long, I cannot say. I suspect that Ghrell has been preparing for this for some time."

"How many?" Goldarrow asked. "What is the size of the force he could bring?"

"I do not know," Dhrex said. "But during our last parade, I saw them. Enough to fill the sky. And Ghrell once said eighteen squadrons, but I do not know what that me—"

"Eighteen squadrons!" Grimwarden thundered. "That...that's close to sixty-thousand! And here we are without the majority of our raptors. We will have to fight without the skies."

Goldarrow said, "We will mount five-hundred ballistas, position our long bows in defense of the private sectors. The first volley of ten thousand shafts should bring that number down fast."

"Yes, yes," Grimwarden said. "Wait, I am sorry, Dhrex. Here we speak of killing your countrymen."

Dhrex said, "No, I've already passed that line. I left my people to warn you. I do not wish any to perish, but there is no honor in our nation's assault."

"Assemble the Fletmarshalls!" Grimwarden commanded. "Goldarrow, see to it. We will need to give them explicit instructions before we depart for the Gnome village. They must—"

"Wait," Tommy said. "I never thought I'd say this but..."

"But what?" Grimwarden asked. All eyes turned to Tommy.

"But, no." Tommy thought sure the old Guardmaster would box his ears for that, but he didn't.

"You don't want us to come with you?" Goldarrow asked.

"I want you to," Tommy said. "But you've got to be here. You've got to guard Berinfell."

"The Fletmarshalls are capable," Grimwarden asked. "You will need our help."

"Not anymore," Tommy said. "You have trained us well. You have trained us to rule. The fight on Earth is not about numbers. Berinfell needs you here."

Grimwarden and Goldarrow were speechless. But they nodded.

"You'll have to excuse me," said Dhrex, "but I must return to Tere Solium. They will be expecting me, and I wish not to raise any suspicions."

"Thank you, Dhrex," said Tommy. "We are forever indebted to you and your sacrifice."

Dhrex puffed. "You can repay me with a bed to sleep on should we all survive, for soon I will certainly be homeless."

A Moonlight Beating

THE SCARLET Raptors soared high in the swiftly reddening Allyran sky. The envoy included the Seven Lords of Berinfell, Bengfist of the Gwar, Jastansia of the Saer, the two Dreadnaughts, Mr. Charlie and Regis, and the Sentinel the Lords called Miss Finney. They were all bound for the Gnome city of Appleheart Village in Moon Hollow.

The flight was long, and the sun set and rose twice and set once more before the Lords caught first sight of the Justice Tree. Tommy flew lead and spotted the hulking moonlit tree. He leaned in his saddle and looked over his left shoulder. Kat was there as usual. He waved to get her attention. *We're here,* Tommy thought, hoping she was listening.

"*I see it,*" Kat thought back. "*I'll tell the others. But, Tommy…*"

Yeah?

"*Back in Berinfell…you never really answered Goldarrow's question. The Tide of Unmaking, remember? If we don't stop it, even Berinfell isn't safe. I get that, but what else is troubling you?*"

Tommy sighed and thought, *It's about Earth, Kat. Even on Earth, there won't be anyplace to hide. The Tide will consume everything.*

"*I don't understand, Tommy. Are you sure? How can it be Ellos' will to destroy everything?*"

It's not His will, Tommy thought. *Not His wish. The Prophecies are clear on that. It's a consequence of a broken world. And even though we were forced through the portals the first time, we've inadvertently pushed both worlds toward destruction.*

"Funny," Kat thought.

Us helping destroy two worlds is funny?

"No, you goof. I mean before, you were coming to me with your doubt… about Ellos, and I basically just told you to have faith. But now…now, you're coaching me."

Iron sharpens iron, Tommy replied. *Isn't that what Grimwarden taught us?*

"Yeah, I guess it is. But when Taeva showed up, well…I thought…"

What?

"Never mind."

Tommy wouldn't let it go that easily. *C'mon, Kat, what about Taeva?*

"No, it's nothing. But there's something else, isn't there?"

Something else?

"Something else about the Tide? You still aren't telling me everything you suspect."

You're changing the subject.

"Yes, I am," Kat thought. "But I need to, and you need to tell me what you've figured out."

Kat knew him too well. This was the one part he didn't want to discuss, and Kat had whittled him right down to it.

The Tide of Unmaking was a terrifying reality, but there was one aspect of it that Tommy could not shake. It was the thing that disturbed his sleep and skittered in the dark corners of his thoughts every waking moment. It was a stark fear…as if his neck were perched upon the base of a guillotine and some masked executioner might pull the cord at any moment.

Tommy relented and told Kat. *There's no escape if the Tide isn't stopped,* he thought to her. *But Asp and his minions are probably still using the portals, maybe constantly. They could be speeding up the Tide. That means that the clock is ticking for us to stop it, and we have no idea how much time is left. It might be weeks. But then again, it might be before we can blink.*

The moment the party from Berinfell landed, they were surrounded by little people wearing leather armor imprinted with the patterns of all manner of foliage, branch, and root. They were the Gnomic Leaf Guard, and in spite of their size, they were not to be trifled with. They bore lethal crossbows, heavy clubs they called *thwack hammers,* and all manner of crippling gadgets and gizmos.

"Halt, Elves!" the leader cried out. His helm was crafted like the thick base of a tree with a few gnarled branches reaching out from it. But it was a tree with a scowling, knothole face. "Invited who did, you to Silverlight Grove?"

"We had no invitation," Tommy declared boldly, hopping down from his raptor. "Nor do we need one, Thorkber, you well-meaning goober!"

The challenging Gnome threw up his grimacing faceplate and dropped his thwack hammer. "Comes, Lord Felheart to visit the Gnomes!" he exclaimed, giving Tommy's leg a swift hug. "Come you, now with me! All of you! Be it not too late!"

Thorkber took Tommy's hand and nearly yanked him off his feet.

"Whoa, Thorkber," Tommy said, "where are...what are we...what's going on?"

"The Thrashing, Elf-boy," Thorkber said with a lusty laugh. "Heh, heh. Are not, you, Elf-boy anymore! Hurry, all of you, hurry now!"

Jast's long Saer fingers scratched curiously at her chin. "Thrashing?"

Bengfist shrugged. "Sounds violent," he said. "Might be fun, heh, heh."

Thorkber began giving orders to his Leaf Guard soldiers to clear the way to the Thwack Pit.

And they did just that. Blowing strange, not-so-tuneful horns and banging thwack hammers upon shields, the group of short warriors led the way for their visitors. They went straight through the middle of Appleheart Village, passed the Justice Tree, and turned a sharp corner that led down into a deep dell.

Cheers like a stout wind rushed up the hill to greet them all. The round hollow was actually a natural amphitheater that now held over a thousand shouting, hooting, laughing Gnomes. And in the bottom center of it all was a grand stage lit from all sides by blazing dremask lanterns.

"Come, you now!" Thorkber yelled and he charged down the aisle.

Tommy and the others followed, drawing awed glances from the few Gnomes who turned away from their fixation on the stage long enough to notice the newcomers.

"Is this what I think it is?" Kat asked in Tommy's mind.

I'm afraid so, Tommy replied.

"What is this?" Taeva asked.

"I am not certain," Bengfist said. "But I LIKE it!"

Jast shook her head and muttered, "Just like a Gwar."

Bengfist feigned resentment. "What?"

Upon the stage stood two Gnome combatants. Each wore a pair of thick leather breeches and a strange harness that secured armor pads over his shoulders and chest. And each wielded a massive thwack hammer.

One charged the other, took a huge roundhouse swing but missed. The other answered but the shot was rushed and bounced harmlessly off the other's shoulder armor.

"Entreaty!" Thorkber cried out. "Hold the contest!"

The two Gnomes doing battle froze in their tracks and turned. Eventually, the crowd noise died down as well.

"Hear, Gnomes!" Thorkber cried out. "To Appleheart, guess you who comes, who comes to witness the championship round of the Thrashing!"

That was when one of the combatants leaped into the air and shouted, "Tommy, Kat, Autumn, Johnny, Jimmy and Kiri Lee! Come the Berinfell Lords to see me trounce old Gilbang here?"

Gilbang snorted. "See we won't that, Barrister Migmar!"

"Migmar," Tommy chided, "what are you doing? I thought you promised to retire from the Thrashing tournament last year!"

Migmar laughed. "Have I still more in my gut. Win, I do, this year and tie me Folgort's record of four Thrashings in a row!"

"Get us back to it!" Gilbang yelled. "Feel you soon like four Thrashings happened to you!"

"Fighting words, eh?" Migmar. "Hmph!" Just then, Migmar took a bite of a stringy, orange colored root.

"Not fair, Migmar!" Gilbang yelled.

"Forbid the rules not dragonroot!" Migmar shouted back. He raised his thwack hammer and charged Gilbang. The crowd erupted in furious cheers.

"Why are they fighting?" Taeva asked. "He's not going to—"

Migmar leveled a wild horizontal swing, but Gilbang spun away from it. As he whirled, Gilbang let the momentum carry him into a strike of his own. His thwack hammer cracked Migmar soundly on the back of the head. There were two odd noises, and Migmar sailed through the air, crashing to the ground some ten feet away."

"Oh, no!" Jast cried.

"This is a barbaric people!" Taeva said. "He's just killed your friend."

Tommy shook his head. "No, not barbaric...just hard-headed."

"What? But he—"

"Just watch."

Taeva looked back into the ring and blinked in amazement.

Migmar laughed and leaped to his feet. "Good one, Gilbang!" he crowed. "Felt it, I almost did."

"That blow would have shattered my skull," Taeva said. "Just look at those clubs they wield."

"Gnomes *really are* hard-headed," Jimmy chimed in. "Skulls and bones are exceedingly hard. Yu can'na hurt them mooch with those wee clubs."

"It's true," Kiri Lee said to the still dubious Taeva. "I once saw a Gnome child fall from a tree, bounce and get up giggling."

"Hey'ya," Thorkber called into the ring, "is what the score?"

"Winning is Migmar, 2-1," Gilbang said, winding up for a charge. "Distract me not!"

Thorkber turned and whispered conspiratorially, "Beat me Gilbang did this year. Hope I that Migmar crowns him, heh, heh!"

And Migmar did just that. He ran a tight circle around Gilbang and leaped over a low thwack hammer swipe. Before Gilbang could turn and defend, Migmar lifted his thwack hammer with both hands as if he was about to split a stump with an axe. He brought the club down hard. It connected smartly with the back of Gilbang's head, making an oddly hollow-sounding wooden THOCK!

"A Blowthark!" the crowd cheered. "Blowthark! Blowthark! Blowthark!"

Gilbang stumbled, took a few disoriented steps, and nearly fell out of the ring. But somehow he managed to regain his balance. The crowd cheered all the louder for that.

"What's a *Blowthark*?" Johnny asked.

Thorkber replied without taking his eyes off the action in the ring. "Was Blowthark a former Thrashing champion," he said. "Did Migmar, his signature move. Call we do it a Blowthark. Come on, Gilbang, fall you out!"

But Gilbang did not fall out of the ring. He came at Migmar ferociously, wheeled off of a block, and caught Migmar with a swift strike to the cheek. Migmar toppled backward and rolled. He tried desperately to grab the edge of the ring, but fell.

The crowd exploded with hoots and shouts. Whistles blew, and a Gnome wearing bright yellow and green stepped into the ring and announced, "Migmar 2, Gilbang 2! Wins the next Thwack!"

Looking equal parts embarrassed and annoyed, Migmar bounded back into the ring. "Fell, I did, for that. Good one, Gilbang, but have you not another!"

"Migmar," Tommy called, "can you hurry this up? We're here on important business!"

"Is, the Thrashing, important business!" Migmar grumbled back.

But not all of the party from Berinfell wanted the action to end.

"Have at it, Gnomes!" Bengfist bellowed. "Thwack him mightily!"

"Sounds t'me like you enjoy violent sports," Mr. Charlie said.

Bengfist's eyes glittered as he turned to the Elves and said, "We Gwar have a similar competition, only with more blood."

Back in the ring, the two Gnomes traversed the circle, battering each other with little pause for respite and no mercy at all. But there came a point when Migmar staggered Gilbang with a lightning-swift, backhand blow. Gilbang did three backward rolls and came to a jumbled stop right at the edge of the ring.

Migmar drew back his thwack hammer low and charged the fallen Gnome. Gasps and an intense chatter buzzed in the crowd. They all knew Migmar's plan. They had seen their Barrister do it before.

Migmar came to a swift, sliding halt a foot from Gilbang, who was just getting to one knee. Migmar swung low-to-high, intending to catch Gilbang under the chin and launch him out of the ring.

Migmar's thwack hammer curled upward with devastating force and connected...

With nothing.

Like a striking snake, Gilbang pivoted on his knee and kept his chin and skull well out of the way of Migmar's stroke. And, not having Gilbang's skull to absorb the momentum, Migmar found himself off balance, teetering on the edge of the ring. Gilbang was up in a heartbeat, swinging his weapon in a hard arc around his body and bashing Migmar in upon the cheekbone. With a yelp, Migmar sailed out of the ring.

The Gnome wearing the bright greens and yellows entered the ring once more, lifted Gilbang's arm, and announced, "Have we a new Thrashing Champion! GILBANG!"

The crowd of Gnomes roared lustily. Bengfist yowled his approval as well.

Tommy felt a tap on his back. He turned and found a grumpy-looking Migmar standing there. He said, "Get, us, to business then."

"Caused Asp, all this?" Migmar asked.

"The Drefids started it," Tommy replied, "when they first opened the portals to get slaves for the Spider King. And the Spider King continued to make it worse by stationing troops on Earth. But Asp has taken it to a completely different level. He's put together armies of who-knows-how-many tens-of-thousands. He's destabilized whatever fabric exists between the worlds. He's violated the will of Ellos to such an extreme that the Tide of Unmaking has already been unleashed."

"See you it...this Tide?" Migmar asked.

"No," Kat answered. "Not personally, but our scouts have. It is moving west to east, consuming everything in its path. It's moving slowly, but it's moving."

"Very ominous, this new Prophecy is," Migmar said. "Come back to Allyra, must Asp and his legions."

"It's the only way," Tommy said. "Either Asp agrees to remove every living Allyran from Earth, or both Earth and Allyra will perish."

"Or, if ole Asp don't see the wisdom in leavin'," Charlie said, "We'll have to take him out."

"And hope his leaderless minions will see the wisdom in our plan," Tommy added.

"Very well," Migmar said. "Come, you have, for Gnomes' help. Offer I will three thousand Leaf Guard warriors."

"Migmar, that is beyond generous," Tommy said. "But we can't take your troops. We can't even take Berinfell's army of flet soldiers."

"Why not?" Migmar asked.

"The Prophecy," Kat replied. "If more Allyrans cross into Earth, it could speed the Tide of Unmaking. We don't dare risk it."

"Besides," Jimmy said, "we'd have t'take an army a' forty, fifty thousand strong joost to worry Asp a bit. We can'na win this by sword and bow."

"Nor by thwack hammer," Migmar muttered. He raised one of his insanely curly eyebrows. "Want you not the might of Gnomes, what then?"

"We need to be invisible," Tommy said. "Asp has stolen your cloaking formula. He's using it on Earth. If we have any hope of ever getting near to Asp, we'll need your paste to do it."

"Wickedly brilliant Drefids!" Migmar exclaimed. "Stole, they did, Gnome bodies from Vesper Crag. Hard they will be to stop invisible. Have, all the paste you need. But one condition."

"Anything," Tommy said.

"Go I must with you," Migmar said with a devious grin. "Must, Gnomes be, represented in this…this fight for Allyra. Is our home too."

Tommy glanced up at the Lords and the others and received the expected agreement. "Done," Tommy said. "Glad to have you with us, Migmar."

"Desperate are these days. Summon, I must, the elders of the village."

"Are you sure you can leave Moon Hollow in Thorkber's hands?" Tommy asked.

"Not that," Migmar said. "Good Gnome, wise is Thorkber. But, approaching, the Tide of Unmaking may be. Ending, it may, all life. Need, my people, to know."

"But Migmar," Kiri Lee said, "won't that cause a panic?"

"Are Gnomes not that way," Migmar said quietly. "In some ways, is this, a good thing. Live, we will, better when the end is in sight."

Tommy sat quietly, thinking. He glanced first at Kat, then to Taeva. But for the differences of their features—Kat's blue skin the mark of Berylinian Elves and Taeva's exotic Taladrim features—they seemed mirror images. Arms crossed tightly, head tilting downward, and lips slightly parted. Their eyes were large with fear and tears streaked solitary lines down their smooth skin.

But neither Taeva nor Kat would share their thoughts.

To the Coven

"I'D COME with yu, if yu asked," Jimmy said, taking Regis' hand.

"I know yu would, darlin'," she replied. "But for this mission, we can'na go with large numbers. Too easily found out, that way."

Jimmy laughed. "Yur doin' it again."

"What?"

"The Scottish accent," Jimmy replied.

Pink bloomed in Regis' porcelain white cheeks. "It's beein' around yu, that does it, lad. I do miss Scotland too. Much like bein' a Dreadnaught. Close community, simple purpose, good people."

"I miss it meeself," Jimmy said. "But this is our home, is'na it? And we've got to do our best to save it and Earth. Yu sure? My future glances might aid yu a bit."

"That they would, Jimmy," Regis replied. "Boot I'll have Charlie with me, and Miss Finney...you remember how she wields a staff, eh?"

"That I do," Jimmy said. "Still."

"I'll be fine, Jimmy me boy," she said. "Now don't yu go making me late." She left a burning kiss on his cheek and was gone.

"What's this, then?" Bengfist complained. "I don't get to bash Drefid heads?"

"I too owe a score to the Drefids," Jast said.

"We all do," Tommy explained. "And if it comes to fighting, we'll all visit the Drefid Coven. But this mission requires stealth. Charlie, Regis and Fin…they are the best at slipping into and out of enemy realms without being noticed. We will remain with the Gnomes. There's literally a ton of invisibility paste to gather."

"Working overtime, my alchemists," Migmar said. "But time requires this recipe."

Bengfist grumbled something unintelligible.

Jast patted him on the shoulder. "We may yet get our chance."

"We'll look for Charlie's team to return in three days," Kat said. "Any longer than that, and we will go after them."

Mr. Charlie sat motionless on his Scarlet Raptor. Regis and Miss Finney had dealt plenty with Drefids, but neither had been to a Drefid Coven before. They waited on their mounts for Charlie's instruction.

"Way I see it," Charlie said at last, "there are two Covens. The closest is south and east, in the barren hills between the Trollmurk and the Gwar village of Witten Crest. The other…is farther away. It's in the stark mountains called the Iron Crown north of Vesper Crag."

"Are you trying to test our Dreadnaught Oath?" Regis asked. "You know the rumors of the Iron Crown. If ever there was a more haunted and fearful place in all of Allyra, I have not heard tell of it."

"Nor I," Miss Finney said. "Growing up, I was afraid even to look east after sundown. Why do I have the feeling, Charlie, that you want us to go there?"

"Well, Ma'am," Charlie said, "you ain't far from right. But I don't *want* to go to either one, especially not the Crown. But it's to the Crown I believe we need to go."

"Why, Charlie?" Regis asked.

"I knew of Asp before," Charlie said. "When he was just one of the Spider King's footstools. If memory serves, and it usually does, the Iron Crown is Asp's Coven. It's where he's from."

"Then we go to the Iron Crown," Regis said. "And may Ellos guide us."

"Amen to that prayer," Charlie said. He nudged his raptor into the air. The others followed, and together they flew east.

The Iron Crown Mountains bore two colors only: black and gray. In shape, they were like any other mountain range in Allyra, but their appearance was startlingly unusual and frightening. The Iron Crown had no proper peak, but rather a ridge of stark stone, knobbed and gnarled, rising, falling and twisting. There were no plateaus, flat and inviting, but rather rows of jagged crags and curving, sharp spires. In truth, the mountain looked like some gigantic dead beast, its gray spine and skeleton exposed as decaying flesh turned black and eroded over time.

Mr. Charlie steered his raptor to spiral down in the shadows among the thicket of tall gray spruce. He dismounted as the others landed. At once they uncorked the long tubes the Gnomes had given them, squirted out the paste, and began to disappear.

"It foams up," Miss Finney said, smoothing the paste over her hands and wrists, and up over the leather armor covering her forearms. "Ah, it…it tingles. How peculiar."

"According to Migmar, the ingredients are quite diverse," Mr. Charlie said. "He told me some a' them. I wouldn't get it in your mouth."

"Good to know," Miss Finney replied, watching the bluish paste fizz and foam. "I look like...what did they call them? Marshmallows? I look like a person made of marshmallow."

"Ah, but the foam is going away," Mr. Charlie said. "I see it now. That's how the stuff covers everything, flesh and material. It foams up and then gets completely absorbed. Every crack, every crevice, every pore. Get your weapons covered too, blades, everything."

"Got it," Regis replied.

Miss Finney suddenly bent over at the waist and hissed.

"What is it, Fin?" Regis asked.

Miss Finney held up a hand. "It's alright," she said. "I'm fine. But putting this paste in your eyes is not fun."

"No," Charlie said, squinting and blinking, "no it is not."

"Great," Regis said. "That's joost great."

At last the Gnome paste coverage was complete. The three Elves stood under the eaves of the spruce and waited.

"I never asked Migmar how long it took," Charlie said. "I was hoping...hoping..." His voice trailed off.

"Dear Ellos," Regis said, staring down at her arms. Her fingers were gone. Patches on her arms grew pale, almost translucent, and then vanished. "I've never seen such a thing."

"Well, that's a way to put it," Charlie's voice said.

But no laughs came. Not even a brave smile. There was, however, grim determination.

"Come on," Charlie said. "The Coven is past the trees and beyond those craggy ridges."

"Is it likely that they patrol this region?" Fin asked.

Charlie replied, "Doubt they get many visitors."

"Still, keep watch," Regis said. "Drefids have a way of showing up where you least expect them."

Rycheswords drawn, the Elves slid naturally into a Nightform combat triangle and advanced soundlessly beneath the trees. As they passed through the twisting gray rock formations that marked the highest elevations of the Crown, they felt a distinct change in temperature. It was getting warmer.

Charlie couldn't see his comrades, but based on Nightform training, he knew precisely where they should be. He knew they would travel at virtually the same speed he used and that they would never likely grow too far apart. But every twenty paces or so, Charlie gave the signal to stop: tapping the tip of his blade one time on the instep of his boot. It made a dull metallic *thang*. He listened, heard the answering taps, and carried on.

When they crested the knobby, spine-like ridge of stone near the mount's highest peak, they saw the Coven for the first time. Charlie tapped twice. They needed to stop, to take this in, and adjust before venturing forward.

The Coven lay in a shallow valley with sharp peaks of stone rising up around it like the skeletal fingers of a hand. Massive trees, long dead and absent of any foliage, stood like ashen pillars all around the dell. From the ghostly trees' limbs hung the mysterious cocoon-like structures the Drefids were known to build but to what purpose, no one knew. They seemed woven, perhaps of Warspider silk, and each one had a round opening cut into its lower quarter.

At the trees' roots, there were dozens of stone cottages that, though they were in a variety of shapes and sizes, all still managed to look like mausoleums or charnel houses. Fires burned throughout the Coven, some beneath massive cauldrons of dark iron. Others flickered hungrily from grated canisters, and some roared in pits.

The Drefids were there too. Hundreds of them.

Few of them were stationary for very long, Miss Finney noticed. They stirred cauldrons, carved diagrams into the sides of buildings, and leaped from one place to another. There was something unnatural about their movements. It was mechanical and insect-like at the same time.

She watched as a Drefid leaped from the ground straight up to one of the cocoons. It clambered around the opening and then slipped inside. She shuddered. Then she heard Charlie's signal to move in.

Charlie had witnessed all that Miss Finney had seen and more. He'd spotted a wide iron barrier on the far side of the Coven. It looked like the opening to an immense cave with a formidable portcullis barring the way. It also had the highest concentration of Drefids which meant, as far as Charlie was concerned, that it was a place worth exploring. But how to do that without summoning a swarm of death, well, Charlie would cross that bridge when he got to it.

"Slight change in plan," Charlie said. "We'll still search the buildings, each a third of the Coven as we discussed in the air. But directly afterward, I want to meet over there." He pointed.

"Charlie, are you pointing?" Regis asked.

"Yes, ma'am," he replied.

"I can't see you, Charlie," she replied. "I can't see where you're pointing."

"Oh," Charlie said. "Oh, right. Look to the western side. There is a vast cave, or so it seems. In any case, it has a serious gate and is heavily guarded. Perhaps what we seek is in there."

"I wish we knew what we are seeking," Miss Finney said.

"We'll know it when we find it," Charlie said. "Books, old scrolls, formulae, recipes—anything related to the Dark Arts or the portals. Anything powerful or dangerous that we haven't seen before."

"With Drefids," Regis said, "that could cover quite a lot."

"Yes, it could," Charlie said. "But we can't have the Lords going back to Earth blind. And I guess I don't have t'tell you fine ladies that stealth is very much the soupe du jour."

"Even if we're quiet," Miss Finney said, "even if we don't take anything, we might still be caught. It could end up a blood bath."

"I know," Charlie said, patting the invisible satchel on his shoulder. "And that's why I brought my tools."

Miss Finney prowled through the northeast third of the Drefid camp. She'd explored five of the tomb-like buildings thus far and found nothing of use. A few diagrams that made no sense at all, several scrolls listing the names of Drefid dignitaries, and a peculiar staff made of black rock and capped with a luminous crystal. She'd thought about taking it, but the three Drefids in that building made it impossible.

If only he'd put the thing down, Fin thought, even for a minute. But he hadn't, and time pushed her to the next building.

One thing that had been conspicuously missing in all her searches thus far was the fact that she had seen no actual graves. The stone buildings really did look like mausoleums. In fact the whole Coven reminded Fin of Innskell, the vast cemetery of Berinfell. And yet, there were no graves in the Coven. Not one.

Fin thought that, perhaps, the cave Charlie had spoken of was actually a passage to catacombs where the dead were buried. Or maybe—and this notion gave her a chill—the strange cocoons hanging from the trees held the Drefid's dead. *Then why did Drefids constantly go in and out of those cocoons?* She shuddered, not wanting to consider the vile possibilities.

Fin scurried between two buildings she'd already explored, waited for a trio of Drefids to walk by, and then raced across the path to the next structure. She'd been in such a hurry, she'd not gotten a good look at the building. But somehow it seemed darker than the others. Maybe it was the sun sinking lower on the horizon? She wasn't sure that was it. It was more than just a variance in shade. It felt darker as if there was something sickly about the building itself.

A thought whispered into her mind: *Maybe I could just skip this one. After all,* Fin reasoned, *I'm a Sentinel, not a Dreadnaught. I've taken no oath to renounce fear. I have fears aplenty, and this place scares the splendine punch out of me.*

Miss Finney edged around the corner of the edifice and spotted another structure she could explore, one that didn't seem quite as menacing. *Wait,* she thought. *What am I doing? I may not be a Dreadnaught, but I am a Sentinel, sworn to protect my Lords. And more than that, I am a servant of Ellos. Running away from danger? That's not how we roll*—Fin laughed at herself, using the phrase of which Lord Hamandar had been so fond.

Then, voices.

Miss Finney flattened herself against the stone wall. She heard more voices, the rasp-chatter of Drefids, and then scraping stone. She watched them walk away and waited until they seemed out of range. She double checked to make sure the Gnome paste was still keeping her totally invisible. It was, so she slid around the corner to the door.

It was a massive slab door, eight feet tall at least. There were strange engravings all around the door. These were Drefid scrawlings. Not their language, but rather symbols of the Dark Arts. She'd seen them before, in Ardfern, Scotland while protecting Jimmy's hometown.

She hoped it wasn't some kind of mystical combination—that she might have to touch them in a certain order to gain access. But the door was slightly ajar. She'd have to move it, only a little, to get in. She checked for Drefid traffic, even checked above to make sure there wasn't a cocoon directly overhead. There wasn't. The coast was totally clear.

Get it over with, Fin! she chastised herself. She took hold of the door and pulled. It didn't budge. Not an inch. She inched her fingers into the opening, getting a better hold on the door's edge. She pulled again, this time, exerting as much force as she could, and the door began to move. It scraped along its familiar path a few inches at a time.

There, she thought. *Just wide enough.*

She pushed her way in, the ragged edge scraping along her front, the frame scraping her back. She pulled herself free and winced.

A sharp pain lanced up from the tip of her finger. Instinctively, she looked down. She couldn't see her fingertip, but there was a growing dot of bright red blood.

She hissed and started to wipe the blood on her thigh...and caught herself just in time. *Idiot! I'll just paint myself visible for the Drefids.*

She turned to look for something in the building to wipe the blood on. But the view of the chamber pushed away all thought about the blood.

The chamber she had entered was much, much larger than seemed possible from the outside. It was vast and deep and seemed like something of a cathedral in miniature. But rather than pews, there were shallow stair steps leading up to the altar where a massive book rested upon a dedicated dark stone pedestal. Large arched windows were spaced evenly, high on the walls.

Odd, Fin thought, *I don't recall any windows from the outside. I'm sure of it.*

But here they were. She drew near to one of them and found them to be anything but transparent—more like polished obsidian stone than glass. She gazed into the dark stone and saw nothing but the reflection of the red dremask brazier that burned on the wall behind her.

She turned and walked toward the altar and noticed that there were subtle hollows in the shallow stairs, pairs of indentations side-by-side, all the way across the chamber. Fin surveyed her imagination as to what these might be for. It didn't take very long. They were places for kneeling, places of worship.

But what did Drefids worship?

Fin looked up at the book upon the altar. As she trod slowly up the steps, her feeling of reluctance grew. She did not want to see this book. But it was precisely what she needed to do. Pressures strove within her: pushing her away and pushing her forward.

Then, she stood before it. The open pages were brine-washed to a sickly tan-yellow, fraying on the edges, and filled margin-to-margin with text. Miss Finney was an expert in dozens of languages, some from Earth, and some from Allyra. But she needn't be for this. The Drefids had adopted the Elven languages from the ancient First Voice to Commonspeak and even the most modern tongues.

She began to read.

> It is always the thirst that moves us. Thirst for blood. There is no greater aim. For to take life from another is to gain it for yourself. Lesser creatures have flesh, blood, and bone only to satisfy our need. Drink deeply of their—

Okay, enough, Miss Finney thought, a tremor working quickly across her body. *I don't need to be reading this section.* She flipped backward through the pages, pausing to look over her shoulder. No one had come in behind her.

She turned to the front of the volume. Best to start at the beginning.

The first page with text had the word Vulrid written in large characters, followed by a series of names. *Vulrid? A title,* Miss Finney thought. *And these, presumably, are the scribes who recorded it.* She turned the page and began to read once more.

> Vulridian sought to make for himself a people worthy of his name, and so he took from the bones of the dead, those accursed by Ellos the Unmaker, and formed the first of Drefid-kind. Vulridian named him Asp-Anthruel and told him to go and kill, that Allyra's blood was his. And should Asp-Anthruel soak the world in blood and be found worthy, then Vulridian shall make him chief among all Drefid-kind and make for him a companion to establish a royal bloodline to prey upon all generations.

Relentless chills rippled throughout Fin's body. The revelation that Drefids worshipped, that they had some kind of misbegotten deity— that would be enough reason to take the book...the Vulrid. But the name, Asp-Anthruel, it couldn't be coincidence. *Could it?* The answer might lie in the many pages of the Vulrid, but she would need time to read, time to scour it further. Time she didn't have now.

Fin checked behind her once more and then took out the tube of Gnomic paste. She hoped it wouldn't damage the book, but it couldn't be helped. She slathered the stuff all over the cover, the binding, and the outer surface of pages with the book closed. She did her best to coat the book evenly, but she rushed.

Miss Finney didn't realize how thin the coating had been on the back cover. She clutched it close to her body and fled from the Drefid temple.

27

In the Realm of the Wicked

REGIS EXPLORED the northwest section of the Coven.

And, she thought about Jimmy.

It seemed so odd that he was twenty-one now, fully grown. On Earth, when time had passed so slowly, she'd watched over him and wondered. First, she'd wondered, *could he be one of the lost Lords?* Certainly his ears had borne the telltale scarring. But as he grew to be a "strapping young lad," as she often called him, she had begun to wonder other things. He was kind and brave and so absolutely sad that it broke her heart.

He'd gone through so much that would have destroyed many strong men. Despised by his parents, nearly murdered dozens of times, torn from the life he'd always known—and yet, he'd not only survived, but he'd grown stronger and braver still. And then, he'd grown up. What—

Regis tripped over some kind of half-buried pipe but managed to keep her feet. She'd need to be more careful or she'd never get the chance to give Jimmy any more thought.

What was that pipe anyway?

Regis held her breath as a Drefid appeared right at her shoulder. It bent low and then leaped up into a cocoon in the tree high above. *Amazing how those things can leap.* Then she knelt down at the pipe and tapped it with her fingernail. Stone or metal, she could not say. It was solid anyway, and as she lay her palm flat upon it, she felt a faint, humming vibration.

Had the Drefids mastered some sort of electrical power? Was this a kind of buried cable system? None that Regis had ever heard of, that was certain. But she meant to find out. The pipe led toward one of the buildings she had intended to explore, the odd round structure with the castle-esque turret on top. It stood out among all the other edifices.

Regis traced the pipe to the building and, seeking a door, followed the exterior wall. She didn't find a door. But what she did find made her curious. There were more pipes. In fact, they radiated out from the building like spokes from the hub of a wheel. Now, she wanted more than ever to get inside. But after encircling the building twice, she'd found no door at all. No ridges in the smooth stonework. No outline where a secret entrance might be hidden. No way in that she could see.

Then from overhead came a loud *whump* and a crackling. Something small bounced off of Regis' head. She looked up just in time to see a Drefid walking across the roof of the building. He disappeared into a round window in the turret.

Of course, she thought. *Drefids don't need doors at ground level.*

Regis wasted no time. She leaped, caught the edge of the roof, and lithely pulled herself up. And there she crouched and waited. If this Drefid came out soon, she'd go and look. If not, well…she couldn't wait forever.

She heard a shriek and some raspy, muffled dialogue. And then not one but two Drefids clambered out of the turret. They spoke for a moment on the rooftop before one leaped up to the cocoon. The other leaped to the roof of another building.

Regis raced across the roof and stopped to listen at the turret. Other than a pronounced humming, there was no sound. If there were Drefids down there, they must have been sleeping. She scanned the cocoons that seemed to be within the Drefids' jumping range. She wanted to be as sure as possible that no Drefid was on its way in the near future. Once she went down below, she'd be blind.

Convinced that no Drefid was an immediate danger, Regis leaped up to the edge of the round entryway and lowered herself inside. She let go, expecting to hit a floor. She did, but it was some twenty feet below. Regis hit hard but absorbed some of the impact by rolling. Dreadnaught and especially Nightform training had taught her how to spread out the force of a hard landing, but still, this one rattled her teeth.

She stood up gingerly and looked around. It was a spartan chamber except for a myriad of violent gashes along the walls, and the apparatus near the far wall. It was taller than she, and looked somewhat like a gigantic dremask lantern or maybe a multifaceted jewel, ribbed with dark iron. The pipes Regis had seen outside clearly attached to this thing. In fact, now she began to wonder if it might be some kind of pump or turbine, driving whatever it was to sources outside.

The humming she'd heard was coming from this device, and cautiously, Regis drew near. Whatever was inside it, it wasn't a dremask flame. It swirled like wisps of smoke or cloud, and churned beneath the thick panes of glass that held it within. It had such peculiar properties that Regis couldn't identify it. One moment, it seemed vaporous. The next, liquid. Once it crackled like a charged thing, but immediately afterward it crystallized like a sudden, hard frost.

At the base of the apparatus there was a small hand-turn above each pipe leading to the exterior. There were also hand-turns above ports that had no attached pipes. Regis wondered what would happen if she turned one of the pipes off. *Probably nothing good*, she decided.

Near the top of the device were three of these unused ports, and between them was a strange two-inch twist nozzle. Without thinking, she pinched it between her thumb and forefinger and gave it a twist.

There was a brief hiss, and she flinched her hand back.

Something escaped the nozzle, a whirling, pulsing red mist. Regis gasped and again, without thinking, twisted the nozzle the opposite direction. It cut off the flow but not before the tiniest wisp of the red mist touched her finger. It felt like the brush of a feather and then...like a hammer blow.

Regis fell to the ground, spasmed, and kicked. She flailed in a writhing circle of agony. Her mind filled with terrifying, violent images. She saw herself taking an axe to people she knew and loved. She saw them dying and saw herself laughing. She saw blood everywhere... tearing, ripping and clawing. There were screams and guttural shouts. Some distant part of her mind registered all of this and realized she couldn't be set free to do this evil that churned within her. She needed to die. That was it. The only way to stop the mayhem she would unleash.

But in that last gasp of hopelessness, it was over.

She couldn't see herself, of course, but she felt herself heaving, gasping and sweating. Her mind was back. She was her own again.

"Dear Ellos," she whispered. "What was that?"

Suddenly, she heard a screech from above. There were scraping footsteps overhead.

Drefids!

Regis spun on her heel, looking for the door. Then, it dawned on her like a swift dagger between the ribs. There was no door. The way out was twenty feet above. A Drefid door. There was no way to get up there. And even if she could, a Drefid was coming in.

She was trapped.

Charlie clambered down the hillside into the hollow, into the heart of Drefid-kind.

Walking into the midst of them, Charlie felt strangely conspicuous. *I know they can't see me,* he thought. *But it feels like a spotlight's shinin' down on me.*

He felt especially exposed near the gnarled roots of the massive, ashen gray trees. He looked up into the boughs and spotted a Drefid cocoon. It swayed slightly and bulged here and there as if something was in it and squirming around. It reminded Charlie of some kind of egg sac. Just then, a Drefid poked its head out of the entrance to the cocoon. It hissed, snuffled at the air for a moment, and then disappeared back inside. Charlie moved on quickly.

A short march later, he walked by a cauldron boiling-full of some putrid green liquid. He leaned over to look and almost fell in as a Drefid brushed by him, actually making contact briefly. Charlie froze and readied his blade. But the Drefid went straight for the cauldron and tossed in a few hunks of some kind of meat. It sizzled a moment and then sank. The liquid seemed to thicken, and when the Drefid stirred it with a long slotted pole, something bruise-colored bubbled to the top.

The smell of the cauldron had been disgusting enough before, but when that gunk bubbled to the surface, it was all Charlie could do to get away without losing the contents of his stomach. He rushed over to a rather square building. He checked the border and looked inside. No Drefids on the way there that he could see, and none inside.

Perfect! he thought, as he ducked into the building. A lone dremask brazier hung high on the inner wall, but it cast only a weak, greenish glow. It was barely enough to see, even in such a small room. But there was plenty to see.

On one side, filling every inch of a series of shelves that went up ten feet, were lidded jars and stoppered flasks of every size and shape. As Charlie drew near to them he hit a wall of scents...most of them unpleasant and the combination of them all, nearly unbearable. Charlie backed away and almost fell into a pile of scrolls. Not a pile. An entire side of the room. Charlie silently exulted. There had to be something of value among these parchments. Hundreds of them, all for the taking. But which ones?

The Drefid dropped to the floor not five feet away from Regis.

Her hand drifted to the hilt of the dagger sheathed at her hip. Killing it, she realized, wouldn't help her situation. If another Drefid came and found a dead comrade, the Coven could get extremely uncomfortable... especially for Elves trapped in door-less buildings.

Regis had the inklings of an idea, but it was so absolutely insane that she shoved it from her mind and kept still and silent. The Drefid was bigger than most Regis had seen. Its shoulders were bony but very wide. Its arms and legs were roped with sinewy cables of muscle, and it towered over Regis.

The thing turned her way suddenly. Regis froze. Its greasy white hair fell across its eyes, but enough of that black hole gaze was visible to send shivers down her spine. It took a step closer. Its head lolled on its neck, tilted this way and that as it sniffed the air.

Regis stopped watching its eyes and focused on its fists. Its talons already protruded several inches from its knuckles and they slowly inched out more and more. The creature raised its fists. Regis drew her dagger. The talons swished...

And the Drefid sneezed.

Something flew past Regis' ear. She thanked Ellos it hadn't splattered on her forehead.

The Drefid wiped its nostrils with its sleeve and turned toward the glowing apparatus at the far side of the chamber. Just as Regis had done moments before, the Drefid went to the device. Its claws retracted, and it reached for the nozzle. Regis heard a hissing. The Drefid bent forward, and to Regis' horror, it inhaled deeply...once, twice, a third time. The red mist seemed to swirl around the creature's misshapen head. Regis heard the hiss of the nozzle closing.

Then, the Drefid released such a shriek that Regis swayed where she stood. The creature unleashed its talons, spun around and growled. Its face was twisted into a maniacal expression, and reddish drool drained from the corner of its slack-grinning mouth. Regis dove out of the way and rolled as the Drefid attacked.

The thing didn't seem to be attacking her, but was rather in some kind of rage state. It smashed into walls and clawed at the stone, snapped at the air with its jagged, half-rotted teeth, leaped and raced back and forth. It was all Regis could do to keep out of the way. Round and round they went: the Drefid, a cyclonic force of talons and teeth; Regis, a ghost trying desperately to avoid the storm.

Then the Drefid came to an abrupt stop. It stood in the chamber's center, panting like a predator after the chase. The breathing slowed, and it retracted its talons.

Regis felt exhausted, but the Drefid did not seem so. *So that explains all the gashes along the walls,* she concluded. It stood there flexing its ropey muscles and grinning. A cold fire burned in its eyes, but much brighter and more potent than dremask. The Drefid held out its gnarled hands and alternately flexed and straightened its fingers. It smacked its hands together suddenly. And when it pulled them apart, a shimmering field of electric blue stretched between them. The Drefid threw its head back and laughed.

The red mist, Regis thought. *It strengthens them.* Then she caught a chill. This was the Dark Arts...it had to be.

The Drefid crouched, ready to leap up to the door.

Regis' insane plan sprang back into her mind. If the Drefid didn't kill her, she thought, Jimmy would...if he found out.

Regis dove, rolled and then leaped onto the Drefid's back just as it vaulted from the ground. Even with invisible Regis in tow, the Drefid easily reached the second story door. It clambered out and shrugged hard, throwing Regis into a painful roll down the roof. She careened over the edge and slammed into the ground, expelling the breath from her lungs and leaving her gasping.

She rolled over with a groan and expected to see the Drefid drop to the ground directly in front of her. She rocked backward, pushed her shoulders against the wall and attempted to stand. A crouch was the best she could manage. She drew her rychesword and her dagger. The Drefid shrieked. She heard its scraping footsteps above. Then it leaped.

...up into the cocoon high above.

In her time in Scotland, Regis had learned many colorful phrases. One of those came to mind now: *Don't look a gift horse in the mouth.* She thanked Ellos, propelled herself away from the wall and sprinted toward the rendezvous with Mr. Charlie.

"Regis?" Charlie asked the night.

"I'm here." A little to his left.

"Miss Finney?"

"Here too."

"Good," Charlie said. "Ya'll took awhile. Was gettin' worried."

They stood among the muffling gray pines down slope from the Coven's western rim, not far from the entrance to the massive cave Charlie had spied before.

"You aren't going to believe what I found," Miss Finney said. She patted the book in her arms. "I know you can't see it, but what I've got right here is the Drefids' religion...their whole belief system. I've only read a little, but it explains a lot. We've got to get this back to Berinfell."

"Now that there's a real find," Charlie said. "Knowing their belief system will help us predict their actions, help us to know just how far they'll go, and maybe what their big plan be."

"You made the right choice, Charlie, coming to this Coven," Regis said. "I found something remarkable as well. I'm not certain, but I believe I discovered the source of the Dark Arts."

"But I thought…I thought it was something they were born with," Charlie said. "Like our Lords and their gifts and such."

Regis shook her head. "I don't think so," she said. "It comes from the red mist."

"Red mist?" Fin asked.

"Right," Regis said. "Let me back up. They have some kind of machine, a pump maybe. There were pipes leading from it to places all over the Coven. Inside the pump is red mist. Hard to describe. It's like red smoke with crystals in it. All I know is that I touched it and…for a moment, I lost my mind. I've never felt such despair, hatred, malice and misery. I wanted to die…and worse, I wanted to *kill*."

"You okay now, darlin'?" Charlie asked.

"Aye," she replied. "It wore off. But I watched a Drefid breathe the stuff in. The thing went berserk."

"Did you kill it?" Miss Finney asked.

"No," Regis said. "I…uh, well…it leaped away, and I escaped."

"This be news for Grimwarden," Charlie said. "Goldarrow and the Lords, as well."

"What about you?" Miss Finney asked. "What did you find?"

"Who, me?" Charlie asked.

"Yeah, Charlie," Regis said. "In the section of the Coven you searched. What'd you find?"

In this moment, Mr. Charlie was glad to be invisible, but he wished he could disappear altogether. "Uh," he said. "I came up empty."

"No way, Charlie," Miss Finney said. "I know you found something."

"Come on, Dreadnaught," Regis said. "Out with it."

"A recipe," muttered Charlie.

"A what?"

"A recipe," he repeated. "For rat pie."

Charlie heard muffled laughter. "Quiet," he urged. "You want to bring this whole Coven down a'top us?"

"So," Regis said, "let me make sure I understand. I may have discovered the key to the Drefids' Dark Arts, Fin brought back *the* book on the Drefids' beliefs…and all you got was a recipe?"

"Look," Charlie said, "we're not finished here. That cave up there's still a'waitin'. I 'spect it'll have something good in it."

"With all due respect, Charlie," Miss Finney said. "What else do we need?"

"We've got to get back," Regis said. "This information can't wait, and we certainly can't risk getting caught."

Charlie was silent a moment. "We came to scout this place out," he said at last. "But ya' both be right. We shouldn't delay much longer. Regis, can you skirt the Coven and bring the raptors back here? Tether 'em to the trees and keep 'em quiet. That will save us time."

Regis said, "Will do."

"Miss Finney," Charlie said, "let's go see about that cave. Just a short look around."

The Drefids stood guard at the cave entrance, three on either side. They weren't the problem. It was the portcullis. Charlie figured he and Fin might be able to get in if they were the size of an Allyran pog lizard. But aside from turning into one of those little orange reptiles, there wasn't much chance of fitting through the sturdy iron that barred the way.

They stood, backs to the stone wall to one side of the cave. Charlie leaned around the corner and checked the horizon. The sun would be along soon. He wanted to be long gone by then. As far as he could tell, the Gnomic paste was still keeping them completely invisible, but he didn't want to wait any longer than he had to.

Drefids came and went, but none of them entered the cave. Finally a small group of Drefids came to the portcullis, but from the inside. They hissed something to the guards, and all six guards responded by manning capstans on either side, turning hard until the portcullis had receded into the roof of the cave. As the Drefids departed the cave, Charlie noticed they were in very different garb. They wore the black trench coats that they favored on Earth. And beneath that, some kind of black armor Charlie hadn't seen before.

Charlie gave Fin a tap. They gave the Drefids a wide berth and ducked into the cave. The portcullis slowly descended behind them.

"You have that part figured out, don't you, Charlie?" Fin whispered.

"What part?"

"The part where the portcullis opens for us on the way back out?"

"I still have my tools," he whispered.

The cave was indeed vast, wide enough for fifty Gwar to walk side-by-side. It was lit only by slightly luminous orbs placed haphazardly along the cave's ceiling high above. Charlie and Fin traveled steadily downhill. They found pods of Drefid guards spaced every sixty paces. These too wore the coats and the armor.

"You saw the coats?" Fin asked.

"Not standard Allyran gear," Charlie whispered back. "Let's keep going."

The wide path continued to slope down. It was as if they were treading upon a huge stone wheel. When the path leveled out at last, three arched corridors loomed ahead. Some kind of unnatural light emanated from them.

"Take my hand," Charlie whispered, reaching backward. "We

can't afford to get separated."

It took Miss Finney a few seconds to find his hand but, when she did, she gripped it tightly.

Charlie took the left-hand opening and proceeded cautiously. Just past the threshold of the corridor, Charlie stopped hard, and Fin ran into his back. He had come just a few steps from falling some twenty feet to the floor of a circular chamber where several Drefid soldiers stood guard. The near fall had been a close thing, but what took Charlie's breath away was the light source.

There must have been twenty or more active portals in the chamber. There came an electrical snap, and one of the portals collapsed. It reopened moments later.

"We need to go," Charlie whispered.

"Why?" Fin asked. "Don't you want to—"

"Now," Charlie said. "We need to get back. If this is what I think it is, it could save the Lords a lot of time. It might even save Allyra."

They turned and moved hastily back the way they had come. This time, they marched up the never ending slope. That's when Charlie thought he heard something. It was a grinding noise with a heavy, intermittent clank of metal.

"Oh, no," Charlie hissed. "We're going to have to run for it. If we lose each other, meet at the pines. We have to run."

"What? Why?"

"The portcullis," he said, and then all she heard were his heavy footfalls.

Charlie saw light up ahead, and it was natural light. The sun had crested the horizon when they were down below. He sped up, trying desperately to keep his steps silent. It might have been due to his own pulse pounding in his ears, but he didn't hear Fin behind him.

Up and up he ran. His heart sank when he finally caught sight of the heavy iron gate. He'd hoped it was on its way up. It wasn't. It was a mere four feet from sealing off any hope of escape.

Still yards away, Charlie clutched his tool satchel to his chest and sprinted. He felt sure the Drefids would hear his passing now, but he had no choice. He ran till he thought his heart would burst from his chest. Just a few yards away now, but the portcullis crept inexorably down.

Charlie careened toward the falling gate, dove and rolled under the sharp metal barbs. He'd done it. He was free. But what about Fin?

He looked back, heard a brief scraping sound and the portcullis slammed into the ground. Charlie was about to despair when something brushed by his shoulder. *Fin!*

Charlie poured it on, dodging Drefids and ducking swiftly between the massive ashen trees that stood sentry on the border of the Coven. Finally, the last leg. He chugged along, hopped a border of rock, and tap danced among the thick, knobby roots of yet another towering gray tree. He came to the ridge and half slid, half skidded down the slope to the pines.

"I thought you'd never get here!" Regis said, her voice drifting out between two trees. "Who are you?"

"It's Charlie," he said. "Fin isn't here yet?"

They heard a clattering from up above. A stream of pebbles came toppling down the slope.

"Fin," Charlie called. As he stared, he saw something very strange. A few feet above the ridge, a brown smudge was hovering. No, it was more than a smudge. It had a right angle, was maybe rectangular.

The book.

It had to be. The book Fin had taken from the Drefids.

"Fin, get down here!" Charlie called. "You're becoming visible!"

"Hold on," Miss Finney called down. "Let me put this book— uhgh!"

A massive gnarled gray hand closed where the book was becoming visible. Blood spilled over the twisted fingers and began to show the form of Fin's legs.

"NO!" Charlie yelled, already bounding up the slope and tearing at the zipper on his satchel.

Suddenly Fin's blood-spattered form was lifted into the air. The towering gray tree. It was a Cragon, larger and stronger than any Charlie had seen before.

Fin screamed again and again. *"Charlie!"*

Driven by dire need, Charlie bounded up to the rim. He had his best battle axe loose from the satchel and slammed it into the Cragon's base. A hunk of gray wood tore free with a gout of black blood. "Let her go, you misbegotten—"

"Char—Charlie," came Fin's voice, garbled and half-choked. "T-take...the book."

The Cragon's roar sounded like splintered thunder, but Charlie didn't flinch. He hacked away at the creature.

"Charlie, no!" Regis yelled from behind. "That thing will bring the whole Coven down on us. Let me shoot its eyes!"

"DO IT!" Charlie yelled. He turned and ducked the Cragon's ill-aimed swipe. But as he came up, he saw.

He saw a blood streaked form in the Cragon's hand. Fin was slumped over and barely held on to the book.

"I...I'm done, Charlie," she said, dropping the book. It hit the ridge and began sliding down the hill.

"No!" Charlie bellowed. He slung his axe and drew two daggers. Just as Regis fired the first arrow into the Cragon's eye, Charlie leaped up onto the base of the creature's trunk. He plunged the daggers in and used them to climb.

The Cragon wheeled about like mad and yanked the arrow out of its eye. But it was no good. The eye gushed a greenish sludge. It was ruined. Regis' second arrow took the other eye.

Charlie climbed the swaying creature until he got to its knobby shoulder. He tossed the dagger in his right hand and grabbed his axe. He straddled his legs around the trunk and swung the axe one-handed at the shoulder joint. "You will not have her!" he cried. He hacked away until he saw the arm begin to tremble. It was losing strength. Charlie gave it one more savage blow and then leaped to the ground.

The arm-limb went limp. The hand opened, and Fin dropped.

Charlie caught her. "Fin!" he called. "Fin! Come on, Fin! Answer me, you no-good Sentinel!"

"Endurance..." she whispered. But that was all.

A sudden clamor from behind forced Charlie to blink his tears away. The Drefids were coming, and it sounded like a lot of them.

Charlie pounded down the slope. "The raptors?" he called.

"Twenty yards past the pines!" Regis yelled.

"The book!" Charlie yelled over his shoulder. "Fin's book—"

"Got it!" Regis yelled.

Charlie burst through the pines and loped to the first Scarlet Raptor. He eased Miss Finney up so that she lay across the front of the saddle. He leaped up himself and gave the raptor a swift kick.

As the first arrows came streaking in from the Drefids, Charlie was airborne. He saw Regis' raptor take to the air, Fin's raptor right behind.

Suddenly, a searing pain struck Charlie's thigh. A Drefid had leaped up and was trying to spear the raptor. Charlie summoned every bit of might and rage he had and bludgeoned the Drefid's face with his fist. The thing gurgled and fell away.

In the air, Charlie noted that the Gnomic paste was slowly wearing off. Miss Finney's face was becoming visible, a peaceful, pale portrait suspended forever in sleep. "Don't you worry, Fin," Charlie whispered. "We're coming back to this place. We're going to take them down. We're going to take them all down."

Chamber of Portals

"THAT COVEN is going to burn," Johnny said, his voice sounding gravelly and thin, spoken through gritted teeth. White-hot tongues of flame trembled in his palms and cast flickering shadows on the inner walls of the Justice Tree.

"Careful," Autumn said, rubbing his shoulder. "Keep your head."

"No, he's right," Jimmy said, the words deep and menacing. "I don'na need to see the future to know that." He buried his face in his hands, but tears found their way through his fingers. Regis gathered him in close and they wept together silently.

"When do we depart?" Taeva asked.

"Yesterday," Tommy replied. "Migmar, please have your Leaf Guard load the remaining invisibility paste on our raptors. We leave the moment they're ready."

"Do, I will, as you say," Migmar replied. "Wish you the Leaf Guard to come with you...fight the Coven?"

"No," Tommy replied. "I won't put them at risk. No one else dies today...except the enemy."

Regis looked up. "What about Grimwarden and Goldarrow?" she asked. "The portals...?"

"I'll send word," Tommy replied. "If the portals can get us to Asp faster...we're going to take them. Grimwarden and Goldarrow need to know we won't be coming back to Berinfell first. They need to know about the Vulrid and the Dark Arts. And..." His voice cracked. "And... Miss Finney needs to return to Berinfell. Migmar, please?"

"Bear her and your correspondence with honor," Migmar said. "Send Thorkber and Sarabell, I will, for coming I am with you."

"Thank you," Tommy whispered.

"The Drefids know we were there," Charlie said. "They'll bolster their defenses. They might bring troops in through the portals. They'll be ready."

"Aye," Jast said. "They will prepare a bloody welcome."

Bengfist stood and hefted his hammer. As he strode from the chamber, he said, "It will not matter how many they are or what they do to prepare. They will never be ready enough for us."

The flight was grueling, both for the raptors and their pilots. They landed about a mile down slope from the Coven, allowed a precious few minutes for rest, and went over the battle plans and objectives.

"Remember," Tommy said, "this is not about avenging our friend. This is not mindless slaughter or lust for blood. If that is why we fight, then we have lost our way and become like our enemy." Tommy's eyes fell gently on Jimmy and then Johnny. "We fight," Tommy went on, "so that Allyra and Earth can survive. If we gain access to those portals, perhaps we can stop the Tide of Unmaking. Perhaps, those we love in both worlds, can know a life of peace. This is why we fight."

Their company of eleven traded solemn nods.

"Well," Mr. Charlie said, "we best paste up. Stuff takes a little while to make us disappear."

"We won't be using the paste for this," Tommy said.

"We won't?" Kat asked. "Tommy…"

"We have no idea how much of it we'll need on Earth," Tommy said. "And besides, I want this Coven of Drefids to see us. I want them to see the combined might of the Elves, Gwar, Saer, Gnomes and Taladrim—the might of Ellos, whom the enemy profanes. No, let them see the grim resolve in our faces. And let them tremble."

Tommy and Kiri Lee flew side-by-side. They came at the Coven out of the sun and swooped down toward the tallest structure, a turreted stone building near the center of the Coven territory. Still some fifty feet above the turret, they both leaped from their raptors. Tommy clung to Kiri Lee as she airwalked to the turret.

The surprised Drefid there didn't have time to shriek. Kiri Lee's lightning-fast side kick laid the creature flat. She pounced and finished it with a dagger. With a brief salute, she was gone, leaving Tommy with the high ground to himself. That's when the noise started.

Johnny and Taeva had been tasked with blasting all the trees. And they carried out their plans with great zeal. Cragons roared and screeched, clawing at the sky in vain as Johnny loosed streams of fire upon them. He drove his raptor on an erratic path that allowed him to keep an eye on the ground. Leaping Drefids couldn't reach Johnny, but arc rifles could. In blurred glimpses, Johnny had seen Drefid soldiers marching in packs or clumping in large groups near certain buildings, but he'd not heard any arc rifle fire. He wondered why, but flew on.

Moments later, Johnny found out why…the hard way. After tossing fire into the upper boughs of a dark gray Cragon, Johnny banked his raptor away, hard to the right. He heard a strange muffled *WHUMP*. Suddenly, something flared brightly in his peripheral vision. He yanked the reins hard to the left. Whatever it was turned the air blistering hot as it passed, and Johnny covered his eyes with his hands. Still, the image burned through his fingers. It was as if a comet had nearly struck him. Johnny blinked and tried to see. That's when it exploded.

A pressure wave surged outward, and Johnny's raptor screeched and tumbled wildly in the air. Johnny held on until the raptor righted itself and then turned back and forth in the saddle, trying to see what had fired at him. It had been like an arc stone—only fifty times larger. It was like an arc *cannon.*

Just as that thought entered his mind, he saw Drefids leaving a long stone building. They left in a hurry but were hunched over. Johnny flew closer and realized they were working in teams of three, rolling very large, dark blue stones as fast as they could. Some went into other buildings. Others went under hastily-built wooden structures covered by tarps. The wind blew up one edge. That's when Johnny saw.

Beneath the tarp was an ominous-looking gray, metallic tube with heavy wheels on either side. Drefids buzzed around it like bees, pouring some luminous liquid into the tube. This they followed by dumping a sack of some sort of powder. Johnny had to loop around to keep watching. He saw that the Drefids struck one of the huge round stones. Sparks kindled, and the Drefids hoisted the stone into the tube.

Dear Ellos! Johnny thought. *They* do *have an arc stone cannon!* Johnny didn't hesitate. He pulled up his hottest flame and launched it at the Drefid weapon. Johnny pulled up just in time to avoid the shockwave from the enclosure's explosion, but a hot vapor-wind still nearly managed to knock him from his seat. He shook all over but finally regained his composure. The raptor screeched unhappily.

"Sorry!" Johnny said. "I won't get you that close again, I promise." He banked the raptor hard to the left, directing the raptor in the general direction he thought Kat might be.

Kat, you listening? Johnny thought, furrowing his brow as if that might help broadcast his thoughts.

"Here," she said.

Tell the team, Johnny told her. *The Drefids have arc stone cannons. Seriously, big ole guns. Steer wide around any shots while airborne. Hit 'em while they're on the ground.*

"Got it," she replied. A heartbeat later, Kat broadcasted the message.

One of the largest Cragons Johnny had ever seen reared up suddenly on the Coven's west ridge. It had only one working arm, but it was so tall that Johnny had to take his raptor much higher. He turned in his saddle and was about to unleash a fiery blast when he heard a familiar voice from far below.

"No, Johnny! Don'na yu do that!" Jimmy yelled. "This one's mine!"

The Cragon took a swipe at Jimmy, but Jimmy had seen it before it happened. He was already moving. He unslung his claymore and began to hack away at the wound Mr. Charlie had begun. Regis joined, chopping at the side directly opposite of Jimmy. They chopped at the base. They chopped at the grasping roots. It was a flurry of sharp steel. Chunks of gnarled flesh flew, and viscous black blood pooled.

Drefids tried to intervene, but Taeva's lightning blasts ruined any that came within a twenty foot radius of Jimmy and Regis.

The Cragon let out a hideous reverberating wail, but it was cut short. "That's for murdering our friend," Jimmy said as he and Regis cut through. The lifeless Cragon fell, and it seemed for a moment that the Coven had gone silent. Drefids scurried to get out of the fall zone. A few could not escape in time. The Cragon slammed into the ground, crushing all beneath it. Taeva weaved electricity from the air and fired two wild streaks at the dead Cragon. The roar of the battle rushed back in like a collapsing wave.

In less than half an hour, every Cragon was either burning and dying...or dead and reduced to cinder. In between a storm of arrows, Tommy watched it all unfold just as they'd planned it. He wondered if Kat had taken position on the bluff overlooking the Coven. He figured he should have heard something if she—

"Company of Ellos," Kat's voice spoke into his mind. *"Cragons are down. Time to bring in the infantry. Watch for the Drefids' new arc cannon, and call out for air support. Johnny, Kiri Lee, Taeva: be ready to bring it from above."*

Like ants in a suddenly exposed nest, Drefids scurried to sure up their defenses. They had expected the Elves to come back, but they weren't prepared for all the Lords of Berinfell and champions from three other races.

Mr. Charlie led Jimmy, Regis, Migmar, Jast and Bengfist in a charge from east to west.

The Drefids tried to leap over their charge to flank the intruders. But Johnny, Kiri Lee and Taeva were waiting above. No Drefid that leaped into the air returned to the ground alive. Charlie and the rest streamed around the bleeding and burning Drefid corpses and raced onward.

Bengfist was a one-Gwar wrecking crew. Ignoring blade, shaft, and talon, Bengfist bowled into the Drefids streaming out from one of their stone buildings. His hammer swept up and connected hard. Drefids flew bodily into the air and crashed in heaps. One Drefid leaped down from a building, trying to impale Bengfist on its talons. But the wily Gwar darted forward, spun and swung his warhammer. It connected just as the Drefid landed. The crushing blow filled the air with the crackling sounds of shattering bones. The Drefid became unhinged and, like a marionette whose strings had been cut, it spun away in an awkward jumble.

Migmar and Jastansia discovered that they worked well together. With the Gnome a safe distance behind her, Jast took two Drefids at a time, whirling her shardstave relentlessly in a dizzying array of strikes and counters. One Drefid lost its sword. The other had its talons cracked. But before they realized they'd been disarmed, the Drefids found their feet swept out from under them, and a maniacal, thwack-hammer wielding Gnome pouncing for the kill.

With fire, lightning and lethally aimed arrows covering them from above, Mr. Charlie and his team advanced across the Coven. The Drefids began to retreat. But when they came to one of the taller buildings in the center of the Coven, they made a stand.

"This is it!" Regis shouted up to Johnny. "This is where the red mist comes from!"

Dozens of Drefids formed a living fence around the building. They fired arc rifles, arc cannons and black-shafted arrows, trying to keep the invaders at bay. Several Drefids managed to leap up to the turret door. They disappeared inside momentarily. Suddenly, one after the other, these Drefids leaped out of the building, soaring to heights the Elves had never seen them reach before. They fell like deadly comets and stood before the invaders.

"Something different about them," Charlie said. "The red mist?"

"It changes them," Regis said. "Be wary."

Six Drefids stood defiantly now between the invaders and the building that contained their precious mist. One of the Drefids exposed his talons, but they glowed white hot. Another's eyes shone like red spotlights. And still another seemed to be tearing a hole in the air.

"This isn't gonna happen," Charlie said. "Kat, now!"

"*Johnny and Taeva,*" Kat's mind voice spoke clearly. "*End this.*"

Two Scarlet Raptors swooped down overhead. "Take COVER!" Charlie yelled.

Johnny and Taeva banked in opposite directions and nearly met directly above the red mist building. Fire and lightning blasted down from their hands. There came the snap of thunder, but then something extraordinary. There was a low hum that throbbed as it got louder. Suddenly, a great flash. For a moment, day turned to night. A frightening silence consumed all sound.

THE TIDE OF UNMAKING

Those still standing—Drefid and Elf alike—fell to their knees, deafened and momentarily disoriented. The Drefids nearest the building screamed and shrieked, but no one heard them. Small fissures of white light began to appear in the turret. They crawled down the tower, across the roof and down the foundation. The fissures pulsed and widened. There came a shrill ringing, and the building disintegrated. The Drefids guarding the building were backlit by white fire for a heartbeat, and then, they too vanished as the voracious destruction spread outward.

The six Dark Arts-wielding Drefids tried to run away but were half devoured from behind. What very little of them was left slowly gurgled into a spreading black pool.

Charlie and his team had fled a safe distance but, aside of Bengfist, they'd all been knocked off their feet. Blinking and dizzy, they stood and gazed upon the destruction spread out a hundred yards in all directions.

Kat, Kiri Lee, Tommy, Johnny and Taeva converged on their friends. "Anyone hurt?" Tommy called out.

"Ears ringin' like Christmas bells," Charlie said, "but other than that, I think we're...uh, fine."

Kat finally spoke what they'd all been wondering, "Johnny, Taeva... what in Allyra was THAT?"

Johnny leaped down from his raptor and stared at his hands. "I...I dunno," he said. "I've made fireballs explode before. Well, you've all seen those...I...I don't think it was me."

All eyes turned to Taeva. "What?" she said, stepping backward. "You don't think—look, I throw lightning bolts. I don't vaporize."

"The red mist," Regis said.

"Must'a been," Charlie said. "Now, listen...we'll have time to ponder all this later, but we still have a few Drefids to clean up." He pointed west with his axe. "And some portals to explore."

"Let's get to it, then!" Bengfist roared.

"Now wasn't that exciting?" said Bengfist, smiling as he wiped black Drefid blood from his warhammer.

"I'm not sure *exciting* is how I'd describe it," said Tommy.

"I thought it was," said Johnny, more than a handful of corpses still smoldering from his handiwork.

"Boys, I think we have more pressing issues before us," Taeva said.

Kat looked over to Kiri Lee and Autumn. *"I'm liking this girl."* The other two smiled.

There were a total of twenty-three portals in the chamber, each roughly fifteen feet wide, each shimmering with an electrically-charged blue aura. Some, however, were less strong than others, a few even flickering.

The Seven approached one of the nearest portals, with Taeva, Regis, Migmar and Mr. Charlie joining them.

Bengfist holstered his weapon and edged close to an adjacent portal. "Where do you think they lead?" he asked, extending a knobby finger toward the glass-like pane.

"Don't touch, your Overlordship," said Autumn.

"Overlordship?" Johnny sneered. "I don't think that's a word."

"No telling where it might pull you," added Kiri Lee.

The Overlord grimaced. "Then how do we know where to go?"

"Well, I guess that's the point right now," admitted Tommy. "We're just going to have to try them."

"Surely not all of us," said Regis. "The Tide."

"I remember," said Tommy. "That's why one of us will need to test each one."

"Each one?" Kiri Lee asked.

Jimmy agreed with Tommy. "How else are we supposed to know which one Asp is using to deliver his minions?"

"Who's to say he's not using all of them?" Kat added.

"So we test them all," concluded Tommy. He squared his shoulders and walked up to the glowing pane directly before the team. The light was strong and steady, emnating so much energy it made Tommy's hair stand up on his arms and neck. It had been almost eight years since he'd gone through a portal; the experience wasn't one of his more fond memories. "I might as well go first."

"Lord Felheart," Bengfist stepped forward. "Let me be the first to go."

But Tommy shook his head. "A good leader cannot ask his followers to go where he has not first dared to go."

Bengfist appreciated Tommy's surprising wisdom, as did the rest of the team, noting it was something he was growing into. "Well said," smiled the Overlord. "Only, let me be next."

"As you wish," said Tommy. He squared his shoulders and stared at his own vibrating reflection.

"Make sure to come right back," Kat burst out. Tommy turned around, slightly surprised at her sudden concern. "Or...or else we'll be coming through with the whole army. You know..."

"Don't worry, Kat. I'll be fine."

"OK," she said, feeling awkward by her outburst. But the concern was genuine.

"Here goes." And with that, Tommy took and deep breath and stepped into the field.

Sam had been waiting her whole life to be at West 53rd and Broadway, sitting in the famous theatre for which all musicals would derive their names.

Broadway Theatre.

For her birthday, Sam's dad and mom had surprised her with opening night tickets to see *The Bohemian*. It'd cost them a small fortune, but it was worth it just to see the look in Sam's eyes.

The upcoming trip to Manhattan was all Sam could talk about at school, and her parents wondered how she slept at night. But the four weeks passed quickly enough, and before long the Masseys were flying to JFK.

It all seemed like a blur, right up until the moment when Sam sat down in *her* seat at the theater. She held the playbill in her lap like a lost Dead Sea Scroll, hardly able to bring herself to touch it. She'd bought plenty on eBay, plastering her room with them, as well as posters of retired musicals whose memorabilia was stuff of legend. But *this* playbill—this was *hers*. It was special, more so than any of the others she owned. She opened it gently and smelled the inside pages, savoring the ink and heavyweight paper.

The lights dimmed, then were raised again.

"It's about to start!" Sam tittered to her parents, nearly exploding out of her seat. She could hear the violins tuning to A440 in the pit. The air was electric.

The lights went down and the audience started their applause as the overture commenced. Sam's dad and mom looked over at her, impressed that she had not magically levitated out of her seat and floated onto the stage already.

The curtain opened on a lonely soul mourning the loss of her father. Her angelic voice paired with the strains of a melancholy cello, the mood soaking the audience in instant empathy. But as the orchestra began to enter, piece by piece, the music swelled with the push of lights and the arrival of new cast members. Before long the stage was magically transformed into a bustling 16th century island square, bursting with color and life and noise.

Sam was thrilled, her smile wider than either of her parents had ever seen. She literally sat on the edge of her seat, nearly pressed between the shoulders of the patrons in front of her.

In the climax of the chorus line, a brilliant blue light exploded about six feet above the stage. The theatre lit up like daylight, and women in the audience screamed. Sam flew back into her seat, holding up her arm against the brilliant light. All at once the orchestra fell apart, strings tapering off and cymbals clashing.

Sam squinted, eyes searching the stage. She'd read the screenplay and stage notes for *The Bohemian* a hundred times; she didn't ever remember this lighting cue. Her eyes were adjusting now, and she could see the actors scattering. There were shouts from backstage, and musicians were fumbling around in the pit.

Something was definitely wrong.

Suddenly the blue light flared. Sam willed herself to keep watching despite the searing pain throbbing behind her eyes. Just when she thought she couldn't bear anymore, a man appeared in the light and fell onto the stage, dropping to his knees.

Gasps went out from members of the audience all around her. She wasn't the only one seeing this. It was as if the man materialized out of thin air, descending from the circular disc of light that lay horizontally across the stage.

Perhaps it was an opening night prank? Or a special one-of-a-kind moment in the performance? She'd heard of things like that happening before. But with all the shouting going on backstage right and left, somehow she figured this wasn't the case.

The man stood up and looked around, apparently as blinded by the stage lights as onlookers were by the aura above his head. The figure squinted, holding up one hand while his other held tight to a bow. He wore a beautiful black cloak, and was outfitted in the most impressive hardened-leather stage armor Sam had ever seen constructed. *Though still not as good as the real thing,* she thought. He turned this way and that, as if looking for something, or someone, then seemed to have a sudden understanding of where he was.

"Oh," he said, loudly enough for Sam to hear at least. "I'm...I'm so sorry, everyone."

People were standing from their seats and entering the isles in an awkward slow-motion retreat.

"I didn't mean to interrupt anything." He looked around the stage. The actors were both awestruck and terrified.

If this is a prank, it was the best one anyone has ever seen, Sam thought. Still, no one said a thing.

"Uh, I'll, um, I'll just be going now," said the man. And with that he raised his hands and lunged up into the blue disc above his head. No sooner had his arms been absorbed into the light, his whole body was sucked up, vanishing as it went. The light expanded rapidly, and then in a brilliant flash it snapped shut with a percussive clap to the air. A dozen stage lights popped, sparks shooting across the stage. More screaming.

In the momentary quiet that followed, the entire cast, crew and audience sat wondering what had happened. Finally Sam's dad leaned over to her and said, "I'm pretty sure that wasn't in the script."

Tommy came back shaking his head. "Definitely not that one," he said.

"Why?" asked Kiri Lee. "How can you tell?"

Tommy looked up at her and said one word. "Broadway."

Johnny started laughing. "You're kidding me!"

"Oh, now that's funny," said Kat. She was laughing too.

"Yeah, next time *you're all* going," Tommy said with a slight smile.

"No, no," Bengfist stepped forward. "I'm going next. I do not fear this *Broadway* warrior. Let me at him."

Autumn was laughing so hard she was crying. "It's not a warrior," she sputtered. "It's a place. For musical performances. Dancing. Acting."

"Ah," Bengfist withdrew a little. "Well then, perhaps I would fear the dancing more than a little."

The Seven were in stitches, their souls happy for the chance at humor.

"You're up," said Tommy, bowing to the Overlord in deference. Bengfist seemed a little more hesitant than he was moments before.

"Earth. It is full of dancing chambers then?"

The Six chuckled. "Not *everywhere*," said Jimmy. "Still, I'd be on your guard."

Bengfist nodded, looking more like an anxious child than a warlord. He held his warhammer in both hands and stepped up to the next portal.

"I'm not sure you'll be needing that," said Kat.

"No, no," Bengfist defended. "If it's a chamber full of dancers, I most certainly will."

"But it can'na go through the portal," Jimmy said. "Unless it's made of natural stooff."

"Heh, heh," Bengfist laughed, patting the hammer's head. "Wood, cord, and stone. Nothing more."

Bengfist was sure his stomach had lodged itself somewhere in his brain, while his shoulders felt like they'd become kindreds of his ankles. While the light display was more spectacular than anything he'd ever seen, he couldn't ignore the overwhelming urge to vomit that sent cold sweats down his back. Or was it waves of heat? With all the rushing wind blasting in his ears it was hard to focus on much of anything.

Suddenly the light grew stronger and Bengfist was sure he was about to lose his last several meals. But the sense of flying was coming to an end, and gravity took over.

The next thing Bengfist knew, he was thrust out of the light and emerged into a small room adorned with strange furnishings and filled with small people that resembled beardless Gnomes. They even wore pointy hats, though the strange multicolored tassels were new.

A few more mature Gnomes who oversaw the smaller ones noticed Bengfist first. Then all at once the entire gathering turned and began shrieking.

These be not Migmar's kin, Bengfist thought frantically. *Some evil cousins, I deem!*

Brightly colored orbs exploded around the room, popping with the lightest touch. Bengfist lost his balance and roared. He stepped on a wheeled board and then fell backward, landing in a heap of white and brown sludge that caked his backside, the central table splitting beneath him. Bengfist cursed himself for falling prey to one of the enemy's diabolical plans.

To add insult to injury, brightly colored boxes toppled upon him, no doubt meant to distract invaders while the vile gnomic race escaped. Bengifst struggled to get up as a pair of the beardless imps began kicking him in the legs, more than one blow landing against his shin bones. He roared again, to which the little minions answered with more shrieking. His warhammer lay across his chest, but was nearly impossible to clutch, what with all the slime covering his hands.

He used his elbows to crawl further back through the sludge, preferring the sticky substance to any further abuse by his assailants. But just as more of the little terrors started bounding toward him, he heard a sharp snapping sound as his head passed through a blue aura. Soon the glow sucked his body backward and absorbed him into a swirling vortex of bright lights.

The portal.

He much preferred vomiting to whatever *that* had been.

"Earth is a terrible, terrible place," Bengfist spat as he crawled out of the portal on all fours, dragging his warhammer.

The Seven were utterly shocked. "What—what happened to you?" cried Kat, a look of genuine concern suddenly transforming to sheer amusement.

"It was horrible!" Bengfist said as he tried to stand. "There was this awful lair of Gnomes!"

"Gnomes?" asked Migmar.

"Beardless ones!"

"Beardless Gnomes?" asked Autumn.

"And they shrieked at me, and used floating arc stones!"

"Arc stones?"

"Yes! All different colors! And then they sent me hurtling into their sludge pit and started kicking me." He began shaking his head. "It was awful, I tell you. Just awful."

Autumn walked up to him and swiped a finger full of the *sludge* into her mouth. "Birthday cake," she said to the others.

The Six and the Sentinels and Dreadnoughts started laughing.

"It seems," Tommy could hardly breathe, "that you were ambushed by a birthday party."

"A *birthday party?*" questioned Bengfist. "I know not this *birthday party.*"

"They were *children,*" said Regis with a wide smile on her face. "*Human* children, in the annual celebration of one of their own. It was a party."

"Vile practice," Bengfist muttered as he walked away to collect himself, brushing the cake off his backside. "Vile practice indeed."

"I think it's safe to say Asp hasn't acquired a sudden love of theatre," Tommy surmised.

"Or invites to birthday parties," added Kat. Bengfist winced at the mere mentioned of the term.

"So all day on this we'll take?" Migmar spouted. "Unacceptable."

"There's got to be a better way to figure out where Asp has gone," added Regis.

"I think there is. Look," said Kiri Lee, pointing out a portal to her left. "That one there is glowing brighter, like those other three across the room, and the two Tommy and Bengfist slipped through." The others hadn't thought much of the variations earlier, but they saw the logic now.

"Those gates are more stable," Taeva remarked. "Like they're less used."

"Right. And I see almost no scuff marks on the floor," said Kiri Lee.

"Like they're of little importance," concluded Johnny.

"Exactly," Kiri Lee nodded.

"Everyone, think," Tommy instructed. "Let's see if we can narrow these down using Kiri Lee's logic. Look for anything unusual." The team spread out, examining each of the gates.

Suddenly one of the portals that had been flickering suddenly disappeared with a loud pop.

"I didn't do it!" said Jimmy, stepping back from the rock wall the portal had covered just seconds before. The team gathered around him.

"What was it doing just before it vanished?" Tommy asked.

"Uh, it was just flickering."

"And look," Kiri Lee knelt down. "Tracks."

"Frequent use of this portal would make it unstable, right?" asked Taeva.

"Yeah," Tommy said. "I think we have ourselves a winner."

As if catering to his proclamation, the portal burst back to life.

"Still wasn't me," said Jimmy with his hands up.

"Anyone want to guess what part of Earth this one spits us out in?" asked Johnny.

The team stepped out of the portal, the trip not nearly as long or as violent as many of them remembered. Even Bengfist was relieved not to have experienced the same nauseating torment his last trip availed him.

Tommy looked around at the cave-like hallway they stood in. "I'm not sure we went very far," he said.

"Seems like we're still in the Coven," added Taeva. There was a narrow pathway before them, and further down around a curve was more blue light.

"What do you think?" asked Jimmy.

"I think Asp needs to get over his blue light bulb fetish," said Kat. "That's my color."

"It's a private entrance," Tommy guessed. "No army is passing through this narrow corridor. You know, like Asp's personal access route or something."

"Personal access to what?" Johnny asked.

Tommy withdrew his rychesword and led the way. "Let's find out. Be on your guard."

The team moved down the hallway single-file and negotiated the long, sweeping curve soundlessly. The glow grew brighter until the pathway spit them out into a massive, empty hall about ten times the size of the large military aircraft hangers Tommy had seen on the Discovery Channel. At the far end, as wide as four football fields laid end to end, stood the largest portal any of them had ever seen. Row upon row of ordered footprints, which came from the hall's main entrance in a cavernous, black space to their left, marched right up to the mouth of the portal and disappeared.

"What in the name of Ellos is that?" Bengfist said, even his whisper reverberating around the hall like a pebble bouncing down a canyon wall.

"I think it's safe to assume that *that*," Tommy cleared his throat and pointed to the monstrous enigma, "is Asp's portal to Earth."

In the Heart of the Beast

THE AIR sizzled and popped as eleven figures materialized and stepped out of the blue portal into a massive hall similar to the one they'd just left. Only something felt different. Felt familiar.

"We're back," said Kat as they looked around. And none of the other lords needed any further explanation.

Earth.

While the new environment posed no immediate threat, as it seemed utterly empty, they still wished the jump to Earth hadn't forced them to part with their metallic weaponry. Only Tommy's bow and dremask-tipped arrows, and Bengfist's stone warhammer made it through. And while sending even more Allyran presences into Earth could japordize everything, Tommy decided Regis, Mr. Charlie, Bengfist, Jast and Migmar just had join the Seven on their jump here. He needed them. Earth needed them.

"Now that was worse than I remember," Jimmy said, turning aside to heave on the cave floor. Johnny joined him.

"The big fuss, I'm not sure what it is," said Migmar. "Much reminds of the morning after a stump stomping, it does."

"A stump stomping?" asked Kat as she wiped beads of sweat from her forehead.

Regis leaned over. "You don't want to know."

"I'm sure I don't. Thanks," Kat replied with a wink.

"Let's keep our voices down and find out where we are," said Tommy.

The team had already spread out, examining the huge staging hall, when Mr. Charlie summoned the team to a large arch cut out of a side stone wall. Within the next room lay a truly exciting find.

"Would yu' look at that…" Jimmy whistled.

"An armory!" said Regis. Jimmy liked a woman that found weapons attractive.

Maces, swords, polearms, shields, warhammers, warfangs and warspikes, axes, staves and slash wheels were all neatly ordered along vertical racks along the walls and the middle of the room.

"There must be thousands of pieces in here," said Bengfist in awe.

"And that's saying something considering it looks like most of it is gone," said Tommy. "Look at all the empty racks. Asp has his forces armed to the teeth. Quick, do the same, but stay light."

"Does that mean I can't bring two of these?" Bengfist asked, holding up additional warhammers.

"Overlord, you already have one," said Autumn.

"I know but—"

"Travel *light* everyone," Tommy stressed again.

"But these *are* light!"

Tommy chuckled at Bengfist. "Let's go."

Regis, Mr. Charlie, Jast and Migmar felt the most grateful for new weapons at their sides, but it was not overly heartening to any. Perspective showed them all that they were a very small force of soldiers set against an enemy ten-thousand times their number.

The team moved out of the armory and toward the rear of the staging hall. Soon the cave floor began a slow ascent, rising toward an ever-glowing cascade of starlight and the appearance of a full moon.

Tommy directed the team to hug the righthand wall, hiding in the shadows. As the team neared the mouth of the cave, Tommy held up a hand. "Migmar, I need some paste."

"Not yet, Lord Felheart," said the Gnome. "Venture a look and be right back, I will." The Gnome stepped past Tommy before the Elven Lord could protest, heading for the open air above.

The rest of the team waited, seeing their breath in the cool night air. The fragrance of pine wafted down from outside, stirring memories for Mr. Charlie and Regis of the night they lost Nelly. Perhaps they were back in Canada once again. It felt oddly familiar.

A few minutes later, Migmar waddled back down the track. "Camped without they were," he said softly. "All throughout the forest and down the mountainside. Prime enemy stronghold, it is. But gone now, vanished they are."

"So we've come to the right place," concluded Jimmy.

"Not necessarily," countered Kiri Lee. "But one would hope. Asp is more than likely with them."

"We'll need to explore," Tommy said. "Stealth will be paramount. Overlord Bengfist, this means we need you to refrain from any urges, no matter how overwhelming, to pummel, grind or pulverize the enemy unless it's absolutely imperative. Not until I give the order."

Bengfist looked like a small child who had just been told he couldn't have cake for a month. "Okay," he muttered.

"I don't want to risk breaking up, so let's stay together," added Tommy.

Tommy led the way up and out of the cave. Just as Migmar had said, the entire mountainside was a massive encampment. Tens of thousands of Asp's forces must have been staged under the tall pines, stretching down into a deep valley. The leftovers of their tents and cocoon-like dwellings littered the forest.

"What are you looking for?" asked Taeva.

"I'm not sure," said Tommy as his eyes surveyed the camp. "But we need to look for clues. Anything that might lead us to Asp's den, or gives any idea of where he took all this." Tommy gestured to the camp with a sweep of his arm.

"Lord Felheart," said Bengfist in his gravely voice from back within the cave. "I think I found something."

Tommy walked back through his team to where Bengfist stood; the Gwar Overlord indicated a cutout in the side of the cave's wall. It was a doorway leading to a stairwell carved out of the stone.

"Well done, Overlord," said Tommy.

"Thank you," Bengfist smiled. "Ready our weapons?"

"Ready? Yes," said Tommy, "but do not let fly until I give the order."

Tommy summoned the rest of the team and they followed him up the winding staircase. Soon they stepped onto a well-traveled path heading straight into the mountain. Small windows carved into the right side of the rock wall gave them a view into the cavernous chamber they'd arrived in far below.

"Observation windows," Johnny guessed. "To track movement."

That's when Tommy heard it.

"Voices. Up ahead." Kat heard them too.

"Everyone down!" Tommy commanded by whisper.

The team took a knee. "Stay here until we get back. Jimmy and Kat with me." If they were going to surprise some of Asp's guards, he wanted to know their thoughts and actions in advance.

The three dark figures used Mandiera and blended in with the cave walls, creeping in the stillness of the shadows. The voices grew louder. The path eventually banked left and opened up into a larger chamber.

"Some sort of command center," said Kat.

Like a medieval dragon's lair meets NASA! Jimmy thought back to her.

On the technological extreme, banks of computer monitors filled four entire tables evenly spaced around the center of the room facing away from the middle; each table highlighted a workstation with mouse and keyboard, as well as a joystick, headset and external speakers. A Drefid sat at each table observing the bank of monitors and talking into microphones; multiple voices were coming through over the speakers. Commands, troop placements and objectives it sounded like.

On the medieval extreme, pools of glowing, red water sat on the outside of each table, tendrils of smoke rising up from their surface. *"Much like the red mist Regis saw,"* Kat imagined. The cords of the computers ran off the backs of the tables and disappeared into the pools.

The most striking feature of all, however, was a giant translucent sphere floating in the middle of the room. It hovered above a pool of water similar to those along the outside, and had etched on it gray horizontal and vertical lines. Within them were the all-too-familiar outlines of Earth's continents in a glowing orange.

"What is it?" asked Kat.

If I had to guess, replied Tommy, *it's Asp's central command.*

HEY! LISTEN TO THIS! Jimmy's voice pounded in Kat's head. She tapped Tommy's shoulder and pointed to his ear, indicating he pay attention to what was coming next.

"We've gained a foothold on the island," came a deep, rasping voice over the loudspeakers. The Drefids seemed to shake with excitement, their eyes riveted to the computer monitors. "We're almost to their financial district."

Ask him whose voice that is, Tommy said to Kat. Kat relayed the question to Jimmy but he simply shrugged his shoulders. Guessing it was Asp, there was only one person in their team who'd heard his voice before. *We need Taeva. Quick!* said Tommy.

Kat took off running down the hall, her footfalls not more than gentle pats on the stone. She sent thoughts to Taeva as she ran, so the Princess was already moving by the time Kat reached the rest of the team. "You might as well all come," Kat acknowledged. "There's going to be some action."

"All right!" Bengfist growled.

"Please, Overlord!" Kat hissed. "You'll lose us our element of surprise."

The Gwar looked to Migmar. "What is this *element of surprise*?"

"Have it, never you will," said the Gnome. "So losing it, you shouldn't be worried of."

"Ah, I see. Thank you for clarifying."

The team followed Kat further down the corridor to the mouth of the command chamber. They knelt in the shadows, listening. Kat brought Taeva up next to Tommy; Taeva no sooner knelt down beside him then her face froze. Tommy looked over. *Ask her what's wrong, Kat!*

Taeva knew Kat was trying to speak to her, but the voice over the loudspeakers had completely paralyzed her. It was *him*. The beast that had killed her father. Her mother. Had decimated her people. Women. Children. All of them. It was his voice filling the room. But he was nowhere to be seen.

"It's Asp, Tommy," said Kat. *"Remember Taeva has no idea about computers; she's looking for him in the room."*

Tell her something! Don't let her attack yet.

Kat put a hand on Taeva's shoulder; she could feel the Princess's muscles coiled up and ready to spring. *"He's not in here, Taeva."*

Practically perspiring with annoyance, Taeva looked to Kat. *What do you mean he's not in here? I hear him, he* must *be in the shadows.*

"It's technology," Kat ventured in a whisper. "Those machines can transfer his voice from anywhere in the world. It sounds like he may be attacking a large city even now. We just needed you to verify it was him."

"It's him, all right," Taeva said. "I'd know his voice anywhere, and I will not forget it until it is silent forever."

Tommy squinted. *Kat, we'll need to be wary. Vengeance could jeopardize our plans.*

"*Agreed,*" she spoke back into his mind.

We need to act, said Tommy. *Kat, tell everyone—especially Bengfist—not to hurt the computers.*

"*I'm not sure he'll get that, Tommy.*"

Just tell him the tables with all the lights on them, Tommy replied.

Kat nodded and relayed the message. Then Tommy withdrew his bow and knocked an arrow.

"Oh, and Taeva," Tommy whispered, "your lightning bolts with those computers won't be a good mix." Tommy didn't see her carrying any weapons from the armory.

"I've always got a knife," she whispered and withdrew a blade from her boot. "Found one in the stash downstairs."

Tommy smiled. He turned back to the rest of the team and held up fingers, counting down from three...

Two...

One...

Tommy's first arrow sailed across the room to the Drefid seated in the farthest chair. The target toppled forward onto its workstation, a fine trickle of blood escaping from where the fletchings protruded from the Drefid's temple.

The other three Drefids removed their headphones and looked

over at their fallen brother. Only two were able to turn back around and see the insurgent force bounding through the doorway: the third and closest Drefid felt a blade plunge into its back. Taeva stabbed a second time into the spine and then threw it to the ground in a heap, slitting its throat for good measure.

The remaining two Drefids leaped up into the air, their natural response for both evading and surveying assailants. But Johnny was ready; the only time he knew he could use his flames were if and when the beasts got clear of the computers. And this was his chance.

Johnny cupped his hands and projected a small but powerful ball of fire. The meteor rocketed across the chamber and caught one Drefid under the chin in mid air, somersaulting it backwards and onto the floor. It was Autumn who zipped around the room to where the Drefid lay and made sure it never got up again.

The last Drefid would go to Tommy, who'd already nocked and released a second and third arrow, one to the upper abdomen and the other to the side. Both drove deep into the Drefid's vital organs, and the creature flopped on the ground like a suffocating fish out of water. Taeva finished this Drefid off, too, plunging her boot knife into the creature's eye.

The Seven and their small band filed into the command center, multiple voices talking over the speakers as if the Drefids were still monitoring them.

"Hey, how come no one left anything for me?" Bengfist complained. He walked up to the first Drefid Taeva had stabbed and dropped his warhammer on its head out of frustration.

"Overlord!" Autumn exclaimed. "Easy. You'll get your chance."

"Asp's command center," Kiri Lee observed. "Jackpot."

"Jackpot?" asked Bengfist.

"Shhhh," said Migmar. "All in time. Years it takes, to learn their vernacular, it does."

"Let's have a look," Tommy said, moving into the center of the room. "What are you up to, Asp?" He slipped into one of the computer terminal chairs that swiveled with his body's motion. The team filled in the center of the control room, admiring the slowly spinning globe, and then watched Tommy go to work.

Tommy touched the mouse. The pointer moved freely between the dozen monitors before him, each highlighting small video images bordered with lots of text. Coordinates possibly. There were also at least three different command windows with dialog boxes, and drop down menus flooded with options. While Tommy liked to think he was good at video games—at least, he *used* to be—there was something far more complex about this system than he had the knack for. And within a few minutes, Tommy was frustrated, unable to get the software to do much of anything. More voices were talking over the speakers now, their tone irate.

"Your pardon I beg," said Migmar, "but a chance I may have?"

"You?" Tommy looked over. But Gnomes did have a way with gadgets, he admitted.

"Understand it, I think I do."

"You know what," Tommy swung out of the chair, "knock yourself out." Just then Benfist stepped forward to intervene. "Not really," Tommy smiled at the giant.

Migmar adjusted the chair to his height, slipped on the headset, and glanced over the keyboard, mouse and joystick. He cracked his tiny knuckles and then went to work. "Be with you momentarily," he hissed into the microphone.

"Too nice," said Kat.

Migmar looked up. "I'm sorry?"

"You're too nice to be a Drefid," she said, indicating the mic. "Try again."

Migmar wrinkled his brow and made his voice more aggressive.

"Shut up, fool you are! Tell you what you need, I will." He looked up at Kat.

"Good enough," she chuckled. "But better to leave the talking to us." She pulled the headset off his head.

Migmar *humphed* and then looked back at the monitors. He chose one of the screens near the center that seemed to display a lot of motion, and clicked on it. The main image enlarged to show a news feed from a street battle in a city. Explosions. Troops taking cover. A tank rolled in the background.

"Looks like one of my old video games," said Johnny. "Sweet."

Kiri Lee leaned in. "I don't think that's a video game," she said. "And it's not the news either."

Tommy looked closer, too. "Seems like a surveillance camera." Soldiers held their position, firing down an empty street. "I think those are US Troops," he said. "See the insignias?"

"But I don't see enemies," said Autumn. "Who are they firing at?"

"Click on that one over there," Jimmy said, pointing.

Migmar moved the mouse up and expanded an image that seemed rather benign.

"It's just a troop truck," Tommy said. "Sitting there doing nothing." The transport was surrounded by skyscrapers, and the men awaiting orders perhaps.

"Watch," said Jimmy. He leaned in. "Look right now!"

The team watched as the troop truck crumpled inward, its front and back ends pitching up, as though a massive telephone pole drove down into the middle of the vehicle and pinned the center to the ground. Soldiers came reeling out of it, others spilled from of the back onto the asphalt. But there was no sign of what caused the destruction; it was as if the truck just imploded on its own.

"What in Ellos' great name was that?" Bengfist bellowed.

A soldier in the front passenger's seat raised his assault rifle and began shooting at the sky. Instead of the bullets disappearing out of view, they ricocheted off a hard surface just above the truck.

More soldiers took to firing at the same invisible object, their molten bullets spraying little more than flashes of light across the invisible surface. Just then two or three of the men were ground to a pulp right where they stood.

Kat turned away. "This is awful!"

As the soldiers continued to fire, a shape began to emerge. The invisibility paste was being blasted away. That's when Tommy muttered the word they all knew accounted for the destruction.

"Warspider."

Migmar brought up more images, each showing different engagements between US Troops and Asp's invisible army. That is except for one shot that confused everyone. Migmar clicked on and enlarged what appeared to be a subway platform underground. A number of humans moved along the stage, sticking what looked like backpacks along the curved wall.

"What are they doing?" asked Jimmy.

"I...I don't know," said Tommy.

"Zoom in," said Kiri Lee. "See that thing in the stairwell?" Migmar clicked on a plus sign in the lower right hand corner of the image. Sure enough it pressed in to the center of the shot. There, half hidden in shadow, stood a Gwar soldier with an assault rifle leveled at all the humans working the platform.

"Curse him!" cried Overlord Bengfist. "A traitor of our people!"

"Peace, Overlord," said Kiri Lee, holding up her hand.

One human furthest from the Gwar and closest to the camera placed their backpack along the wall, and then started looking up and down the subway tracks.

"Uh, oh," said Tommy, noticing how nervous the man looked. "I don't think this is going to be good."

Suddenly the man ran off camera and presumably leaped down onto the tracks. The Gwar warrior came bounding down the platform and then raised the rifle. Migmar tried to use the joystick to follow the man, but the camera was stationary. The Gwar aimed, and then squeezed a steady burst of lead from his weapon, bullets pounding down the tracks after the man. A second and third burst discharged from the firearm, and then the Gwar lowered the rifle with a smile on his face.

Bengfist stepped toward the table, warhammer poised. "I'll kill you myself, traitor!"

"Bengfist, no! Stand down!" cried Tommy. "You'll have your chance. But *not* now."

"So Asp is using humans too," Kat said. "I can actually read their thoughts somewhat."

"Really?" asked the others, quite surprised.

"Yeah. It's strange too. All of them there were saying they'd never even been to New York before. *'What a way to see the Big Apple,'* one of them said."

"So they're tourists," guessed Johnny. "That's not unusual."

"That's just it," said Kat. "They're tired. And one of them was thinking about the nightmare they've been living through, especially passing through the *wormhole.*"

"Worm hole?" said Johnny. "Like, Star Trek worm hole?"

"One could assume so," she said. "Probably means *portal.*"

"Slaves," said Kiri Lee. "Asp's taken humans as slaves. Possibly from all over the planet."

"I certainly wouldn't put it past him," said Regis. "That was the Spider King's plan long ago."

"So what do you think those are?" Tommy pointed to the backpacks on the walls. Then he noticed the Gwar was gone and the humans were huddled on the platform, two of them crying in fear. A beat later and an explosion burst from the farthest backpack. Then, the camera went dead, the screen all static.

"In the great name of Ellos!" Mr. Charlie exclaimed. "No!"

Simultaneously another video feed further down the table showed a plume of dust shooting skyward in a street. The corner of a building began to cave in, and the next thing the team knew, an entire building was listing sideways on a slow-motion descent into a cataclysmic swatch of destruction. Those among the team who knew and even lived through the history of 9/11 watched in horror as the collapsing building brought back a flood of memories. The slogan had been well coined: they would never forget.

"There he is!" Taeva tapped on a screen on the far left side of the table. "Migmar, quick!"

Migmar grabbed the image and brought it to the center, expanding it over four or five screens. Caught by a skyscraper roof-cam, a figure sat atop a Warfly that hovered above a street battle.

It was Asp.

He was still half hidden by a dark cloak, but his otherworldly shape, angular joints and arachnid features gave him away.

"Bold," Tommy said. "He is the leader of all of this, and yet he stays visible and out in the open."

"Arrogance, more like," Jimmy replied.

Asp seemed to be presiding over his invisible army's advance down a street of overturned cars. Tanks fired in the distance. As Asp turned his head, Tommy could see a small headset microphone protruding from under his hood. A voice came over the loudspeakers.

"Advancing further inland," Asp said.

A shudder went through all those gathered. It was as if Asp was right there in the room with them, bigger than life.

Migmar glanced over and saw Bengfist with his warhammer held high over his head. "Overlord, you are doing what?"

"Finishing this here and now!" cried the Overlord.

"Woah, woah, woah!" Regis reached over and tried to help Bengfist ease his weapon down. "It's just a *projection* of Asp. He's not really in front of us."

The Gwar Overlord looked extremely confused. "I don't understand. We should kill him while we have the chance!"

"First off," Tommy said, "we need to persuade him to return to Allyra, remember? Killing him may be necessary, but we have to try diplomacy first. Secondly, you'd just be destroying the equipment that's giving us observation powers from afar. Like Regis said, he's not *really* in front of us."

From behind, Autumn tapped Tommy on the shoulder. "What's up?" he asked.

"Do you think the pulsing orange dot on the globe has anything to do with the image we're currently looking at?"

Tommy turned around. "Hmm. Well, that's New York City onscreen. No doubt about it. And that dot over New York State's southeastern point looks right on the globe."

"Here," Kat walked over to another table of computer screens. "I'm going to click on another image. Autumn, see if the dot changes." Kat used the mouse to click on an image of a strange piece of architecture surrounded by old, elegant buildings.

Suddenly the globe spun, then slowed, and a new dot pulsed. Autumn examined the globe.

"Why...that's Paris!" Kiri Lee exclaimed, using the proper French pronunciation of the city, *Pah-ree.*

"What?" asked Tommy moving to look at Kat's screen. "You sure?"

"Absolutely!" Kiri Lee looked between the globe and the screen to confirm what she saw. "That shot's just above the Louvre! See the glass pyramid?"

"Where is Pear-ree?" asked Bengfist to Migmar, to which the Gnome simply shrugged his shoulders.

"It looks to be a great city," Jast said. "Like Thynhold Cairn… without the mountain."

"Why would Asp have a camera feed of the Louvre?" asked Mr. Charlie.

"There are caves," said Kiri Lee. "At least those are the rumors. Miles of caves beneath the museum underground."

"A perfect place to amass an army," concluded Tommy.

"Precisely," said Kiri Lee. "That's what I would do if I was going to attack Paris."

Feeling more curious than ever, Tommy stood up and moved to another table, clicking on all the screens. One at a time, each of them lit up displaying a new camera image. Likewise, the globe spun smoothly, displaying a dozen pulsing orange lights. Half the team examined the globe, while the others were taken with the images.

"There's Tokyo," Kiri Lee pointed. Three different feeds of the city corresponded with a pulsing dot on the globe. Kiri Lee leaned in closely. "Wait. What's that?" She was tapping the respective screens. "Tommy, zoom in."

"Uh, I just clicked," Tommy protested. "Migmar?"

"Migmar coming," said the Gnome, leaping from his chair and running over to jump in the one Tommy steadied for him.

Migmar moved the mouse, grabbed the group of three camera shots and expanded them. One of the images, taken from atop a tall building, showed what looked to be a giant lens flare behind the cityscape in the distance. It was a common solar aberration that some photographers liked to use in their art.

"Migmar, can you use the joystick to turn a camera?" Kiri Lee asked.

Migmar reached for the device with his left hand, right hand on the mouse. He selected an image with the mouse and then tried the joystick. Nothing happened. At least at first. About five seconds later the camera moved to the left as Migmar had instructed it.

"There's a delay," Tommy said. "Makes sense." Though Tommy had forgotten to research exactly where they were at present, he presumed they were far away from Japan.

"Quick then," Kiri Lee pointed to one of the cameras without the sun flare showing. "See if you can rotate this camera in the same direction as the other here."

Migmar selected the camera shot and inputted movements to the joystick. Five seconds later the camera responded. But it wasn't enough.

"Keep going," Kiri Lee said. "All the way around."

Migmar moved the joystick more. But the camera eventually stopped, unable to get the view Kiri Lee wanted.

"Try the other one," she snapped.

"Easy, girl," said Johnny. "What are you looking for anyways?"

"A hunch," she said. "A bad one."

The camera continued around. But the image was distorted. The buildings disappeared until the city was gone, replaced with a solid wall of glimmering, prismatic light.

"Something's wrong with the camera," Jimmy said.

But Migmar shook his head. "No, wrong with the camera, there is nothing." The wall of light inched toward the camera.

"It can't be," said Autumn.

"But it is," whispered Kat. "Just as I had feared. The Tide of Unmaking. Exactly as the scouts described it."

No one breathed. The screen turned to violent static.

"It's here on Earth too," Autumn whispered. "And now Tokyo is... is *gone*."

"I fear it is so," Taeva said, her eyes flitting relentlessly. "There is a logic to it. Our two worlds are connected with the portals now. What happens on one affects the other. We're bound by a common fate."

"The Prophecy told us," Tommy said dejectedly. "We spoke of it before, but to see it…"

"Everything will be destroyed," Kat said. "Unless we get Asp to return to Allyra with his forces."

"So let's get him!" cried Bengfist.

"We will," said Tommy, nodding back to the other set of screens that tracked Asp. "We know he's in the air somewhere over New York City, but we've got to figure out exactly where he is. Unless we can find a portal that goes right to him, we may have a long trip from here to there."

"Where is here anyway?" asked Jimmy. "And how did Asp get there from here?"

"Good questions," said Tommy. "I think we can figure it out." He and Migmar moved back to the first workstation with all the images of Asp's attack on Manhattan. Tommy remembered something in the text on the bottom of the video shot that showed Asp, the video shot that was connected to Asp's headset. "Right there," he pointed.

FREQ: 915MHZ
BROAD: 42.430N / 74.350W
RECEP: 52.176300N / 117.23470W

"That's latitude and longitude," Johnny said, remembering it from Boy Scouts.

"And ten bucks says that abbreviation means *reception*," Tommy added. "Where the signal is being *received*." He looked down at the listing of coordinates from all the video cameras and saw what looked to be a search field. "Migmar, type those numbers in that box there," Tommy pointed.

Migmar entered the *"RECEP"* latitude and longitude integers and hit enter.

"Woah, it's spinning again," said Autumn standing back by the globe. It rolled to a stop with a blinking orange light in the Canadian northwest.

"We're in Canada again," said Mr. Charlie, suddenly remembering the jaunt he and Regis had taken.

And Nelly.

Mr. Charlie and Regis locked eyes. How could either of them forget? They'd lost her that night...she'd sacrificed herself so they could escape...with the map of Vesper Crag. Too much like Miss Finney's death. "But that was on the east side," Mr. Charlie added.

"What was?" asked Kat.

"Our passage to the Spider King's first stronghold on Earth. Northern Quebec if my memory of the French province serves me correctly, and it usually does."

"It was under Asp's command," added Regis, "long before any of us really knew his name."

Jimmy laughed nervously, "We sure do now."

"So judging by the portal downstairs, and the pools of glowing slime up here," Tommy peered over the table as he talked, "I'm guessing Asp has figured out a way to tether his Dark Arts with human technology."

"Eh, come on Tommy, he'd need to be a software engineer for that kind of thing," said Johnny, rubbing the back of his neck.

"Or he'd need to kidnap software engineers," said Autumn.

"Exactly." Tommy clicked on an image of New York and sent the globe spinning from Tokyo back to New York. "And I'm guessing that pulsing dot is exactly where the portal downstairs would spit us out if we walked through."

Out of nowhere Kat burst out with, "It can't be!"

"What?" Tommy asked, spinning around with the others to see her hovering in front of a monitor on the far table.

"There," Kat pointed, clicking on the image to expand it. "Right there." Everyone walked over, eyes fixed on an image of a formidable estate surrounded by a white picket fence and bathed in morning light.

"What are we looking at?" said Bengfist. "I don't understand."

"It's an Earth home," said Regis. "In North America." Regis turned around to find the corresponding dot on the translucent globe. "Right there. North Carolina."

Tommy took an exasperated breath; what did this have to do with Asp? "I still don't get it, Kat. What's so special?"

Kat stepped up and put her finger on the metadata of the image. Tommy looked closer.

TIME: 04:21:15
ADDRESS: 3296 BELLEVUE RIDGE CR., GREENVILLE, NC 27609
NAME: GREEN, AUSTIN AND HAZEL

Six of the Seven froze. Their eyes went from the home to the address back to the home.

Tommy muttered, "Jett's home."

Autumn approached the monitor and placed a hand on the image. "I don't understand," she said. "Why would Asp be watching Jett's home?" She turned back to Tommy. "Are the rest of our homes up here?"

Migmar stepped in front of Kat and got on the keyboard. He started scrolling down the list of thumbnail images and addresses on the central lower screen, expanding the metadata. Tommy watched closely. Cities all over the world appeared, and monitors on the other tables came to life, displaying cityscapes and mountain refuges. But as far-reaching and diverse as the images were, no other single-family homes were displayed.

"Only Jett's," Tommy said finally.

"What does that mean?" Kiri Lee asked, turning to look at Tommy's face.

"It means that Jett's family is in grave danger," he said. "For all we know, our Earth families' homes aren't listed because they've already been—"

"Don't say it," said Kat.

Tommy nodded. "We have to assume Asp not only wants to conquer Earth, but make sure he personally eliminates our heritage here, too." He glanced up at the image again; pristine lawn, perfectly manicured gardens. "We've got to warn them."

"But what about Asp?" Kiri Lee asked. "The mission?"

"Well, if those shots from Tokyo are any indication, the Tide is about to move into the Pacific. That buys us a little time."

"Do you think...could it have anything to do with Jett coming back?" Kiri Lee asked. "Remember?"

"I wish I knew, Kiri," Tommy said. "I don't like this at all. At the very least, we need to investigate. If we can get the portals to take us where we want, I say one group of us investigates Jett's place. Those who stay, keep an eye on Asp and wait for him to make a mistake."

"Sounds like a plan," said Kiri Lee, "though I don't like the thought of letting Asp spend one more minute here, nor prolong the Tide's destructive path." She pointed to the Tokyo monitors. "Those are innocent lives. An entire nation, gone."

Tommy nodded. "I know. Neither do I, Kiri. But if we make a mistake now, it means the end of *everything* as we know it, not just Japan."

"I think it's a mistake already," said Taeva.

"What?" asked Tommy, starting to bristle at Taeva's tone. "Why?"

Taeva grew incredulous. "That's Asp! Right there!" She looked over at the monitor. "Let's use his portals to get close to him now. We must kill him now!"

"Taeva," Tommy protested, "it's not that easy."

"Of course it is!"

"Have you been to New York City?" Tommy questioned. "Do you even know what a *skyscraper* is? You seriously have no idea, Taeva. I mean that with utter respect. But snagging Asp out of the air there will be next to impossible."

Taeva stood there, eyes furious. She looked at Kiri Lee. "Well, *she* agrees with me! People are *dying* every minute we delay. I say it's a mistake to go to this Northern Caroleena."

"You are one of us, Taeva," Tommy said, trying to mute the anger in his voice. "But you have not been with us from the start, and you do not lead us. All of us owe Jett Green our lives. If his parents are in danger, if Asp has some vile plan for them, we must discover it and defeat it. We will split up. Some of us will go, but we will not be away for long."

Taeva blew out an exasperated breath and turned away.

"Right then," said Kat trying to bring the conversation back around to Tommy's plan. "Who stays and goes?"

"Well," Tommy stood up and looked at her, "I think you, Mr. Charlie, Bengfist, Jast and Migmar should stay here. Keep an eye on Asp. The Seven will go to the Greens." Everyone nodded. "Except you, Taeva."

Everyone looked from Tommy to Taeva...as if the conflict between them wasn't already heated enough.

"You want me to stay stuck in here?" she spat.

"Well, I certainly don't want someone's emotions jeopardizing a tactical mission," Tommy replied.

"Emotions?"

Tommy let her reaction speak for itself. Taeva balled up her fists and Tommy thought she might explode in a fury of lightning bolts. She turned on her heels, bolting for the door.

"Just where do you think you're going?" shouted Tommy.

"Let her go," Kat said placing her hand on his shoulder. "Give her some space. She'll be okay."

"I was just trying to do what's best for the team."

"I know," said Kat. "Just...just give her a few minutes."

Tommy sighed. He didn't understand girls very much. They frustrated him at times just like this. What did he do wrong? He really liked Taeva...thought she liked him too. Until now.

"Better move," said Mr. Charlie. "The Tide isn't slowing down any."

"Right," said Tommy. "Lords of Berinfell, let's see if this computerized portal contraption will take us where we need to go."

While the Cat's Away

RILING UP these three teens was easy as stirring up a bucket of pigmy pucker-nosed fish: plunge a stick into the water and start swirling—in less than ten seconds the fish would as quickly devour each other as they would the stick.

Like most Nemic, temper clouded vision, making them easy to distract. Dhrex often wondered if that was the reason he entered the Priesthood, to escape the inherent temper of his people. Perhaps this was why they lost the war against the Elves so many moons ago. And if he had anything to do with it, it'd be the reason they lost this time too. Ghrell was mobilizing faster than expected, and Dhrex would not have a chance to get back to Berinfell in time to alert Grimwarden and the Lords. So the best he could do was strip Ghrell of the element of surprise and force him to move before he was ready.

At least, that was his strategy. Only Ellos knew if he could pull it off or not.

"Can you believe what they did out there?" Dhrex pushed again, recovering ground he'd tilled just a few minutes before. "So many innocent lives."

He sat at a table in an eating house with three young Nemic warriors, all nearing the age of twenty, each in their last year of the

Logosic Warrior Way. *The Path,* as the tribes referred to it, was mandatory for all young men to embark on. It spread out over ninety-six moon cycles, or eight years, and covered the Nemic history, culture, hunting, trapping, desert survival and, of course, the flying fighting arts. But most of all, it endeavored to connect them to Allyra, a discipline Dhrex had long ago decided could only be obtained with complete dedication. In this way, *the Priesthood,* he argued, was far superior to The Path. It was the *true* path.

Ghrell had never seen this. War was all he knew. War and revenge. And now he had his chance. And so did Dhrex.

"I want to attack them now!" said Khril, the leader of the three Nemic warriors, pounding his fist into his palm.

"What?" Dhrex sat back agast. "I caution you against speaking with such passion," he raised a finger.

"Such passion?" Kril spat back. "Was it not you who spoke so passionately a moment ago of just how many innocent lives had been taken?"

Dhrex nodded. "That I did."

"Then how can you, a mere Priest, assume passion, when it is I—a defender of Allyra, a warrior of the illuminated path—who is called to act with even greater passion!" Kril stood from his chair now, spilling his porridge.

"Come, come," Dhrex motioned him to sit. But when the young warrior refused, Dhrex made the sign of the spirit realm and threatened him with a curse.

"All right, all right," Khril said annoyed, "don't have to get all mystical on me."

"I wish not to harm you," said Dhrex, lowering his voice, "only to counsel you in your way."

Kril lightened at Dhrex's gesture. "What sort of counsel?"

Dhrex cleared his throat and looked around. The three warriors took this to mean he was about to share something profound and leaned in. Dhrex had them right where he wanted them. *This is too easy.*

"Your passions are well-placed, lads," he began. "Whereas those of our esteemed leaders are waxing thin. Even now they appear to make war, but without the zeal afforded to some." He raised an eyebrow and paused. "There comes a day in all generations when the elder generation must bow to the foresight and enthusiasm of the younger. Tell me, how often have they asked for your ideas?" Dhrex looked between them. "How often have they sought you out? Surely, you have things to say, strategies to offer for the good of our people. Why are you overlooked?"

"Well, possibly because—"

Dhrex cut Khril off. "Because they're stubborn and old. They're the past, while *you*," he pointed at each of them, "are the *future*. You will lead us."

"You've seen it?" Khril clutched the table.

"I've seen it, as it was foretold."

The three warriors held their breath. *Could it truly be?* they wondered. Khril fought the overwhelming urge to believe wholeheartedly. "What are you up to, Priest?" he said. "What's in this for you?"

"For me?" Dhrex sat back, apparently put off. "Why, young leaders of my people, I'm saddened. There is nothing in this for me."

He lied.

"Power? Riches?" Khril suggested. "A place in our new kingdom?"

Our new kingdom. Dhrex had them. "No such thing, my brothers. Only that I am obedient to the spirit realm. That is all."

The three looked between one another, evil smiles growing wide on their faces. Dhrex's manipulation was almost complete. He let them savor the moment, setting to hook.

"So how would you counsel us, Priest?" Khril asked.

"For one, Ghrell is threatened by you. They all are. But I know of your strategies. I've seen them," He tapped the side of his head.

The three were enamored now, amazed at the Priest's ability to read their thoughts—though precisely what strategies he was talking about, they had no idea—they merely wanted to kill some Elves. But if the Priest saw it, then strategies they had!

"*Now* is your time to lead, to set the example," Dhrex's voice remained a whisper yet grew more forceful, a technique he'd honed over the years delivering homilies in the temple. "Yes, Ghrell makes ready for war, yet for all his anger, he is lax and his methods are dated. If the *people* are to desire new leadership, they must *see* new leadership."

"But how are we supposed to do that?" the youngest of the warriors questioned.

"That I cannot say," admitted Dhrex, "as I'm not the foretold leaders of the Nemic, only a servant of Allyra." He shook his head as if he wished he had more to give them. "Perhaps there is wisdom found in an ancient Nemic proverb: *A pebble is only overshadowed when rolled behind the boulder.*"

The three sat mulling over the proverb. Dhrex was hoping these three were as stupid as he'd hoped, but with the amount of time it took them to wrestle with the fake proverb he'd made up, he worried his plan might never come to pass.

Khril's eyes finally lit up. "Tell me, Priest, when did Ghrell say we'd fly on Berinfell?"

"What? Why?" Dhrex said, his brow furrowed.

"When is our army leaving for Berinfell? Surely you'd know such a detail."

"You mustn't say I told you."

"Do not fear, Priest; you've already proven yourself faithful, and we will not soon forget that."

The Priest relented. "Tomorrow at dawn, I believe. Why, what are you thinking?"

Khril looked to his two compatriots. "I'm thinking we give our people a display of bravery the likes of which they have never seen."

Dhrex sat back in his chair. "How very noble of you," he said. *Gullible pucker-nosed fish.*

The sun had nearly finished descending from the sky bowl when Ghrell stood on his portico. He could never sleep on the eve of battle. Nerves too tight. But he knew better than to starve his body from rest. Doing so could prove fatal after long hours of warring in a distant land. He'd need every measure of strength he could get.

"Ghrell, come to bed," his wife said from inside. "The battle can wait."

"I know," said Ghrell, unable to take his eyes away from the flaming sunset. "It's just that—"

"That your Commanders are finishing the preparations you've instructed them to. Everything will be ready by first light. Have they failed you yet?"

Ghrell relaxed. His wife had a way of reading his thoughts like no other. "You're right, Nhada. As you always are."

"And yet you seem surprised," she countered.

Ghrell turned around and walked back into their spacious bed chamber. "Only surprised at myself for not listening sooner."

Nhada sat up. "Not listening to me? Or to the voices telling you to go to war?"

Ghrell looked at her from across the room. "Whatever do you mean by that?"

"Come now," Nhada said. "We both know you've been meaning to wage war against the Elves your entire life. Now it's the eve of your attack and you wonder why you can't sleep? You give me more credit than I'm due for reading your thoughts."

"And still, you think I should question the voices in my head summoning me to war?"

Nhada didn't flinch. "I do."

"Ghah, you're just like that Priest."

"Does that surprise you?"

Ghrell turned back to the portico. "I suppose I'd more readily agree to your mutual counsel if things weren't as they are."

"We both feel for you in our own way. I as your wife, he as your friend."

"He is not my friend," Ghrell spat. "Dhrex was there with me as that Elven spawn swallowed our people with his Dark Arts. Dhrex saw him in the distance just as clearly as I did. For him to deny it is treason."

"Ghrell, please..."

"I shall not entertain your shallow words tonight, Nhada. You know not of what you speak. The Elves have made their last assault on our people, and it shall be my reign that will be remembered for ending it."

"Or remembered for dying in a naive attempt at revenge."

Nhada's words cut deep. And normally she was right. Except this time. This time his wife was wrong. She'd see. They'd all see.

There was a knock at the door.

"This better be good," Ghrell spat, more thankful for the break in conversation than he let on. He hovered over to the door and opened it.

"Vault Minister Ghrell," came the nervous voice of messenger.

"What is it, spawn? You dare to bother my wife and me in our chamber?"

"I know, I know, and I'm terribly sorry. Terribly sorry." The messenger couldn't even look his leader in the eyes.

"Oh, stop groveling, spawn. What is it?"

"Your presence is requested at the staging grounds."

"My presence? *But I just left there.*"

"Yes, your Vaultship, it's just that—"

"Come, that's not even a word," Ghrell said.

"Yes, I beg your pardon."

"Well? It's *just that* what?"

Another voice came down the hallway. "It's just that there's been a development you should be aware of," Dhrex said. The messenger turned to see the Priest coming; the poor soul slid away into the shadows, praising Allyra at her providence for sending the Priest to rescue him.

"Priest," Ghrell stated blandly. "What kind of development?"

"It seems you don't have as much control over your army as you might claim."

Ghrell winced. "Such a sharp jab from one who cares for me in his own way?" he glanced over his shoulder at his wife on the bed. Then back to Dhrex. "What merits such words?"

"Deserters."

"WHAT?" Ghrell stepped forward.

"Three of them. They were seen flying north, carrying terrain bombs stolen from the armory."

Ghrell couldn't speak. Three warriors, leaving for the frontline prematurely, with their most destructive weapon...

"Our element of surprise will be destroyed," Ghrell whispered to himself.

"Precisely," replied Dhrex.

"Well, did someone try and stop them?"

"We sent our best fliers to—"

"Oh, out of my way, Priest! This will be our undoing!"

As the door lingered open, Dhrex caught the eye of Ghrell's wife on the bed. "Yes," he said softly, looking into his sister's face, "this will be our undoing."

The first of a thousand screams came in the middle of the night.

A stone-shattering explosion jolted Grimwarden out of a deep sleep. He flung off his covers, donned his Mandiera battle garb and bounded down the hallway of the palace.

Some of his flet soldiers had already found their feet in the midnight hours and met him in the courtyard. Grimwarden's oldest friend was there as well.

"What is it?" Goldarrow asked as she synched up her belt.

Grimwarden searched the skies. A tower to the East, on the wall near the Gap, had lost most of its turret and burned wildly. At first there was no sign of whatever had done the damage.

"There!" he pointed at last. "Right there!"

Something jagged across the star-lit sky and, for a moment, was backlit by the moon. Goldarrow thought it was a giant moth; it was not uncommon for them to grow quite large in the Thousand League Forest. But then something fell from its clutches.

Crrrrrrack-boom!

More screams. Shouting. Pandemonium spread across the waking city.

"WE'RE UNDER ATTACK!" roared Grimwarden. "DEFENSES!"

Fletmarshalls within the courtyard unholstered their horns and began signaling their respective troops; those calls were echoed further down the ranks and were answered quickly by each and every guard post within the city.

"I'm going to scourge the watchman who fell asleep on this one," spat Grimwarden as he headed for the ramparts of the palace wall, hoping for a better view. "Man the ballistas, nock and fire on sight! Archers, line the rooftops! NOW!"

Goldarrow followed him up, and withdrew an expandable brass telescope from her hip pouch. She blinked twice and steadied her hands against the beating of her heart.

"It is as we feared," she said. "The Nemic."

"What? Already?" Grimwarden turned. "Dhrex said we'd have more time."

"Here," Goldarrow passed him the device. Sure enough, three Nemic fliers circled over the eastern portion of the city. Two of them seemed empty of payload, having already dropped their explosive cannisters of powder-filled sandstone onto the sleepy tower and the homes behind the east wall. But the third Nemic was coming back around, head twitching this way and that, looking for a target.

With solemn satisfaction, Grimwarden watched as the three fliers—including the one with the stone—were riddled with Elven arrows. The bat-like forms tumbled out of the sky and crashed into the city, yielding a flash of orange light. More screams.

"This is not encouraging," Goldarrow said. "They have us either way. Let them fly, and they drop their exploding weapons; shoot them down, and the weapon explodes where they fall."

Grimwarden didn't reply directly. He pulled the telescope away from his eye. "Why only three?"

"Three? What do you mean?" Goldarrow reached for the glass.

Grimwarden explained, "Dhrex said the whole army would engage us. Where are the rest of them?"

"Perhaps Dhrex's warning was premature," Goldarrow said, still searching the sky.

"Perhaps," replied Grimwarden. "Though he was convincing enough."

"I mean, I don't doubt there are those who still harbor bitterness toward Elven kind," she mused. "But maybe he overestimated the situation."

"Perhaps," Grimwarden said again.

Goldarrow lowered the glass and looked at him. "What is it with you and *perhaps*?" Grimwarden raised his eyebrows. "Must you always fear the worst of situations?"

"It is my job to expect the worst," said Grimwarden.

"Perhaps that's why you've never asked me to go to dinner."

Grimwarden paused. "What?"

Goldarrow raised the telescope back to her eye. "Always fearing what will go wrong instead of what will go right."

Grimwarden worked his mouth as if to say something but couldn't find words. Only a woman could think of such things during a potential invasion. He shrugged, glad she wasn't looking at him anymore.

"Guardmaster," came a messenger below.

"Yes," Goldarrow and Grimwarden both replied. The messenger looked confused.

"Sorry. Goldarrow," Grimwarden deferred to her with a nod.

"Yes, flet soldier," she replied. "What's the news?"

"Descriptions of the invaders, Guardmaster. And a message from one of them on the throes of death."

"A message?" asked a curious Grimwarden.

"Well, don't keep us hanging, son," said Goldarrow. "What is it?"

"All three were very young, nearly twenty years I'd wager." The flet soldier cleared his throat for the next bit. "And he whispered something before slipping into unconsciousness. *This is just the beginning,* he said."

Grimwarden and Goldarrow looked at one another, then Grimwarden nodded to her and looked back to the messenger. "Assemble the Fletmarshalls. Fifteen minutes."

"For the unforeseeable future, I'm extending my Guardmaster privileges of leadership to include Grimwarden," announced Goldarrow to the room full of Fletmarshalls. "You will hereafter refer to him according to his previous title until the time that the Lords of Berinfell negate my actions, should they so desire. Understood?"

The Fletmarshalls clapped in acknowledgement of the move and then quieted down as Grimwardem stepped forward. He nodded to Goldarrow, then mouthed the words *thank you.*

"It's an honor to be among you again, lads and lasses," Grimwarden declared to his band of Fletmarshalls. "As always, I count it a rare privilege to lead you.

"While our intelligence is unconfirmed on this, we need to plan for the worst: an attack by the Nemic, echoing what we saw here tonight. As such, I want the fire wall raised to maximum height. All rampart crossbows need to be re-calibrated for extreme elevations. And pull out every bolo-net we have. I don't care if we use the ones for fishing; let those Nemic smell like the rotting carcasses of the sea for all I care. But we'll take every single one of them out of the sky, and I don't want any more terrain bombs landing on our city. Any questions?"

"I thought you said we'd have more time than this," said one Fletmarshall. "Before, you mentioned nine days."

"According to our intelligence, we did," replied Grimwarden. "But it seems that time table may have moved up considerably. And I won't treat this potential threat idly. I'd rather we take every precaution possible only to find out it was a lie, than not prepare and find out we were wrong. Anyone else?"

The Commanders shook their heads in quiet agreement.

"Guardmaster Grimwarden," said Thorkber. "In particular is there, anything for which the Gnomes you'd desire doing?"

Grimwarden smiled at the ever-eager, child-like face of Migmar's Chief Soldier and Second in Command. "Well, that depends, Thorkber. Is there anything the Gnomes would prefer to oversee?"

Thorkber's eyes lit up. "Indeed, indeed!"

"Then I shall trust you to your cause. Anything else?" Grimwarden searched their faces until he was satisfied. "To your stations," he said. The command room emptied until only Goldarrow remained beside him. They shared a moment of silence, then walked back down a corridor leading outside, presenting a stone stairwell that led to ramparts overlooking the city to the south.

"So what do you think that first attack was about?" she asked.

"I don't know," said Grimwarden. "The reports were as you heard. Teen warriors. Not more than twenty years. Overzealous, I assume. That, and poor discretion."

"Which fits with the Nemic disposition," Goldarrow agreed. "But to preempt the entire Nemic army?"

"I know," said Grimwarden. "It's either something meant to distract us...or benefit us."

"Benefit us?"

"I pray Ellos himself stirred up those headstrong fliers to set upon our fair city at such an hour. For it's He I'm thanking that we were not awakened by a much larger force—a fate I fear we'd never have survived. Perhaps these impatient youths' premature strike forced the rest of their brethren to come at us unprepared."

"At least one could hope," agreed Goldarrow.

The two of them stood there, looking out over the city that was quickly preparing for war. Darkness spread over Berinfell like a blanket, kept at bay by thousands of torches that indicated embattlements under construction. The air was crisp, and night-sounds filled the forest surrounding the city. That's when Goldarrow noticed something.

"Wait," she withdrew her spyglass and held it to her eye. "THERE THEY ARE!" She thrust the telescope toward Grimwarden.

The Guardmaster took an icy calm breath and put the glass to his eye. Something wavered near the starry horizon. It seemed at first like a heat mirage, an undulation in his entire field of vision. He scanned the telescope left and right, trying to gain a reference point for the distortion. Then, at last, he understood what Goldarrow saw. And it was no mirage.

The horizon, the *entire* horizon, was alive with Nemic fliers. Thousands upon thousands of them, enough to raze Berinfell to the ground. He slowly lowered the glass and turned to Goldarrow. "I fear Dhrex may have underestimated Ghrell's intentions," the Guardmaster said, a faint thinning in his voice. "The Nemic don't mean to attack us. They mean to annihilate us."

A Knock at the Door

AUSTIN AND Hazel had just sat down for dinner. Hazel's twelve-hour rump roast had been tantalizing Austin his whole day off. Instead of playing golf, he decided to stay home—forcing himself not to turn on the TV—to take care of a few projects around the house for Hazel. The reward: she was making his favorite roast. But it was torture, especially with Hazel's strict *no-tasting* policy.

He tried sneaking a fork full of the tender meat at least twice, but his wife had the uncanny ability to catch him in the act.

"Elwood Austin Peruses Green," she called out, using his entire given name, "just what do you think you're doing?"

Austin looked up, a small mound of tender meat nearly to his opened mouth. "Uh...I was...making sure you properly spiced this roast."

"I see. And may I ask you if I've *ever* improperly spiced my roasts?" Hazel's hands were planted firmly on her hips.

Either way, Austin was caught. *No* meant he had no reason to doubt her abilities this time; *yes* meant he wouldn't be having *any* dinner tonight. He knew better. Austin acquiesced and handed his wife the fork.

"Good boy," she said with a love pat on his rear. "Remember now, good things come to those who wait."

"Oh, don't I know it," Austin replied gloomily.

"But don't forget the second part," she said. "Those who don't wait get a pile of crackers on the back stoop."

But now, the threats were behind, and the waiting was over. The lights were low, and the lid was finally—blessedly—off the pot. Austin thanked the Lord for the food, and for the sudden turn of events that had brought their lives back to normal. *Almost.*

Hazel dished out a steaming chunk of beef, covering it with vegetables and gravy. He was inches from his first bite when the doorbell rang.

"For crying out loud," Austin grumbled.

"I'll get it, dear."

"No, no," he said, reluctantly placing his fork on his plate. "I'm sure it will just take a second."

Austin folded his cloth napkin and pushed his chair out. He weaved through the dining room, around the corner of the kitchen, through a hallway and then into the main entry hall. He glanced at his watch to double check the assertion he'd be making to this unexpected guest that they were calling on the Green Home far too late in the evening. *7:38pm.* Well, at least too late for his tastes.

He opened the door.

"May I help you...?" he began to ask, his tongue and lips mumbling the final words.

Six figures stood on the front stoop. Their garb resembled a strangely executed Halloween costume mixture of the Three Musketeers, The Matrix and The Lord of the Rings. Which was especially strange considering the group looked to be in their early twenties.

"Sorry, wrong month, wrong house," Austin said, rolling his eyes as he swung the door closed.

One of the young men caught the door with his hand. "Mr. Green?"

Austin looked up, not as surprised that some strange kid knew his name but that this upstart had the audacity to prevent him from closing his own door. "Best take your hand off the door, son."

"I'm sorry, but I wouldn't be so forward unless—"

"Unless you had no respect for my family. Step away."

"Austin," came Hazel's voice from behind, "what's going on?"

"These kids were just leaving," Austin said, trying to push the door shut against the intruders again.

"Mr. and Mrs. Green," the young man pleaded, "we're friends of Jett's and we need to talk with you." Tommy had rehearsed the opening line a dozen times, but it still came out wrong. Mr. Green glanced up at them, his face a conflicted mix of anger and pain.

Hazel took a few steps forward. Placing a hand on Austin's shoulder, she looked at Tommy and said, "That's awfully kind of you, dears, but we're just sitting down for dinner. Would you mind making an appointment with Austin's agent, and we'll be happy to meet you—"

"Mrs. Austin," Kat stepped forward. "It's of utmost importance we speak with you right now. It will only take a few minutes, and I really think you need to know what we have to say." All of them, including Kat, knew that much was a lie: it might take a lot longer than *a few minutes*.

Hazel looked up at Austin, her eyes silently coercing him.

"You have five," Austin said.

The Six sat around the oblong living room with Mrs. Green in a leather couch chair and Mr. Green sitting on the arm. Tommy shared a couch with Kat and Johnny; Jimmy, Autumn and Kiri Lee stood next to the arm. All three rocked on their heels.

Tommy wasn't sure how to begin, but Mr. Green's impatient eyes forced him to start talking.

"Mr. and Mrs. Green, I know this is going to sound extremely strange, but I'd ask that you give me just a few minutes to explain without interruption. Then you can ask as many questions as you want, I promise."

"Well, you have four minutes left young man," Mr. Green replied, glaring at his wristwatch.

"Austin," Mrs. Green rebuked her husband gently. "Please...let him speak."

"I'm trying to," Mr. Green said with his upturned hand toward Tommy.

Tommy decided to cut right to the chase. "We're not from Earth."

The mood in the room instantly shifted. Mr. Green's hard face didn't change much, but Mrs. Green's went flat.

At least they weren't laughing, Tommy thought. "We're from a world called Allyra. All of us," Tommy gestured to the rest of the group on the couches. "We were abducted from that world when we were babies and adopted by families here on Earth. But eventually we were taken back to Allyra when we were each about thirteen."

Kat looked to Tommy. *"They're taking it surprisingly well,"* she told him. *"Almost like it's not the first time they've heard this."*

Tommy wondered if this would be easier than he thought. "Mr. and Mrs. Green," Tommy continued, "your son, Jett, was one of us." He paused, searching their faces. The Greens hardly blinked, but refrained form interrupting as he'd asked. Tommy plowed forward. "Once in Allyra, all seven of us were reinstalled into the roles for which we were born so many years ago: to be the ruling Lords of Berinfell, a race of Elves meant to serve, protect and lead the whole of Allyra. But it was in that pursuit...of protecting our people...that your son perished."

Kiri Lee stood up and interrupted. "Your son saved my life," she said.

Kat put her hand on Tommy's shoulder. *"Let her tell it,"* she told him. Tommy nodded. *"Go on, Kiri,"* prompted Kat.

Kiri Lee's eyes already glistened as she began the story. "We were fighting the sworn enemy of Allyra, a mutated murderer called the Spider King. But I was captured and then poisoned…it was a mortal wound. I was moments from death." Kiri Lee shuddered, the emotions of that moment flooding her memory. Tears welled up in her eyes, and a lump caught in her throat. "Jett—" she swallowed. "Your son saved me."

Kiri Lee cleared her throat and wiped her eyes with the back of her hand. "Each of us, the Elven Lords, have gifts," she said, gesturing. "Jett, he had two gifts: superhuman strength and healing. He could heal himself. He could heal…anyone he wanted." She looked down. "And in that moment, he decided to heal me. But it cost him…"

Kiri Lee could hardly finish the sentence. Tears flowed freely. Telling Jett's parents in person what had had happened played out far differently than she'd imagined. How many times had she rehearsed the words and phrases? How many times had she envisioned Jett's parents and how they might react? But now, really here, really saying it…well, words were harder, the well-practiced lines caught on hooks in her throat.

"It cost him his life," she finally got out. "He traded his life for mine." Kiri Lee looked hard into Austin and Hazel's eyes. "I was healed, and the poison killed him."

The Greens bore expressive masks, mixtures of deep-seeded grief and utter confusion.

"Jett is a hero to all of us," Tommy continued. "And he was our friend. We wanted you to know what happened to him, but…there's more, there's another reason we came to you."

Tommy couldn't remain on the couch. He stood up and moved to the side of the room where a large picture window overlooked their side yard. "The Spider King is dead, but from his ruin, another enemy rose. He is a creature called Asp, and he has raised an insurmountable army that, even now, threatens our world and Earth. We are here to stop him, but we discovered that Asp, for reasons we do not yet know, is watching you."

Mr. Green made to speak, but Hazel squeezed his shoulder, then looked back to Tommy. "I'm sorry," she said. "Please continue—what did you say your name was?"

"Tommy."

"Please continue, Tommy."

Tommy ran a hand through his hair. *Blank expressions now,* Tommy thought. *Hard to read, but they seemed to be taking all this rather well.* "Anyways, we need to get you to safety," he said, "at least for the time being. I know it all sounds crazy, I'm sure. But that's the long and short of it."

Austin and Hazel looked at each other, both with hesitant smiles. The Lords weren't sure what they were expecting as a reaction, but this wasn't it. Secretly, Tommy figured, they'd either freak out and require some fantastical display of the Lords' otherworldly powers to convince them otherwise, or they'd freak out and call the police.

But there was no *freaking out* going on here.

"Thank you for coming," Mrs. Green said. "All of you. We truly appreciate it." She looked to her husband.

"It took a lot of courage to share all that with us," said Mr. Green, "and who knows what you went through to even get here."

"Excuse me, excuse me," Kat stood and waved her hands. "You mean to tell me *this doesn't sound crazy to you?*"

"Kat," Autumn cautioned her friend.

"No, no," Mrs. Green said, gesturing to Autumn, "it's okay, dear. I understand."

"You do," said Kat doubtfully.

"In fact, we believe most all of your story," said Mr. Green.

"You believe most...wait, wait, really?" Kat was incredulous. She turned to Tommy, to Autumn, to the others. "I'm having a hard time with this." She was flicking her hands in the air like a runner warming up for a sprint.

Kat! Tommy called through his thoughts. *Get a hold of yourself. You're doing enough freaking out for everyone.*

Kat didn't reply. She simply stood their gaping like a fish out of water.

"Mr. and Mrs. Green," said Kiri Lee, "did Jett's Sentinel—the one assigned to protect him—talk with you?"

"Mr. Spero," Mrs. Green said, nodding fondly. "He did indeed."

"We freaked out on him at first," said Mr. Green.

"See! Right there," said Kat. "They freaked out. I knew they would."

Ignoring Kat with a tentative smile, Mr. Green continued. "But after *those Dredded things* broke into our house and tried to kill us, we knew it was real. All of it."

"Really?" asked Kat.

"Yes, really," said Mr. Green.

"What *things*, exactly?" asked Tommy.

"Creatures with wintry white hair and blades for fingers," he said. "And monstrous trees, near tore our house to pieces."

"What did you do afterward?" asked Kat, still incredulous.

Mrs. Green stood up off the side of the chair. "What could we do? We either went insane, trying to piece it all together, or we took Mr. Spero at his word. After all, we saw what we saw. Austin buried the dead creatures on the property."

"Maybe we're crazy," said Mr. Green. "But I guess being Christians like we are, we believe in some pretty crazy things anyway. At least that's what the world thinks."

"We call it faith," said Mrs. Green. "And that counts for an awful lot in life. So we prayed. And waited. Publicly, of course, we continued to use the media to try and get Jett back because…well…that's what the world expected of us. My husband is well known, you see. Our whole family is well known. Since Jett wasn't dead, and there was no body, we had to continue to act like concerned parents."

"Even though you knew there was nothing you could do about Jett being taken to another world," concluded Kat.

"Precisely, my dear."

There was a long pause in the room. It would have been awkward had not so many minds been processing so much valuable information. Finally, Tommy walked back to the center of the room and spoke up.

"Mr. and Mrs. Green," he said, now very curious, "if you don't mind me asking, you said you believe *most* of our story. What part don't you believe?"

"We take a lot by faith," Austin said, winking to his wife. "But there are some things you just have to see with your own eyes. Follow me." Austin and Hazel swept out of the living room and waved for the Lords to follow.

Holding hands, the Greens took to the stairs. They waited for the Lords to catch up and then turned down a long hallway. They passed several open doors: guest bedrooms, and a sewing room from the look of it. But they came at last to one door that was shut.

Mr. Green glanced at Tommy and gave a sharp knock. "This," Mr. Green said, "is the only part of your story that doesn't add up." He turned the knob and pushed open the door.

Furious Flying

THE FIRE wall was an impressive tactical feat of Elven engineering. Spread along Berinfell's defensive perimeter sat large crossbows fed by specially banded clusters of arrows. One arrow in the bundle deployed a parachute upon reaching its flight apex; three arrows held lightweight flasks that sprayed a pressurized oil over the long, ten-minute decent to the ground; and a fifth arrow in the center was tipped with flaming dremask so that it set the oil aflame as it spewed from the flasks.

The effect was a constantly cascading wall of fire that swept below each bundle of arrows. When set in sequence with other bundles beside it, and replaced with newer bundles above it, the effect was a wall of glowing fire that risked dowsing flying enemies, like the Nemic, with a nearly inextinguishable, napalm-like coating.

Because the Elven invention was fairly recent, inspired to combat the Warflies in the wake of the Spider King's rule, the Nemic had never encountered it, and were caught by surprise. The first wave of terrain bombers closed within two-hundred yards of the city before the first volley of clustered arrows was sent skyward. The Nemic viewed them as any other bow attack, and steered clear.

That's when the wall appeared.

Only a scant few made it to the other side before the wall of liquid fire burst to life. Those beneath the clusters were immolated in a shower of flames. Every beating wing that attempted to extinguish the blaze added more air to the fire's fury, until each flier had been engulfed in a pulsing shroud of angry red and orange.

The Nemic fell from the night sky like bloody comets, plummeting to the ground just in front of the walls. Terrain bomb after terrain bomb exploded upon impact, jarring the heavy fortifications and jouncing the archers atop the ramparts, but doing little real damage.

Those Nemic not engulfed in the first round watched their brothers perish in fiery explosions but pulled out of their approach to avoid the same fate.

As new arrow-clusters took the place of those descending to the ground, Ghrell realized his army would need a new strategy. "Higher still!" Ghrell spat to his Commanders. "Their shafts cannot out-climb us! I want half our bombers to scale the heights. The rest, encircle the perimeter. There must be a breach in their fiery net. Find it, and exploit it!"

"But sir, won't dividing our attack make it more vulnerable?" asked a Lieutenant named Chorlic.

"If we divide," Ghrell said, chewing on his calloused lip, "they must divide to counter. We will stretch them to the point of breaking, and then swoop in for the kill."

The new orders were delivered, and the next wave of fliers were split into three groups: one that would assail the right flank, the second over the top, and the third to the left flank.

But the Elves were waiting.

The first group that climbed over the fire wall had a dizzying descent to overcome, all the while keeping hold of their terrain bombs. The force of gravity alone made pulling up after the rapid drop-and-release, necessary for an accurate explosion, nearly impossible. Many

Nemic aborted the precision they had practiced and opted for a blind drop from a thousand feet.

Some few survived long enough to release their weapons. But most found a forest of arbalest shafts flung up to meet them, followed by a swarm of arrows. Impaled Nemic fliers fell like some morbid downpour. But each falling Nemic still managed a parting gift for the Elves. Terrain bombs shattered walls, gouged buildings and scoured the cobbled stone streets.

The Elves managed to reduce the damage somewhat, utilizing bolo-nets to catch some of the terrain bombs in midair and detonate them prematurely. Finely woven from cables of lightweight kassek fiber and perfectly weighted with round stones in the four corners, the bolo-nets were normally used in trapping and fishing. But when fired from an arbalest or the larger ballista, the nets served as a swift catch-all for the enemy terrain bombs. The weighted nets forced the weapons to loose their fury long before they reached the ground. A similar invention captured the bombs and pulled them unexploded, dangling from the walls on spring-loaded tethers.

Still, there were far too many bombs to get them all, and each shot required pinpoint accuracy. Berinfell began to feel the Nemic attack, enduring an assault such as it hadn't seen since the Spider King's invasion.

Grimwarden watched from atop the palace ramparts with Goldarrow, surveying their defenses through her telescope. With the waterfall of fire at the southern-most point, hundreds of Nemic spilled into the sides of the city like swarms of cluster flies descending on an animal carcass.

"This may take every arrow we own," said Goldarrow. She zoomed in on a battalion of furiously firing archers, sending shaft after deadly shaft into the naturally hardened, exterior shells of the Nemic fliers.

"Good thing we have a reserve of Gnomes," Grimwarden replied with a grin.

"And Bear," said Goldarrow. The giant wolf did his best to join the fray, racing along open stretches of the ramparts and snagging any Nemic that flew too low in a death grip.

Grimwarden smiled, then set off down the stairs. "Seems I'd better get Thorkber's plan situated."

"I, uh, don't understand," said the crossbowman. He fumbled with the awkward plank of wood Thorkber handed him.

"Just do as he says," said Grimwarden. "And tell all the other operators to do the same." He leaned in to the crossbowman's ear for added emphasis, "And trust me, you don't want to make a Gnome angry."

The operator raised his eyebrows, then stared at a smiling, winking Thorkber. "Yes, sir."

As Grimwarden walked away, Thorkber scrambled up onto the thick beam of the crossbow, then stood on the center of the curved bow. "Here," he said. "To me, hand it."

The crossbowman offered the strange-looking plank to the Gnome and watched as Thorkber laid it along the central beam. The lower portion terminated in a tail piece exactly like the end of a bolt, while the front was rounded to a point. Folded along the sides were spring-loaded wings that extended once airborn. A wooden block rose from the plank a third of the way from the bottom, while a dowel protruded toward the top. Once it was securely in position, Thorkber climbed onboard. He lay on his stomach, feet braced against the block, hands wrapped around the dowel.

"You've got to be kidding me," said the crossbowman.

"Me," Thorkber thumbed his chest, "aim!"

"You're not serious."

"Serious he is," said another Gnome standing beside the

crossbowman, his own plank in hand; and behind him was a line of Gnomes filing up the rampart stairs.

The fire wall was no doubt raised in anticipation of the Nemic attack, no thanks to the unfortunate announcement of their arrival. *Unfortunate only for those youthful spawn,* thought Ghrell. Still, Ghrell had sent his minions over the top, knowing the Elves would never expect it, though also knowing it meant certain doom for those who were ordered over the top. Assaulting the flanks would be a far less tragic objective, though still riddled with danger. And other projectiles.

The most frustrating part of the fire wall was not being able to see what was happening in the city beyond. So Ghrell moved his hovering Conclave of leaders to the left flank, hoping to get a better view of things as he rose higher into the night sky.

The fire cast a warm, orange glow over the southern portions of the city and, with his multi-occular vision, Ghrell could see the legions of Elven Archers posted along the ramparts, on building summits and further down into the streets, making good the evacuation of Berinfell's citizens to the north.

It was then he noticed that many of his glorious terrain bombs were not detonating. His fury grew as he squinted against the chaos to see some sort of spring loaded netting reaching out to snag the bombs and often the fliers too, pulling them to safety along the wall. He ground his teeth, and without realizing it, was flying closer and closer to the front.

Dangerously close.

"Send them in faster!" Ghrell roared.

"Faster?" questioned a Commander. "But they are already—"

Ghrell's temper got the best of him. He pulled his bolt pistol from his hip and fired a pin-pointed stone dowel into the Commanders forehead. The Nemic warrior flipped backwards and disappeared in the darkness below.

"Any other questions?" The remaining Commanders shook their heads. "Good, push them. We must flood the city until the Elves suffocate under our weight!"

Ghrell had no sooner got the words out of his mouth when a piercing heat drove between his shoulder blades, the force of which spun his body in the air. He roared in pain, shock getting the better of him. He managed to correct the spin, but his wings were failing, and he was losing altitude. That's when he realized something was on him. And it was alive...and screaming.

Thorkber saw a lone warrior in the southwest sky descend from a cluster of Nemic fliers. His rich battle garb and the fact that he had hung back from the battle seemed to mark him of some importance, so Thorkber directed his crossbowmen to aim in that flier's general direction.

"You sure about this?" asked the operator.

Thorkber nodded, then said, "Loose!"

The crossbowman shrugged his shoulders. "Suit yourself," he said, then pulled the lever. The braided cord snapped taught with a *thwack!* and sent the Gnome-bearing plank hurtling skyward, wings extended.

Thorkber suppressed his desire to yelp, knowing it might alert his enemy. Instead he held tight to the plank and leaned right to correct a subtle change in trajectory. Flying closer, he prepared his body for the leap. Muscles tensed. He only had one chance.

Thorkber lunged away from the plank, his little body in free-flight, plummeting toward the unsuspecting Nemic warrior. Thorkber reached for the knife in his belt, and clutched it—blade out—with both hands.

The blade sank between the flier's shoulder blades before Thorkber's body even made contact. But when he did, his momentum twisted the Nemic warrior in midair. Thorkber held onto the knife for dear life, praying it was deep enough to hold. When his target finally righted itself, Thorkber sat upright and let loose a terrible war cry.

Still in near-debilitating pain, Ghrell started skittering across the sky in a vain attempt to rid the terrifying creature from his back. How had he been bested so easily? Despite his violent efforts, the thing would not relent, and the pain between his shoulder blades grew more fierce. With every twist and turn, the burning spread, driving deeper and wider. And still the beast wailed with a terrifying shriek.

What demonic spawn have the Elves loosed upon us? Ghrell thought as he descended lower and lower.

"Where'd you send him?" Grimwarden came back to ask the crossbowman.

"There!" the crossbowman said, raising his finger.

Grimwarden looked at a lone Nemic flier now hurtling toward the city with Thorkber clearly holding on for dear life.

"That's him," Goldarrow stated. "That's Ghrell."

"You're sure?" Grimwarden asked, his voice tense. "But how could Thorkber have known?"

"Known what?" asked the crossbowman.

"You sent him to the Vault Minister of the Nemic race," Grimwarden informed him.

"Thorkber knew what he was getting into," said Goldarrow. "It's crazy enough as it is."

"Right. And he didn't need to make it worse by mounting the most violent warrior in the lot!"

Ghrell was fighting to stay aloft now, unable to control his direction. That's when he noticed he was flying over the city. The archers looked up at him, but refrained from delivering a barrage of fatal arrows. *Why?*

Suddenly the archers from below started to howl...*in triumph*. Raising their fists at Ghrell. Shouting. Cheering. The Vault Minister was incredulous. How had these Elven spawn identified him and lured him out so easily? *And now they praise my demise.* It was confounding.

Suddenly the beastie upon his back began chanting, and the Elves echoed his cry...

They aren't cheering for my demise, Ghrell realized. That's when the travesty of it all prevailed upon him. *They have no idea who I even am! They're cheering for the spawn on my back!*

Just when things couldn't get any worse, Ghrell cast a fleeting glance behind him. Nemic were falling from the sky everywhere. And not a single arrow was sent up toward them. That's when he noticed a small colored lump on each Nemic's back.

Gnomes.

Some hung from wingtips, knives shredding the thin Nemic skin. Others dangled from legs or arms. Still more rode precariously, knives embedded deep into the shoulder blades—just as the Gnome was on Ghrell's back.

"GNOME SPAWN!" Ghrell roared in a desperate attempt to rid himself of his passenger. But the Gnome would not be dissuaded. Ghrell saw he was headed for a tall building. If he could not wrest the beastie from his body, he'd make a go of crushing it, even if it meant perishing himself. From the amount of blood soaking his chest he figured he was dead anyway.

The Nemic leader was alive, but flying out of control. Grimwarden knew this was not going to end well, and estimated the point of impact. He bounded down the rampart stairs four at a time, turned at the bottom and raced into the streets.

The flet soldiers started cheering, and Grimwarden looked up to see Thorkber pass between buildings, hooting and hollering from atop his mount. Ghrell looked weak, heading straight toward a tall building just ahead. Grimwarden forced himself faster.

A sickening thud echoed down the street ahead and to his right.

"I'm right behind you!" yelled Goldarrow.

Ghrell managed three more beats from his weak wings, then tucked his knees in, rolling on his side. The move presented the Gnome to the broadside of the building, followed by a bone-crushing collision. He hit harder than he imagined, knocking the wind from his lungs. But he felt the Gnome share the impact. The pair fell to the stone street below.

All was quiet.

Ghrell coughed, sending shooting pains throughout his cracked ribcage. The taste of blood filled his mouth. He blinked, trying to get his bearings.

The Gnome.

Ghrell rolled over, lifting his head. The street was empty save for the flickering glow of the fire wall in the distance. He attempted to rise to his hands and knees, but the pain was overwhelming. That's when he noticed the Gnome laying beside him.

"It seems the tables—" Ghrell coughed, then spit blood to the side. "The tables have turned." The Gnome had just enough life in him to open one bloodied eye. Ghrell grinned against the pain it took to lift his clawed hand to the Gnome's throat. "You have bested me, Gnomic spawn. But not before I kill you first." Ghrell squeezed his claw, pinching off the airway and making the Gnome's eyes bulge.

Grimwarden took the corner too fast and slammed into the stone building. Just ahead of him lay Ghrell, one arm reaching over to Thorkber's motionless body.

Grimwarden raced forward, seeing Ghrell squeezing Thorkber's throat.

That's when Thorkber saw Grimwarden, his eyes widening.

Ghrell suddenly realized the Gnome's bulging eyes were not from his strangulation, but from surprise. Something flashed in the Gnome's dilated pupils.

Jolted by a new blast of adrenaline, Ghrell released his grip on the suffering Gnome and rolled to his opposite side. He recognized the two Elven leaders from the Conclave. Grimwarden, and behind him was Goldarrow. *Wretched spawn!* They raced toward him, swords raised above their heads.

Ghrell summoned his energies and withdrew a fusillade from a leather pouch on his hip. He rolled five metallic *draws* along the street, the balls whizzing past Grimwarden, then whipped a handful of *shards* high above. The shards spun as they gained their bearing, then flew toward the irresistible draws. Ghrell smiled as the tiny blades cut Grimwarden's skin to ribbons.

"NOOOO!" Goldarrow screamed. She flew forward into a spray of blood, watching Grimwarden stumble to the ground. His knees hit the stone as his sword clattered down the street.

Her first instinct was to attend his wounds, but she was all too aware of the lethal enemy gaining his feet. Goldarrow paused long enough to see light in Grimwarden's eyes, and hear his forceful admonishment: "*Get him.*"

She looked up. Ghrell was nearly erect, reaching into his pouch for another handful of shards. But Goldarrow countered, having produced her bow and nocked an arrow in the time it took Ghrell to stand. Goldarrow relaxed her string fingers.

"Shoot me and these shards fly free," Ghrell growled. "And we both know where they'll go." His eyes looked down to the draws pinned under Grimwarden's already battered body.

Goldarrow stayed the arrow between her fingers, her heart beating loudly in her ears. Ghrell was losing blood, a lot of blood, and she wondered how much longer he could remain standing even if she didn't shoot him. There was no way she could move Grimwarden's body in time, and throwing herself in front of the shards was pointless: they'd still travel through her and hit him. Nothing but a granite wall could stop them.

That's when she realized she'd been outwitted. It was over. She secretly hoped some Elves had followed her and Grimwarden down the street, but based on the boisterous cries of the flet soldiers, they were too distracted, celebrating imminent victory. The Gnomes' little invention had apparently swung the balance in their favor. She chuckled. *Who would have thought Gnomes would have been so good at flying?*

"Why are you laughing, Goldarrow?" Ghrell hissed, the air coming out a puncture in his throat. His hand loosened on the shards.

"We beat you. We beat you with *Gnomes,*" she said. She lowered her bow.

Goldarrow watched Ghrell's rage consume him. He shook, face contorting, limbs fluttering. His blood pressure squirted fluid from the wounds on his chest. The last words she ever heard him say were, "I DESPISE YOU, ELVEN SPAWN!" And with that he opened his hand and released the shards.

Ghrell realized he would probably never walk out of this alleyway. But at least he was certain Goldarrow and Grimwarden would die for their treachery against his people. Liars. Deceivers. All of them deserved to die. At least he would get the pleasure of seeing two of Berinfell's leaders bleed out right before his very eyes.

Goldarrow had infuriated him for the last time. He felt his body expand with rage. It rose up inside of him like a geyser issuing up boiling water from the deep. He had few words left, nor the energy to speak them, but he would be true to his heart.

"I DESPISE YOU, ELVEN SPAWN!"

His hand opened, and he watched as the shards tumbled into the air. When they found their bearing, Ghrell eyed them. They were pointing toward him.

Impossible!

A moment later two dozen new holes had been opened in his torso. He didn't feel them. There was already too much adrenaline coursing through his body. He glanced up to Goldarrow, his mouth filling with blood.

"Like I said," she smiled, "we beat you with Gnomes."

Ghrell wobbled, his head growing dizzy. He blinked, trying to focus, then slowly turned around. There stood the Gnome from on his back, holding one metallic ball in each hand, each protruding with a dozen bloodied shards.

Ghrell fumbled a hand into his pouch and noticed two draws were missing. "How...how did you..." but he was too weak to talk.

Impudent Gnomes...

Friendly Fire

JETT GREEN sprawled back on his bed reading a book about motorcycle racing. He looked up and frowned, seemingly annoyed at the invasion of his space. There were, after all, six strangers at the door, strangers who were gawking at him.

Autumn burst into the room first. "JETT! YOU'RE ALIVE!" she cried, hurling herself at him, arms wide.

Tears filling their eyes, Kiri Lee and Kat both cupped their mouths with their hands. Johnny placed a hand on Jimmy's shoulder, and Tommy threw an arm around Johnny's back.

"I...I can't believe it," Tommy said, the words a joyous sigh. "Thank Ellos."

Jett rolled off the far side of his bed and ducked under Autumn's embrace as if she were some crazed football fanatic.

Autumn froze, stunned by Jett's obvious avoidance...as well as, his cold expression. The Lords filed into the room behind her.

"Jett, honey," Mrs. Green said, "these are your friends."

Tommy frowned. *Something's not right here.*

Jett stood, arms to his sides, staring at all of them.

"Jett?" Autumn pleaded. "Are you...are you okay?"

Jett examined her, but he wore a blank face. No look of surprise;

worse still, no look of recognition.

"Jett, it's me," Autumn said, taking a step closer to the bed. Jett withdrew even more, pressed against the far wall.

Kiri Lee came forward next. "Jett," she said. "You remember me, don't you? You came to me in Berinfell and again in the Thousand League Forest."

Jett blinked, stared at the floor for a moment, and then looked up... it was the tiniest flicker of recognition.

Kiri Lee reached out. "I knew you would remember." But he flinched away from her hand as if it was a white-hot branding iron.

Tommy stepped forward. "Jett, it's Tommy. Tommy Bowman," he said. "Felheart Silvertree, I'm here for you, man. We all are," Tommy gestured to the others. "We've come to get you."

The room grew silent. Jett backed up a step, cornering himself between the end of the bed and a bifold closet. He glanced warily about the room and finally said, "Get me? No one will *get* me. I am home."

Tommy looked at the other Lords, all manner of questions popcorning in his mind. He stepped in front of Autumn, but Jett balled his fists.

"*Tommy,*" Kat's voice spoke into his mind. "*I wouldn't.*"

It's fine, Tommy spoke back. Then he spoke to Jett, "Whoa, easy man. Everything's cool."

"No, everything's not cool," Jett said, his face contorted. "Who are you people? Why are you troubling me?" Jett glanced to his parents.

"Honey," Mrs. Green said, "these are your friends. From Brenafield."

"Berinfell," Jimmy corrected her with a whisper.

Jett squinted, struggling with something in his head. "I...I don't know any *Berinfell,* and I do not have any friends."

"Yes, you do, Jett," Autumn reached out her hand past Tommy's side, reaching once more for Jett. "You do. I'm right here. *We're* right here."

The moment of wonder at seeing Jett alive had been utterly crushed. He was there, right in front them him. He looked older than when they'd buried him seven years ago, but he'd aged no more or less than they had. He was Jett, in the flesh. But he did not know them.

It was some type of amnesia, and sometimes amnesia was reversible. But often, it was not. Jett was alive, that would have to be enough for now. Exactly *how* he was alive was another story. But that could be answered later.

"Jett," Tommy asked, trying to relax and keep his frustrations invisible, "what exactly do you remember?"

"Remember?" Jett barked back. "About what?"

Tommy said, "About Allyra. About the Elves."

Jett blinked, looking down at the floor.

"Keep going Tommy," said Kat.

"About the Age of Reckoning, the Prophecies of Berinfell, about the Spider King and—"

"STOP! STOP!" Jett held his hands up. "You are absurd. Leave, now."

"Don't you remember who you are?" Autumn pleaded. She was crying now, as were Kat and Kiri Lee.

Their joy had morphed into sorrow, like a butterfly reversing its metamorphosis and climbing back inside a cocoon. Jett was dying all over again right in front of their eyes. Kiri Lee sobbed into the corner of her arm.

That's it, Tommy said to Kat.

"What's it?" she asked.

Tommy approached the bed and started walking slowly around the end, his hands up. Jett tensed. "Jett, who are you?"

Jett's eyes darted between Tommy's slow steps and his outstretched hands.

"Tommy, be careful," Kat cautioned.

"I'm…I'm Jett Green," Jett said flatly.

"And?"

"And what?"

"Tell me your other name," Tommy said, as he eased closer. "The name you were born with, your Elven name."

"Stop talking to me!" Jett cried, fist balled tight.

"You are an Elven Lord of Berinfell!" Tommy declared, inching closer.

Tommy! said Kat.

"You're Lord Hamandar, born of Vex and Jasmira Nightwing. And Ellos granted you gifts of untold strength and miraculous healing."

Jett clenched his eyes shut, his hands covering his ears.

That's when Tommy got an idea. Sometimes a physical sensation could trigger memories. *Maybe,* he thought. *It might work…or, it might get me flattened.*

Get ready, he told Kat.

"Tommy, what are you doing? Don't do anything stu—"

Tommy made his move. In one swift motion, Tommy drew a dagger from his belt. He trailed it lightly across Jett's exposed forearm, leaving a thin red line.

"GAH!" Jett yelled. His eyes bulged, and he glared at Tommy.

"TOMMY!" Jimmy yelled. But it was too late. Jett took one step forward and shoved Tommy in the chest with two hands. The force of the blow knocked Tommy off his feet, through the sheetrock wall, to a sickening crash into the two-by-four studs of the next wall.

"JETT!" Mrs. Green screamed. The room filled with dust and debris, Jett's parents coughing.

Kat raced to the hole in the wall, looking for Tommy, while Autumn tried to plead with Jett. Johnny was out the door, racing across the hall, and found Tommy crumpled in a heap and powdered ghostly white with drywall dust. Johnny glanced at the exit hole Tommy's body had made.

"Great Ellos," he whispered. Then to Tommy, he said, "Hey bro, talk to me. Come on, man. You're tougher than that."

He patted Tommy's face, trying to get him awake. A trickle of blood appeared at the corner of his mouth. "Come on, Tommy. Wake up."

Tommy's slack expression tightened into a pained wince. "What—what hit me—Jett...why?" He coughed, then clenched his teeth trying to catch his breath. His entire chest burned.

"Easy does it," said Johnny. Jimmy and Kiri Lee came to his side.

"Is he okay?" said Jimmy.

"Oh," Kiri Lee said. "Oh, no."

"I think he may have busted a rib," Johnny said. "A concussion, maybe too. He's awake, but I think he might need a hospital."

"Oh, this is not good," Kiri Lee fidgeted. "Not good at all."

"I have an idea," said Jimmy. "Stay here with him, Johnny. You too, Kiri."

Jimmy bounded back into Jett's bedroom where Kat and Autumn were pleading with Jett who was pacing in the middle of the floor. Mr. Green was holding his wife in the corner, both distraught.

"Kat," Jimmy motioned her over. "Tommy's in a bad way." Kat looked up, but Jimmy kept talking. "He needs Jett, or else we're going to the hospital, and I don'na need to tell yu how that could turn out. I'm thinkin' yu could use yur gift to talk to Jett, and maybe get him to heal Tommy which—"

"Which might trigger Jett's memory," Kat finished.

Jimmy gestured toward the hole in the wall, "As if that display wasn't enough."

"You're not far off," Kat shook her head. "He's doubting everything...like there's a veil over his eyes. I'll see what I can do."

Kat turned around and started talking to Jett's mind. *"Jett, it's me, Kat."*

Jett froze, a female voice loud in his head.

"Over here," she said, waving her hand at him.

"What are you—how are you in my head?" Jett backed into his closet doors.

"It's my gift, Jett. You have strength and healing, and I can hear a person's thoughts and project my voice into their head."

"This is insane," Jett muttered. He looked to his parents.

"Listen to them, Jett," Mr. Green said. "Can't ya' see they know ya', boy?"

Jett's eyes narrowed.

"Recognize the truth, Jett. Everything Tommy told you is true. And Tommy needs you right now. He's in the hallway. You hurt him, who knows how bad. You're the only person who can heal him."

"Heal him?" Jett exclaimed. "You...you are crazy."

"Who sent him through a wall?" Kat pointed to the hole even though Jett didn't need to look. *"And how did your arm heal so quickly?"* He looked at the gash Tommy made; Jett's eyes widened as he realized the wound was completely healed. Not even a scar. Jett put a hand to his head. He took a step backward into the closet doors once more.

"Oh no you don't," Kat said, stepping toward him and grabbing him by the arm. *"You're not getting woozy on my watch. You have a job to do."*

"This...this cannot be happening," said Jett.

"Come with me!" Kat pulled him out of the room, around the corner to Tommy's side. Johnny remained crouched beside Tommy's body. The gaping hole in the wall looked like the exit wound of a cannon blast.

Kiri Lee looked up to Jett and moved aside. "He needs you, Jett," she said, ushering him closer. "He needs you right now."

Jett was hesitant. "But I don't know how," Jett confessed, genuinely at a loss. "How could I send him through that wall? How might I repair his damage?"

"Here," Kat said, taking Jett's hand and placing it gently on Tommy's head.

"No, no!" Jett pulled away. "I cannot do this! You have all lost your minds."

"Jett, please!" cried Kiri Lee. "He needs you! *We* need you!" She stood up and grabbed his hands. "I know it's you in there. Somewhere. You saved my life, Jett." Kiri Lee started sobbing again, her hot tears dripping onto his knuckles. "And you remember, don't you? That's why you appeared outside my window. That's why you found me in the Thousand-League Forest. Please, Jett!"

Jett pulled away from her. "I cannot help you," he said. "Leave me alone."

"ENOUGH!" cried Mr. Green from the end of the hallway. He kept Mrs. Green behind him with an arm, her fearful eyes gazing around his bicep. "I want you out of my house!" he roared with the same kind of authoritative tone he'd honed over years on the football field.

"But Mr. Green," Kat began.

"You are disturbing my son. He's already told you he cannot help you."

"At least tell him to heal Tommy!" Johnny demanded, rising to his feet.

"You deaf?" Mr. Green asked, his face blooming a furious red. "He said he can't do it. Leave him be."

"Austin," Mrs. Green pleaded with her husband, but he'd have none of it.

"But Tommy's fair hurt," Jimmy said. "Yu can't just leave him like this."

"Look, son," Mr. Green said. "Jett can't heal your friend. But I don't think you need to worry. I've seen worse. Tommy will be okay. Just needs a week of bed rest, that's all."

The hall fell silent. The Five looked up at Mr. Green. Jett retreated slowly into his bedroom.

Tommy stirred. "Help me...help me up," he said. When they did, he glared at Jett's parents. "Let's go. There's no help available here."

"Asp will be coming for all of you," Johnny said as they turned to leave. "Please…for your own good, come with us."

"We're staying right here," said Mr. Green.

"Then at least let us take Jett," Kat pleaded.

"You took him from us once," said Mr. Green, pulling Jett close. "You won't take him again."

The Phantom Blitz

GENERAL CAERFASZ sat on his Warfly, hovering six-hundred feet above the southern bank of the Thames River. The Warspiders and warworms, as well as the infantry they carried, were in position in the network of sewers beneath the city of London.

What a beautiful scene, Caerfasz thought of all that unfolded below him. The grand old city at night was lit with tens of thousands of lights. Every imaginable color. Every possible brightness. And many of the lights were in motion. The cars and trucks on the Westminster and Waterloo Bridges were especially mesmerizing to watch. Other lights moved as well, winking and blinking, sliding and bouncing. Even round and round. Caerfasz locked in on the amazing observation wheel known as the London Eye. It was his first target.

Asp had ordered two kinds of attacks. The primary goal was to eliminate England's formidable military threat, especially the Royal Air Force. General Scarvex had been given the larger of the two invasion forces for that task. Caerfasz was easily a better pilot than Scarvex, but was more than agreeable to let that assignment go to the advancement-happy general. Caerfasz and his squadron, on the other hand, had a relatively easy mission, but one that was sure to be satisfying. If only the minutes would go by faster.

Caerfasz had been staring at the luminous face of Elizabeth Tower (formerly Big Ben) for close to an hour, and the hands had moved so slowly. Asp had been very clear: the coordinated attacks all over the Earth were to begin at the stroke of midnight, London time. And Caerfasz had obediently waited. It had been painful, but he'd waited.

The last five minutes seemed to be the worst. It was like the hands of that gigantic tower clock had stopped moving. Caerfasz couldn't stand it. Then, at last, a viable excuse arrived. A military helicopter had been spotted, racing in from the east. At its current speed and heading, it would likely plow right into the invisible, hovering squadron. Premature discovery was not acceptable. Nor was signaling the whole squadron to move out of the helicopter's way. Caerfasz wouldn't let that happen.

So, at two minutes to midnight, Caerfasz lifted the war horn from his chest and winded it. The sonorous, moaning horn was an eerie cry in the night. And the entire invisible squadron, six-hundred Warflies strong, surged forward to carry out their mission. Caerfasz drove his mount into a dive. He saw the crowd below, thousands of unsuspecting humans, milling about at the base of the London Eye. Perhaps, they were waiting for their chance to ride. *What a shame.*

Caerfasz pulled up suddenly and cracked two, tear-shaped arc bombs together. They flared to life, and Caerfasz let them fall. The bombs kindled brighter and brighter, a searing blue to an intensifying white just as they struck the concrete foundation beneath the Eye. The arc bombs shrieked when they exploded, followed by blinding light and a thunderous report. A shockwave rippled out into the crowds. A wave of screams answered.

Then came the groan.

The steel A-frame legs of the Eye had been superheated by the initial blasts. They groaned against the tension created by the six backstay cables holding the great wheel in place. But the blasts hadn't been enough.

Caerfasz had already circled back. This time, he dropped three separate bomb pairs. One after another, they crashed down and exploded. Anyone on the ground who hadn't been flash incinerated by the first two bombs, disappeared now in successive walls of white fire. The steel glowed like it had come fresh from a forge. Then it buckled.

The backstay cables went suddenly slack as the A-frame bent backward, and the wheel crashed in upon itself. The cable spokes ripped from their hub and slashed the nearby Jubilee Gardens and the Film Museum across the road. Passenger capsules slammed into the concrete, exploding. Some snapped off and flew into the Thames River.

The London Eye was no longer recognizable as a wheel. Amidst the fire, there was only a gigantic skeleton of twisted steel. Sirens sounded from every area of the city. The rest of Caerfasz's squadron had been busy as well.

The Tower of London had been obliterated, and Elizabeth Tower would never tick past two minutes to midnight because it now lay in ruins. *Yes, this mission is satisfying,* Caerfasz thought.

"Terror," Asp had said. "I want you to create terror."

Niloth Fel, nephew of the former High Councillor Grundin Fel, sat atop a red Warspider downslope from Shanhaiguan Pass in China's Hebei Province. These deadly beasts were normally reserved for Drefids, but Fel had so distinguished himself among the Gwar that he had been awarded this steed. Unlike his more diplomatic uncle, Niloth had seen very little point in negotiations. When the leadership of the Taladrim and the Saer hesitated to support Asp, Niloth had advocated the wholesale annihilation of each race. And when Asp needed to eliminate great numbers of these beings to make a point, he had turned to Niloth to see that it was done.

And so, Niloth sat upon his red Warspider, an invisible general with invisible legions behind him, and waited for the signal.

WHOOSH. A single red skyrocket surged into the heavens. Scores of tourists, strolling along the Great Wall or climbing the Zhendong Tower, watched it go up. Some gasped. Many cheered. It was all part of the experience, and they reveled in it. After all, it was a popular saying among the Chinese that, "He who has never been to the Great Wall is not a true man."

Leaving a trail of orange sparks behind it, the rocket raced ever higher until, *FOOM!* One thunderous clap of power, and the Shanhaiguan Pass was bathed in red light.

Niloth Fel grinned, lifted his war horn, and loosed a fearsome call. A strange hush traveled rapidly from the tower down the length of the wall. If his engineers had done their job correctly, Nilhoth knew the silence was very much temporary. *Any moment now,* he thought.

There! The first flash of an arc stone charge, at the base of the wall beneath the Zhendong Tower. It blazed to life, brighter and brighter, until Niloth couldn't stare at it any longer. Then, it detonated.

Twenty-three-hundred year old stone sprayed into the sky. Screams rang out from the tower as the foundation trembled. The second arc stone charge had been activated by the first. It exploded, and the tower foundered. It crumbled as it fell, collapsing in a cloud of fire, smoke and dust.

The third charge went off, and another section of the Great Wall erupted. The chain reaction had begun. Niloth watched with a mixture of fascination and pride as charge after charge exploded. To the far west, there were bright flashes, and Niloth knew his comrades had begun their assault as well. As per Asp's orders, Niloth and other teams all across China were systematically destroying the Great Wall of China. It would be a blow to their national pride. And it would send a signal to the Chinese and the world that their enemy was immense and well-armed.

Any foe who could simultaneously obliterate fifty-five-hundred miles of ancient stonework, was a force to be reckoned with.

Niloth winded his war horn once more. It was time for the Warspiders to move in...to pick off the survivors and answer any military response the Chinese might offer. Niloth laughed to himself. *As if they could offer any real resistance.*

Had Niloth known that the nation to his east had just been incinerated by a force of destruction not even Asp could compare with, perhaps he would have thought better of scorning the Chinese resistance at all.

The Collector

"HE HAS returned," the Drefid at the console said. "Just as you said he would, my Lord."

"Are you certain, Zirile?" Asp asked. His long cloak rippled and, in a blink, the Drefid ruler stood by the bank of computer monitors. This field setup wasn't as elaborate or as powerful as his Canadian encampment deep in the mountainside, but it at least gave Asp a bird's eye view of his other theatre of war. And in this particular case, it gave him a lead on the elusive pet project he was so eager to capture.

Zirile smiled wickedly. "Your word is certain, Lord Asp," he said. "But I know better than to speak theories to you. According to the digital recorder, he first arrived yesterday morning. See here in this first segment."

Zirile's long fingernail moved slowly on the optical pad, causing the still-moving image to zoom. "You see," he said. "Right here. He's on the front steps. Now he turns. There!" He tapped a button, and the image froze.

Asp leaned closer, eerie blue light from the monitor illuminating his skullish face. "The size and frame are correct. The color of his flesh… could be Lyrian."

"*Is* Lyrian," Zirile said, his fingers flying across the keyboard like spiders' legs. "I took the liberty of looking up photographs from Jett's time on Earth. It seems he was rather the local hero. Many, many photographs in the news. I scanned those into the facial recognition software I modified and...see for yourself, my Lord. A perfect match."

"Lord Hamandar Nightwing," Asp said. "Welcome back to the world of the living."

"If there was any doubt," Zirile said, "you can see how his parents fawn all over him when they open the door."

"There is no doubt, Zirile," Asp said. "You have done well."

"Thank you, my Lord. I am moving Cragons in as we speak."

"Surround the house," Asp said. "But do not attack. I want to collect Hamandar myself."

"Jett, honey, eat a little more," Hazel Green said. "Pot roast with onion gravy is your favorite."

Jett's eyelids were only half open. He held the fork in his hand, but didn't move it toward the food his mother had generously piled onto the plate.

"Let 'im be," Austin Green said. "He's been through a lot."

"You mean today?" she asked.

"No, I mean all of it."

"Just how much 'a that you think is true?"

Mr. Green glanced at Jett, then back to his wife. "C'mon, Hazel," he said, standing up. "Let's give Jett a little peace."

He led his wife into the study, a place he figured would be out of earshot for Jett. Once he closed the French doors, he said, "You know I don't want to believe them any more than you do. Shoot, they're all freaks to me. But I know a liar when I see one. And those kids, not a one a' them is lying. They might be crazy, but they ain't lying."

"But they said..." her voice thinned and cracked. "They said he died. They said our boy died."

"Maybe they thought he did," Mr. Green said. "They sure believed it. You see the look on their faces when they saw Jett? Especially that Asian girl. What was her—"

"Kiri Lee."

"Right, Kiri Lee. That look on her face near broke my heart. Reminded me of the look on your face. Remember the game against the Raiders? Ole Jack Granger put that hit on me, knocked me clean out. I woke up, saw that look in your eyes."

"I thought you were paralyzed," Hazel said. "Thank God you weren't."

"I know one thing," Mr. Green said. "Our Jett would'a given his life for a friend. He wouldn't a' thought twice about it."

"Jesus said 'Greater love has no man than this: that he give up his life for a friend.' Jett always liked that verse. I 'spect you're right about—"

"Shh!" Mr. Green held up a hand. "You hear something?"

She shook her head.

Mr. Green opened the French doors a foot and leaned out. He listened a few moments and then ducked back in. "Must be gettin' windy. That strip a' siding's still loose. Anyway, after all we've seen, I can't see why we shouldn't believe those kids. Except..."

"Except that Jett's alive."

Mr. Green nodded. "Yet he doesn't seem right. He doesn't talk much 'cept when he's angry. Didn't know his friends either, if they were his friends. Not even sure he knows us, not really, not like he used to."

"He found his way back home, didn't he?"

"That's promising," Mr. Green said. "I'm gonna give Chad Riley a call. He's one of the Panthers' new docs. He's supposed to know a lot about brain injuries, kind of a specialist they hired 'cause of all those concussions. Bet he could steer us in the right direction."

"Good idea," Hazel said. "Can you call him tonight?"

"I will. Now, let's go sit with our boy." Mr. Green opened the door, and they walked back toward the kitchen.

"Y'know, it's funny," Hazel said. "But after losing Jett once, I just don't want to let him out of our sight—"

Mr. and Mrs. Green stopped and stared. They'd been gone only a few moments. But Jett's food was untouched, and his chair was now empty.

"Hamandar Nightwing, we meet face-to-face," Asp said. The Drefid lord stood between two massive, swaying trees just inside the fence to the Green's property. Lightning lit the night. Thunder sounded eventually, a long, low rumble like a distant avalanche. Cold wind swirled. "You heard my call."

Jett stood unmoving for several moments, a massively built, shadowy figure. Then, he nodded slowly.

"I was afraid that you were perhaps beyond reaching," Asp said. "But then, the healing gift is strong in your family line. Very strong indeed. You aren't the first to come back, you know."

Lightning lit Jett's face, his eyes embers of violet fire.

"Several generations back," Asp said, "one of your line was buried and forgotten, only to rise again in time to meet his grandchildren. It is a curious thing. You didn't actually die, you know. Oh, it was a mortal blow that you absorbed. It shut down every system of your body, but began recreating you immediately. Cell by cell. It took years. It would have taken at least another year or two had I not...sped up the process a bit."

Asp held up three fingers. A red electrical arc wobbled at his jagged fingertips. He held his bony fingers to his lips and blew. The spark became a dancing red strand. It floated through the air and landed on Jett's cheek. It snaked its way up Jett's face and disappeared into the corner of his left eye.

Jett smiled.

"You like it," Asp said. "That is the taste of power. And there is much more for you, Hamandar…if you serve me well. Come."

Jett tilted his head sideways, down to one shoulder and then the other, cracking vertebrae. He began to follow Asp when there came a metallic clicking from behind.

"Don't you go another step, Son," Mr. Green said. "Not with that monster anyway." He lifted his shotgun and pointed it at Asp's chest.

Asp looked closely at the gun. "A Mossberg 835, smooth bore 12-guage—I have made a point to study the weapons of your world. Good choice, Mr. Green. Perfect for home protection."

"Good enough to wipe that grin off your face," Austin Green said.

"Perhaps," Asp said. "But if you fire, you might hit your son."

"He'll heal," Mr. Green said. "But you won't."

The cold wind intensified, rustling dead leaves between them. Lightning flash-lit the yard, creating shadowy faces in the shrubs and in the trees.

Asp stepped toward Mr. Green. "I sincerely apologize that you've become attached to Jett," he said. "But he is no longer your son. In fact, he never was."

"Shut your slack-jawed mouth," Mr. Green commanded, bracing the shotgun against his shoulder. He switched off the safety and slid his finger from the guard to the trigger. "Don't you come any closer!"

Asp moved slowly, but didn't pause in his movements. "Jett is Elven," Asp said. "Not human. He was never meant to come into your world. Regrettably, there were weaker vessels of my kind who brought Jett here." With each step forward, Asp's talons slowly began to extend. *"One man's loss is another man's gain,* I think you say. I have simply come to reconcile the error, to ah…collect what is mine."

Austin Green had made many important decisions in his life. But he'd never taken such a risk as this one. Asp stood just in front of Jett now, and those sharp talons were emerging.

"You said Jett belongs to you," Mr. Green said. "That's where you're wrong. You can't own a man."

He fired.

The shotgun blast should have ripped the Drefid's left side to shreds. But the buck shot stopped in a swirling cloud of red mist just inches from Asp's outstretched hand. Storm-driven wind blew the mist away, and Mr. Green's shotgun blast went with it.

"That was valiant, Mr. Green," Asp said, still advancing. "I wasn't sure you had it in you. Now, you can fire again and again, use every round you have, and watch me blow them away. Or you can rescue your wife."

Asp pointed to the Green's home. Mr. Green turned, keeping Asp in his peripheral vision. But when he saw the massive dark trees moving in on his home, his heart fell. He'd seen first hand the damage that Cragons could do, and these were bigger than the others he'd seen.

"Isn't this fun?" Asp asked. "You cannot save Jett or your wife. But you have to try. Am I right? Those Cragons are already ripping up the roof of your home. You told your wife to wait there, didn't you? Probably in the basement…a storm cellar, I imagine. But Cragons are not like some mindless tornadic wind. Their gnarled fingers snap timber and crack stone. They will search out every corner, every crevice until they find her. And then…"

Austin Green looked down at the shotgun. He looked at his son. In the lightning flickers, Jett's stare was sullen…cruel.

"Son, you don't have to go with him," Mr. Green said. "We're your family! Don't let him own you. Jett, don't you know me, boy? Please."

Jett cracked his neck again and then, almost sneering, he said, "Go home, old man."

If someone had sucker-punched Austin Green in the gut, it wouldn't have had nearly the impact of those words.

CRACK!

Mr. Green turned, saw a section of what had been their family room collapse, two Cragons mercilessly crushing and tearing.

"Let me make this easy for you, Mr. Green," Asp said. "You have no weapon that can harm me. Jett has renounced you. I will leave with him. You really have but one choice."

Asp slashed the air with his talons. A shimmering portal opened behind Jett.

Mr. Green's eyes grew huge and plaintive. He looked back and forth between Jett and his home. Back and forth. No hope versus little hope. Back and forth.

Lightning blasted. Somewhere very close. Thunder crashed instantaneously. And Mr. Green turned and fled for his home.

Asp laughed quietly, put his arm around Jett's shoulder, and led him into the portal. "Come, Hamandar," Asp said. "We have much to do."

When Kingdoms Crumble

SKAX TURNED his Warfly out of combat and brought it to hover so that he could think. The attack on Russia's Pacific Fleet had gone exceedingly well. Stationed at Petropavolvsk on the Avacha Bay, the Pacific Fleet Base had an aircraft carrier, six destroyers, and more than a dozen nuclear submarines. *'Had' being the operative word*, Skax thought.

Asp's senior general did the calculations. Yes, it was true he'd lost a dozen Warflies, mostly due to the MiG-31 Interceptors flying about like hornets. The Russians had made cunning use of their forward cannons, each plane capable of strafing the skies with close to ten-thousand rounds per minute. And several Warspiders had been burned up by the ship-based artillery. The destroyers had found the right range once, but only once.

Any casualties the Russians inflicted were by chance. Nothing more. Skax smiled. The Russians, on the other hand, had suffered a humiliating loss. Four of the destroyers were ablaze and sinking. The nuclear subs had submerged and scattered, but arc charges disabled most of them before they got too far away. Warworms finished them off. Avacha Bay was a radioactive mess now. It was almost too easy.

But, something must be said of Russia's valor, Skax thought. *They are doomed, and yet they fight on. To the last man, perhaps?*

"Well, so be it," Skax said aloud, turning his Warfly into a dive.

He emerged from a cloud bank and smiled again at the destruction. Skax cracked several pairs of arc bombs together and released them. The aircraft carrier already burned in several places. A huge fiery balloon of smoke boiled into the sky from its cracked hull near the conning tower. *FOOM...FOOM...FOOM!* Three helicopters still on deck went up in flashing fireballs, one after the other.

Skax looked for another target. He found a tight formation of three MiG-31 fighters screaming in from over the bay. Skax couldn't keep up with them, and he certainly didn't want to stay in front of their ridiculous cannons for long. He gave his Warfly a sharp tug, and the beast responded with a darting upward movement...the kind of aerial movement of which airplane pilots could only dream.

Satisfied with his altitude, Skax smacked two large arc bombs together and looked up. The MiGs were nearly upon him. He dropped the arc bombs and yanked on the reigns. The Warfly zipped upward and zigzagged out of range. The arc bombs exploded directly in front of the three MiGs. Angry orange fire churned within the larger white flame burst, and the Russian fighters were gone.

From his current altitude, Skax saw two things: a serious rain front was moving in from the west, and the Russians had mobilized their armored cavalry at last.

The rain was somewhat troubling. Skax had seen the Gnomic invisibility paste tested. It was waterproof, so the rain shouldn't matter. But Skax didn't want to take a chance. Losing their invisibility would be more than a little problematic. He looked up at the dark mantle of cloud, just now sweeping in over the western volcano range. Something looked odd about the clouds and the rain curtain beneath them, but Skax couldn't identify the issue.

Thunderous artillery fire below jerked Skax's attention back to the tanks and other armored vehicles crawling over the battlefield. He knew the Warspiders would be scurrying to get out of their way, but he also knew the tanks wouldn't stop. They would set up a skirmish line and press forward, firing ordnance at varying ranges until they hit the Warspiders. Skax knew that wouldn't take long. And, agile as they were, the Warspiders wouldn't be able to maneuver forever.

"Time to have a little fun," Skax muttered. As he drove his Warfly into a dive toward the tanks, he recalled the Dark Arts commands he'd need. Russian soldiers marched in fire teams behind the tanks. But their attention was straight ahead. Those who did look up didn't see Skax bringing his Warfly to a frantic hover in front of the tanks.

Skax put his knobby hands together. He uttered a series of rites and stretched his hands apart. Some thirty feet below, directly in front of the line of tanks, a seam tore open in midair. Bluish electrical arcs danced on its jagged perimeter as the portal window ripped wider and wider. The Russian tanks rumbled forward. Sparks flew and the portal flared as tanks edged into the hole.

Skax watched with glee as each and every tank that drove even a few feet into the portal became disabled. The portals, he knew, wouldn't allow anything but organic materials to enter. Skax slammed his hands together. The portal collapsed, sheering off portions of tanks across the battlefield. Skax opened the next portal across the middle of nine armored vehicles. Then he brought the portal to a crashing close, gutting the enemy. The remaining tanks and the soldiers opened fire, but hit nothing.

SCREEEE!

A chorus of shrieks and screams came from the west, but not far. Skax knew those sounds: dying Warspiders and Warflies. Had the enemy gotten lucky with their artillery once more?

The cacophony of pain rose in strength and pitch to the point that Skax's Warfly began to buck wildly. Skax nearly fell but, with a few swift kicks, managed to force his mount to submit. He couldn't blame the creature. The cries were as disturbing as they were continuous. Skax snapped the reigns and raced west.

The storm had been moving much faster than Skax anticipated. It had already crossed over the westward volcanoes and was even now intruding upon the field of battle. Skax felt a cold chill. He'd been right to fear the rain. The Gnomic paste must have failed. The rain water washed it off, and now the Russians could see—and attack—the invaders. Skax winded his horn three times—the signal for retreat—and drove his Warfly west at top speed.

Skax looked down at the terrain blurring beneath the Warfly. Based on their battle plan, he knew that he was flying over a sector where there should have been hundreds of Warspiders and half a legion of Gwar and Drefid soldiers. Of course, they were all invisible. Still, Skax raced on. The storm front and the volcanoes loomed ahead.

"NO!" Skax yelled. He yanked the reigns. The Warfly tried to respond, but couldn't make the turn in time. Its left wing slid into the rain curtain. The creature shrieked and jagged hard. It began to spin out of control. Skax leaped from his saddle just as the Warfly buried itself in rocky, half-frozen ground.

Skax hadn't gotten much lift. He extended his talons and flailed at the limbs of a tree as he sailed by, but that only served to throw him further off balance. There was no way to land on his feet, so he tried to roll. The angle was all wrong. He hit his shoulder, heard a sharp snap, and screeched his agony into the wind. He rose unsteadily to his feet. Pain throbbed along the right side of his body, but he didn't acknowledge it. He couldn't. His mind was consumed with the sight before him.

"What...what is this?" he asked in a scratchy whisper. What he saw made no sense. The storm front...the rain curtain...it was destroying everything it touched. Skax blinked at the series of startling flashes before him. And in the instant of each flash, there had been just the briefest of shadow images—Warspiders and soldiers—silhouetted in the moment of death.

There were more flashes higher on the rain curtain. *Warflies, no doubt,* Skax thought with what reasoning he had left. *They weren't able to turn away in time and burned up.*

But he still could not understand what he was watching. He'd been over and over the reports. Except for nuclear warheads, the Russians had no weapon of this magnitude. Skax looked at the approaching curtain of death. It scorched the ground as it came, devouring turf, tree and stone. It seemed to make no difference. There came a rumbling behind him.

It was the thunder of a large group, an army. Skax turned to the east but saw nothing. The sound grew louder and louder. It was all around him. "NO!" Skax yelled. "Turn back! Turn back!"

It was his own army. Hundreds of Warspiders and thousands of troops. He had sounded the retreat, and now they all raced west...into certain death. He spun and looked for his war horn. He'd lost it in the fall.

He limped down a hill. He had to find it. Something banged into his shoulder, spun him around, and knocked him to the ground. "NO!" he screeched. "You fools, turn ba—!"

The Warspider's foreleg pierced Skax's breastplate, impaling his chest, and then tore free. The second limb crushed his skull. He hadn't seen it coming. And his army raced west, not realizing the doom that was upon them.

"Flee!" Irethor cried out. "Take only what you absolutely need and only what you can get swiftly! The Tide is upon you!"

The scout from Berinfell stood under the eaves of the highest bell tower in Wooten Vale and shouted from the depths of his lungs. In between yelling out warnings, he rang the colossal bell. Down below, the Elves who lived in this village at the western edge of the Thousand League Forest, ran from storage buildings and from their homes. They were running for their lives.

Irethor wished he had five-hundred Scarlet Raptors to bear the village into the sky and out of harm's way. But he had only one flying mount. His mind raced as he screamed more warnings. He knew he'd arrived at Wooten Vale just in time. If the villagers moved swiftly, they could escape. And, if the need were upon them, Elves could travel through the trees more rapidly than most of Allyra's races.

Irethor looked up. The need was most certainly upon the Elves of Wooten Vale. The Tide of Unmaking loomed just a few hundred yards from the village. Irethor watched as one of the scattered trees on the other side of the village wall vanished in a blue-white flash. That tree had lived for over a hundred years and now, in the single beat of a heart, it was gone.

Irethor blinked. *That cannot be right,* he thought. *The Tide was just outside the wall. It cannot be here already.* Irethor stumbled backward, striking the bell. "No, no," he whispered. "Its speed has increased."

Irethor grabbed the bell rope and heaved. The peal was louder and more frantic than before. Irethor yelled, "Forget your belongings! Go now! Flee for the trees! Flee for Berinfell!"

He leaped out of the bell tower, slid down the rooftop, and dropped hard to his feet. His raptor shifted nervously as Irethor climbed into his saddle. Then, he was in the air. He looked down at the Elves as they fled into the Thousand League Forest. He prayed for them to make it safely to Berinfell. Then, as he rose above the treetops, he looked into the hazy east. Berinfell was there. But what safety would that grand city provide against the Tide of Unmaking?

Echoes Uncertain

"WHAT DO yu mean she's gone?" Jimmy asked. "She's a Lord now. She can'na just leave."

"Leave, did she indeed," Migmar replied.

Bengfist shrugged his shoulders and said, "She must have been watching Migmar work the moniterds, and when our backs were turned, she went right out through a portal."

"I knew her grudge against Asp was strong," Kat said. "But I never thought she would go after him on her own."

"I don't think she ever really believed diplomacy would work with Asp," Tommy said. "In her mind, Asp has to die. She should have waited for us. She's going to get herself killed."

"Uhm…" Migmar said. "Thinking me not that reason she left."

"What?" Autumn asked. "Of course that's why she went. Why else would she leave?"

Bengfist held out a small leather-bound text. It looked tiny in his massive hands. "What my backwards speaking friend here means," the Gwar Overlord explained, "is that Lady Taeva left this behind." Bengfist handed it to Tommy and said, "It does not paint a very promising picture."

Tommy passed the book on to Kat. "Do your thing, Kat," he said. "Broadcast it."

Bengfist snatched the book back. "It is long," he said, flipping the pages with remarkable dexterity given his thick fingers. "Very long. But...hmm, no...a moment, yes, here! Here, read these pages. They are the most...informative." He handed the book back to Kat.

"I have a feeling I'm not going to like this," she said.

"No," Migmar replied. "Like it not at all."

November, 1445

As near as I can tell, two months have passed since my last entry... since just before the birth. The poison he gave me forced the child from my womb prematurely. Thank Ellos she was conceived before the venom, for she appears in every way normal. As normal as the child of an Elf maiden and a halfbreed Elf Gwar could be.

But whatever she is or might become, she is my child. She is precious to me. A ray of light into this dark place. So smart she is. She quiets with a touch and mimics my every expression. Brave too. For she looks upon me without fear. In fact, she loves me. I have named her in First Voice, the oldest Elven language. Her name means Spark of Life. Her name is Taeva.

I have come to bitter terms with my fate. This thing that I have become, this wicked spider-like monstrosity, will never be able to mother another child. I feed Taeva but fear what might travel from my body to hers. And I do not know my own strength. Each time I touch her I am afraid I will wound her... or worse. No, as much as I long to do so, I cannot be the mother precious Taeva needs. And this, this dark cavern cannot be her home.

I have delayed our parting out of selfishness. So far, I have kept her hidden from him. But for how much longer? And so it comes to this day... this cursed day. I have made arrangements with a Drefid who, among all the beings of Allyra, are most skilled in stealthy movement. His name is Asp. I am not certain if he is loyal to my cause or just to his own private agenda. In any case, he is clearly not loyal to my husband. And that is enough for me.

In exchange for such treasures as I have left, Asp has agreed to bear

Taeva safely from Vesper Crag. When I implored him to deliver Taeva to a family of means, he insisted upon the Taladrim, who have no heir. I have never trusted the Taladrim, but then, what of my judgment? History will never show me wise.

Tomorrow, before dawn, I will gaze upon Taeva one last time. And then, Asp will bear her away. My only love will be taken from me...my last strand of hope leaves with her.

As one, the Lords looked up at Bengfist with a twisted expression of both recognition and fear.

Tommy blinked the fog from his eyes and asked, "Is this who I think—"

Bengfist nodded. He took back the journal, paged through it to a place much later in the book, and then handed it to Kat. "Now, now read this," he said. "And brace yourselves."

Wretched. I am a misbegotten creature from a misbegotten race. All those useless words about honor and nobility! Elves and their beloved Ellos! Where are they both when I need them? Vesper Crag stands as a haughty insult to all of Allyra. And the Elves? The Elves are hiding! Faithless and fearful, they hide.

Allyra is left to rot, and I am left to languish...to fester. More than twenty years have passed! And he uses me to breed a race of savage creatures. I have become his brood mother...a Queen of spiders.

Curse the Elves! Curse the so-called Children of Light! If I could, I would reach across this world and poison them all!

Maybe one day, I will.

In this imprisonment, I have grown powerful. Though now my body is so wracked with venom I fear my writings may soon end, such is the impediment of my faculties. The Elves have forgotten me...forgotten and forsaken me. But before all has ended, I will make them remember my name. Navira will haunt their steps until the end of this age.

"Navira," Kat whispered.

"The Spider Queen," Tommy said. "Taeva's mother."

"But," Johnny said, "that would make the Spider King...*her father.*"

Tommy nodded and stared at the ground.

"And Asp was the one who took Taeva to safety," Kiri Lee said. "He brought Taeva to the Taladrim."

"Taeva used us," Tommy said. "The whole time...all she was was a spy for Asp."

"That can'na be right," Jimmy said. "She helped oos against Asp's forces in Thynhold Cairn. She came to oos for help. I mean, Asp killed her people, for cryin' out loud!"

"They were never *her people*," Tommy said. "Not really. If Taeva had her mother's journal all this time, there is no doubt she shares her mother's hatred of the Elves."

"I don't know, Tommy," Kat said. "I never read Taeva's mind, but I thought sure that...well, that she had a good heart. She's wounded, but I thought—deep down—she was...I don't know. Ugh, this is so hard to take."

"So she's gone to Asp, is it?" Jimmy said.

Bengfist nodded. "I fear it is so. Migmar and I have read a little more of the journal in the time you were gone, but these two passages you have now read, they speak plainly the message of the whole."

"We should'a never made her one of oos," Jimmy said.

"I tried to tell you that," Kiri Lee said. "We should have waited for Jett. Maybe that's why he doesn't remember us. Maybe Ellos is punishing us for choosing on our own!"

"Yu can't know that!" Jimmy shot back.

"No, none of us can know," Tommy said. "And none of us should presume to know Ellos' judgment."

Jimmy nodded slowly.

"But it was the Spider King who poisoned Taeva's mother," Autumn said. "It was that Dark Arts poison! Taeva should despise the Spider King! She should hate Asp too. He's a Drefid, and he's all mutated like the Spider King, right?"

"Maybe she did hate the Spider King," Tommy said. "But he's dead. Vesper Crag is thrown down. But Asp was there before. He was there with Navira...aided her to bear Taeva to safety. And now Asp is mutated just like Navira and bent on destorying Elven kind, along with the humans...maybe that's why Taeva's sympathetic to him."

"I don't buy it," Johnny said. "She fought with too much vengeance. She can't be all friendly with Asp now. Or maybe that was just to impress us."

"Too many *maybes*," Autumn said.

"One thing's certain," Jimmy said. "We're in big trouble."

Communication Breakdown

"TROUBLE," TOMMY said, "doesn't begin to cover it."

"Right," Johnny said. "Asp is already blastin' Earth with who-knows-how-many legions."

"The Nemic are marching on Berinfell," said Kiri Lee.

"Taeva's gone and betrayed us," Bengfist grumbled.

"Oh, and let's not forget," Jimmy said. "We have a wee wall of electrical energy fair eatin' oop both worlds unless we can stop it."

"Wait," Kat said, a strange look on her face. "There's still more. The Prophecies of Berinfell tell us that we have to get every last Allyran being off of Earth and back to Allyra."

The Lords and their friends stared at each other for a moment, a weary smile—very out of place—spreading.

"And count us," Autumn said, barely containing a giggle. "Just six of us, right? And the prophecies say we've got to be Seven again, or the Tide will destroy everything!"

It happened all at once.

Laughter.

Spontaneous, exhausted, gut-wrenching laughter. Asp's subterranean fortress had probably never seen such a display of utter tomfoolery. Jimmy cackled so hard that he fell out of his chair. And that, of course, set Bengfist to howling. Autumn and Kiri Lee leaned on each other and giggled so hard that tears poured.

Tommy held his sides, winced and coughed while he laughed. "Ow, ow, ow! Don't forget, I'm hurt so bad I can barely walk! So we have that going for us too!"

Migmar, usually the most jovial of them all, failed to see the humor. He munched pensively on a piece of dragonroot and said, "Stop you this foolishness! Need we a plan!"

Eventually, the laughter decelerated. Except for a few sniffles and whispered sighs, the chamber grew quiet once more. That's when they heard a peculiar sound.

"Oh, ah, that's an awful smell," Jast said.

Bengfist nodded and scrunched his face. "It...it's like a maladon curled up and died around here."

They all turned to Migmar.

"What?" Migmar objected.

Laughter roared anew, and it was several minutes before anyone could speak coherently.

"Okay," Tommy said at last, "I think we all needed that. But now, we need to get serious. Now, we need a plan."

"I think I have one," said Kat, turning toward Migmar at the controls. "Migmar, you said you can open a portal anywhere in the world, right?"

"Of course," he grinned. "Kat goes where?"

"It's not where *Kat* wants to go," she countered, "it's where we want Asp to go."

"Why didn't I think of that before?" said Tommy.

"Oh, brilliant!" replied Autumn. The group gathered around the table, riveted to the monitors.

"Okay, Migmar," Tommy said, "where's Asp at?"

"Here," he brought up a window as before; Asp was hovering high over a section of midtown Manhattan.

"Wait until he's steady," Tommy's eyes narrowed. "Just use his coordinates. With any luck he'll either fly right into it, or the portal's gravity will snag him if you get it close enough." *Such a simple idea,* Tommy thought. "Then we'll send him...where do we want to send him?"

"Vaporlize him!" said Bengfist.

"It's vapor*ize,* Bengfist," corrected Autumn. "Vapor*ize.*"

"Not so fast," Tommy said. "Remember, it's better if we can convince him to move his armies back himself. They'll listen to him more easily than us I'm guessing."

"And then we vapor-eyes him," added Bengfist.

"Everyone be on the ready," said Tommy. "We're bringing him back here. Weapons drawn." The group readied their arsenal of combat skills and weaponry. Blades glimmered, fire danced, arrow points focused, stone hammers swung, all aimed at the open space above the Kevlar pad. "No one shoots until I give the signal. Remember: talk first, shoot later." He nodded to Migmar.

Migmar entered the appropriate data and initiated the action command. He pressed the *Enter* key.

A small *burp* rang out as a pop-up message filled the window.

Unable to complete task.

Tommy glanced over, frustrated. "Unable to complete—? Try it again, Migmar."

Migmar entered the same data, being sure he'd typed it in properly. *Enter.*

Unable to complete task.

"Blocking it, something must be," said Migmar. "Not sure."

"He's got some sort of jamming gadget I bet," said Autumn. "Or just the Dark Arts would do it, I'm sure."

"Some bright idea that was," said Kat.

"Hey now, it was a great idea," Jimmy corrected her. "Joost not the right one. We need a better one, that's all." Everyone stayed their weapons and relaxed.

"No,"Kat thought, "now…right now we need to pray." The other Lords exchanged glances, their eyes speaking what they all felt: shame for not thinking of prayer in the first place.

They bowed their heads and quieted their hearts. And each, in his or her own way, searched for Ellos.

Their prayers ended. They were silent a minute. Some glanced at computer monitors. Others watched the luminous line that represented the Tide of Unmaking as it crept slowly but inevitably across the holographic globe.

"I have to admit," Kat said, "I had a hard time praying."

Autumn and Johnny looked up sharply. They glanced at each other and then back to Kat. "You, too?" Autumn said.

Kat nodded. "Maybe it's being back on Earth," she said. "Or maybe it was our trip to Jett's house, but as soon as I closed my eyes to pray, I couldn't stop thinking about my parents…my human parents that is."

Tommy sighed. "I kept asking Ellos to give me a plan…to show me how to defeat Asp or stop the Tide. But I just kept thinking about this fishing trip my parents took me on when I was like eight."

"Looks like we we're all thinking of our folks," Johnny said.

"Not all of oos," Jimmy said.

Kiri Lee looked up but said nothing.

"Sorry," Johnny said. "I wasn't thinking." Jimmy waved dismissively.

"Maybe we could visit them," Kat whispered. "They have a right to know what's happened…and what's happening right now."

"Least we can do," Johnny said.

"We don't have time," Tommy said. "The Tide is advancing. People on Earth, in Allyra too...they are dying by the thousands. Maybe the millions."

"I know," Kat said. "You're right."

Autumn made eye contact with Johnny and said, "This could be it, Tommy. Asp, the Tide, the Nemic...the end of everything. You know that, right?"

Johnny nodded. "We're not givin' up," he said. "But...just in case... don't you want to see your folks, your human folks, that is...just one more time?"

Kat's moist eyes glimmered with hope. "We'll never have another chance like this," she whispered. "The portals. We can go wherever we want...in a heartbeat. And be back just as fast."

Tommy found no comfort in the eyes of his friends. Grief, despair, ache, fear—these things he saw. It was like looking back in time...before they were all Lords. Tommy saw them as they might have been as children. How frightened and needy they all were.

Or maybe, he thought, *maybe that's just how I feel.*

If this was the end of all things, and Tommy knew it very well could be, it would mean a lot to see his Earthly parents one last time. *Maybe,* Tommy thought, *it might just be what we all need to finish this.*

"Ten minutes," Tommy said.

"What?" Kat asked.

"We portal to our parents for ten minutes," Tommy said. "We can't spare any more time. If you can't find them, just come back here. Agreed?"

They all nodded.

Migmar had clearly grown adept with the controls. His small fingers raced across the keyboard, and the luminous globe spun to the Eastern Seaboard. Tommy gave Migmar the street address of his family home. The instruments in Asp's fortress tapped into several satellites and, in moments, Migmar had a portal open.

"Is ready," the Gnome said, taking a bite from a twig of dragonroot.

"Glad I'll be gone for a little while," Tommy said with a wink. "Go ahead and open the link."

A few clicks from Migmar, and a shimmering, vertical seam opened above the octagonal Kevlar footpad in the corner of the chamber. The seam spread open, forming an opening the size and shape of an arched door. Flickers of blue and white electricity danced around its border.

Tommy looked to the other Lords. "Ten minutes," he said. "That's all. No matter what."

They nodded, and Tommy stepped into the portal.

A flash of light. A dizzying array of patterns. Nausea. Tommy kept his stomach in check, but suddenly, he was falling.

Only a few feet, it turned out. He hit the turf and rolled to a crouch. He looked up and felt a pooling heaviness in his stomach.

He was home.

As much as he wanted to take in the surroundings—the carport where he'd hit tennis balls against the side of the house and yelled at thunderstorms, the sycamore tree he'd climbed, the one that leaned in from the Ledbetter's yard so conveniently, and the little sewer vent in the side yard where Funny Face, the family cat, had first appeared—he just couldn't waste a moment.

Strange, he thought, climbing up the front steps. *It looks exactly like I remember it.* He glanced at the driveway. *Ha, my parents still haven't even gotten a new car.*

Then, it dawned on him. *Seven years, Allyra time. But on Earth, I've only been gone, what? A month and a half?* He laughed.

Tommy knew the door would be unlocked, but he knocked anyway. Didn't want to startle them.

She came to the door, looked through the sheer curtain, and gasped. She opened the door slowly and whispered, "Tommy?"

"It's me, Mom," he said. "I know I look older and—" He never finished the sentence.

His mother crushed him in an embrace and wept on his shoulder. "Thank you, thank you, thank you, Jesus," she said, squeezing him tighter and tighter. "I thought we'd never see you again!"

Tommy's father was there in an instant. Soon his strength added a few more ounces of crush to their embrace.

"I missed...you...too," Tommy said. "But...can't breathe." They released their son and pulled him inside.

The den soon became a jumble of half-spoken sentences and phrases. Tommy kept an eye on the clock. He had just three minutes left.

"The scroll you left," his mom said. "It's all true then...oh, my gosh, look at your ears."

Tommy laughed. "All true."

"You look so much older," Mr. Bowman said. "A man now, really. Elf...er, Elf-man?"

"Seven years passed in Allyra," Tommy said. "I know it doesn't seem like that long to you, but—"

"Long enough," Mrs. Bowman said. "Don't you ever—"

"Mom, I can't stay," Tommy said gently. "I only have a few minutes left."

Fresh tears ran down her cheeks. "Why, Son?" Suddenly she was hugging him again.

Tommy did his best to explain it all, using up as few words and as little time as possible.

"That explains a lot," Mr. Bowman said. "The attacks. They've been on the news. Terrible things, Son. All over the world. Thousands and thousands dead. And that, what did you call it? Tide? Scientists are saying it's a geothermal vapor wave caused by global warming."

If the moment hadn't been so utterly grim, Tommy might have laughed.

"I have to stop it, Dad," Tommy said. "Ellos, uh…God…told us how to in His prophecies. But…we lost our Seventh Lord. And I have no idea how we'll even get close to Asp. And we can't fight him. It's just—"

"Shh, shh, shh," Mr. Bowman said. "I know it seems hopeless, Son. But you listen to me. I don't understand much of what you said, but I do know that the darkest times are when God can use you to shine the brightest."

"Thank you," Tommy said, embracing his father. He stood up. "I needed to hear that right now, needed to hear it from you. I'm sorry, but I…I have to leave now."

Wiping her tears on her sleeve, Mrs. Bowman hugged Tommy once more. "You go do what you have to do, Son," she said. "We'll be praying for you."

They followed Tommy outside to the lawn. The portal appeared. This time, closer to the ground.

"Mom, Dad," Tommy said. "If we stop it…if we stop the Tide, I won't be able to see you again. And if we fail…everything…everything will be gone."

"That's not true at all, Son," Mr. Bowman said. "If you stop the Tide, it'll just be a little longer…until we see you again."

Tommy's lips trembled as he forced a smile. He knew what his father was talking about. *I can trust you, Ellos,* Tommy thought. And he stepped into the portal and was gone.

"This is maddening," Bengfist grumbled. "With every flicker of this...what did they call it? Moniterd? Every time the picture changes, I see the destruction caused by Asp's forces...and there's nothing we can do to stop them. I wish there were something more productive we could do while the Lords are away."

"Agreed," Jast said. "But at least it is to be only ten minutes." She looked over at Migmar, but the Gnome seemed lost in thought. She glanced downward. "Migmar," she said abruptly. "Why is that light blinking?"

She pointed at a red light flashing on one of the monitors. On screen there were at least four Drefids standing in what looked like the husk of a burned-out house. "Migmar?"

The Gnome blinked at last. "Sorry," he said. "Know not this." He reached up and pushed on the screen with his finger. The red light stopped flashing.

"...much longer," came the raspy voice in mid sentence. "So if you'll kindly open a portal for us."

The Drefids seemed to be staring right through the screen.

Migmar ducked beneath the console. "See us, Drefids can!" he whispered urgently.

"I do not think so," Bengfist said. He brazenly slid into Migmar's chair so that he sat directly in front of the screen where the Drefids waited impatiently. He grabbed the headset from Migmar and spoke into the mic. "We, uh...have had some...moniterd problems," Bengfist said. "Can you see us?"

The hiss that came through the speakers made the hair on Bengfist's forearms stand up straight. "Of course we cannot see you," the Drefid said. "This is a keyhole camera, dolt! Now, give us the portal to the New York Armory, or I will report you to Lord Asp myself."

"Ten thousand apologies," Bengfist said, trying to make his voice raspier. "We will open a portal...right away. Uh...where are you?"

The exasperated Drefid practically screamed the address.

"You get that?" Bengfist whispered to the Gnome. Migmar nodded.

"English military is upon us!" the Drefid screeched. "Now! Give us the portal, now!"

Migmar jumped back into his seat. His fingers raced over the keys.

A small blue circle appeared on the globe. It completely surrounded England but shrank for several seconds until it was directly over a tiny corner in the northwest. Then, the globe spun slightly. A new circle appeared over Italy.

Migmar kept typing away. He hit the final key with a hearty laugh.

Bengfist, Jast and Migmar looked to the monitor. The Drefids were already entering the portal Migmar had opened within the burned-out house. Soon the room was empty, and the camera switched off.

"Where'd you send them?" Bengfist asked. "The New York Armory?"

Migmar shook his head. "Opened, I did, the portal right above Mount Etna in Italy. Is an active volcano, explosively."

"You sure you don't want to take the 12-gauge with you?" John Briarman, Johnny's dad, asked. He leaned out of the shadow cast by the barn's roof and held out the formidable looking shotgun. "It'll fix those Dref-varmints, and good."

"We can't, Dad," Johnny said. "It's got a lot of inorganic stuff. Won't go through the portal. Besides, I have a little more firepower than that now."

"You're not going to show off, are you?" Autumn asked.

"Just a little."

"I think you both should show off, my gems," Mrs. Briarman said, still drying her eyes. "A little."

They got up off of the bales of straw, and rounded the back of the barn to the field where the Briarman's had once grown corn. A severely weather-beaten scarecrow leaned on its post at the field's edge. Its head was an old throw pillow with a Jack 'O Lantern's face drawn upon it.

Johnny pointed at the scarecrow and asked, "Do you need that anymore?"

"Nah, Son," Mr. Briarman said. "Do your thing."

Johnny cracked his knuckles.

Autumn muttered, "Oh, brother."

"You might want to back up a little," Johnny said. He held out his hands, palms facing upward. A flicker of white flame formed in his left hand; a ball of orange fire in his left. He flicked his hands, and the two fireballs crisscrossed. Back and forth they went. A red ball of flame joined them. Then a blue one. Soon, he was juggling fireballs.

"Mom said *a little* showing off, Johnny!" Autumn grumbled.

Johnny winked and turned toward the scarecrow. The circling fireballs intensified to a ring of flame. Johnny yelled and heaved his hands forward. The ring of flames became an inferno and surged into the scarecrow like a freight train made of fire.

It was flash-incinerated. The heat washed backward, but Autumn raced forward. Her lean legs churned like pistons, becoming blurred as she moved faster than the eye could steadily follow. She encircled the blaze. The flames dimmed instantly. The faster Autumn went, the faster the flames were starved for air. In a matter of seconds, the blaze was out.

Autumn skidded to a halt in front of her parents. "Well?" she asked.

"I always knew there was something special about you," Mrs. Briarman said. She gathered Johnny and Autumn into an embrace. "No, that's not quite right. You were special long before you got these powers."

Mr. Briarman joined the embrace. He spoke haltingly, emotion choking his words. "Johnny, Autumn," he said. "We're both so proud'a you."

Just then, a black shape raced around the other side of the barn. It moved swiftly. Autumn sidestepped it, but the thing barreled into Johnny. He sprawled backward with the thing on top of him. There was a flash of teeth at Johnny's throat and then...

Laughter.

Johnny grabbed the big black shape and hugged it. "Sam!" he yelled, half laughing, half weeping. "Oh, Sam, where on Earth...or Allyra have you been?"

Autumn threw herself at the black lab and gratefully accepted a few face-licks from her old friend. And, with Mr. and Mrs. Briarman looking on, the three of them rolled happily in the hay-strewn dirt. It was just like old times.

"Migmar, look!" Bengfist pointed. "Now a red light on the other moniterd."

"Good," Migmar replied. "Send more Drefids, maybe I will, to a volcano."

Upon the screen, standing in front of the burning wreckage of a massive truck, stood more than a dozen semitransparent Gwar soldiers. A pair of Drefids stood in front of the Gwar and seemed to be screaming at the screen.

"They don't look happy," Jast said. "Should I?"

Migmar and Bengfist nodded, and Jast reached over and tapped the screen.

"...hours overdue!" the Drefid screamed. "Where are our reinforcements?"

"Send them, I will soon," Migmar said. He'd made his voice more of a screechy-hiss, but that didn't help.

"Who are you?" the Drefid demanded. "Where is Varlex?"

Migmar looked to Bengfist and shrugged. Bengfist shrugged back.

"Fixing, Varlex is, the western portal," Migmar said.

The Drefid's black eyes narrowed. "What western portal?" he asked.

"The...one in...uh, Western Canada," Migmar said.

The Drefid reached toward the screen and seemed to take it into his gnarled hands. "Listen to me," he said. "I don't know who you are or how you infiltrated our command center. But I assure you, you will not leave it alive. We will come for you, Gnome!"

Migmar looked up at Bengfist and Jast. "How he knows I am Gnome?"

Bengfist frowned. "I wonder."

Migmar turned back to the screen. "Try, you can, all you wish," he said. "Give you, I won't, any portal to come back here."

The Drefid laughed wickedly and said, "Fool. We already have one."

"Only ten minutes?" Mrs. Simonson said clutching her daughter by the shoulder. "But your father's at the office. There's no way he could get home that fast. He has to see you!"

"Mom, I'm so sorry," Kat said. "But I can't wait...there's so much going on. So much to tell."

Kat's mom released the embrace and took out her cell phone. "I have to call him, at least let him know. It won't be the same, but at least he can video chat." She hit speed dial and waited. "C'mon, pick up." The phone went to voice mail. "Oh, no. Not today."

"Mom," Kat said. "Just text him."

Mrs. Simonson's fingers flew across the keypad. "There," she said.

"There, he'll get this for sure." She pushed send.

There was a faint tinkling sound. "What was that?" Mrs. Simonson asked.

"I don't know," Kat said. "Came from the den, I think."

Mrs. Simonson raced away without another word. When she returned, she had a second cell phone in her hand. "It's his," she said. "He left it on his desk...again."

Kat stared at the ground. "Mom, I—"

They both froze. The front door of the house opened, and Mr. Simonson walked in. "Hey babe, I just realized I forgot my—" He saw Kat and dropped his briefcase. "Thank you, God," he whispered and ran to his daughter.

Tears fell, they embraced again and again, and at last, they collapsed onto the plush sofa. There they rested, spoke and listened. But in the end, Kat saw the time.

Her parents saw her expression. "You won't be able to come back," Mrs. Simonson said. "Even if you throw out all the invaders?"

Kat shook her head. "I'm Elf-kind," she said. "I have to stay in Allyra. But I can speak across worlds...I can think messages to you, sometimes."

Mr. Simonson took his daughter's hand. "There's so much of your future," he said. "So much I always thought I'd see. Graduation...a career...even walking you down the aisle." He looked down a moment. "But look at you. You're all grown up. There's not already someone, is there? Someone special, I mean?"

Kat's blue skin blushed purple. "Actually there is," she said. "He just hasn't figured it out yet."

The Six Lords returned all at once. It was fortunate for Bengfist,

Jast and Migmar who were fighting a losing battle to keep the chamber's iron door closed.

"What's going on?" Tommy yelled.

"A pair of Drefids," Bengfist grumbled. "And a bunch of my estranged kindred."

"Let them in," Tommy said.

"No way," Jimmy said. "Yu're in no condition to fight hand-to-hand. You stay back, Tommy. Put out their eyes from a distance. Let oos do the dirty stuff up front."

Tommy was about to argue, but knew Jimmy was right. "Keep them clear of the portal controls!" Tommy warned. "Now, let them in."

Bengfist, Jast and Migmar stepped backward, letting the door fly open. Bengfist stuck out his foot, and the first Gwar went sprawling to the floor where Jimmy beheaded him with his claymore.

The next two Gwar fell with arrow shafts protruding from their eye sockets. A Drefid's Dark Arts blast spewed into the room like red, molten stone. Johnny's flames met it in midair and pushed it back through the door. Both Drefids were caught and seemed to boil in a cauldron of flame. One Gwar made a break for the portal controls. He raised a huge axe, but it never fell. Autumn sped passed him, looping a chain around the Gwar's neck. Her momentum jerked the chain free but crushed the Gwar's throat.

The enemy fell quickly. The Lords emerged without so much as a scratch.

"We were fortunate," Bengfist said. "Those had just returned from battle. They were already half spent and careless. Others will come."

"Still, we need to hold this chamber," Tommy said. "You see what power we have from here."

"You all came back, am I glad, when did you," Migmar said.

"All?" Tommy asked.

"Jimmy?" Kat said. "Kiri Lee? Did you leave here also?"

"We went back to North Carolina," Jimmy said. "We have to have Jett back. We have to have a Seventh or—"

Kiri Lee interrupted, "It was my idea. We went back to get Jett to change his mind. I just knew he would, but he didn't, Tommy. He...no, no, no! It's all worse now."

"Worse?" Kat asked. "What happened?"

"When we went to Jett's parents," Jimmy said. "The Cragons had torn the place oop, but Jett's parents...well they put oop a good fight. Lit the Cragons all afire, they did."

"Did Jett help?" Tommy asked.

"Aw, no," Jimmy said. "No...he did'na help one bit. When we got there, Jett was already gone."

"Gone?" Kat blurted out. "What do you...was he, was he dead?"

"Worse," Kiri Lee said, covering her tear-streaked face with her hands.

There was a moment of stunned silence as the group pondered anything that might be worse than death. And even in their darkest thoughts, they never considered a development so bleak and fearsome as the news Jimmy then spoke:

"After we helped Jett's parents finish off the Cragons," Jimmy said, "we had a chance to talk. Jett's dad told oos that Asp himself came to their property. Mr. Green confronted him, brave man, he is. Asp told him that he was the one who brought Jett back from the dead. Ellos help oos, Tommy. Jett's working for Asp now."

An Immovable Object

"SO LET me get this straight," Tommy said, rolling his head between his shoulders. "Not only has Taeva left us to join Asp, but so has Jett?"

"I'm afraid so," said Kiri Lee.

"There must be some mistake," Autumn said. "I mean, this is Jett we're talking about."

"Perhaps not the Jett we all remember," Kat pointed out. She reminded them briefly of the incident at the house.

"Still," Autumn said, refusing to back down, "the real Jett is still in there. He is. Maybe…maybe Mr. Green misunderstood the situation."

Kiri Lee shook her head. "There was nothing to misunderstand, Autumn. Jett willingly left with Asp."

"So we're fighting Asp, Taeva *and* Jett," mumbled Johnny. "Just great."

"More time grumbling, more time losing," added Migmar. "Attacking your giant green woman, Asp is."

"Giant green woman?" Tommy looked at the Gnome. The team gathered around Migmar as he tapped a screen with his stubby finger.

"He's attacking the Statue of Liberty!" Autumn exclaimed. The arial camera they viewed from, presumably affixed to a military or news network helicopter, circled the giant Statue. While Asp's forces were still invisible, their destructive intent was not. A series of small explosions fired off in a circle around the wrist of Lady Liberty's outstretched torch-bearing arm. The team gawked at the monitor as the torch and hand toppled over. The hunk of metal, glass and cables plummeted along the length of the Statue's body and crashed into the small patch of island at the base.

"He's taking her apart piece by piece!" Kat protested.

"Aw, see, now that's just low," said Johnny.

"We've got to stop him," said Tommy. "Right now. Migmar?"

"Portal you have," said Migmar, his fast little fingers pecking away at the keyboard. The blue gateway snapped open above the Kevlar pad.

"Wait," said Bengfist, "what about the command center? The Drefids and my infernal kindred will not give up. More will come."

"Right," said Tommy. "Bengfist, will you and Jast stay? Protect Migmar—"

"Not protection Migmar needs," interrupted the Gnome.

Tommy rephrased his request to Bengfist. "Will you and Jast stay to protect the portal system in case Asp's forces return?"

"Consider it done," said Bengfist.

"Johnny," Tommy added, pointing to the doorway, "care to give them a little insurance?"

"My pleasure," said Johnny. He stepped away of the computer equipment and spread out his hands. An intense, narrow stream of white fire shot from his palms, a stream that traced the outline of the door, welding the metal and molten rock together.

"That should buy you some time," Johnny said. "No one will get through that weld."

"Depends on who Asp sends," said Bengfist.

"Now that's comforting," said Autumn.

Into the thick of it I send you.

That was the last thing Migmar had said before depositing them all on Liberty Island.

"HE WASN'T KIDDING!" yelled Kat as she ducked for cover beneath a half-crushed gazebo. The rest of the Six joined her, surveying the scene around them.

Lady Liberty towered directly above them, the base of the monument about one-hundred feet inland. Asp's invisible attack had been temporarily slowed by two US DDG51 Class Destroyers that had opened fire with their 57mm Close In Guns (CIG). The fact that the ships hadn't used any of their larger weapons systems, like the mammoth 155mm deck guns or Vertical Launch Systems, proved they had no idea what they were firing upon, and didn't want to risk further damage to the population around them.

Though they doubted the ships' Commanders knew what they'd hit, the Six spotted at least a dozen Warflies thrashing in the water, their invisibility paste washing off.

"There he is!" Jimmy pointed. "On the backside of her head!" The team spotted Asp right where Jimmy'd indicated: Asp clung on the far side of the Statue's head, out of sight from the destroyers. He was, perhaps, the only assailant not cloaked in invisibility paste.

"He's bold," said Johnny.

"Or just arrogant," replied Autumn. "If he was bold, he'd be flying around those destroyers, not hiding like that."

The Six looked on as Asp and his Warfly suddenly leaped off the back of Lady Liberty's head and dove onto the conning tower of the nearest Destroyer.

"Nope, he's bold," Johnny stated cheerlessly.

"And he's bringing a whole mess of those right jolly boogers with

THE TIDE OF UNMAKING

him!" exclaimed Jimmy. While they couldn't make out the forms entirely, the Six were familiar enough with the Gnome's paste that they could see the subtle transparent change in texture against the sky. The CIG boomed from the Destroyer's deck again forcing the Six to cover their ears.

"We've got to stop him!" yelled Kiri Lee.

"Agreed," said Tommy. "But we can't fight what we can't see."

"Think the Rainsong would work here on Earth?" asked Kiri Lee. Tommy shook his head. "We're only Six."

Kiri Lee blew a few strands of hair off her face, disgusted by the hopelessness of it all.

"Wait a second," Johnny said, tapping Tommy's arm. "Wait a second! I got it!"

"What?" asked Tommy.

"The Destroyers! I built models of them when I was a kid." He realized that according to Earth time, that was only a few weeks ago. Shrugging off the irony, he went on: "I remember that they had high-pressure water hoses, to fight fires and keep away smaller ships, you know."

"We could use them to wash the paste off," concluded Tommy. "The Rainsong revised."

"Exactly!"

Tommy felt a plan forming. "OK. Kiri Lee, I need you to get Kat and Jimmy onto one of those Destroyers. Kat, it's your job is to convince the Captain to use those hoses. It won't be easy, but they're probably more desperate than we are. Use whatever means necessary. Jimmy, you call the shots as you see them. Johnny, you stay here with me and Autumn; we'll keep these creatures busy on the island. Any questions?"

"Yeah," said Jimmy. "Do I get to fire one of those big guns?"

Kiri Lee carried Kat over first. Airwalking was impressive enough as it was; but carrying a person over open water and landing on a moving US Destroyer in the midst of a gunfight topped it all.

More than one Marine leveled an assault rifle on them as they landed on the deck. But it was Kat, still twenty-five hovering feet to the ship, who saved them.

"*Stand down,*" she said, remembering the term from war movies and hoping it was actually something real soldiers said, not just a Hollywood-ism. She could see the Marines look at each other in bewilderment, more than one of them tapping the communication device in their ear. "*They're friendlies.*"

A beat later, the weapons slowly lowered.

"We need to address your captain," she said as they touched down. "We have critical information about the enemy you're facing."

"Begging your pardon, miss, but why are you blue?"

Kat glared at him. She was half-tempted to tell him she was from Mars, but instead she said, "It's stealth warpaint."

The other Marine said, "But how did you both do that? You were… like walking in the air. Howzzat?"

"It is ehm, how do you say?" Kiri Lee began, lapsing into a thick French accent, "new technologies from France, n'est-ce pas? No time to explain."

"This is a matter of national security," said Kat, using more movie lingo.

The closest Marine took out his sidearm and stepped forward. "I'm sorry, ladies, flying powers or not, no one gets on the bridge. Consider it a miracle you haven't been shot already."

"*I don't think you understand what's happening here, sir,*" Kat spoke into his mind, utilizing amplified mental projection.

The Marine with the pistol looked around uncertainly.

"*I'm not here to hurt anyone,*" Kat went on, "*except our enemies, the ones currently assaulting the city. As for you, I'm already inside your head. You don't have a choice on this issue, unless you want me to get really angry and liquify your internal organs."*

"Right this way, miss," said the Marine.

"Kat, I will return post haste with Jimmy."

"Don't give her any problems," Kat commanded the remaining Marines. "Please see that she and the young man who arrives are brought to the bridge as well."

The Marines nodded and Kiri Lee stepped into the air.

Tommy withdrew his bow and looked around the air above them. "Pretty hard to see them," he said to Johnny and Autumn. The Destroyer's guns boomed over and over, trying to connect with the elusive enemy. "Or hear them," Tommy added, his ears ringing.

"Well, no time like the present to light up the sky and see what we get," said Johnny. "We've got to draw some of their attack if we're going to save Liberty."

"In more ways than one," Autumn said.

Tommy looked to her. "Autumn, with your speed, think you could make it up the surface of the Statue?"

"I'll give it a shot," she said.

"Great. See what kind of trouble you can stir up. Johnny, you flood the sky with fire and see if you can hold them at bay until Kat and the others get those hoses going. As soon as I begin to see targets, I'll stick them up with my bow."

"Sounds like a plan," said Johnny. He leveled his hands with the ground, pushed pulses of flame from his palms, and blasted skyward.

Autumn sped away from the gazebo's wreckage, and Tommy began searching for the best vantage point from which to snipe the enemy.

Once he'd gained enough altitude and upward momentum, Johnny raised his palms over his head and shot a broad blanket of flames billowing upward. Right away at least three Warflies screeched, climbing away from the expanding bloom of fire. One didn't make it and was overwhelmed by the flames, its wings disintegrating end to end. Its charred body dropped from the sky like a stone.

The other two Warflies, however, managed to bank away from the fiery plume. That was, until Tommy spotted their retreat and sent arrows into their lower abdomens. The giant insects twisted violently in a vain attempt to dislodge the shafts. One of the Warflies unmounted its rider, the Gwar soldier crushing an information booth below. The last Warfly careened out of control, slammed into Lady Liberty, and knocked its rider unconscious; both Warfly and Gwar fell to their deaths on the island.

Tommy looked skyward and spotted the faint trail of Autumn speeding at an upward angle across the surface of the Statue, slicing through two Drefids who appeared to be planting explosives. They dropped away from the Statue in twin sprays of black blood and, for good measure, Tommy put a shaft in the eye socket of each Drefid as they fell.

His attention on a burning Warspider, Johnny was broadsided by an invisible Warfly, sending him spiraling out of control.

"JOHNNY!" Autumn yelled, halting on the Statue's shoulder.

Johnny shot out a few blasts in an effort to stabilize himself, but managed only to propel himself sideways. Fortunately, he landed with a splash in the water just off shore.

Autumn had been so distracted by Johnny's fall that she didn't anchor herself to the Statue. Something slammed into her shoulders and sent her off the edge. Her quick reflexes saved her, however, at least momentarily. While still in mid air, she spotted a half-visible Gwar and its Warfly mount hovering just below. Autumn stretched out until she felt the untucked, leather thong of the Warfly's stirrup pass through her hand. She grabbed on and was pulled aloft, floating high above the scene. The Gwar above noticed the unwelcome rider and started jabbing with the butt end of his spear.

Autumn dodged as best she could, blows glancing off her arms and shoulders. But one wayward jab in particular was just the opportunity she needed; the Gwar overcommitted and lunged off balance. Autumn grabbed the spear shaft and pulled down, twisting the Gwar from his saddle and throwing him into open air. The warrior yelled as fell to his death.

Despite the small victory, the Warfly's bucking wouldn't allow her to climb up. Instead Autumn decided to make her own way down. She flipped the spear in her free hand and drove it up into the Warfly's belly. The creature shrieked. Suddenly Autumn was upside down, the Warfly spiraling out of control.

"Oh, bad idea!" Autumn shouted, trying desperately to hold on.

"LET GO!" shouted Johnny, now flying along beside her. "I'LL GET YOU!"

Autumn released her grip, flung wide of the doomed bug. She expected Johnny to catch her straight away.

But he didn't.

Autumn gained speed, the island's rocky shore coming up fast.

"JOHNNY?!"

No answer.

She was falling fast. She arched her back, trying to right herself for what would surely be a crippling impact.

"Got'cha!" Johnny grunted, pulling her tight with one arm. He used his left hand to blast the ground with a dizzying, swirling wash of fire, slowing the pair until he could swing Autumn into an open patch of turf. She released, rolled and came to a kneel on the blackened swath of grass, still smoking from the fresh blast.

"Cut that one pretty close," she said, breathlessly.

"Sorry, you just got all squirrelly up there."

Tommy came running up. "You guys okay?"

"Yeah," said Autumn standing. "Seems Asp has a bit more than we can handle up there. And who knows how many arc charges he's already planted."

"Or where they are," Johnny added. "I can wash Lady Liberty with fire, but I'm afraid I'll melt her or set off arc charges I can't see."

"I hear you," Tommy said. "We need those hoses."

Just then, there came a thunderous blast overhead. It was followed by an agonizing wrenching of metal. The three lords looked up to see a huge segment of Lady Liberty's shoulder tumbling down her torso right toward them.

Unexplained creatures of the deep, yes.

Water spouts and tsunamis, sure.

But in over thirty-two years at sea, Admiral Blackburn had never encountered such a being as this: a blue Elven maiden who could cast her thoughts directly into his brain.

It begged military action. But what? He had no earthly idea.

The Admiral realized he'd better honor her strange request. After all, she wasn't asking to commandeer his ship, kill his crew, steal his nuclear rods, or fire his deck guns. She wanted the boat's fire hoses.

"*Admiral,*" she'd pleaded, "*there may yet be time to explain all this in the future. But if you're a man of action, as I think you are, turn the fire hoses on the Statue.*"

He'd hesitated at first. But she'd been very persuasive.

"*If you're as tired of not seeing what you're fighting as I am,*" she said, pointing out through the command bridge windows, "*do it.*"

The Admiral gave the order, and what he saw next made even the blue Elf maiden seem inconsequential.

Johnny shot a two-palm blast at the hunk of greenish copper. It didn't flash melt or even slow, but it did slightly alter its angle of descent. It was enough.

Autumn took Tommy by the waist and drove him well out of the way. Johnny launched himself backward, and the wreckage crashed just inches away from his feet.

And that's when it began to rain.

"By Ellos, she did it!" said Tommy as he watched the plumes of water arc out from the destroyers, showering the Statue and most of the island. Then his hopes crashed.

The pump-propelled jets of water seemed to be blasting the right locations, but at first, nothing appeared.

Please tell me, he thought despondently, *please tell me they didn't make the paste waterproof.*

For several long moments, nothing appeared. The wounded Liberty Statue had been soaked and glistened, but there were no creatures to be seen, flying or climbing. Nothing.

"I don't see them," Autumn said sadly.

"Dang it," Johnny said. "The Rainsong worked. This should'a worked too."

"Wait!" Tommy shouted, pointing. "Look!"

At first ten, then twenty, then one-hundred, then more Warflies and Gwar and Drefids appeared out of nowhere. Materializing as if by magic, the sky was suddenly full of giant insects, each carrying its particular rider.

With the invisibility paste washing away, Tommy, Johnny and

Autumn had their targets picked and went to work. Jimmy called out shots on board with the Admiral, who tried more than once to convince Jimmy to join the NAVY given his display of talent. Kat communicated to all to make sure their attacks were coordinated...and to make sure Johnny, Tommy and Autumn were never in the line of fire.

Tommy had just dispatched five Warflies and their riders, and was beginning to feel the battle had shifted to their favor, when a massive explosion rocked the nearest destroyer.

It was the same destroyer Kat and Jimmy were on.

Jimmy had been calling out shots as fast as he could. The radio men were translating his target descriptions and finger pointing into coordinates relaying the numbers to gunmen along the ship. But when Jimmy went mute, the gunnery officer didn't know what to do.

"Sir, where—?"

Jimmy had seen the events before they happened, but it was so sudden and so unexpected, he'd not had the ability to shout out a warning. He watched in horror as a dark being swung up onto one of the massive barrels and began squeezing the steel barrel shut.

The order was given to fire.

The trigger pull on the control handle sent the computerized system into action, slamming home the firing hammer on the massive brass casing, which in turn initiated the near instantaneous combustion of the gun powder. The rapid pressure buildup sent the explosive round rifling down the now closed-off barrel. With nowhere left for the gasses to expand, the barrel flared open like a metallic flower. The back pressure tore a gaping hole into the gun deck and killed at least four sailors.

The explosion cracked the glass in the bridge. Jimmy was knocked off of his feet and lay sprawled and dazed for several moments. Finally he gained his feet and stared down at the bow.

I can'na believe it, he thought hard in Kat's direction. *It's Jett.*

There, standing with his hands on his hips, was the unmistakable Seventh Lord of Berinfell, gloating over the chaos he'd just caused.

"Uhm, Tommy, Kiri Lee, Autumn, Johnny," Kat called with all her projecting might, *"we need you here...now!"*

Tommy was about to loose an arrow when Kat's thought came to him. *Can it wait a few? I've got a pesky Warfly in my sights,* he replied, never quite sure how well she could pick up his thoughts over distance.

"Jett's here, Tommy."

Tommy let the arrow fly, but it sailed well wide of its intended target. *Send Kiri Lee for me; Johnny will take Autumn,* he said. *We're coming.*

Johnny and Autumn touched down midship, as did Kiri Lee and Tommy. Kat and Jimmy raced down to join them, with Admiral Blackburn leading the way.

Jett remained where he was, practically daring everyone to attack him. Dozens of sailors and heavily armed Marines had filled the decks and trained their weapons on him.

"Hold your fire," Kat voiced to all of them. To the Admiral she added: *"I hope that's okay."*

"You'd better have a good reason, young lady," said Admiral Blackburn. Kat smiled thinly.

"This is complicated, Sir," Tommy said. "And it could get ugly."

"Well, whatever you have planned, might I suggest you do it now," replied the Admiral.

"Right," Tommy nodded. "I'll go."

"We all go," said Jimmy. "We don'na stand a chance, noone of oos do alone."

"Fair enough," said Tommy.

The Six strode out toward the bow, the Admiral raising his hand to stay his men.

Jett spotted his companions making their way toward him. Kat was sure she saw something register in his eyes, even if very slight. *"Jett, you need to stop this,"* she said. *"No one wants you to get hurt."*

"Stay where you are!" Jett yelled from the bow.

The Six stopped momentarily, but Tommy took another step forward.

"I said STOP!" Jett cried.

"Jett, I don't want to have to do this," Tommy withdrew his bow and nocked and arrow, keeping both low.

Johnny took his cue and put his hands on the ready.

"Tommy, no," said Kat. "Not until we've got no other option." Tommy looked to her, as did Johnny. *"We must reason with him…if we can."*

Tommy thought about it. Jett seemed far from reasonable. Still, trusting Kat had always proven to be a blessing, even when he didn't agree. Tommy sighed, then took the arrow from the bow.

Jett put a hand up to his ear. "Yes, Lord Asp," he said. "I will delay them at the very least. It will be safe to proceed."

"Dear Ellos," Kiri Lee said. "He's talking to Asp."

"Kat," Tommy said. "What's Asp saying? What's Jett thinking?"

But Jett cut the connection. "Not that easy, Elven kind," Jett said.

"We're not stopping, Jett," Tommy said finally. "You're our friend, and you'll always be."

"I have no friends!" Jett roared from up front, and with that, he hammer-fisted the solid steel deck. Jimmy warned everyone but his voice was lost amid the bone-jarring noise of bending steel. The metal buckled in front of Jett, then a wave of energy rippled through the ship. Kiri Lee stepped aloft, avoiding the tremor, but the others weren't so lucky; Elves, sailors and Marines alike toppled over like bowling pins.

"He's getting away!" Kiri Lee pointed as Jett whistled for a Warfly.

"Not on my watch!" yelled the Admiral from his side. "OPEN FIRE!" But the shower of gunfire was delayed as his Marines were still trying to find their feet.

Jett leaped off the boat for the hovering Warfly.

"I got this," said Johnny. He focused two thin streams of fire at Jett's body, blasting him in the shoulder. The sheer force sent Jett head over heels, toppling down into the sea.

"YOU WEREN'T SUPPOSED TO KILL HIM!" Autumn shrieked.

"I didn't!" said Johnny, shielding himself from her barrage of blows.

"Easy there," said Tommy. He yanked Autumn off Johnny and pulled her toward the rail. "Look."

Jett was thrashing in the water, the Warfly buzzing down to pull him out. Jett climbed on. Johnny's flames had been extinguished, but the damage had been done: Jett's entire left side had been charred with the puckered flesh of third degree burns.

"FIRE!" came the Admiral's voice again. The Six covered their ears as automatic weapons fire burst to life, drilling the water's surface with hundreds of bullet holes.

"NOOOO!" screamed Autumn. Johnny held her from diving off the boat. She beat his chest, willing him to let her go, but Johnny's grip held.

To the Six's amazement—and to the Admiral's—Jett's Warfly darted into the sky and avoided the withering assault from the ship.

"After him!" said the Admiral.

"We'll see to Jett," Tommy said. "You just finish off the force on

Lady Liberty. Shouldn't be a problem now that you can see your targets."

Admiral Blackburn hesitated, but knew he couldn't argue with forces he couldn't explain. He decided to stick with what he could explain, and pulverizing a visible enemy attack was much more his style, even if that force was a fleet of bizarre creatures flying around on giant insects.

"Where do you think he's going?" Kiri Lee asked.

"Asp," answered Kat. "I heard him think it."

"And where do you think Asp is?" asked Autumn.

"Only one way to find out," Tommy replied. He puled out a small video handset Migmar had given him before they left. Ironically, he thanked Ellos that Asp had managed to create some kind of Dark Arts coating to allow the device to pass through portals. But he shuddered to think what more Asp could do with the coating if given more time… what he could do with Earth weapons on Allyra. *We won't give him the opportunity,* Tommy concluded. "Migmar, you there?"

The small video screen sparked alive; Migmar's pudgy face filled it up. "Here is Migmar," the Gnome said.

"Migmar, do you have a fix on Asp?" asked Tommy.

"Migmar fix Asp good, he will."

"No, Migmar, do you know where he is?"

The Gnome smiled. "Always know where he is, Migmar does."

"Then we need a portal there, fast!"

Migmar's face withdrew from the screen for a moment and Tommy could here the clicking of the keyboard. After a few seconds, Migmar grumbled.

"What is it, Migmar?" Tommy asked.

"Hmph. Like prevented me before with Asp, something did. Same it does now. Very close, I can't get you."

"As close as you can is fine," Tommy replied. "Hurry."

"Very well," said Migmar. Just then a blue portal popped to life on the Destroyer's deck. "Go fix Asp, you will."

"Thanks, Migmar," Tommy said. "We're going in." The team was just about to walk through when Kat stopped them.

"Hey, Tommy, there was something different about Jett this time."

"What?"

"Before he was...well, adamant," she said. "Completely resolved... and angry. There's something different now. He's powerful and knows what he's capable of, but he's also...he's hesitant."

"Begging your pardon, but he didn't seem too hesitant about destroying my ship," said the Admiral.

"I know, I know," Kat waved off the comment. "But inside, he's aching. It's like the kid who takes pleasure in bullying because that's the only way he can feel in control of his life."

"You heard him think all that?" asked Tommy.

"No, not all of it," Kat answered honestly. "But reading minds has helped me to recognize mental emotional patterns in people. I don't know, maybe it's just a hunch."

"Think we can change him?" Autumn asked.

"No," Jimmy said, "but Ellos can."

"If Jett doesn't die of those wounds you gave him, Johnny," Kiri Lee muttered.

"Hey now," Tommy said, "we don't need any sarcasm among us. Kiri Lee, relax. Jett will heal those burns easily." Tommy winced and put and arm gingerly to his side. "I just wish he'd have healed my ribs."

Tommy was the last through the portal, hesitating before he made the leap. He knew that, somewhere on the other side of that shimmering sea of Dark Arts technology, the Lords of Berinfell would have to face Asp. But somehow, the possibility that they would face Jett again...was worse.

The Confrontation

TAEVA SNARLED, racing up the city street jammed with humans and their impossibly slow-moving wheeled vehicles. The yellow ones were the most vexing. She took to climbing on top of them, running and leaping from their roofs. She snarled again, mentally chastising herself for not watching more closely when Tommy and the Gnome worked the portal controls.

When she first arrived, she'd thought she'd missed New York City altogether. She'd found herself in a massive forest. But after wasting precious minutes combing the area, she discovered that she was indeed in the city, just a wooded area called Central Park. A reluctant human had told her there was fighting somewhere up a road called 7th Avenue.

But thus far, she hadn't seen any warfare. Still, she sprinted through the city, listening for explosions and searching for destruction. If she found that, Asp certainly wouldn't be far away.

Taeva leaped from the roof of a yellow vehicle and crashed onto the hood of another. Just then, something buzzed by Taeva's ear. Then something clipped her shoulder. Searing hot pain lanced down her arm and up her neck.

Taeva summersaulted off one car, landed on the street between two large trucks, and spun around. There were humans, dozens of them all dressed in blue, racing toward her with strange black instruments in their hands. They were yelling at her.

Some screamed, "Stop!" or "Don't move!" Others yelled "Freeze!" And that, Taeva didn't understand. She started to run but heard sharp claps of sound behind her. She thought of the instruments these humans were pointing at her.

Weapons! she realized. *Of course.* Taeva stopped immediately and turned to face her pursuers. *I wish you no harm, humans,* she thought. *But I cannot be waylaid.* Her hands began to weave the air. Sparks leaped from fingertip to fingertip. Then, she thrust both hands, palm up, toward the sky.

A massive bolt of lightning flashed down from above, striking a nearby newspaper stand not far from the humans who had been giving chase. Three smaller strikes walked backward toward them. The humans made a terrible ruckus and dove for cover.

There, Taeva thought. *Now leave me to my business.*

She continued down 7th Avenue without interference but chose to run on the sidewalk rather than atop the vehicles.

An explosion. Not far ahead. At last! Taeva sprinted forward, weaving in and out of storefronts, taxis, and pedestrians who were now sprinting away from the danger ahead. They slowed her down, and she noticed that many of the humans were bleeding.

At last, she found herself in the middle of a huge crossing between the humans' buildings. There were massive signs and all manner of glowing lights. There was also fire.

Screams came from the east. Another explosion. Taeva looked up and saw the high building in the middle of the road. Sparks flew from it. Lights blinked in impossible-to-follow patterns. Then she saw it. An arc stone raced through the air. It hit the structure where it was already burning and exploded. Three more struck it, and the building buckled. It wrenched sideways, cracked and fell in a debris cloud to the street below.

Human soldiers raced into the street. They had dark green vehicles following them. They didn't know where to fire, but fire they did.

Orange fire and smoke flew across the intersection and rose into the sky. Blue arc stones crisscrossed their flight. There were more explosions on both sides.

There! Taeva saw a Warfly take a hit. Its burning shape careened wildly into the base of a building. She launched herself across the intersection, dodged flaming debris, and came to a stop near the Warfly. She found the Gwar pilot, but he was already dead. Cursing her misfortune, she craned her neck to look down the next side street. It was oddly clear except for a great many trampled humans.

Then, she understood. Summoning all her strength, Taeva began to weave lightning. Bolts scattered down in a wide pattern. These were not of killing potency, but they did the job. After the roar of thunder, there came the ghastly sounds of screeching Warspiders, shrieking Drefids and screaming Gwar. And the lightning had charred enough of them that Taeva had a decent sense of where they were.

She raced around the corner, rammed her forearm under the chin of a Gwar soldier and then dragged him into an alleyway. Taeva slammed the Gwar up against a brick wall and held him there.

"Where is Asp?" she demanded.

"I will tell you nothing!" the Gwar growled back.

Taeva pulled one hand free from the Gwar's shoulder. In it, sparks of lightning began to dance. "Care to see how I can make this move inside you?" she asked.

The Gwar swallowed hard. His huge eyes seemed to double. "Grand Central Terminal it's called!" he bellowed, lifting an arm to point. "That way!"

"Thank you," Taeva said. Then she slammed a backfist into the Gwar's jaw. He dropped like a sack of flour.

�֍

Asp stood on the edge of a skyscraper and overlooked his progress. The Times Square assault was underway. The United Nations had already been reduced to rubble. A Warfly zagged out of the spectral clouds and swirling smoke far above.

"Right on time," Asp muttered.

The Warfly landed, crushing a spinning air duct with a clawed forelimb. Two passengers dismounted: a Saer and a dark-skinned Elf.

"He isssth...amazing," Sardon said, pointing to Jett. "Healssth them with a touch of the hand. Inside of three hoursssth, he emptied our field infirmary."

"Did I not tell you?" Asp said. "Lord Hamandar is nearly unmatched."

"Don't call me that," Jett said, his tone deep and commanding. "That name sickens me."

"Ah," Asp said. "I should have guessed. The less to remind you of the wretched Elves, the better. But, understand...Hamandar...I will call you whatever I see fit. Do you understand?"

"As you command it, Lord Asp," Jett said.

"Indeed," Asp said, "but if you had your will, what would you have me call you?"

"Jett."

Asp nodded. "Still a soft spot for those pitiful humans back in North Carolina, eh? They're dead now, of course."

"I care not," Jett said. "But I took the name as mine."

"Are you loyal to me, Jett?" Asp asked.

"I am," Jett replied.

"Sardon," Asp said. "You left a position of command to serve me. Do you understand why?"

Sardon's red goat-like eyes shifted. He crossed his arms. "You hold the power, my Lord," he said.

"Yes," Asp replied. "But you do not understand yet the extent of my power. You see Jett here. Do you realize he was once one of the Lords of Berinfell? He was my sworn enemy and aided his countrymen in slaying my predecessor."

"I wasssth not aware," Sardon said.

"He stormed Vesper Crag with the other lords," Asp said. "But he was slain...or at least, poisoned to the point of death."

"I do not follow," Sardon said.

"No," Asp explained. "Nor should you. Hamandar—Jett, is of the Lord's healing bloodline. A long, unbroken line that is very significant to the Elves. There have been many gifts among the Lords of Berinfell, but in each generation there is always a healer. That line must continue or the line of Lords itself will fail. I suspect the Elves are not themselves aware of this. It is written in one of their sacred Prophecies, a singular document my ancestors removed at the foundation of their grand city."

"It seemsssth we have document theft in common," Sardon replied. "We Saer have one of their Prophecies in our chief archive."

Asp nodded approval. "Yes, well this particular document explains the importance of Jett's line. Without a healer, the Lordly bloodline will become soiled and impure...weakened. That is why the healers are next to impossible to kill. When Jett was stricken, his own kin left him for dead."

"Extraordinary," Sardon said.

"Jett appeared dead," Asp explained as he circled Jett. "In fact, he was in such a deep state of inner rebuilding that no one could have roused him, not for years. He lay beneath the ground, but Jett was not decomposing like a corpse. He was *recomposing*. It would have taken at least another year, but I found several rites in the Dark Arts to be infinitely helpful. I sped up the process and made certain that, when Jett emerged from the dirt, he would be malleable to my will." Asp paused and glared shrewdly at the Saer. "Would you like to see precisely how malleable he is?"

Sardon shook his head. "That won't be necces—"

"I will show you," Asp said. He held up a fist and, with a shrill, grating sound, the boney blades extended. "Jett, look at me."

Jett turned his head. His violet eyes fixed on Asp.

"To whom do you belong?" Asp asked.

"I belong to you, Lord Asp," Jett replied.

"Even to the point of death?" Asp asked.

"Even then," Jett replied.

Asp placed the jagged tips of his claws against Jett's chest. "I am going to test you," Asp said, and he pushed his fist forward a few inches. They slid through the leather jerking and pierced the skin.

Jett winced, but continued to stare at Asp.

"Really, my lord," Sardon said. "You don't have to do thisssth."

"I do," Asp replied. "Watch." He pushed more. Blood trickled out of the puncture sites and ran in dark red rivulets down the armor. Jett groaned, but Asp kept pushing. The blades sank deeper. Jett fell to one knee.

"No, no," Asp said. "We aren't quite finished."

He pushed the blades in more and, with a crimson spray, the points burst through Jett's back. Asp put a boot on Jett's shoulder and shoved his body off the blade. Jett fell backward and curled into a protective ball.

"There," Asp said. "Now we are finished."

"You..." Sardon stammered. "You killed him."

Asp said, "Heal, Jett. We have much to do."

Jett clambered to one knee. Then to his feet. He flexed his chest muscles and there was a last spurt of blood. He took off his leather jerkin and showed the pink marks where the blades had penetrated.

"You see," Asp said. "Obedient to the point of death. I expect an equal measure from you, Sardon."

The Saer wobbled a moment. "Yesssth, my Lord," he said.

"Are the barrel caravans en route?" Asp asked.

"Indeed," Sardon replied. "They approach the human'sssth Grand Terminal as we speak."

"Then, we had better join them," Asp said. "There will be vermin to clean out."

Finished in 1913, Grand Central Terminal became one of New York City's architectural marvels, with the commonly misappropriated Grand Central Station referring to the subway station beneath it. The limestone facade on the terminal's southern side was modeled on a Roman triumphal arch, a triumph for rail travel and a gateway to the city. But, sprinting east on 42nd Street, Taeva approached the terminal and felt anything but triumphant. She'd betrayed the Elves...their Lordly vows...and perhaps, even herself.

Even now, as she raced ahead, she found it impossible to clarify her own motives. All manner of uncomfortable thoughts swirled in her mind. There were questions and urges...each one begging for action. She forced her focus back to the terminal ahead. *Best not to get too far ahead*, she told herself. *I'll know what to do when I see Asp.*

Asp's forces had already wreaked havoc on the structure. The police force housed within had attempted a defense, but they had been overmatched. Their bodies mingled with those of pedestrians and travelers flung all over the street outside the huge, barrel-vaulted building.

Taeva winced, reminded of the destruction at Taladrim. She came to an abrupt stop. Asp's forces had no doubt set up a defensive perimeter, but where were they?

Rushing in would be deadly, but Taeva didn't have time to wait. She began to weave. Thrusting her hands skyward, she sent arcs of electricity toward the station. She walked them in, and the lightning sparked and smoked whenever it made contact. Gwar infantry and Warspiders began to appear in flickering, ashen shadows. As soon as Taeva spotted them, she intensified the bolts and aimed them with lethal accuracy.

A bright white stroke blasted from her right hand and struck a taxicab and the Gwar soldier who had been hiding behind it. The taxi exploded in a boiling fireball, engulfing two nearby Warspiders.

Taeva advanced quickly. She ran through plumes of smoke and sent tangles of electricity ahead. She managed her way between cars and smoking fires and escaped under the shadow of the Park Avenue access bridge. She clambered through a blasted-out door frame and raced ahead, respectfully avoiding the bodies strewn all over the concourse and the stairs.

There were Gwar and Drefids among the dead, she noticed. *Good for the humans,* she thought as she went to step by them. *More resilient than I thought.*

Then she stopped and reached down. She took a short hacking sword from the Gwar and a wickedly curved dagger from the Drefid; there wasn't always time to weave.

At last, she emerged in a cavernous chamber with a great vaulted ceiling that she thought had to be at least one-hundred feet high. Three colossal windows on the far side glowed with late afternoon light. Huge, half circle windows lined both sides of the massive vault, but the western side's windows projected streams of ethereal light down into the chamber.

Taeva gasped. She looked upon the vast ground floor that teemed with completely visible soldiers. *There must be close to a legion gathered here,* she thought. Dozens of Warspiders clambered about also, some already webbing up corners as if they planned to stay there for some time.

The activity was frenzied and yet still organized. Some soldiers stood in orderly rows, a hundred astride or more. Others were busy carting huge crates and barrels from one side of the chamber to the other before disappearing into shadowy corridors. Some Gwar sat atop their Warspiders and appeared to be dismantling just about anything they could get their claws into. Still others were busy shoving pods of captured humans around. At least a legion, and yet the cavernous room seemed to suck away the sound until only a whispery buzz remained.

On the far side of the chamber, hanging beneath a huge red, white and blue flag, there was a circular pavilion of glass and stone. And on top of it, sat a gold clock with four luminous white faces. The Gwar soldiers were thickest there. "That's where he'll be," Taeva muttered to herself. But it didn't seem to matter much to know where Asp was...not anymore. There was no way to get to him.

If I had the Lords of Berinfell with me, she thought ironically, *I could plow through this crowd. But now? No chance.*

"If you have come seeking me!" a voice rose above the crowd and echoed subtly, "I am here. Come, Taeva. Come, daughter...I am waiting."

The Lords of Berinfell ran through New York City on their last legs and yet, they knew that soon—somehow—they would have to summon even more strength. *Ellos help us,* Tommy prayed. He winced as he twisted to avoid a sign post. The pain had mostly dulled to a kind of throbbing ache, but he knew there was something wrong still. He tried not to think about it.

A hundred times grateful for Asp's coating on the video handset, Tommy called out to Migmar. "THIS is as close to Asp as you could get us?"

"Bounced something the signal," Migmar called back. "Now, no fix can I get on Asp."

"He's still blocking us somehow," Kat said.

"Well, where was he?" Tommy demanded of Migmar. He heard the clicking of computer keys.

"Terminal, it was," Migmar said. "Grand Central Terminal."

"Okay, thanks, Migmar." Tommy called to his friends. "We have a bit of a run ahead of us."

A chorus of groans answered him.

The sidewalks were jammed. Tommy and the Lords dodged civilians fleeing south on Park Avenue. Many of them were wounded: bruised, cut, burned and bloodied—some of them just children. Tommy wished they could stop and help each one, but to do so would allow catastrophe on an unimaginable scale.

Maybe there's nothing we can do to stop it, anyway, Tommy thought. He could only guess what manner of destruction waited farther north. *But we'll spend every last heartbeat trying...every last one.*

He held up a fist to stop and then led the Lords into an alley between a barber shop and a deli. He reached into the satchel on his hip and took out a squat, cylindrical jar. "I think it's time we disappear," he said.

The Lords took out their Gnomic paste jars and began the application. The slow process gave each Lord time to think. Too much time for some. For others, not nearly enough.

"Yu, know," Jimmy said, smearing the paste on his chest and up his neck, "I really thought this was over. I mean, when we put down the Spider King...washed him down that blasted mountain, I really thought we'd have peace. I can'na believe how bad it is now."

Already fading into invisibility, Kat put her hand on Jimmy's shoulder. "And I never thought Taeva would betray us."

"The worst thing..." Autumn said.

"Is Jett," Kiri Lee whispered.

"I can't believe he's fightin' for a Drefid," Johnny said. "Fightin' us!"

"I don't think he can help himself," Tommy said. "You heard him. He's talking nonsense. He doesn't know us anymore."

"It's that Dark Arts stoof," Jimmy said, waving a disappearing hand in front of his face. "Evil...pure evil."

"We can't think about Jett," Tommy said. "Keep your mind on the plan. It's not much of a plan, but it's what we've got."

Completely invisible now, Kat said, "So we get past Asp's minions... charge right up...and then what?"

"We tell 'im, right?" Jimmy asked. "We tell 'im about the Tide. I mean, he's not stupid. Given the choice t'fight oos back in Allyra or burn oop, I think he'll do it."

"But if he doesn't?" Autumn asked. "If he turns Taeva and Jett on us..."

"Could you do it, Tommy?" Kiri Lee asked. Her face hadn't quite vanished yet. He dark eyes looked huge...and haunted. "I mean, if he won't stop...could you, could you kill Jett?"

Tommy's throat and mouth felt suddenly dry. His mind reeled. *Could I?*

A dozen happy memories with Jett flashed before him. In truth, Tommy didn't know the answer to that question...that terrible question. *But I'm the leader of the Lords of Berinfell,* he thought, *there's no pawning this off.*

"If it comes down to it," Tommy said, "if there's no other way...I don't want any of you to have to do it. It's on me."

Daughter.

So many connotations to the word, and Taeva's heart became the epicenter for them all...tremors spreading outward to the point where she could barely grip her weapons. Her hands trembling, she slid the sword and dagger into the sheaths strapped on her thighs. They fit awkwardly, but it would do. Better than dropping them. *Get a grip on yourself!* she admonished. *He's lying.*

"You've come at last!" Asp called out. "I was beginning to...to be concerned."

She could see him now, standing on the ceiling of the information counter. He rested one hand on the top of the golden clock. His shock of Drefid-white hair danced eerily on some unseen current of air. Two others stood there as well, just on the other side of the clock, but Taeva didn't recognize them.

"Come, my daughter!" Asp called, his voice rich with authority. "Advance and take your place."

"I am not your daughter!" Taeva yelled back. "And I've come to kill you."

"Kill me?" Asp replied. "As amusing as that is, I know it isn't true. You've come to bring me information. The Lords of Berinfell are here, this I know all too well. You know their plans now. And, you've returned to me at last to bring me the information, just as I asked."

"We never agreed!" Taeva yelled. She found herself descending the white stone stairs to the floor of the concourse.

"They will not hinder you!" Asp called, and the teeming soldiers parted, giving Taeva a clear aisle of approach. "After all, you are family."

"Stop saying that!" Taeva screamed. She kept her hands at her sides, sparks beginning to dance between her fingers. "My father is dead...and so is my mother, no thanks to you."

Asp leaped high into the air. His cloak flapped as he descended. He landed with eerie grace a dozen paces from Taeva. The other two figures leaped down from the information center and advanced just behind their leader. She recognized one: Sardon, the Saer leader from the Conclave of Nations. And the other...a Lyrian Elf to be sure. Taeva thought that this one must be Jett. Her eyes blinked back to Asp.

"I rue Navira's death just as you," Asp said, striding forward. He stopped a little more than arm's reach from Taeva. "The Spider King, even before his Dark Arts accident, was quite mad, I assure you. I was there, and I knew him. He was a bitter and demented being. And he slew Navira while I was a world away."

Taeva winced each time Asp said her mother's name, but found herself crumbling inwardly. "I hate the Spider King!" she said miserably. "But he was my father...not you."

Asp smiled patiently and said, "Did Navira...did your mother... ever reveal him as your father? Did she ever say his name and call him your blood father?"

Taeva rocked on her heels. She thought back to the journal and cursed herself for losing it in the fortress back in Canada. She'd read it so many times though, and her mother had always implied...well, they were husband and wife...it had to be. But, the silence screamed out something new. Her mother had never actually revealed the father's name.

"NO!" she shrieked. She lunged at Asp, electricity flying from her hands.

But the white-hot bolts never connected. Asp lifted his hands, and blood red arcs of electricity erupted outward and blocked Taeva's blasts.

Taeva used both hands and wove a massive bolt that flashed down from above. Asp pointed his fingertips at the floor and a huge red bolt rose up to meet the other. Thunder rocked the concourse, and gasps rose from the crowd of soldiers assembled there.

"You see," Asp said, rising from a defensive crouch. "You even share my ability to throw lightning. Did you never wonder how you came to such gifts? Surely it is not from Ellos. Surely you are not an Elven Lord."

Taeva growled and spun a kick into Asp's midsection. The blow landed solidly and Asp flew backward.

"My Lord!" Sardon yelled, leaping forward. "Jett, see to him!" Sardon lifted his staff and whirled toward Taeva.

"Stay back, Sardon!" Asp commanded, rising easily. "You'll only get yourself hurt."

But before Asp finished speaking, Sardon cracked Taeva smartly on the jaw with his staff. She reeled backward. Sardon charged in and tried to sweep Taeva's legs. But his staff swept nothing but air. Taeva leaped and, at the same time, drew out and slashed the jagged short sword across the Saer's throat.

Sardon's goat eyes bulged, he clutched his throat and fell in a heap. Asp stepped casually by the fallen Saer. "Jett," he said, "heal the fool."

Taeva gazed at Sardon's body, still twitching. His fingers made little ripples on the pool of blood spreading beneath him. Jett put his hand on Sardon's neck, and the twitching stopped.

"Too late," Jett said, rising and wiping his hand on his tunic. "He is already dead."

"That," Asp said, glaring at Taeva and exhaling deeply, "was less than kind."

"He shouldn't have come between us," Taeva said.

"No, no he shouldn't have," Asp agreed. "This was not his concern, but really, Taeva...have you not figured it all out by now? I thought for sure when we met in Taladair that you would come around."

Taeva didn't answer. She hadn't had much time to learn from the Elves, but Mandiera, the Nightform, had been something of a revelation. She had never seen a combat method so lethal. So Taeva had relaxed herself completely. To Asp, she would appear nonthreatening, almost at ease. Like a tree limb whipping back, she sprang. From motionless to speed of thought, she attacked.

Asp crossed his fully extended claws in front of his chest, easily deflecting Taeva's first thrust. She spun and slashed, but he blocked again. She tried every angle, darting and chopping, but always his claws were there. Her final attempt left her breathless for more than one reason.

Taeva leaped into the air, diving toward Asp. She wove a jagged bolt of lightning with her left hand and, with the sword in her right, carved a deadly arc toward Asp's neck. There was an awesome red flash, and Taeva's white bolt dissipated. And yet, Asp managed to block the sword with his claws also. And somehow, something hit her midsection, and she sprawled backward onto the floor.

"How…" she muttered, gazing up at Asp, then she gasped.

Asp's cloak was spread wide now, and she could see his segmented body armor, the way it opened up revealing four shoulder joints, two on each side. For Asp had four arms, and each hand had the Drefids' characteristic extended claws.

"A little evolution," Asp said. "Courtesy of the Dark Arts. Now dispense with these feeble attacks and listen to me. You, Taeva, owe everything to me. You've read Navira's journal, you know that I rescued you as a child and took you to a safer home with the Taladrim."

"Only to wipe them out?" Taeva mocked. "They raised me as their own. They were my people and you annihilated them."

"I wouldn't have," Asp said, "if you had done your job. They perished because you did not do as I intended. The Taladrim had an opportunity to join me, but they did not. They were not your people anyway. What of them? I rescued you from Vesper Crag. I am the one!

"Did you never wonder how, at eight years of age, you received your mother's journal? I delivered it to you. I wanted you to know your true enemy. All this time, I have been grooming you from afar. I wanted my daughter to have a choice, but the time has come for you to make that ultimate decision."

Taeva shook her head. "But…you cannot be my father," she whispered. "Look at me…I bear Elven features…some Gwar even, but there is no Drefid blood in my veins. I have no claws embedded in my fists!"

"Have you ever tried?" Asp asked, his four arms gesturing independently, almost as if he were working a spinning loom. "The claws may lie dormant unless you command them."

Taeva looked at her fists and blinked.

"Try," Asp said.

She shouldn't, she knew. *What's the point?* But she decided to anyway. To mock him. To spite him. To prove him wrong.

Taeva dropped her sword and clenched her fists. He brows beetled in concentration. She groaned...and then gasped.

The skin of each knuckle burst open, the skin puckering but without blood. Thin points emerged slowly. Tears streamed down her cheeks, but not from pain. The bony blades extended a foot from her fists and glistened in the beams of sun from the high windows.

"I...I can't believe it," Taeva whispered, silently weeping. She looked up at Asp. "It's true then?"

Asp nodded. He folded both sets of arms across his chest, covering a red, crystal talisman which hung from around his neck on a cord. "You see?" he asked. "All along, I cared for your mother, even when to do so aroused the ire of the Spider King. I hid her when she was pregnant with you. I carried you off to safety. I helped pen her journal when she was no longer physically able, and then brought it to you, only to seek you out among all the leaders of the world."

Taeva flexed her fingers and let the claws retract. "It all makes sense now," she whispered.

"Now, won't you come with me," he said, "tell me what you know of the Elven Lords and their plans?"

Terror Dawning

GRIMWARDEN HAD lost more blood than Goldarrow cared to think of. As had Thorkber. Now it was up to her to get them both to safety where they could be treated.

Goldarrow stared up at the night sky. "Where are all my flet soldiers?" she called to the darkness. "We need help!"

"They...are engaged otherwise, I'm afraid," Grimwarden said softly.

"You save your strength, you old codger," she commanded. "And be quiet so I can think." She saw his faint smile and knew he understood.

Thorkber was the easier of the two to manage, as all Goldarrow needed to do was lash him to her chest with her cloak, like swaddling a child. Grimwarden, however, wasn't even able to sit up on his own. She tried to push her right shoulder beneath his chest, to will his massive body upward. But the blood made his arms and armor hard to grasp, and eventually she had to face the reality that she could not lift him...not without crushing Thorkber.

How can I do this? she half-thought, half-prayed. *I cannot carry him.* She glanced down at Grimwarden and then glared at the sprawled body of Ghrell, the dead Nemic ruler. "It's your fault!" she growled. "You sanctimonious fool. You put blasted plants and dirt above our people, the creation before the creator!" She was so angry that she slammed the toe of her boot into Ghrell's shoulder joint. "You deserve worse, you...you..."

Her voice trailed off as she stared at that shoulder joint...and the outstretched wing. "Dear Ellos," she gasped. "It might work."

Guardmaster Goldarrow was no butcher. She killed in the line of duty, but she never took a blade to the dead. Not until now. She bent low to Grimwarden. "I'm going to borrow this for a bit," she said, gently removing his battleaxe from his backhanger. Grimwarden did not reply.

Goldarrow took the axe and set upon Ghrell's shoulder with a vengeance, hacking and chopping until, after the seventh blow, the limb broke free from his torso. Goldarrow tossed away the axe and grasped the wing by the exposed bone. She dragged the wing to Grimwarden's side.

The wing was massive, larger than it needed to be and ribbed with bony spokes. "I'm going to roll you over," she told Grimwarden, but still he did not answer. It took all the leverage she could manage, but she did it. She let his upper body fall gently upon the wing such that his head lay about a foot from the severed joint. Then, she swung his legs up so that his entire body rested on the wing.

Thorkber swung out from her chest precariously as she hoisted the bony wing joint up to her shoulder. But the cloak-sling held, and Thorkber did not spill out. Then, bending at her waist and harnessing all the power of her lower body, she began to drag the wing.

Every step was a mighty chore, and while the army all about the city cheered with each Nemic flier they dispatched, Goldarrow's heart sank, cursing the irony that two of Berinfell's heroes were dying within their own city and no one knew about it but her.

Grimwarden coughed up blood, showering the paving stones in front of them.

"Don't you die on me, Grimwarden!" she scolded him. "Keep yourself awake, or I'll kill you myself."

He turned his head ever so slightly to smile at her. His voice was a mere whisper. "I'd like to see you try."

Goldarrow choked. Grimwarden's humor always melted her. And now she was going to lose him without him ever truly know how she felt. *No, I'm not going to lose you,* she corrected. Grimwarden coughed again. Goldarrow faltered, her knees hitting the ground. Thorkber groaned. She struggled back to her feet and looked back. "Stop coughing, you big oaf," she said. "Just hang in there!"

"Goldarrow," he whispered, shaking his head a little. "Not...this... time."

"Olin," she said, suddenly aware she was crying. "I won't have you talking like that."

But still, Grimwarden shook his head, his hands trembling, reaching forward for her. Goldarrow cried out and lowered the makeshift litter. She was tired. And deep in her heart, she knew this was the end. She gently laid Thorkber down and pulled the sling off from over her head. Then she turned, knelt beside Grimwarden, and grabbed his breastplate, soaked in blood.

"Just who do you think you are, anyway?" She could hardly speak now, forcing her words through agonized lips. "You go off rescuing the realm of Berinfell, acting like a hero, only to rally the hopes of your people? And make every girl fall in love with you?"

"Not...every...girl..." Grimwarden breathed, "just...you."

Goldarrow was beside herself now, her emotions as unguarded as they'd ever been. She closed her eyes, trying to shut out the pain... the noise... the battle din in the background, the shouting of her people, the barking of dogs. Why could she never have a moment to herself with him?

"I do love you, I do," she sobbed. "As I always have. Never another." She placed her head against his.

And then she heard from him the faintest words, words that would ever ring the loudest in her memory.

"And I you."

Goldarrow picked her head up off Grimwarden's chest; it no longer rose and fell. She couldn't tell how long she'd lain there holding him. She looked over to Thorkber who lay motionless on the stone road. *Where are you, Ellos?* Goldarrow sighed. Too tired to move, too sad to try.

She heard the dog barking again. Only this time much closer.

The cheering stopped. All of Berinfell froze, including the Nemic invasion, at least for a moment. To the west came a haunting glow in the sky; odd because it was still far from dawn. Dazzling lights started to flicker against the horizon, like a brilliant shaft of light split into a million directions by the prisms of a crystal chandelier.

The Nemic invaders paused to observe the strange phenomenon. Being students of the sky, and given their position high above the Elves of Berinfell, they could see the light play from north to south without breaking. It was exactly as their scouts had seen earlier. *The Curtain of Doom.*

The Tide was coming.

That Terrible Question

THE LORDS watched in fearful paralysis as Taeva shook Asp's hand. They shook firmly, like statesmen celebrating some final agreement after years of tense conflict. There was also an air of smug finality, Tommy thought, as if Taeva and Asp had completed some final victorious stroke.

Still grasping Asp's hand, Taeva bowed her head slightly. It was an act of deference, a recognition of ultimate authority and a sign of submission. *It's ten-thousand ways wrong,* Tommy thought. *How could she bow her head to the one who slaughtered her people?*

Asp's grin widened to a sickening gloat, and he turned his burning orb eyes to the crowds of soldiers. He declared triumphantly, "At last, my daughter has come home!"

Daughter? Tommy heard Kat speak the word in his mind even as he thought it himself. *No, it can't be. We would have seen...*

But Tommy couldn't finish the thought. His eyes locked onto motion.

Taeva yanked Asp toward her. At the same time, her left hand appeared. She held some kind of blade and it seemed to be crackling with sparks of electricity. In that flash of movement, she rammed the blade under his lower shoulder joint. She pushed it in to the hilt and gave it a wicked twist before Asp backfisted her. She fell backward and rolled to a wary crouch, even as Asp fell backward...stricken.

Taeva sensed movement from behind. She quickly wove a dozen charged arcs between her fingers, swung around and threw a scattershot, splintering bolt that slammed into the approaching soldiers. None of the strokes were powerful enough to kill, but she'd knocked enough of them off their feet that perhaps they would think twice before their next approach.

She turned back to Asp and watched him pull the dagger free from his side. A gout of blood so dark that it might have been black spurted out of the wound and continued to trickle as Asp let his head loll backward.

"Why, Taeva?" he asked, his voice weak and raspy. "Why?"

"You continue the ruse until the end?" Taeva said, her fingers crackling with sparks. She took a step forward and laughed. "All this time you thought you had a marionette, and yet, you failed to see the strings upon your own limbs. Don't you understand? I knew! And I've known for years. Ever since I realized that my mother's journal was missing more than a third of its pages. You cut them out and rebound the book, but there were phantom imprints left on so many of the pages. The humidity of Taladair showed me. I couldn't read them, of course, but I knew there had been other pages.

"I imagine those pages did not paint a flattering portrait of you, Asp. You were the one! You were the agent of chaos behind it all! You gave the Spider King the Dark Arts. You poisoned his mind with paranoid fear of my mother. It was by your whispers that he locked my mother away, poisoned her with that Dark Arts venom, and forced her to be broodmother to a teeming swarm of Warspiders. You didn't rescue me. You took me and used me as a pawn, delivering me to the Taladrim to sway their loyalties.

"And my mother knew you would try something of that nature. That's why she pasted a false page into the back cover. It was all there, Asp, everything you did. My mother's word against yours. So I made plans and I played the role. And here at last you unveiled your empty gambit. You called me daughter.

"Tell me, Asp, how long after I gave you Berinfell's plans were you going to kill me?" Taeva smiled and looked at her fists. "You'd have had to kill me soon. It wouldn't have taken me very long to figure out that the claws that came from my fist were just a Dark Arts parlor trick."

Asp groaned, leaned up on one elbow, and said, "You are right, Taeva. I would not have waited very long to kill you. But this way is so much better. This way, I will have to torture you to get the information I need."

"You won't touch me," Taeva hissed. "I studied Drefid anatomy, and I knew just where to hit you. My dagger found the coil of your heart, Asp. You are minutes from death."

And Asp began to laugh. They were more like wet, heaving breaths, but nonetheless, he laughed.

"Did you...did you think you could kill me?" Asp asked. "Just like that? Amusing little wench." Keeping his eyes on Taeva, Asp tilted his head a little and called out, "Jett, heal me!"

"NO, Jett," a voice came, seemingly from nowhere. "Don't heal Asp! Not yet!"

Tommy's cry echoed throughout the hall. Every head moved to look in his direction, but saw only empty space. The Six had already snuck within twenty paces behind Taeva, Asp and Jett.

Jett had already moved to within arm's length of Asp, but he froze when he heard the voice.

Asp's two left arms came up. There was a flash of red light and a flurry of red embers, like in a fireplace after a smoldering hunk of wood snaps in half.

Tommy looked down, shocked. The embers danced all around him. His arms were rapidly reappearing. The red embers continued to swirl until he was fully visible. He looked back over his shoulder. The other Lords stood there, completely uncloaked.

"Jett!" Asp commanded. "Heal me!"

Jett took another step.

"Don't!" Tommy ordered. In a blink, he had an arrow nocked and pointed at Jett. "Not an inch farther, Jett. I don't want to shoot you, but I will. And you know I will not miss."

"Tommy!" Kat exclaimed.

"What are yu doin', mate?" Jimmy asked.

"Put the bow down!" Kiri Lee said. "Please."

"Jett!" Asp called. "I command you to heal me!"

Jett looked from Asp, back to Tommy and the razor-tipped arrow. His eyes narrowed, but he didn't get any closer to Asp.

"Asp!" Tommy yelled. "Your life hangs in the balance!"

"As does yours," Asp said weakly. He gestured dismissively with his hand.

Tommy saw from his peripheral vision that the many hundreds of troops had formed an uneven circle around them. And they were slowly moving forward. It was like the tightening of a noose.

"More have come back," Bengfist said.

"How many more?" Jast asked.

"What I saw," he said, "on this moniterd, I saw two, perhaps three dozen. Maybe more. It was crowded. I cannot say for sure. But mostly my derelict kinsmen and Saer. I saw only two Drefids."

"Saw them, I too, and more from the outside," Migmar explained. "Be here, the enemy, all too soon."

As if on cue, the trio heard muffled screams, grunts and shrieks from the other side of the chamber door that Johnny had welded shut.

"What will we do?" Jast asked.

"Hope we that the door holds," Migmar replied.

Bengfist grunted. "Or we die drenched in enemy blood."

"Guys!" Tommy called out. "I need time."

"Got it!" Johnny said. He stepped out to Tommy's left and held out his hands, palms up. Fire danced immediately. "Come any closer, and you burn!" he told the Gwar.

Kiri Lee leaped into the air, climbed until she was high over the enemy, and nocked an arrow of her own.

Jimmy missed his claymore but he made a decent show with the twin bladed staff he'd taken from a Saer on Liberty Island.

Autumn drew two daggers. In a blur, she sped back and forth in front of the enemy line. She smacked each one of them on the jaw with the handle of her blades. "Next time," she said, "it will be the blade. And, next time, it will be your neck."

"Our lives are all at stake," Tommy said to them all. "But Asp, hear me out. We didn't come here to fight you. I will let Jett heal you. But you must listen."

"Let Jett heal me?" Asp snarled. "You are deluded." He coughed up more blood. "But still, I am curious. Speak, Elf! I grow weary."

Tommy chose his words carefully but explained to Asp the damage the cross-world portals had caused. He spoke of the Tide of Unmaking ravaging both worlds and of the desperate need to get all Allyrans out of Earth for good. Tommy finished speaking and found himself panting from exertion. He still had the arrow nocked, the bowstring drawn back to his ear. The muscles in his back felt close to knotting up. Sweat dribbled down his forehead and threatened to drain into his eye. He had to finish this quickly.

"We will allow Jett to heal you," he said. "We will allow you to return to Allyra without interference from us. You can regroup, attack Berinfell, try to finish this...but only on Allyran soil. You have to make certain that every last one of your soldiers departs Earth."

Asp coughed, and pressed both right hands to the still leaking wound. "Let me be certain...that I understand," he said. "You believe that I...that Drefid-kind has, by using Dark Arts portals over the ages, caused a tearing of the veil between worlds. And that in so doing, we have unleashed the Tide of Unmaking, a kind of wall of energy that will utterly consume both Earth and Allyra. Is this correct?"

Tommy nodded, blinking away sweat. Back, shoulder, arm, hand—all burned from keeping that bowstring back, keeping it still. "If you don't believe us," he said, "check the news broadcasts here. There are visuals already...Russia, Japan and—"

"I have seen the moving pictures," Asp said. "But until now, I had no idea what the wave of destructive energy was. I feared it was some new Elven weapon, something you would use against me. And to think I expended so much energy to woo young Taeva...for information the Lords of Berinfell themselves would so freely give. So many things now become clear."

Tommy swallowed. He was beginning to lose sensation in his fingertips. "So you'll do it then? You'll depart Earth? There isn't much time. It has to—"

"You are Felheart Silvertree, are you not?" Asp asked. "Your family line is ancient, all the way back to the beginning of the Allyra. Did you know?"

Tommy shook his head. Sweat stung his eyes.

"Yes, one of the oldest Lordly lines. But did you know there are other ancient bloodlines? Powerful bloodlines not connected to the Lords of Berinfell whatsoever? Yes, in the pages of the sacred Vulrid, I have learned much of my own family line. I am Asp-Anthruel the Sixth, beloved of Vulridian and destined to do many great deeds."

He coughed again. Blood dribbled between the fingers of the hands covering his wound. "You see, Taeva was right. I was the one who brought the Dark Arts to the Spider King. I used the Dark Arts to twist his mind toward vengeance. He became my puppet, even imprisoning and poisoning the Elf maiden he so deeply loved. Oh, yes, I was the one who fanned the Spider King's hatred of Berinfell to an inferno. Pity he could not finish the job. But, he did keep his side of the bargain to me. Or at least his corpse did. The venom fermented...matured within him until, at last, I found him in the wreckage of Vesper Crag. That venom now flows in my veins."

"Enough!" Tommy yelled. He could barely hold the bowstring any longer. "Will you take your armies and leave Earth, or not?"

"No," Asp replied. "Ignorant Elf! You do not understand me. You have never understood. We will not leave Earth! In fact, as soon as Jett heals me, I will command my soldiers under penalty of death NEVER to leave Earth! I will open new portals and shuttle human slaves to Allyra by the thousands. Let the Tide of Unmaking hasten! According to the word of Vulridian, let the world—both worlds—be soaked in blood!"

"Wrong!" Tommy barked. "Jett will not heal you. We won't let him."

"So be it," Asp said, laughing. "Then I will enjoy my last sights, watching you murder the one you once called brother in arms. And I will die knowing that I have done as Vulridian asks, and for my service, I will reap reward beyond reckoning! My soldiers, KILL THE ELVES!! Jett, heal your master, NOW!"

Jett lunged toward Asp.

"NO!" Tommy screamed. The moment came. That terrible question. Jett was two seconds from Asp. But Tommy couldn't do it. He couldn't release the arrow and kill his friend. He started to let the bowstring relax when—

THWANG!

The bowstring left his fingertips. The arrow flew. "NO!" Tommy cried out again. He hadn't meant to let the arrow go. But his fingertips were numb. The arrow was gone. And Tommy knew it would fly true, pierce Jett's eye, and sink into his brain, killing him instantly.

The arrow was gone. There was no bringing it back, Tommy knew, and at this close range, there was no hope of changing its course. *I've killed him,* Tommy thought hopelessly. *I've killed Jett.*

Tommy shut his eyes.

But Autumn didn't. She'd seen Tommy struggling to hold the bowstring. She'd already made up her mind what she would do, if it came to it. But she'd relaxed for just a moment, simply exhaling, when the arrow flew. Her speed, her reflexes, and her reactions were all superhuman—even ten times the speed of the nimble Elves. In a blink, even as the arrow began its single heartbeat journey, Autumn was off.

She flashed toward Jett to intercept the arrow, but she knew. She knew she'd left a split-second too late and at the wrong angle. Still, she forced every ounce of speed from her legs, leaned forward, and dove in front of Jett.

Autumn struck something, stumbled and hit the ground hard. She rolled and felt a sharp pain in her shoulder. For a moment, as her body finally tumbled to a halt, Autumn thought she'd succeeded. But she reached up to her shoulder and felt her flesh slick with blood. But no arrow shaft. She closed her eyes. She'd failed.

But Kiri Lee hadn't.

Kiri Lee also had been watching Tommy draw back the bowstring with the deadly shaft pointed at Jett. She'd seen the anguish in Tommy's expression, the strain in his neck and forearms as the confrontation with Asp went on. Kiri Lee had been patrolling the air above it all.

But when she saw Tommy falter, she launched into a swift descent. Not just falling, but propelling herself downward by pushing off the air. And still, she feared it would not be fast enough.

Something struck her foot, and she felt herself twisting. At the same time, a burst of agony radiated outward from her gut like a corona of flame. She landed on her side and skidded to a stop.

Major General Anton Velashzny had never seen orders like these, not since the training exercises many years before. That and a recurring nightmare shared by most senior officers of the Russian Strategic Missile Command.

Anton swiveled in his chair and said, "Chekov, did you...can this be right?"

Chekov—whose eyes were barely visible under two dark, caterpillar eyebrows—replied, "The security codes are accurate and they are today's."

"But...but, you know what this will do," Anton said. "This will start—"

"World War III has already begun, Anton," he said. "Have you not heard? Have you not seen pictures of Petropavolvsk?"

"But the Americans? Intelligence would have briefed us if the Americans had developed a new weapon."

"Who else could it be?" Chekov asked. "The Americans are the only ones capable, technologically speaking. We have lost the race."

"And when we do this," Anton said, "the world will lose."

Chekov nodded and removed a key chain from his breast pocket. He consulted a leatherbound logbook. "Insert key," he said. "Execute one quarter turn to the left."

The two senior Commanders inserted their keys and gave their fist turn.

"Proceed three-quarters turn right."

Each Commander did so. And each action elicited the same response: a four-inch door slid open just inches above the Commander's key hand. A chrome half-sphere rose up from the panel and its cap popped open to reveal a small red button.

"Three times, Anton," Chekov said. "Are you ready?"

Anton swallowed. His face felt numb. He tried to swallow, but it felt like a fist-full of screws had lodged in his throat. Sweat pouring down his brow, tears from his eyes, Anton nodded.

Together, they pressed their red buttons. Once. Twice. After a pause, the third time.

BOOM. BOOM. BOOM. Silo hatch doors began to open. The red light on the control room's ceiling began to spin. Anton turned to his friend and said, "May God forgive us for what we have unleashed."

"Just following orders," Chekov replied, lighting a cigarette.

"I wonder," Anton replied, "if perhaps, hell is most populated by men who were just following orders."

Meanwhile, above ground, smoke thrust upward from each silo, and heat emissions flash-melted snow into steam. One by one, the SS-25 Topol missiles rose slowly from their silos. Then, having cleared the opening by fifty feet, the first stage booster fell away, and the second stage ignited.

The first wave of nuclear intercontinental ballistic missiles had begun their flight to North America.

Tommy opened his eyes and didn't understand what he was looking at. Autumn and Kiri Lee were sprawled across the floor, and Jett was still standing. He had his hands on Asp's shoulders. Then, Tommy saw the fletchings of the arrow he had fired. The arrow was deep in Kiri Lee's stomach.

"No," Tommy whispered, running toward her. "No, no, no!"

"Kiri Lee!" Kat and Jimmy cried out and raced to her side.

Johnny and Taeva, a combination of fire and lightning, burned up scores of enemy soldiers as they tried to bring aid to Asp.

"Don't know how much longer we can keep them out!" Johnny yelled.

"Finish this!" Taeva cried out.

Tommy stopped, crouched to check on Kiri Lee. Her tunic was already dark with blood from the wound. It seemed to be seeping.

Kiri Lee's eyes opened. She glanced at the wound and smiled. Then she looked at Jett.

Tommy stood. Wincing, he drew his sword. It wasn't as strong as his Nightstalker blade, or even his rychesword, but it would do the job.

"How touching!" Asp said, blood dribbling from the corner of his mouth. "She saved you, Jett. Did you see? Felheart—your friend—sent that arrow for a place in your brain."

Jett's eyes burned with violet fire. His fingers flexed upon the muscle of Asp's neck.

"Don't!" Tommy said, his voice cracking. "Don't heal him, Jett."

Asp let out a coughing laugh. "Of course, he will heal me," he said. He glanced over his shoulder. "Make this quick, Jett."

"Don't!" Tommy yelled.

"Don't worry," Jett said. And with a quick but powerful jerk of his hands, he broke Asp's neck. Then he shoved the corpse aside.

An audible gasp went up through the entire hall. No one moved.

"Jett?" Tommy whispered. "Jett, do you know me?"

"Are yu, are yu yourself?" Jimmy asked.

"Some things are clear," Jett said. "Some aren't. But I know my friends, and I know that Ellos is my only Master."

Feeling joy beyond his own understanding, Tommy spun on his heels. "Johnny, Taeva, hold on! Jimmy, Kat, we need to help them keep the enemy out!"

"But, Kiri Lee?" Kat said.

"We can't help her," Tommy said. "But Jett can." He looked questioningly at Jett.

"You bet your trigger happy fingers I can," Jett said.

"JETT'S BACK!" Autumn cried, raising her hands in the air with overwhelming glee.

Jett leaped over Asp's body and rushed to Kiri Lee's side. He reached his hand toward her wound.

"NO!" Kiri Lee exclaimed. "No you won't. Not this time!"

Jett held his hand up. He shook his head, not comprehending.

"You took the poison for me, Jett," she said. "Don't you remember? You took what would have killed me and put yourself in a grave for seven years. I've spent all that time wishing you hadn't. If I am to die, then I should die...not...not you."

"Don't worry," Jett said, gently moving her hands away from the arrow's shaft. "I'm stronger now. A lot stronger."

✳

"The door will not hold much longer!" Jast said, pacing with a sword in each hand.

Shrieks and howls continued just outside the chamber door. There was another muffled boom, and this time a seam of blue fire appeared on one edge of the door.

"Let them come!" Bengfist growled as he hefted his battle hammers. "If we must perish, then let us perish fighting for our friends!"

"Not fond, I am, of the whole perishing thing," Migmar said. His head bobbed from monitor to monitor, and his fingers flew across the keyboard. Every few tip-taps on the keys, and the Gnome swiveled in his chair to look at the luminous globe. "Not fond at all," he repeated.

Another explosion outside, and the seam of bright blue light tripled in size. The upper left-hand corner of the door warped and bent in. A thick Gwar hand reached in. With a running start, Bengfist slammed a hammer against the intruding hand.

The crunching sound was nearly as loud as the howl that followed.

"That'll teach you!" Bengfist yelled at the blood-spattered gap in the door. "Rest of you traitors want some of that, you just keep on coming!"

Then, a thread of white mist seeped in through the growing hole in the door. Within two heart beats the vapor materialized into a full-sized Drefid—right inside the control room! Bengfist was stunned and fumbled with his warhammer. Jast swung, but the Drefid's talons caught her blade and twisted it awkwardly in her hands.

"Wisp, it is!" Migmar shouted. It was the first anyone had seen in years. "First Voice! Old words!"

Bengfist balked. "First what?"

"Everything must Migmar do?" yelled the Gnome, sliding down off his chair. He grabbed a dagger and sped around behind the faux-Drefid while Jast kept it busy. "Watch you, Bengfist." The Gnome thrust the blade into the back of the invader's calf and began spewing words so fast Bengfist had no idea what the Gnome was saying. The truth was, even if Migmar had slowed his speech down, Bengfist *still* wouldn't have had a clue.

Suddenly the Drefid squealed and writhed, contorting in all manner of odd movements. Finally the body dissipated and vanished in a puff of white mist.

"Like that you just do," said Migmar with an annoyed tone in his voice. "So simple," he muttered as he walked back to his chair. "No one teach old ways anymore, so simple."

More pounding assaulted the iron door.

"This is far from over," Bengfist bellowed. "I've just begun to fight!"

"Let them through!" Migmar yelled.

"That's the spirit, my little Gnome brother!" Bengfist yelled. "One final stand together!"

"Not quite," Migmar said. "Mean I something else! But when they come, step away!"

"I do not understand," Jast said. "We aren't going to give up...are we?"

An arc stone flew through the opening in the door and rolled toward the luminous globe map.

"Aiiee! Get you that out of here!" Migmar shrieked. "NOW!"

Bengfist pounced on it, but Jast was faster. She grabbed the arc stone and hurled it back through the door opening.

FOOM!! Incandescent blue light filled the chamber, followed by a string of screams, whimpers and Gwar curses.

Jast clutched her burned hand. "Now that was almost worth scarring my hand."

An immense crash, and the chamber door bent inward suddenly. Another hit, and it tore free of its upper hinge altogether.

Migmar tapped away on the keys. "Almost...almost...just...

about...there!"

The door blasted free...and vanished into a shimmering pool of electricity. More than a dozen soldiers surged into the chamber. They brandished weapons and screamed in fury as they charged forward.

And one by one, the enemy soldiers left Canada.

"A portal?" Bengfist blurted out. "You opened a portal right in the doorway? You evil genius!"

"Evil, I am not," Migmar said. "Genius? Maybe."

Jett tossed the bloodied arrow away in disgust. It clattered on the concourse floor. Then, he placed his hands firmly on Kiri Lee's abdomen, and closed his eyes.

He heard Tommy yelling commands. He heard the roar of Johnny's flame and the crashing of Taeva's thunder. He heard the clamor of battle between his friends and the combined Gwar, Drefid and Saer forces. But it was all muted, smothered in gossamer peace.

Jett felt the blood drain from his face, the odd cool sensation on his flesh. He heard Kiri Lee groan. Then, he opened his eyes and lifted his hands.

Kiri Lee sat up, blinking as if waking from a dream. "I don't feel any pain," she said. "Any pain at all."

"I told you," Jett said, "I am stronger now." He stood up straight, took a deep breath and roared, "And I am AWAKE!"

Then, Jett turned and looked at the teeming enemy, threatening to overwhelm them. "Kiri Lee," he said without looking at her. "You hang back until you feel well enough to fight. I'm going in."

Kiri Lee watched Jett lumber away. She realized he didn't have any weapons. But amidst the fire and lightning, Jett didn't seem to care. He charged into the fray. Immediately something changed. Enemy combatants began to fall in heaps. One minute, they were there, holding up shields and brandishing weapons. Then Jett came, and they went down. It looked like some bizarre form of dominos.

Suddenly, a voice cried out above the clamor, "HOLD! HOLD FAST! I declare a cease fire!"

Kiri Lee leaped to her feet, grinning at the ability to do so, but desperate to see who was doing the ordering. She sprinted up behind Tommy.

He glanced and then did a double-take. "Kiri Lee?" he said. "You're healed?"

"Good as new," she said. "Better, even. What's going on?"

"Don't know," he said. "One of the Gwar generals just ordered his troops to stand down."

The front lines of the enemy parted. A massive Gwar appeared and came forward, casting his shield aside. He wore a stone helm with a bone face guard and a light armor vest.

Tommy thought he looked like a Roman centurion...crossed with the Incredible Hulk, minus the green skin that is.

"Pointless carnage!" he bellowed at his soldiers. He glared left and right, staring them down, one after the other. Then he came away from the crowd. "Elves, who is lord among you?"

Tommy stepped forward. "Uh...we all are," he said. "We are the Seven, uh...Eight, the Eight Lords of Berinfell."

"Yes," said the Gwar, "well, that much was clear by the way you fought, but I mean, who speaks for your group? Is it you?"

"It is," Tommy said. For a moment, he wished Grimwarden or Goldarrow would suddenly appear. But the musing passed quickly, and Tommy stepped forward. "I am Felheart Silvertree."

"I am Eragor, General Commander," the Gwar said. "I do not speak for Asp's forces worldwide. But Grand Central is my command. And I ask you your terms."

"Terms?"

"We do not surrender," Eragor explained. "But it is pointless to fight on while precious minutes pass by. What good is victory if this battlefield, if Allyra, is consumed by the...what did you call it?"

"The Tide of Unmaking," Tommy said.

"It is a fearsome thing," Eragor said. "Asp had a force on the ground in a place the humans call Russia. The military base there and two legions of Asp's eastern army were utterly wiped away. It is a fearsome thing. So I ask again: what are your terms?"

"It's simple," Tommy said. "You, me, we all need to leave Earth. The Tide will continue so long as even one Allyran remains here alive."

"That will not prove easy," Eragor said. "There are legions scattered all across this world."

"Don't you have some sort of communications?" Tommy asked.

"Of course," Eragor replied. "Each legion Commander has a communication device. I believe they are called cells."

"You have to contact them," Tommy said. "Every one of them. You have to convince them to get everyone out. We control your portal center in Canada. I think we can open a portal wherever your men need them."

"How can we trust that you won't portal us into a volcano or some such thing?"

Tommy thought a moment. "For every ten soldiers who enter the portal," he said, "have one come back to report safe arrival. We'll put you in Allyra wherever you wish. You can all band together and attack Berinfell at your convenience. Though, we'd rather you didn't."

Eragor laughed. "Don't mistake this, Elf," he said, his voice lowering. "We are not allies, nor are we friends. I have no love for humankind either. If there were some other way to stave off annihilation, I would take it and then gut you."

Johnny bristled. "You try that, and I'd roast you to a charcoal—"

Tommy put a hand up to caution Johnny. Then he nodded to

Eragor. "Understood," he said.

Eragor walked over to Asp's corpse and snapped something off from around his neck. "First you'll be needing to get rid of this," he said, holding up a red crystal. "Keeps portals from opening anywhere within one-hundred paces."

"So that's what was stymying Migmar," Jimmy said.

"Shield it with Dark Arts, and it's useless," continued Eragor, "or just do this." The General dropped the crystal on the floor, and in one swift motion of his warhammer, he pulverized the talisman into powder on the marble floor. A small wisp of red smoke emanated from the floor and then vanished.

"Well, Migmar will be happy now," said Johnny. The others smiled at this fortunate turn of events. "*Thank Ellos,*" Kat said among them.

"So," Tommy held out his hand to Eragor, "the cease fire holds until the very moment we are all back in Allyra and the final portal is closed for good. Do you accept our terms?"

The Gwar reached out as well. "On behalf of our combined forces, I accept—ughnn!" Eragor lurched forward, arched his back, and spat blood. Three Drefid talons pierced his chest.

"Traitor!" a voice rasped. The Drefid appeared behind Eragor and shoved the Gwar off his claws. "You are a pack mule! Nothing more! How dare you take authority here. Lord Asp's plans will not be violated! I, Cyndred, will see to that!"

Tommy drew his sword and stepped forward.

The Drefid held out his arms and his extended claws kindled red, shrouded in writhing, whirling sparks of crimson. "Stand aside, Elf!" Cyndred commanded. "You may strike me down, but you cannot stop what we have begun. Even now, eighteen trains are hurtling toward massively populated human cities. Each of these trains is loaded with the very same venom that turned Asp into the power that he was! When these trains reach their destinations, they will detonate...and the Dark

Arts will rule here on Earth as it is in Allyra!"

Suddenly, Jett lunged at the Drefid. Cyndred's clawed fists came up fast, but not fast enough. Jett intercepted both of the Drefid's arms at the wrists and began to squeeze. "Tell us which trains!" Jett demanded.

"You cannot stop them!" Cyndred hissed.

Jett's grip constricted even more, producing audible cracks and pops. "WHICH...TRAINS?"

Cyndred's voice cracked into an anguished wail. "You are doomed! The trains, the missiles, the Tide—one way or the other, you are all doomed!"

"What missiles?" Jett demanded, beginning to twist the Drefid's wrists.

The Drefid's agonized shriek transformed into a maniacal laugh. Jett wrenched his arms. There was a loud, wet *SNAP!* Cyndred screeched, and his clawed fists fell limp. Jett shoved him into the crowd of Gwar soldiers.

They threw the Drefid to the ground. A scarred and still-bleeding Gwar stepped out of the crowd. He hoisted an enormous battle hammer into the air and brought it crashing down on the Drefid's skull.

"Pack mule, bah!" the Gwar grumbled. He spat on Cyndred's remains and then looked back to Tommy. "With any luck," he said, "that puts an end to any further interruptions. Now, Elf, what do we have to do?"

/

The Elven Lords and the Gwar leaders had gone in search of the train station's communications center. From there they intended to contact Migmar and the others in Canada and begin the process of opening portals to evacuate all Allyrans from Earth.

Taeva stood near the information center, half in sunlight from the

high window and half in the shadow of the golden clock. There were so
many variables that her mind could barely track them all. After many
dark years of waiting and plotting, she'd exacted her revenge on Asp. But
that had only been one part of the plan. The other...lay within reach. Her
eyes stole down to Asp's body.

His head and body were unnaturally contorted. His mouth was
open. Venom dribbled from his pronounced fangs.

But do I still want this? she asked herself. She had no definite answer.
The Taladrim were all but gone. And what of the Elves? The Lords had
been kind...foolishly trusting, even. The door might still be open in
Berinfell; Tommy certainly extended their number to *Eight* just a moment
ago...on her account. *He still believed.* But then again, the Elves had much
to answer for as well.

Taeva couldn't decide, and so she chose to delay the decision. But
that meant taking some action now. She reached into the drawstring
satchel at her hip and withdrew a small stoppered vial. She knelt swiftly
to Asp's side, turned his head and placed the vial beneath one fang, then
the other, until the vial was nearly full. Then, she stoppered the vial and
hid it from sight.

Each generation gets stronger, she reminded herself. Her mother was
first to endure the Dark Arts venom. And, in her body, it became more
potent. *She bit the Spider King who became a mighty force. He, in turn, gave his
strengthened venom to Asp. And now,* she thought, *I have the most powerful
venom of all.*

Taeva left the shaft of sunlight and walked into the shadows to
await the Lords' return.

Turning the Tide

BENGFIST AND Jast stood mere feet away from their enemies. Separated by a transparent blue film that sizzled and popped, neither force dared cross it for fear of where it would take them.

"How long will it hold?" Bengfist asked Migmar without looking over his shoulder.

"Enough, long," replied the Gnome.

A voice crackled over the communications system. *"Migmar, are you there?"*

Migmar lowered the mic to his lips and searched the monitors. "Yes, Tommy. Migmar this is. Good it is, hearing your voice."

"And yours, friend. Listen, I need a favor. A whole lot of them actually."

Tommy filled Migmar in as fast as he could, detailing the eighteen subway cars headed out of New York City, the remaining pockets of Asp's forces scattered across the globe, and even the airborn nuclear missiles he suspected were headed for the US, which—up until a few moments ago—he and the others knew nothing about. *That could have been a real bummer,* Tommy noted to himself. *Thank Ellos for Cyndred's big mouth.*

"See them, I do," said Migmar about the missiles, noting the small orange blips traversing over the globe. "Three to the north, two more from the east, and three from the west, I see." Migmar quickly realized

Tommy's plan was flawless: the portals would disintegrate the inorganic composition of the missiles and the trains, and easily usher every pocket of Asp's forces to whatever destination they desired. Migmar muttered under his breath, wishing he could send the lot of them into a volcano as he'd done before.

"*Get those first,*" said Tommy, speaking of the nukes. Migmar's impish fingers flew across the keys, eyes tracking coordinates and maps. "*Migmar? Please tell me you're making progress.*" There was only heavy breathing in the mic. "*Migmar?*"

Migmar pushed *Enter.* "Lord Tommy," he said, spinning his chair around and glancing at the globe. Even Bengfist and Jast stepped away from their growling enemies and eyed the glowing orb. The three of them watched as, one by one, the orange lights representing the missiles disappeared. "It is done."

"He got the missiles!" Tommy turned around with a fist raised in the air. The small group of leaders around him gave a shout, even the Gwar leaders were enthusiastic...which was saying something, as they didn't even know what nuclear missiles were. Then Tommy cupped the ear piece with the palm of his hand and signaled Migmar. "The trains?"

"*Pushy, Elves are,*" Migmar grumbled. A few minutes passed, and then, Migmar said, "*Gone, the trains are.*"

Tommy gave a thumbs up to all who hung on the news. "Finally, all Allyrans, Migmar. We all must go home. But not before—"

"All the humans are free, your lordship," interrupted one of the Gwar Commanders, tired from a long run from deep within the bowels of the station. "Just as you ordered."

"Thank you, Commander." Then Tommy looked to the newly appointed-by-default Gwar General, Teneth Kilmauran, and had him call his team leaders from the mobile communication device.

"I'm going to miss this place," said Johnny, looking around Grand Central. "Well, I mean, not *this place*."

"I know what you mean," said Kat. "It's been home for us all. At least, it *was* home. But knowing we...we..."

"We can never come back," Kiri Lee finished. "Yeah, that's hard." She took a deep breath.

Tommy was listening to the headset. "Migmar says Asp's forces are all walking into the portals he's opening," he said. "Good job, General."

The team cheered again. It felt so good for things to be going right. Tommy looked at each of his teammates, even to Taeva; he was so proud of them, proud to be counted among them. He didn't know what awaited them in Berinfell, but seeing this chapter come to a close was bitter sweet. To leave Earth—to know he'd never be back, he'd never be here to help these nations recover from their tragic loses—was something he'd never get used to. But to save everyone, even to save himself, it had to be done.

Minutes passed. An hour. Two. The hands on Grand Central Terminal's famous clock went round several times. "Almost done," Migmar said.

Tommy sighed and watched the shadows lengthen on the terminal floor. It seemed like an eternity, and Tommy couldn't help but wonder how many people were dying on Earth while Allyrans lingered. He tried not to allow another thought, but it insisted. When they returned to Allyra, would Berinfell still stand? The Nemic or the Tide...either way, there was a very real possibility that the Lords would be orphaned once more.

"We won't be orphans," Kat whispered into Tommy's mind.

How do you know? Tommy asked.

"Because we were never orphans to begin with. We are Ellos' children."

If sunshine could beam its golden rays within, if it could warm and sustain from the inside out, then that is precisely how Tommy felt.

Kat's words were beyond true. They were transforming.

Tommy smiled at his friends and listened to the ear piece for the signal that would end his final moments on a planet he'd so come to love. He looked at Kat's face, so beautiful and unique; a face he'd fallen in love with if he was honest with himself. Johnny's face, large and strong and faithful. Autumn's, like smooth porcelain. Kiri Lee's, dignified and ever delicate. Jimmy's, pale and speckled, yet always alert. And Jett's, rich and formidable. Even for all her elusive ways, Taeva's face—mysterious and exotic—she was still one of them. And they'd won. They'd done it.

"*Here you go,*" came Migmar's voice in Tommy's ear. A massive blue portal erupted above the main steps in the station. The entire army turned to address it and obeyed orders to march through.

In less than five minutes the entire force had retreated back to Allyra, arriving exactly where Kilmauran had specified. The Eight walked the General to the portal to see him off.

"Don't think this let's you off the hook, Elf," said Kilmauran.

"I wouldn't dream of it," Tommy replied with a grin. "And don't think we won't defend ourselves."

The General smiled. "I wouldn't have it any other way." He stepped through the portal, and both he and it vanished without a trace.

A beat later and a new, smaller portal arrived in its place. Tommy checked with Migmar just to confirm their arrival location. "And make sure your exit takes out the command center."

"*Bengfist asks if the mountain leveled you wish.*"

"Negative," said Tommy. "I think the Canadians are partial to it."

"*Understood.*" With that, Migmar signed off for good and Tommy heard the ear piece go silent.

Tommy looked to the others with a tired, but genuine smile. "Time to go home," he said. "This time for good."

✳

The portal spit the Seven and Taeva out in the Lords' Throne Room, the very chamber where all this had begun so many ages ago. They'd been taken as infants, now they returned for good as Lords. Migmar, Bengfist and Jast arrived a moment later, then both portals vaporized in unison.

The group looked around at each other.

"We're home," said Autumn, and took a deep breath.

"And home is still here," Tommy said. "Thank you, Ellos."

But the revelry was short lived. Though faint, the group could hear something in the distance.

"Shouting," said Jimmy. "Lots of shouting."

"Under attack, you are," said Migmar.

Tommy reached for his sword, but it'd been swallowed by the portals. "Quickly! To the ramparts!"

The team rushed from the Throne Room, and ran down the main corridor to the outside where the voices of thousands upon thousands of Elves hollered in the darkness.

"Up, up!" Tommy yelled, heading for the stone steps. As soon as they mounted, they noticed a radiant light spilling over the city from the west. And all below them, Elves and what looked to be Nemic retreated to the east in terror.

"THE TIDE!" Autumn pointed. "But I thought it'd be finished!"

"As did we all," Tommy growled. He ran a hand through his curly hair, mumbling under his breath. He watched in horror as the Tide was slowly consuming the westernmost flanks of his beloved Berinfell. The city's main wall was gone, and now dwellings were disappearing. Tommy could only assume the sight of so many Nemic meant they'd attacked in his absence; but whatever war had been waged it'd prematurely ceased for a far more deadly foe, one that did not discriminate. "I—I don't understand."

"Time it takes," said Migmar. "Wait and see."

"Or maybe we missed some of Asp's army?" surmised Kiri Lee.

"Impossible," Migmar said. "All of them I snatched. You'll see. You'll see."

Suddenly Kat took off running. "Kat!" Tommy yelled after her. "Where are you going?"

"It's Grimwarden!" she hollered over her shoulder. "He's—he's almost gone!"

"What?!" Jimmy replied.

"She must have heard his thoughts," Tommy said. "Come on!" The team raced back down the rampart stairs and twisted around through the main gate. Kat was a good twenty paces ahead of them, darting off the main thoroughfare and zigzagging down side streets. But she was heading dangerously close to the Tide.

"Kat!" Tommy yelled. "Watch where you're going!" All he heard in reply was a faint, "I know."

When the others thought Kat had completely lost her mind and was about to walk head-on into the Tide, she stopped at the entrance of a narrow street. The rest of the team caught up with her as she knelt before two figures, and a third half the size.

"Grimwarden!" Tommy yelled. "Goldarrow!" The couple lay in a growing pool of blood with a Gnome swaddled nearby in Goldarrow's cloak. There was so much red that no one could be sure exactly who was injured and who wasn't.

Migmar rushed toward the fading face of Thorkber. "Stay with me you shall," pleaded Migmar, holding the weak Gnome's face in his pudgy hands.

"Oh Kat! Tommy!" said Goldarrow, her face sparking to life at the sight of all the Lords. "Praise Ellos! I was sure we'd perish here!"

"What, what happened?" asked Kat.

"No time," replied Goldarrow. "If that doesn't devour us first, there will be plenty to tell." She pointed a blood-soaked hand toward the wall of dazzling light now towering over them.

"Quick!" ordered Tommy. "We've got to get them out of here!" He picked up Grimwarden with Johnny's help; at first Grimwarden's chest was so still, Tommy thought he was dead. Jett helped Goldarrow to her feet, relieving her of Thorkber.

The team made a slow retreat on Grimwarden's account. Too slow. The Tide was gaining on them. Entire homes were vanishing in the wake of the radiant wall.

A weak Grimwarden tried talking: "Leave...me..."

"Not today," replied Tommy. "Not any day, for that matter. We'll make it. Keep moving everyone!" But every time the team took a turn onto a street that ran parallel with the Tide, the wall moved closer.

It was chewing through the building directly beside them now, and their next turn away from the Veil was still forty paces ahead at best.

"We're not going to make it," said Jimmy.

Tommy glanced at him. "Was that a *we're not going to make it* because our pace is slow, or Jimmy's gift telling us we're *actually not going to make it*?"

"I'm just saying," replied Jimmy with a fatalistic shrug.

The Tide was a few feet from entering into the street.

Tommy looked ahead: twenty-five paces. "Whoever can get down that street, leave now! Autumn, that's you first!"

"No way! If one dies, we all die," she shouted.

"Autumn!" Tommy roared, his body heaving Goldarrow along. "GET OUT OF HERE!" As soon as he spoke, there was a thud behind them.

"For crying out loud!" Kat exclaimed. She'd fallen to the ground and smacked her head on the stones. She tried to get up but her limbs wouldn't obey; she squeezed her eyes shut against the pain and saw stars twinkling behind her lids. Fresh blood sprang from a gash on her forehead.

"Take her, Johnny!" Tommy said, passing all of Goldarrow's weight to him. "Keep going!"

"Leave me!" Kat said, rising to all fours, dazed.

The Veil was in the street now, less then six feet away. No heat, no noise, just dazzling light that left an abyss in its wake.

"I'm not leaving you, Kat. Ever. I love you," Tommy said.

Kat raised her head and stared at him. The wall of light made his eyes glow. She didn't know what to say, but at least they'd have eternity to talk about it.

Tommy knelt before her and pulled her close. They'd never make the turn now. And the rest of the team had lost enough time turning back to see what the commotion was that they wouldn't make it either.

Tommy wiped the blood and hair off Kat's face, then kissed her. "Had I to do it over again, I'd have asked you to marry me a lot sooner."

Kat cried. Tears of joy, letting them run freely down her face. Then she laughed. "Thank you."

"Thank you?" Tommy questioned. "For what?"

The Tide was three feet away now.

"For loving me just the way I am."

The Elven leaders, those who replaced Grimwarden and Goldarrow in their absence and presumed death, reluctantly gave the order to abandon the city in light of the destructive wall sweeping in from the west. Whatever Nemic invaders remained were given a wide birth to flee with the rest of the living, their treacherous assault all but forgotten though only hours old. Yes, the Elves had beaten them, but not even they wished this mystical fate upon their neighbors to the south.

The shouts and cries of Flet soldiers, parents and children filled the city. There was no escaping the slow-moving wall of light that chased them, and no guarantee it would stop in Berinfell. It certainly wasn't a Nemic creation of war, as they were just as terrified. This was surely one of Asp's doings.

"Flee to the east!" was the only order passed through the Elven city, with no destination in mind. *Just east*. It passed from home to home, family to family, until every living soul was on their way, flooding the city gates with whatever they could carry.

More than half the city had been successfully evacuated when the strangest of things occurred. All at once, as if someone snuffed out the faintest fire on the thinnest of wicks, the wall of light vanished.

Gone. The Tide of Unmaking had disappeared.

The sudden presence of complete darkness silenced the living with a corporate exhale of wonder. No one moved. Nothing stirred.

Just stillness.

Then the whispers began. No one dared speak it too loudly in case their pronouncement should curse providence and summon the heinous blaze back to life. But as the moments ticked by, the Elves' assurance that the deadly wonder had truly ceased took root, and whispers became murmurs became statements became declarations became celebration. Whatever *it* was, it was no more. And they only had Ellos to thank.

But had they known of who the real heroes were in that moment, they would have uttered the names of their champions along with that of their Great God.

44

Revisiting the Past

THE ELVES reentered their beloved city slowly at first, worried that the mysterious aberration might pop back to life one step in front of them. But with each passing minute that peace remained over Berinfell, the inhabitants' confidence grew, and their steps became more swift.

It was the bravest of these souls who first noticed a bedraggled band of Elves, two Gnomes, a Gwar Overlord, a Saer Shardbearer and a giant wolf walking out of the dust. They appeared like spirits at first, half-hidden in the twilight hours of dawn, creeping down a side street in the shadows of the western portion of the city; but soon their fleshly disposition was confirmed by the sight of blood and the sounds of coughing.

"Well, don't just stand there, fetch us some water! These are heroes of Berinfell!"

"Y-y-yes Lord Felheart!" said an astonished young flet soldier. "Right away, your lordship!"

Soon a crowed had gathered, and that's when the cheering began, with no one quite sure when, if ever, it stopped. The sight of the Lords and Guardmasters and beloved Gnomes emerging from the ruins of Berinfell turned the city into a hysterical, thriving celebration that lasted for weeks.

And then some.

The palace was emptied of food and drink for the benefit of all, and every home in the city became a sought-out destination, with family after family bidding one another congratulations and exulting in their world's good fortune, delivered down from the Mighty Hand of Ellos.

And at the center of it all were the Lords and their noble kinsfolk, who would be heralded for all time as the Redeemers of Berinfell, second only to the Great Redeemer Himself. Their names would never be forgotten, but rather championed and lauded in stories and books for all time, as they still are to this day.

Taeva had enjoyed the celebrating as much as anyone, or at least as much as a foreigner could in an all-Elven world. True, she was accepted as part-Elven, and forgiven for whatever wrongs she had appeared to enact while operating on her own. And she was even allowed to keep her title, albeit an honorary one; *the Seven, plus One*, it was often mused. But still, there was a restlessness in her that no embrace, no kind word, could quell.

A week had passed and the constant din of music and laughter had numbed her. Without so much as a soul noticing, she took her leave and slipped out of Berinfell. She knew exactly where she needed to go.

Vesper Crag was dark, even in broad daylight. And now that it was utterly abandoned with Asp's Gwar armies resettling their homelands, it seemed even darker. *Profound emptiness,* Taeva thought. This mountain had soaked in the blood of many, and had housed within it unspeakable evil.

Which was exactly why she needed to go back.

Taeva knew she had to go to the very heart of it all—to the last place her mother had breathed air. She didn't know what she'd find, but something called her. Perhaps it was the secret she held inside her belt even now.

She hiked the mountainside in fading light, the storm clouds gathering over the Lightning Plains for their evening display. The first bolt kissed the ground far below her with a deafening crack, washing the entire mountain face in white light. There, just above her, was the gaping mouth of the Crag, set like the yawning jaws of a lion. Taeva stole herself to enter the black labyrinth and soon found a discarded pile of torches. She weaved some electricity around the shards of canvas and pitch until they were lit, then held the firelight above her head.

She'd never been here, not since she was an infant, and as such her mind told her she was a fool for coming. Surely this place was an unimaginable lair of unending routes and chambers that not even an Elven map could adequately articulate.

Still, something prompted her...begged her onward.

Taeva moved deeper inside the mountain, her heart leading her forward whenever she confronted a fork in the path. Eventually she came to a high set of stairs, rotten and tarnished with years of neglect, but surely grand in their day. They led into a series of ornate parlors, each decorated with lush tapestries and thick carpets, though by the smell, mildew and mold had taken their toll.

At last she came to a small room with a large chair in the middle. It faced a wide picture window. And beyond? A massive empty space that not even her torch could illuminate. Her free hand touched the chair, and then she moved to the viewing window.

A chill went up Taeva's spine. *Something's alive in here. Or once was*, she thought. Perhaps *it* was what called her, from the realm of the living…or the dead.

She shuddered—then lost her grip on the torch. She fumbled with the shaft, almost burning herself, but dropped it out the window. The fire slipped down a long, sloping stone surface before striking the ground and spinning to a halt some fifty yards below.

"You've got to be kidding," she said, her voice echoing out in the vast expanse. Other than weaving lightning for the thirty minutes it took her to get in here, her only light source for getting back out was now a long way down. And yet it seemed like the fire called her.

Taeva straddled the window sill then swung both legs over the side, palms against the steep slope under her. "Here goes nothing," she muttered. She gave herself a little shove forward, and within seconds she was speeding along much faster than she liked.

Her clothes hummed along the smooth stone surface, all the while her body braced for impact as the torch raced up toward her.

Taeva's legs crumpled into her chest as her joints smashed against the stone floor. She tumbled into a heap, pain jarring her limbs, chest and head to the point she had trouble catching her breath.

Finally, she managed to sit up and assess herself. *No broken bones.* The torch was about fifteen feet away from her, having skittered a little farther than she had. She crawled forward on all fours and reached for it.

Her hand came up short.

There, on the wall in the glow of the fire light, was a drawing. A very strange drawing. Carved into the granite with deep lines was the image of a large spider, *uniquely female*, Taeva thought. And hidden within the lines, as if intentionally kept out of sight, was a baby.

A baby girl.

"It's me," Taeva whispered. Her fingers touched the heavy marks, and tears flooded her eyes. She wiped them away to keep visual contact with the drawing, but it was nearly impossible. Somehow she knew— she knew her mother had made this. *Even in her imprisonment, her enslavement...she still thought of me.*

She ran her arm across her nose and cheeks, trying desperately to compose herself. The torch flickered, and her eye caught a glimpse of more markings.

Another drawing.

This one showed the spider asleep. No, worse. *Dead.* Taeva didn't know how she knew it was so, she just did. And the baby girl was no longer an infant...she was an adult. Strong. With long hair. Though the drawing was crude, Taeva sensed innate beauty in the form.

But the woman was also powerful, and she stood on top of a mountain with lightning bolts dancing around her.

Taeva's fingers brushed over the lines reverently. For all she knew, this was her mother's resting place. The very air Taeva breathed now could have been last inhaled by her mother. The connection was strong, she could feel it.

"Is this me, Mother?" Taeva asked aloud. "Was this what you saw me as?" *Strong. Beautiful. Powerful.* That's when Taeva withdrew the secret in her belt.

The vial of Asp's venom.

The glass tube seemed to burn in her hand. She noticed she was still crying a little, and her arms shook.

"I would be...the most powerful yet..." she muttered to herself. She looked back at the picture. The picture *of her* standing atop Vesper Crag. *Victorious.*

The Elves. *What about the Elves?* They had shown her acceptance, even genuine concern at the loss of her people. No, not her people. *The Taladrim.* A noble race, but not *her people.* This was her people, here. Her mother's bloodline, her father's. The Dark Arts that surely coursed through her veins. She could rule everything.

"I could end this all," she whispered. "No more war, no more death." She let the little vial roll around in her hand, feeling the heat of it kiss her flesh. This was Asp's venom, yes, but it came from her mother, from her father. It was *alive*. And it belonged in her.

She held the vial aloft and stared into its depths.

The Seven sat beneath the stars on a grand portico gathered around a flaming brazier. The summer night was alive with the sounds of the woods, and throughout the city the valiant tales of epic battles as told by minstrel bards rang out. They enjoyed evening drinks atop the heaps of food that sat in their bellies from a long night of feasting, no thanks in part to Mumthers' beloved handiwork.

"May we join you?" asked Grimwarden, escorting a very lovely Goldarrow on his arm.

"Why of course!" Tommy exclaimed, standing with the others in honor of their beloved friends. Jett and Johnny pulled over more chairs as Goldarrow was seated and Grimwarden limped to his designated chair.

"You're very kind," he said to Jett, laying his cane across his thighs.

"Feeling stronger?" asked Jett.

"A little everyday, thanks to you," Grimwarden replied.

"It's my honor, Guardmaster. I expect you to be walking on your own within the week," said Jett.

Grimwarden leaned in. "Let's not make it too fast," he said, "lest Goldarrow here stop doting on me." Everyone had a good laugh with Goldarrow casting him a sly smile.

A short time later Taeva joined them as did a few others. Regis strode over and casually sat on the arm of Jimmy's chair, and Mr. Charlie took a seat on the floor close to the fire. Bengfist and Jast walked in later, both opting to stand, and Migmar and Thorkber shared a single chair. The night carried on with toasts and laughter, recounting of stories both old and new, and endeared itself to all of them as one of their more memorable nights. One they'd soon not forget—Grimwarden would make certain of that.

"Well, well, before I head off to bed, as it's been a fine evening you've provided us, my Lords," he dipped his head in deference, "I confess that I have a small gift I've been saving for you." Grimwarden's face grew a bit solemn. "I'd feared I might not be able to give it to you. And surely I wouldn't have, had it not been for the students I trained back in Whitehall who have saved my life—saved all of our lives—on more than one occasion."

"Whitehall," Kat reminisced. "Those were wonderful days." The group all nodded.

"Indeed they were," Grimwarden continued. "And it's from Whitehall that this gift comes."

"Oh? How do you mean?" inquired Tommy

Grimwarden sat back a little in his chair and took a deep breath. "There was an exercise I had you do, the very first one, as I recall." He looked among the Lords, waiting.

"The blind walk," Autumn piped up. "In the cave!"

"The very same," Grimwarden confirmed.

"I got so mad at you, Johnny," said Autumn.

"We all got mad at each other, as I recall," added Jimmy. "We were a ramshackle lot, we were."

"You were, you were," laughed Grimwarden.

"And I never heard the end of it," Goldarrow added. "He brought that one up every day for weeks!" The group chuckled.

"So did you ever wonder?" Grimwarden asked. The group grew silent, looking at each other. "Well, did you?"

Johnny wrinkled his brow, and asked, "Wonder about what?"

"Why, wonder what was in the clay pot I had you retrieve, of course."

"The clay pot!" exclaimed Kiri Lee. "I'd totally forgotten about that!" Everyone else nodded in agreement, excited that Grimwarden might soon tell them.

"Are you going to tell us?" Kat felt like she was thirteen again. "Are you?"

Grimwarden just smiled.

"Well, are you?" asked Johnny.

"No, no, I suppose not," replied Grimwarden, to which the group replied with a rumpus round of cajoling and clapping. "Easy now, easy now," said Grimwarden, trying to get everyone to settle down, all the while clearly enjoying the process. "I'll not tell you anything. But I will show you."

And with that, Grimwarden reached inside his cloak and produced a single, white piece of paper, holding it gently in his lap face down. It had some strange marking on the back, Tommy noticed.

That's when Grimwarden flipped it around for all to see. It was a post card, with a picture of Earth taken from the Hubble Space Telescope.

All at once the Lords held their breath and slowly got out of their seats. They moved reverently toward Grimwarden and knelt around his chair like children marveling at a bedtime story.

The sight of Earth, suspended in all her glory amidst the star-speckled black depths of space, brought tears to each of their eyes.

"Where—where did you get this?" Tommy asked, clearing his throat.

"You had it all along?" asked Kat.

"While we were hunting for you, I found it in a shop. I was struck with the beauty of the planet Ellos made, and that the human race developed technologies that allowed them to see it from His perspective."

Grimwarden flipped the card over for himself to see. "It's so sad that their kind have the ability to see it just as He sees, yet still refuse to believe He cares about them." The old war hero shook his head. "Anyway, I didn't know how things would go at the time, but I thought you should remember the world that Ellos saved you on."

Kat reached for the post card, receiving it from Grimwarden as if handling a page of text from the original Berinfell Prophecies. *"It's so beautiful,"* she said as if too many words might make it disappear. Looking up to him, she added, "Thank you, Grimwarden. We will cherish it always." Kat flipped it over and read the printed text in caption.

"Go ahead," Grimwarden said, "read it aloud."

Kat swallowed, then mustered her strength. *"For by Him were all things created, that are in heaven, and that are in the Earth, visible and invisible, whether they be thrones, or dominions, or principalities, or powers: all things were created by Him, and for Him: and by Him all things consist."* Kat sat back. "Colossians 1:16-17," she finished.

"Thank you, Grimwarden," Tommy said, echoed by all the others. "While we know we can never go back, somehow, this helps a great deal. And we will never forget."

"Nor should you," said Grimwarden. "How fitting that you had to work together, fighting your way through darkness, to bring me a clay vessel that housed the Earth, only for you to *be* clay vessels that saved the Earth in the midst of great darkness. Such was your call from the very beginning."

The Seven sat for a long time, gathered there at Grimwarden's feet, starring into the fire and getting lost in the stars above. It had been an adventure they'd never forget.

"I would'na trade it for anything," said Jimmy finally. "It was all worth it."

"That it was," said Tommy.

It was Kat who sat holding the post card for a long time. She muttered something under her breath.

"What'd you say?" asked Tommy.

"Sorry, it was nothing," Kat brushed it off.

"No, really. What'd you say, Kat?"

Kat sighed. "Well, I was just thinking. We've become something, you know. We were nobodies, and now look at us. Lords of Berinfell, saving whole planets. So I just got to wondering about *them*."

"Them?" asked Kiri Lee.

"Yeah," Kat held up the post card. "This story isn't over. Not here. Not back on Earth. I just wonder what the next generation will become."

THE END

TO OUR READERS

This is the end . . .
. . . but the stories have just begun.

From the very beginning, we never felt that this story was our own. By virtue of the fact that we were co-writing these books, there has always seemed to be a strong sense of community surrounding *The Berinfell Prophecies*. From the many real people, places and circumstances that inspired us, to the Elves of The Underground who helped shape the plot and encourage us along the way, these stories were never *owned*. They were *shared*.

As a result, we are doing something that has never been done before in the history of publishing, at least in as much as we know. We are turning *The Berinfell Prophecies* over to you, our faithful readers.

We believe there are far more authors out there who the world needs to hear from than the traditional publishing model has ever allowed. With the astonishing rise of self-publishing from *vanity publishing* to *preferred solution for established authors*, it's never been easier to reach people with stories than it is today.

We've purposefully left a number of threads undone in this final installment in the hopes that those writers, perhaps even *you*, would pick up where we left off...that you'll pen the tales we never could.

Like any true *passing of the mantle*, there are a few guidelines we insist you follow. Should you choose to self-publish a work of your own, it's imperative that you apply the same values we have in developing books:

1. **Work hard on writing-craft.** Like artisans of old, we believe that fine art comes from dedication to the respective disciplines of the trade. We're not perfect writers, but together we've penned *tens of thousands* of words in our joint collection of titles. This represents *years* of our lives. We read good writers (and avoid bad ones), study their styles and adopt sound habits. We meet together with other writers and share our work for critical review. Don't have a writing group in your area? Start one yourself. Look for others in your family, your church or your school who share similar passions, and make a point to connect with them. Be truthful, and say everything with kindness.

2. **Let lots of eyes read your manuscript.** Once you've written what you feel is a Berinfell-worthy book, put it in the hands of others. Save your money and let a qualified editor read it and pick it apart (it will be one of the best investments you ever make); we both have editors who we recommend and you can always ask around The Underground. With or without an editor, you should also gather a group of Proofies like we do. These are readers who are very familiar with the story, and can point out everything from plot and formatting inconsistencies, to bad grammar, to poor sentence structure. Your goal should be to make your manuscript as clean as you can, knowing it will never be *perfect*… that's because it's *art*.

3. **Create a strong end product.** There are many tools available to you to help create both physical and digital books, with more emerging all the time. But trial and error and your critical eye will be techniques that ensure your final presentation to the public is a good one. Now, we don't expect every Berinfell story from this point on to look and feel exactly like ours; they need to be your own. But they always must strive for excellence, which is simply *doing the best with what you have in the time you have it*. We recommend using the services of BookJolt.com if you do

not have knowledge of formatting books for print or e-readers. There is also a wealth of information that outlines exactly what we've done for *The Tide of Unmaking* in Christopher's ebook on how to self-publish your manuscript (see christopherhopper.com for more details). The steps are not hard, but they do require time and dedication. By taking your time to produce solid material for readers, you'll take major steps in ensuring the long-term success of your story and building an audience that wants to read what you have to say.

So have at it! You have our expressed written permission. These characters, these places, these themes are all yours. Dream, write, publish. Do what we never could, and go further than we are today. Our hope is that an entire library of *Berinfell Prophecies* will emerge over the coming years, and that the threads of truth in them all will bring people closer to knowing the Savior of the world.

Endurance and Victory!

Wayne Thomas Batson and Christopher Hopper

Thursday, August 16, 2012
Eldersburg, MD and Clayton, NY, USA

ACKNOWLEDGMENTS

From WTB and CH:

To all the Elves of The Underground: Endurance and Victory! Special thanks to the continued inspiration and enthusiasim of EaglesWings, Goldarrow, Millard, The Seventh Sleeper, Jake, TAK, SciFiAuthor, Chris, Vrenith, Hark, The Golux, Manny, Brianna, Anduril, Seth, Anna, SilverLake, Alastrina, Jared, Pingpong, ElvenPrincess, Squeaks, Seth E, and Olivia—as always, you rock!

To our publicist, agent, and friend, Gregg Wooding—we are forever in your debt for getting publishing doors to open, keeping them open, and encouraging us when they close. God's richest blessings to you, our friend.

A special thanks to Thomas Nelson Publishing (Laura Minchew and AnnJanette Toth in particular) for inviting Christopher and I to write together on this series and for allowing us continue it with *The Tide of Unmaking*. Thank you to editors Beverly Phillips and June Ford for helping us make the first two books of the series sparkle. Christopher and I truly hope we've continued the story with quality storytelling and high standards that would make you all proud.

A shout out to our fellow Spearheaders, Christopher and Allan

Miller in Seattle, and to the amazing Athena Dean: you've been a tremendous source of encouragement and a boon of knowledge in the leap to self-publishing. We truly cherish you three.

To Rachel Harris, Marisa Miranda, and Ryan Paige Howard, thank you for all the help promoting the books...and for being cool.

Facebook Fans (esspecially Jamie Gil): thanks for making sure this book got finished by frequently offering threats of great torture as penalty for NOT finishing it.

Special thanks to the fine establishments that have allowed us to darken their doorstep with our laptops and consume tables all day and all night: Barley Creek Tavern in the Poconos, The Banshee and Backyard Ale House in Scranton, the Brickstore in Atlanta, the Blind Pig in Champaign, O'Llordan's in Westminster, Martin's Grocery and Panera Bread here in Eldersburg, and probably a dozen other places.

Jeff Hanson, Squid.org, Sam Stoddard at Rinkworks, and The Donjon for making the coolest fantasy name generators on the planet!

Lastly, to our faithful Proofies, who made sure we stayed on track and kept the manuscript sparkling: Jake Buller, Tim Vehrs, Sarah Pennington, Glade, Noah Arsenault (Winter's Read), Abigail Goenner, Emma McPhee, and the infamous Billy Jepma – your names will be forever emblazed on this manuscript (aka: bragging rights for life).

From WTB:

To my Wife: thank you for supporting this new venture of ours. To leave the safety of conventional publishing is both wonderful and scary, and I couldn't take the risk without you supporting me. By God's mighty grace, we have weathered a very stormy season of life. Through it all, your devotion to God and to me is a blessing I can scarcely describe. I love you. 1C13

Kayla, Tommy, Bryce, and Rachel: God bless you, young

adventurers. Boys, may you be tender warriors for the Lord, and girls, swordmaidens for truth. You aren't little kids anymore, which makes me sad. But at the same time, I know this is really where God's amazing plans for you will begin to take shape. I can't wait. Thank you for putting up with your author Dad so that I can pursue God's plan for me on this giant spinning mudball. I love you.

Mom and Dad: Thank you for your continuing support of me, my family, and my books. Thank you for setting such a great example of marriage and companionship. And…let's play cards soon. Much love!

Leslie, Jeff, and Brian—So grateful for you and your families! Stoked to watch your adventures unfold!

To dear friends/family: Ed, Deanna, Diana, Andy, Lorraine, Olin, Jordan, Christian, Matthew, Tyler, Abigail, Deborah, Annalise, Daniel, Samuel, Nikki, Ashley, Dillon, Patti (Lil Tyler), Sadie, Lochlan, Kaitlin, Josh, Kaleb, Luke, and Lydia. Dave, Heather, Doug, Christine, Chris, Dawn, Mat, Serrina, Susan, Alaina, Chris, Leslie, Jeff, Eric, Alex, Noelle, Todd, Dan, Warren, and so many others who enrich this adventure.

To Bill Russell: thank you for believing in BIG things. In you, I've always seen reflected the fact that God is not small, nor weak, nor shortsighted. He is mighty. He is spectacularly HUGE and is willing to include us in the greatest plan the world has ever known. Iron sharpens iron, bro.

To the administrators, faculty and staff, my friends at Folly Quarter Middle, thank you for never settling for less than the best for our students. Thank you for the incredible support and understanding, knowing that I am a man divided by three passions: family, teaching, and writing. Each one of you inspire me to be better at all three.

To my students, past and present: 22 years times @120 students per year. Whoa! That is a lot of kids. Please know that I am grateful for every one of you. You are dynamic, intelligent, magnificently strange…and you are all precious to me. Thank you for reading my stories…even before they were actually any good. Pip pip cheerio!

Sir Christopher Hopper: can you believe it? By God's grace we've penned a trilogy together. Howzzat for coolness, eh? What a strange adventure this has been. I'm so grateful for your friendship and steadfast faith. I'm a little bummed not to be teaming up with you again, but seriously stoked to see you turn your fiction voice loose with your next several novels.

Thanks to Bob Vogel for listening to all my new "doubt bombs." Your wisdom has given me peace and stability.

To David Larson for smoking me in a Word War. Dude has speedy fingers.

To the Thrice Blessed Starseekers - **Icemen**: Jake, Elizabeth H, Livia Hess, Merry, Allissie, Ciara, Lauren, MaryanneM, Malorieke, and Kendra; **Lumenos**: Anna G, EmilyJ, Talfagoron, Tari Verya, Christina D, Silver Angel, Ciara, SuperSmiles, and Loranna Skyfire; **Phoenix**: Aaralyn, Varon, Adam D, Mary D, Maggie Q, Xyno Xyaxis, ElizabethC, Destiny Fire, and Theodora 'Eru Nenharma' Ashcraft; **Pureline**: Silverlake, Aarathyn, Ethaecia, Aaron W, Qaosqar, Eyes of Fire, Staci, and Melanie; **Silvertree**: Abigail M. Goenner, Rachel (RAMH), Caitlyn "Earendil" Gehman, Nathan R. Petrie, Noah Arsenault (Winter's Read), Henry Hollow, and Chayal Dresdove; **StarryElite**: Wolf-Dragon-blade, Elven Princess, Jaryn, Sunflower, Winterbane, Lady Clumsy, FlyingFalcon, Myrianalya, LadyReadsAlot, JellyMan, and Saerwen; **Starfire**: Ryebrynn, Andrea M., Arwen_of_Rivendell, Pathfinder, Ryan Paige Howard, Elizabeth Dresdown, Rebekah Gyger, Caleb M., and Nichole White.

I'd like to thank the following bands for their EPIC music. I listen to you constantly while I write and you never fail to inspire: Majestic Vanguard, Beyond the Bridge, Anaxes, Neverland, Borealis, DGM, Mendel, Mirrormaze, Vanden Plas, Anthriel, Dream Theater, Seventh Wonder, Circus Maximus, Echoes, AsWeHuman, and Supreme Majesty.

From CH:

To Jenny: Thank you for parting with me for the many long hours I spent sitting on the couch in the red room while you were "Mommy." Your selflessness and faithfulness are the stuff of legend. You've always believed in my writing, even more than I have, and I can't imagine walking this path without you. Thank you for being my number one supporter, friend, confidant, fan, and even critic. I'm a better man because of you. i2i2

To Evangeline, Luik, Judah and Levi: thank you for parting with your Daddy so I could write this story. As such, you've invested into thousands of readers who are just as much a part of your legacy as they are mine. May you reach exponentially more souls for Jesus in your lifetimes than I ever could have in mine. Your sacrifice is their blessing, and God does not blink at that.

To the people whose enthusasim and encouragement continue to inpsire me: Kirk Gilchrist, Chris Mooney, La Famille Sureau, Shane Marolf, Matt Dumont, Joseph Gilchrist, and Postmaster Jill.

And lastly, to my dear friend, Sir Wayne Thomas Batson. This final installmenet will always be a reminder to me of your patience and grace. Without your faithful plodding and continual encouragement, I'm certain this book would not be. I'm honored to call you friend, and beyond grateful to the Lord for knitting us together when He did. Here's to flatulent barrister Gnomes everywhere!

 WAYNE THOMAS BATSON is the author of numerous best-selling novels, including: *Isle of Swords, Isle of Fire, The Door Within Trilogy,* and *The Dark Sea Annals.* His books have earned awards and nominations including Silver Moonbeam, Mom's Choice® Silver, Cybil, Lamplighter, The Clive Staples, and American Christian Fiction Writers Book of the Year. A middle school reading teacher in Maryland for more than nineteen years, Wayne tailors his stories to meet the needs of young people. When last seen, Wayne was tromping around the Westfarthing with his beautiful wife and four adventurous children. For more info on Wayne, go to enterthedoorwithin.blogspot.com

 CHRISTOPHER HOPPER, whose other books include *Rise of the Dibor, The Lion Vrie,* and *Athera's Dawn,* has gathered awards and nominations including Silver Moonbeam, Lamplighter, The Clive Staples, and The Pluto. He is also a multi-album recording artist, pastor, visual designer, and restaurateur. His prolific writings in both book and blog form have captured the imaginations of loyal readers around the world. He lives with his wife, Jennifer, and their four children in the 1000 Islands of northern New York. To find out more about Christopher, go to christopherhopper.com

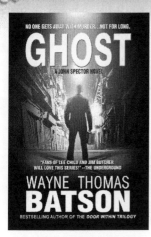

The Elves
of The Underground
await you . . .

heedtheprophecies.com

Made in the USA
Lexington, KY
19 May 2014